IN FOR A POUND

Also by Richard Marinick

BOYOS

IN FOR A POUND

A NOVEL BY

RICHARD MARINICK

KATE'S MYSTERY BOOKS
JUSTIN, CHARLES & CO. PUBLISHERS
BOSTON

ISBN: 978-1-932112-51-1

Library of Congress Cataloging-in-Publication Data is available.

Published in the United States by Kate's Mystery Books, an imprint of Justin, Charles & Co., Publishers, Boston, Massachusetts
www.justincharlesbooks.com

Distributed by National Book Network, Lanham, Maryland
www.nbnbooks.com

Printed in the United States of America

Book design by Boskydell Studio

2 4 6 8 10 9 7 5 3 1

IN FOR A POUND

PROLOGUE

DELRAY MCCAULEY'S NIKES SLAPPED the pavement hard as he ran, all out, one hundred feet behind the shadowy figure in the grimy, narrow alleyway that seemed to go on forever. He didn't cry out to him or scream "stop" like in the movies, he just ran, surprised at how easily he breathed, the effortlessness of his gait. He hadn't run like this since college. But for all of it he was getting no closer to his quarry, who was not just elusive, visible only when darting around Dumpsters hugging the wall, but quick and seemed to bound like a kangaroo through the puddles of moonlight.

Skidding to a stop at the end of the alley, McCauley pressed his back to the wall, simultaneously pulling his Glock. Both hands gripping the weapon, his heart uppercutting his chest, he snapped his head around the corner then back, around the corner then back. Nothing but darkness. He leveled the weapon shoulder height and took in a deep breath and leaped.

Instantly he was hit by a light so bright he saw yellow stars in front of his eyes—before he felt the heat.

From somewhere a voice, which sounded like it had been brushed by alcohol, barked, "Skin, show some skin, McCauley." The order was followed by a metallic bang loud enough that McCauley had to cover his ears. The voice growled, "Come on, McCauley, you know the drill."

Rolling from his side onto his back, McCauley pulled his hands from under the covers and made a fist with his gun hand, which he raised up into the Maglite's steady beam. Flicked up the middle digit hard enough he could have lost a fingernail in the process. A louder bang followed his raunchy salute as the guard drove the butt of the flashlight against the steel door.

Which only energized the finger.

Now it made tiny circles in the air, as if stirring the sonic vibrations.

"McCauley, you fresh cocksucker," the voice outside said. "Lucky it's your last night behind the walls, or ex-cop or not you'd be headin' to the hole."

The light blinked off.

Dropping the arm, McCauley pulled the thin state-issue pillow over his head but still heard the footsteps recede, shuffle to a stop at the next cell of the 2-1 block of Norfolk State Prison. And there was a loud metallic bang.

ONE

UNDER THE STEADY HUM of the fluorescent light, Enfield Higgins looked over his shoulder at the lone figure in white down the far end of the corridor. Close to the wall, his arm above him at an angle, he seemed to wave at it slowly, like to a cruise ship backing its ass out of the Black Falcon Terminal.

He gave Dinny McLintock a look as he laid his roller with the six-foot extension across the top of the rectangular cart between them and wiped smears of blue paint from his palms on the thighs of his white Carhartt overalls.

Dinny took a nervous step sideways and shrugged, the back of his hand gliding across the tip of his nose, smudging the drop of Pearly Gates white there onto his cheek. He said, "Hey Ennie, calm down, was an accident, right?" looking past him down the corridor.

He avoided Higgins's glare as he squatted down quickly. Scooping the rechargeable SawzAll off the floor, he slid it onto the open-sided cart's interior shelf, tucking it behind a half-empty can of Stain Kilz and two full ones of primer.

Dinny, afraid he might kick him, looked up at Higgins and said, "Can't believe I forgot it was inside the drop cloth." Keeping his eyes on him, he covered the SawzAll, a small sledge-hammer, pinch bar, and a couple of screwdrivers with the paint-splattered drop cloth.

He peered down the corridor as he slowly stood up. Looked at Higgins, said, "Re-lax, Ennie, Froggy down there's Perc'd outta his mind, the loser heard nothin'. Wouldn't have noticed I burst into flames."

"Don't give me ideas," Higgins muttered, wheeling the cart past him in the opposite direction.

In front of the elevator doors, jabbing the button, Higgins turned just his head, following Dinny's lazy approach, thinking, Did three years of a nickel to get paroled and end up with a shit head like *him*?

Turning his attention back to the doors, Higgins said, "Remember now, we're dropping two floors. Anyone gets on in between, we tell 'em we had to go back down to seven to touch up some crown molding."

"Why not just tell 'em left our scrapers down there, pretend that we're morons," Dinny said, grinning, bobbing his head.

Higgins burned him with his eyes as the doors glided open. "Because you ain't pretendin'." He shoved the cart in and poked at the button.

A few seconds later the doors opened at seven and Dinny stuck just his head through, turning it both ways. "Looks like all clear," he said as Higgins moved past him, turned right, wheeling the cart quickly down its tan carpeted length.

He looked at his wrist. "It's two twenty-five, it shouldn't take us more than a couple of minutes to get the thing out."

The corridor ended at a floor-to-ceiling wall of glass. Two doors in the center, each with shiny brass handles shaped like palm leaves. To the right of them, in shiny gold letters, outlined in black, the words COTTER, MCBRIDE & COTTER.

Higgins pulled a silver key from his pocket and looked over his shoulder back up the corridor.

"We still lookin' cool?" Dinny said.

"Wouldn't matter it wasn't," Higgins said, slipping the key in the lock beneath one of the palms, twisting. "We're goin' in, Godzilla ain't stopping us now."

"How about Mothra? You stop for Mothra?" Dinny said, grinning, coming behind him with the cart.

Higgins pictured the flying monster. "Why would I?" he said "Didn't Godzilla kick the shit outta Mothra?"

Now in the reception area: colorful brass framed prints on pastel-colored walls — a law office or art studio? — a huge, seafoam-colored vase, artificial flowers erupting from the top, standing next to a desk. The desk was one of the fancy new ones, all stainless steel and Lucite, the phone with more buttons than an accordion.

Brown leather couches, matching chairs, they passed a glass table in the center piled with *House and Garden, Forbes, Golf Digest* — boring rags that wouldn't confuse you, knock your lies out of order before you spoke to your lawyer — heading east down a corridor, lined either side with closed office doors.

Stopping in front of the door at the end, Higgins pinched at his pocket, winking at Dinny as he reached in and pulled out a key.

Dinny blinked like he'd just watched a card trick. "Was thinking we had to jimmy the door, where'd you get *that*?"

"I need you to think I'll stick the key in your ass," Higgins said, pointing the tip towards the ceiling. "Got it from Froggy, our steward, remember? The little junkie that's eating our Percs? We're painting the whole building, you gotta have keys. Do you think some super, who's *supposed* to be carrying 'em, gonna be up runnin' around at two in the morning?" Waved the key. "Naw, he hands them to Froggy and says, 'Do your own thing.' Which Froggy, of course, does. And all it cost us was a couple of Percs. He thinks we're down here shooting dope."

"Love it, the way the Percs get ya perks," Dinny said, bobbing his head. He shoved the cart through the dark doorway as Higgins fished for the light.

It was plain this lawyer wasn't a slouch. The fancy rug, leather couch and chairs, oversized desk in front of a bank of huge windows overlooking the waterfront, the lights of the World Trade Center Boston twinkling out there, a gash of yellow moon over the harbor beyond it. In a corner, one of those big painted globes on a stainless-steel pedestal. And other weird stuff too. Dinny eyeballed the huge hatchet attached to a wall.

Almost everything in here had some kind of red. Red leather couch, chairs, the wood of the desk, the huge Persian rug, even the books on the bookshelves filling an entire wall. Red must mean power, money. Higgins's guts gave a jump and he started to smolder. He hated this lawyer. Living like this while he sat in a cell rotting.

Three years in Walpole for carving up some squid in the Navy. Who didn't *belong* in Southie, the Beer Garden, in the first place. Hell, with an accent like *that*, didn't belong in the Navy. How they take 'em like that when they can't understand English?

Understood the end of his knife.

In front of the desk Higgins thought back to the first time they came here, a big contract, union paint job. How he figured then there had to be something worth grabbing even if they had to come back like tonight, later.

And boy did he find it.

Higgins looked at his watch, "C'mon," he said and gave Dinny a "follow me" sign. Turning the knob of a door in the wall he paused for a second as it swung back on its hinges. Threw a hand up the wall tripping the light, sucked in his breath and held it. Hit him the same way it did the first time they came here two nights before — to paint the place legit — like the staging area for a Radio Shack clearance sale.

This room was narrower, mostly taken up by a table and chairs, and a *ton* of electronic equipment: computers, flat-screened monitors, with the sticky tags on them, some still in boxes, all stacked on a table beneath the tall windows.

On a shelf below them at least a dozen Dell laptops still in boxes, and there was other electronic stuff that he couldn't figure. At the room's other end, over what looked like one of those old-fashioned cabinets — his grandmother called them arm-wahs — a sixty-inch plasma attached to the wall.

Behind him Dinny was saying, "Still think we oughta come back here and grab all of this shit?"

"Thinkin' again?" Higgins said, maneuvering the cart around the end of the table "You must be feeling somethin' sharp in your ass."

The table — twenty feet if an inch — was surrounded by ten black, high-backed leather chairs you could sleep in real easy, probably worth something too.

"Looks like one of them boardrooms where the governors sit and figure how to fuck up the country," Dinny said, bulling the cart between the wall and the chairs, stopping before he rounded the opposite end.

Using his foot to shove a chair out of the way, Higgins slid in front of the wardrobe. He ripped open the door on the left, sweeping aside the wooden hangers in front of his face. Stared at the safe. Yep, knew the type well, had *danced* with them before.

1st pass

Model called a Gardall, probably lag-bolted into the partitioning wall. Nothing too tough to take out.

Remembered the first time he saw it, almost dropped a fat one right there in his pants. Now resting his fingertips on the dial, turning it slightly. He looked at his watch. They had to get back up to the ninth before Froggy came looking. He nodded at Dinny and held out his hand.

"Screwdriver," Higgins said, taking the tool, positioning the edge against the inner back panel, six inches over the top of the safe. Stuck the hand out again. "Hammer," he said, Dinny slapping the tools into the palm like a surgical aide.

Higgins worked quickly, punched in two holes in a row — close enough together almost looked like one — took the Sawz-All from Dinny and inserted the blade.

The sound of the saw and vibrating wood filled the room as he circled the safe, drove in the pinch bar, and popped out the wood, exposing more of the safe and the lag bolts behind it.

Higgins stepped back; quickly changed the saw blade from a wood one to metal. Peering over the other man's shoulder, Dinny's head floating now in front of the safe, he said, "How many lags we got?"

Shifting the flashlight up at an angle, Dinny said, "Four, looks like four," sounding like his face was pushed in a pillow. Grunted as he backed himself out.

"Good," Higgins said, bending back into it, extending his arms. "Then it's four and the door," he said and leaned into the saw.

TWO

THE ROOM IN EDGEWATER STATE HOSPITAL was pink, all of it, even the floor, which was sticky. The mattress was streaked with shit, and some kind of liquid was pooled in the creases. On top, shredded remains of what appeared to be boxer shorts, on the fragments the word "Edgewater" in red displayed in small letters.

1st pass

The room's only window was secured inside by a thick wire screen; outside by heavy steel louvers, cracked only a few inches, like they waited to strangle any hint of a breeze that might have tried to sneak through.

The door to the room consisted of two doors. The first one solid steel, like something in a submarine, its thick plastic window bearing a permanent rainy day look. The inner one was just steel bars, what you'd see in a cowboy jail, with a slot cut halfway down that allowed for the passage of food.

There was no sink in the room, no toilet, and no running water. Mid-October, it was hot and airless, and flies, as big as hummingbirds, collected at the ceiling and floor — particularly around a hole in the floor.

A flat metal disc rose from the center of that neatly cut hole. On it and the floor a collection of semi-dried turds, scattered like someone was moving fast when they dropped them.

Jarvis Reems, six foot six, two hundred seventy pounds, naked, and in the "down" position for his fortieth handstand push-up, looked up past his long legs and feet at the ceiling. Flecks of fresh excrement dotted its surface, forming a crappy constellation that, to anyone with an eye for such things, was a fair representation of Ursa Minor and Pisces.

He welcomed the sting of sweat rolling up into his eyes as he pumped out another ten push-ups, swung himself down, and came to rest on his knees. He stretched his arms overhead and lowered his torso; pressed his palms flat to the floor. Breathing shallowly, closing his eyes, he reveled in the burn in his shoulders. His thoughts were like tracer rounds mangling midnight; he sensed the image before it was there.

Carrying a chopped-down M16 at portarms, dressed in desert BDUs, Jarvis was running now down a narrow angular path that cut, like an appendix scar, through a small settlement of cinderblock huts, corrugated steel roofs. Still early morning, an arid ninety degrees, when he heard the first shot. The first shot was always exciting.

But not half as exciting as the first scream.

Stopping in front of one of the huts, squatting under a window while others like him ran silently past, communicating only with hands, he focused on the doorway.

A young Sunni leaned out, and like a trapdoor spider Jarvis was on him, stitching him with a burst of white fire from his groin to his chin, launching him into the doorframe. He crumpled like a broken kite to the ground.

Straddling him, Jarvis giggled and tapped him twice more in the head, tossed a phosphorus grenade through the door. He heard wails, the pop-whoomph of the grenade, and the wails turned to screams. He shot the first flaming figure who stepped into the light.

And the next three.

Jarvis was the milkman leaving things in dark doorways that burst into flames behind him. He laughed as he killed on the run.

Found it all strangely comforting.

Behind him a large brass key slid into the lock and the outer door swung back on its hinges. Leather soles shuffled close to the bars and Jarvis stopped chuckling, aware now of the sound of the circling flies.

"We've got problems, Jarvis," the voice said behind him.

Like a call to prayer the kneeling man nodded. He got up and stood facing the window. The floor was hot, like there was a furnace beneath it, and Jarvis imagined the flesh falling from the bones in his feet.

"Jarvis, I thought it was over but sadly it's not — they don't seem to learn."

Jarvis inhaled deeply. Swore he could taste cordite on the back of his tongue.

"They never learn," he said softly, balling his fists. His hands made the crackling sounds of Rice Krispies in milk.

"We've another government mess to clean up."

"Another," Jarvis replied, his voice a gray monotone.

Now there was a hint of cologne in the air, mixing with the smell of the cordite and shit.

Jarvis turned just his head, saying, "Team 6, will I be working with them?" unclenching his hands.

"No, as usual, it will be only you."

Jarvis gazed blankly down at himself.

"I'll need underwear," he said.

"As always you'll get what you need, but in the meantime,

Jarvis, you must behave, you hurt the guard badly. Had he died, I couldn't protect you."

"When?" Jarvis said, looking up at the window.

"Soon," said the voice. "We're gathering intelligence, developing patterns. Like the others, this bad man's a creature of habit. We'll talk again *soon*."

Jarvis closed his eyes and raised his chin towards the ceiling. He opened them and gazed at Ursa Minor and Pisces. Curling his lips into a crooked smile he sang out softly. "Hun-gry hippos. Get your hungry hip-pos."

"What was that, Jarvis?"

". . . hungry, hungry, hip-pos," Jarvis repeated, deeper and louder this time.

"Yes, Jarvis," the voice said, "the hippos *are* hungry again."

Jarvis grinned and covered his ears. He sang some more, and couldn't have cared less when the door closed behind him.

THREE

TWENTY MINUTES BEFORE THE ALARM went off, the telephone's insistent ringing woke Delray McCauley from a restless sleep. He rolled over and reached, knocking it from the small bedside table. He groaned and said, "Son-of-a . . ." and rapidly blinked, trying to shake the sleep from his lids. He picked the phone from the floor and flipped it open.

"Ya?" he said sharply, and coughed into the mouthpiece.

"McCauley, you awake?"

McCauley recognized the voice. Conway Lilly was a captain in the Boston police. They had worked together with the feds years before on the Bank Robbery Task Force and Lilly was one of the few men on the planet that he'd trust with his life.

"Jesus, Lilly," McCauley said, scratching his chest, looking around for his watch.

Nuala, the gray Persian, jumped onto the end of the bed, making eye contact with him before gingerly pressing ahead across the light blue comforter towards him. She belonged to the tenant downstairs and visited him regularly through a back window left open for her.

Nuala pushed into his hand. "What time is it?" McCauley said, stroking between her ears.

"You weren't still sleeping? Christ, McCauley, it's after seven, what time you go to work?"

McCauley kicked off the comforter, ruffling Nuala, and swung his feet over the side of the bed. "I work days, usually, open the bar around ten," he said, the "ten" coming out as a yawn. "But last night was special, I filled in for someone."

Lilly laughed. "Christ, you got it easy."

"Hey, while you were home watching Letterman, I was busting my ass in a roomful of drunks, I didn't get home until three."

"I can't stand Letterman."

McCauley looked at his wrist, around the bed, patted the covers.

"But I've a hellava memory," Lilly said, "and remember as a cop you loved to work nights. Of course you staties, unlike us city cops, had it easy, hiding off the highway in the bushes all night until — what — rush hour began around five?"

McCauley pulled his watch from between the blanket and sheet. Pried open the flex-band with the fingers of one hand, and said, "Ya, and the bums who pass for cops in Boston couldn't *find* the damn highway unless a Dunkin' Donuts was on it."

McCauley collapsed back on the bed, dangling his feet over the floor. "Okay, Lilly, enough of the smart aleck exchanges, what's up?" stroking Nuala again, the cat arching, sticking her tail in the air.

"Not like my life isn't busy enough, but something's come up," Lilly said. "Like to swing by the bar to discuss it if I could, may pique your interest."

"What are we talking?"

"Not on the phone, brother, too many details. I'll stop by for a coffee — you do serve coffee?"

"Coffee, ya. What time you figure?" McCauley said.

"Got a meeting with the deputy super at nine," Lilly said, rustling papers. "Some paperwork and calls to make after, I'll be there around ten thirty, and you'll be awake then?"

"Bring me something from Dunky's, I will."

"Large regular?"

"Got it."

"See you at ten thirty."

As McCauley thumbed the phone shut, Nuala was in the process of settling down at the end. He tossed it on the extra pillow, exhaling slowly as he looked at the cat. "Smart girl," he said and fell back on the mattress, swinging his legs back under the covers. He looked at his watch, it was quarter to eight. He'd sleep for another hour.

FOUR

BANG, BANG, BANG! "Come on, McCauley," somebody shouted. Then it was Bang, bang, "Hey, Mr. McCauley, wake the hell up."

Mr. McCauley?

McCauley sat bolt-upright in the bed, flipped off the covers. The same dream again? His heart pounded like a base in a Latino low-rider as he scanned the bedroom interior. Nothing but bright sunlight through the windows opened a crack, a cool breeze tussling the faded brown curtains.

Bang, Bang, BANG.

Nuala hit the floor running, disappeared through the doorway.

The front door sounded like it was coming off its hinges.

Clearing his voice, McCauley said, "Ya, who the hell is it?" and swung his feet to the floor. Cursing, he pulled on some boxers at the foot of the bed.

He moved quickly from the bedroom and down a short hallway past a kitchenette on the right, stopping at the edge of a small foyer, the front door just ahead. Could see the peephole from where he stood but wouldn't use it. McCauley knew a guy once who, under similar circumstances, did and got gut-shot through the door.

Following the wall, he moved closer. "Ya, who is it?" he said.

On the other side of the door a boyish voice said, "It's me, Michelin. Got your *Herald*, McCauley, you're owin' me for more than six weeks." A sound like a tapping shoe on the floor.

McCauley shook his head, grinned. He opened the door. Staring up, a kid about thirteen, five four, on the light side of a hundred. Wearing a red cotton, long-sleeved tee, black double oversized pants, blue suede sneakers, he waved a rolled-up newspaper like a magic wand in front of McCauley's nose.

"Put your mitts on this paper, the beginnin' of *seven* weeks," Michelin said.

"You got heavy hands, kid, oughta be a fighter," McCauley said, snapping the paper out of Michelin's hand.

"Huh?"

"At ease, kid, I'm getting your money," McCauley said, turning.

"Hey, McCauley, you don't look so good," Michelin said to his back.

"Maybe because I don't *sleep* so good," McCauley said over his shoulder.

He came out of the bedroom with a wallet, pulled out some bills. He said, "How much I owe ya?"

Looking everywhere but at him. "Forty-five bucks," Michelin said.

"Forty-five bucks?" McCauley scowled, counted slowly. "Sorry kid, no tip today."

Using just a finger and thumb to tug the money from McCauley's hands. Michelin said, "That's what I figured so tip's *included*."

McCauley leaned towards him, saying, "Hey!"

Smirking, Michelin folded the bills with one hand, and stuffed them down into his pocket.

"See ya later, McCauley," he said with a flip of the hand, turning. He stopped at the top of the stairs. "Enjoy today's paper, got some interestin' readin'," he said without turning. "Some statey — you was one, wasn't ya — got busted over the weekend with

a pound of coke. And some Beacon Hill snot got it *real* good."
He turned and gave McCauley a look. "Said a couple of years
back he murdered his girlfriend." Stuck a finger inside of his
cheek, popped it, and bugged out his eyes. "Maybe it was her
ghost who done it?" He pulled another *Herald* from the canvas
bag on his hip, folded it in half.

"This," he said, slapping his palm with the paper, "is for Mrs.
Slattery." Waved to Nuala as she ran out the door and past him
down the stairs. "Mrs. *Slattery* always pays me on time." He
gave McCauley a suspicious look. "Hey, what're you doin' with
the old lady's cat?" Before he could answer, Michelin said, "See
ya later, McCauley."

As Michelin's footsteps receded down the stairs, a slight breeze
floated up them, passed through McCauley's cotton boxers, cool-
ing the sweat on his groin. He left the door open and entered the
small living room, dropped into the brown leather recliner. His
eyebrows rose as he scanned the front page.

The headline read: "State Cop's Coke the Real Thing!" Mc-
Cauley scrutinized the photograph of a handcuffed man, late
thirties, in just pajama bottoms being led down the outside steps
of a building. He recognized the face. Sergeant Clifford Downey.
He had been on the Violent Fugitive Apprehension Team. Mc-
Cauley was thinking he should have been angry, but wasn't.
There was a time he would have been embarrassed, taken it personal, a *genuine* bad egg making the entire job look bad. But
those days were gone.

McCauley folded the paper and was half out of the seat when
his eye caught a small image near the bottom. It was a photo,
grainy black and white, of an apartment hallway somewhere,
and it appeared as though a giant slug had tugged itself down its
checkered linoleum length, sliming the walls as it went. But it
wasn't slime that caught McCauley's eye — the caption below it
said it was blood.

And it was more blood than any human body ought to con-
tain.

McCauley forced air through his lips without whistling and
sunk back against the new leather cushion, read the heading that
screamed:

Industrialist's Son Victim of Beacon Hill Butcher

It went on to say:

Caleb Whitehead III, 33, son of investment brokerage house magnate Caleb Whitehead, Jr., of Marblehead, CEO of Whitehead Investments, was found dead late yesterday afternoon in his Joy Street apartment, the victim of an apparent homicide.

Boston Homicide detective Dennis Conley said, though he declined to go into detail, that the murder scene was one of the most horrific he'd witnessed in his eleven years as an investigator. When pressed, Conley stated, "Body fluids (blood) had been splattered around like some satanic version of the Blue Man Group had been practicing there."

Three years previously, Whitehead, no stranger to violence himself, was charged with a daylight shooting that resulted in the death of his fiancée, Melissa T. Holmes, 28, formerly of Manchester-by-the-Sea. Whitehouse, later found not guilty by reason of insanity by an Essex County jury, was sentenced by Superior Court Judge Emmanuel Brooks to an indeterminate time at Edgewater State Hospital, the maximum-security state prison for the criminally insane. Committed for just under a year, Whitehead was later released by a panel of Edgewater doctors who, after treatment, determined him fully competent and no longer a threat to the community.

McCauley's eyes drifted up to the crooked cop story. The guy had no clue what he'd be facing in prison. Dropped back to the photo of the bloody Beacon Hill hallway. Compared to the cop, Caleb Whitehead was lucky, everything had been taken in the end.

For the cop it was just the beginning.

McCauley checked his watch. It was nine fifteen. Enough time to shower himself completely awake, and to wash the dirt from the news from his hands.

FIVE

S QUINTING UP AT THE CLOUDLESS SKY, McCauley descended the front steps of the three-story beige clapboard on G Street. Stretching his arms, he paused to admire the black Mustang in the driveway.

Once inside he fired it up and sat there listening to the engine's dull rumble as it warmed itself, loosening its muscles like a fighter getting ready to bang out some rounds. Even at age forty, McCauley thought, there was still something about the scent of high test fuel exploding in a modified engine that made him want to go — *yeah*!

He backed into G Street and went up the hill past Southie High, where students huddled out front in groups like nicotine-addicted pigeons. Rolling down the other side, he turned left onto East Eighth Street, followed it along past block after block of single- and multi-family homes, many caught now between stages of demolition and rebuilding in the process of gentrification.

For the past decade there had been a construction boom in Southie to accommodate all the new faces who wanted to live there and were willing to pay big bucks for the privilege. The changes made McCauley uncomfortable. Growing up, Southie was made up of just Southie people. "Outsiders" rarely moved in. Nowadays it was different.

Everything was condos, find an empty twelve-foot patch of land and throw up five *luxury* condos. Yeah, today everything's *luxury,* McCauley was thinking as he pulled to the curb on the corner of K Street across from Joseph's Market. He got out and crossed the street into Joseph's.

Paulie, one of the owners, was in his usual place behind the counter and gave him his usual nod and grunt before reburying his nose in the sports section of the *Herald*, as McCauley headed to the back of the store.

He returned moments later, shaking a bottle of Yoo-Hoo that

he put on the counter just as Paulie was driving his heel into the floor and muttering something in Italian before switching back to English. "Lost again," he said, "fucking Red Sox — fighting." Turned his palms to the ceiling, hunched his shoulders, and growled. "Are we talking boxing?" he said, throwing uncoordinated punches at an invisible target. "Nooo, this is *baseball*." Now Paulie swung an invisible bat. "We lost because two of these. . . *bums*," jabbed the paper with a finger, "got tossed from the game. I say you wanna fight, put on the gloves, go up The Munie, you wanna fight. What do you say, McCauley?"

McCauley cracked the Yoo-Hoo and raised the bottle to his lips. He swallowed and twisted the cap back on. "The Munie's been closed for years," he said, wiping his mouth.

Paulie gave him a look of utter contempt.

"Then go down Triple O's," the older man sneered. "*Plenty* of guys love to fight down there."

"Closed that about month ago too," McCauley said, dragged the cold bottle across his forehead.

Paulie yanked his hands from the paper like it carried an electric shock, dropping his chin past the collar of his starched white shirt. With both hands, he pulled off his glasses and dropped them on the counter.

"You're missin' the point here, Del-ray. Baseball's a fucking *game*, see, you do it with a ball, bat, and glove."

Shook his head, sighed.

McCauley hoisted his shoulders and held them a moment before letting them drop.

Said apologetically, "Paulie, you know about me and sports. I don't follow them, never have, not a lick of interest. Know why? The time I'd waste on sports would take from the things I really like."

Paulie gave him the eye.

"And that's?"

"Messing with old guys like you."

Paulie slipped on the glasses and rolled up the *Herald*. When he swung it, McCauley ducked under, sliding right, grabbing a *National Enquirer* off the scandal rack near the door. He slapped a five on the counter.

Paulie took off the glasses again. "Ever gonna buy anything other than Yoo-Hoo," he said, ringing up the sale, scooping change out of the register, "and a friggin' *National Enquirer?*"

McCauley took his change and washed the room with his eyes. "Not here for the merchandise, Paulie, I'm here for the colorful commentary" he shrugged, "and *that* I get for free."

Outside on the sidewalk McCauley opened the tabloid. The headline read: "Brad and Jen Secretly Dating Again?" McCauley smirked. He certainly hoped so. He'd read only last week that she was a lesbian.

Enquirer under his arm he started across K Street but stopped in the middle, at the sound of a car racing towards him. As its front bumper abruptly sucked down towards the street, he attempted to see through the green Lincoln's dark windshield. When the side window went down, he recognized the driver — sunglasses, blue tank top, large hands draped lazily over the wheel — as Mike Janowski, chief lieutenant to Southie mob boss Jack "Wacko" Curran.

Janowski's long arms were free of tattoos, hard and lean like they swung an ax for a living. His tricep flexed briefly, like a current shot through it, when one hand floated away and tugged the black wraparounds to the tip of his nose. Janowski's grin frozen, he locked his eyes on McCauley's.

He said, "Gotta look both ways before crossin', McCauley. Ain't you aware the streets can be *dangerous?*"

McCauley squatted, still keeping his eyes on Janowski, and put the paper and bottle down on the street.

"Your point, Janowski?" McCauley said, straightening.

Janowski smirked and pushed the sunglasses back up.

Dude'd gotten big. All that working out in the can. Keeping up with it too, not letting himself slide.

"My point?" Janowski said, snorted, and looked back at the windshield. "Always questions, just like a *cop.*"

He turned his head back to him and ripped off the glasses, his eyes boring into McCauley's.

"Fucking pig, I'll make my point when we can *discuss* it in depth."

McCauley subtly rolled his shoulders, tilted his head side to side, loosening the neck muscles. "I'm looking forward to it, Mike." Gently foot swept the Yoo-Hoo out of the way, heard it tinkle-roll behind him to the curb. He stepped back and gave the other man room to get out. "You want, we can talk here," he said, "right now in the street. They tell me I'm good at debating."

Janowski gave McCauley a mirthless grin, slid on the glasses, and dropped his hand to the shifter. "Isn't debatin'," he said, pulling it down into neutral, "when there's a guy in the middle separatin' the two arguin'?"

"So they say."

Janowski pursed his lips, nodded. "So-they-say," he repeated like he wanted to be sure.

An electric motor whined and the door glass ascended, stopped halfway up. Janowski put the car into gear. He said, "Time comes, McCauley, ain't no one going to separate us."

With a chirp of tires the Lincoln roared off.

McCauley followed it with his eyes. Something telling him the wait wouldn't be long. "I'll hold you to that," he said.

SIX

IN WHAT WAS ONCE A SMALL KITCHEN, Jarvis Reems stood at the window and parted the blinds with two fingers. Shafts of sunlight pierced the interior daylong dusk as he stared out watching cars pass a hundred yards away on Sea Avenue. Just the rooftops, over the hulls of the small shrink-wrapped boats up on stands for the winter, were visible through the rusted chain-link fence that surrounded the boatyard. This time of day, traffic was light but picked up after five, like a slit artery spewing rush hour commuters heading home after work. After five was the best time to leave.

The last time he took care of the Beacon Hill boy — couldn't call him a man. A woman would have given him more of a fight. Sea Street, Quincy Shore Drive, the expressway into Boston. In town he had parked on Charles Street, in front of a high-end bakery. The odor wafting from it smelled good enough to go in before.

He decided to wait until after.

Then, enjoying a fresh black coffee — not like the waste water they served down in Edgewater — the pretty red-haired counter girl asking him, "Cream sir?" All very civilized. Him shaking his head, saying, "No, I like it *dark,* wouldn't happen to have a blueberry scone?"

He was sitting at a counter in front of a window, watching himself eat when the text message came telling him, "Return to the boatyard." That was six days ago and Jarvis hadn't heard from the good doctor since.

Jarvis extracted his fingers and the blinds snapped together, choking the light.

Early evening now in front of the TV, spooning from his third can of cold Chef Boyardee, Jarvis watched Oprah. Today's guest a fat blonde, her dress a paisley puptent, gold earrings like barbells. Bitching about how her Welsh corgis were stolen at gunpoint. Oprah, in a thin phase now, saying, staring into the camera, "What kind of man? What kind of . . . *creature* does something like that?"

Jarvis scraped the can good enough Ma would have been proud, put it down next to the chair on the flimsy TV table, printed flowers on sheet metal riding hollow gold legs. Licked the back of the spoon, thinking, Maybe the kind who key taps his way into a Joy Street apartment and hacks off a head?

He got up and crossed the room to the window again. Thought about the good doctor, Noah Durning. There was something about him . . . soft, he was too soft. Never trust a man who wasn't in shape. Something in his eyes too. But the Company never said anything about trusting your contacts. He'd played the damn game, eight years in a cell awaiting his assignment.

Time to move on.

Jerry "Stuffa" Finneran twisted the end of the mop into the mouth of the ringer and tugged down on the arm, leaned the mop against the wall. He unhooked the wringer from the side of the deep yellow bucket, then, with no small effort, dumped the dirty contents into the sink.

Drying his hands on a bar towel draped over his shoulder, he glanced at his watch. It was almost ten and his cousin Del would be here any minute. He came out of the kitchen through two swinging doors and went behind the bar. Grabbed a sharp knife and started to cut limes and lemons, murmured softly to himself as he did, "Cut 'em once in the middle, cut 'em again, then those sections in half."

After he'd done six of each, he heard a sharp rap come from the front window. Stuffa looked up and saw McCauley with his nose to the glass and almost stabbed himself waving him in.

"The alarm on, Stuff?" McCauley said, folding his keys into his pocket, pushing the door closed behind him.

Stuffa stopped cutting, held the hand up with the knife like he was readying to conduct a swing band.

"*Yes*, Cuz, go through the same bullshit whenever you work." Little side to side, the band was in motion. "The alarm's *on*, fucking junkies everywhere." Tossed the knife into the sink and turned on the tap. "You forget, they robbed Meany's joint only last month, *in the mornin'*. Shot old man Doherty in the ass?

"Christ, I always cancel the motions when I come in here at seven, but reactivate contact alarms on the doors." Shook his head. "No one's gettin' the drop on ol' Stuffa while he's swab bing the floor."

McCauley punched a number into a keypad over a framed autographed photo of Mayor James Michael Curley. He leveled Curley's head, stepped back marveling.

"An autographed James Michael Curley," he said, "can't believe nobody's swiped it."

"They *have*," Stuffa said, drying the knife with a bar towel. "Got a half dozen others upstairs in Walter's office *I* signed the one you're lookin' at."

McCauley frowned, then said, "The bar was busy last night," walking towards him.

Stuffa shrugged. "Yeah, seemed it. Packed some Buds, bunch of Bud Light, Heinies, Miller Lites in the coolers earlier. Couldn't tell how busy from the bathrooms though."

"Meaning what?" McCauley said, taking off his jacket, laying it on the bar.

"Meanin', can usually tell how busy it's been by how much puke's in the bathroom — and *this* mornin'? Both were clean as a whistle, go figure."

Like colossal caterpillars, Stuffa's eyebrows suddenly flexed. "Hey, I cut up some fruit for ya, Del," nodded at the pitchers, "just the way ya like 'em."

McCauley looked. He said, "Just the right size. Done a good job the two months you've been here. I'll talk to Walter about training you for the bar."

Pumping McCauley's hand, Stuffa said, "Been *waitin'* to hear that, Cuz, thanks." He held up a finger like he was testing the wind, counted strokes in the air. "Washed the floors, packed the coolers, made the coffee, ordered the rolls for lunch — do *that* every morning — and . . ." stomped his foot, shot a fist at the ceiling. "I forgot — fucking ice."

"Relax, I'll get it," McCauley said, starting towards the kitchen.

"Na, na, na, nooo, *I'll* get it," Stuffa said, grabbing a white plastic bucket from under the bar. "You mixologists gotta conserve your energy, brain's gotta be sharp gettin' them drinks just right." He ran into the kitchen, came out through the back swing.

"And that's gonna be soon, right, the bartender job, me a mixologist?" He rubbed his palms together, said, "Keee-rist, Del, I love it," and disappeared again.

Going behind the bar, reaching, McCauley pulled a cigar box from behind a stack of dishes on a shelf. Opening it on the bar, he counted the bills he took from it.

Returning, Stuffa watched him as he dumped ice in the bin.

"The bank, huh?"

McCauley nodded. "Yeah, start every day with a hundred fifty." Turned and clicked open the register behind him.

Watching him stick the bills in the slots, Stuffa said, "Usually *end* my days like that. Me up the Quencher handing Morgan Daly a C-note for a game that I lost on, and him stickin' it into *his* register."

Stuffa picked up the empty cigar box, looked wistfully into it saying, "Be nice to have money in the mornin' again, even if it's somebody else's." Pulled on his jacket.

"Well, I'm outta here, Cuz, off to make me some money."

"So you can hand it to Morgan?"

"*Please*, Cuz, don't jinx me, didn't have bad luck, wouldn't have any. They say luck runs in spurts," thought for a moment, "thinkin' *my* luck's got bum knees." Shrugged. "Speakin' of runnin', my pal, Paulie Paint Chips? That lame that he runs with, his cousin from Charlestown, Tooky? Ticky? Whatever-the-fuck, grabbed a box-truck of Reeboks last night in Revere. I'm gonna help them unload them today. Heading to Dorchester, Quincy — stayin' the hell out of Revere. What size are ya?"

"Thanks," McCauley said, "but I'm all set for sneakers." He opened a can of grapefruit juice, poured it into an opaque plastic bottle, and placed it on the speed rack next to the sour mix. His eyes tracking something outside the main window "I'm set for sneakers, but maybe he's not," nodded towards it.

Turning, Stuffa made a face like he smelled something foul and said, "Looks like a fucking cop to me."

Captain Conway Lilly, the edges of both hands over his eyes, shifted his head side to side as he squinted in through the glass.

"Hey, I was a cop," McCauley said, waving the other guy in.

"Ya, key word is *was*, I'm outta here, Cuz."

"Bet the captain needs sneakers, ask him his size."

"Keep being fresh, I'll rat you to your mum."

Lilly came through the door shaking a white paper bag near his shoulder. He said, "Top o' the morning, Del." As he approached, he gave Stuffa a curious look, kept his eyes on him as he shook McCauley's hand. "I have to apologize, should have brought more," he said, taking two cups with plastic covers out of the bag.

Stuffa gave an awkward grin, did the hand jive in front of his chest, said, "Na, na, na, noooo, thanks, I was just . . . *leavin'*," he said. Looked at McCauley. "See ya, tomorrow, you workin'?"

"Yeah, I'm working, how you set for cash?"

Stuffa grinned. "I'm good, gonna be better real soon, like I told ya, *I'm* workin' today too." He turned towards Lilly and offered his hand. "Jerry Finneran's the name," he announced grandly, "some call me Baked Stuffed, others just Stuffa."

As they shook, Stuffa tilted his head towards McCauley. "Had no choice in the matter, the fact I'm his cousin."

A damp bar towel hit him square in the chest.

McCauley stared after him as Stuffa walked out the door, said, "He's a good guy, Lil, as kids we were close, was at our house more than his. His mum had the curse, almost drank herself to death before finally going on the bright. Never knew his da."

Lilly blew on his coffee and said, "It's tough when the hard times start early."

"Amen," McCauley said, tugging the top off his cup, letting it sit. "Stuffa had problems later in life: drugs, petty crime, did couple of small bids at South Bay, but he finally got his act together. A month after I started, I got him a job here cleaning the place."

"An English guy," Lilly said, blowing on his coffee, "a fop, Oscar Wilde, said something about how it's not the problems that we get into in life, that it's more what we do as a result." He looked in McCauley's eyes, nodded, and brought the cup to his lips. "The guy had a point," he said, pushing McCauley's cup towards him.

"You have to move on," McCauley said, brought it to his lips and sipped. He held it in his mouth a moment before swallowing. Suddenly jerked up his eyebrows and stared at Lilly.

"You're not here for the coffee, Lil, especially when *you're* buying, so what can this ex-con, ex-cop do for you?"

Lilly shot down the rest of his coffee and squeezed the cup until McCauley heard cracking sounds and watched the insides touch. Lilly said, "Got a little case, for lack of a better word, I figured you might be able to help me with."

McCauley straightened and pulled back his shoulders. Said with an edge, "Case?" And put his cup down. "Think you're doing me some kind of favor?"

Angry, but as calm as he could, McCauley said, "I'm not a cop anymore."

Lilly's eyes dropped to the bar, and slowly rose until they met McCauley's.

"I know that, but this is personal, Del, I got a friend who needs help."

"Who is this guy and what kind of *help*?"

"His name's Esmond Cotter, he's a lawyer with a hellava practice down on the waterfront, heard of him? Last week his office got hit and they pulled out the safe."

McCauley shook his head in time with the finger that he swung like a metronome in front of his face. "Number one, I-don't-like-lawyers," he said. "Two, I'd rather do work for the Klan."

"The Klan's no good, but Cotter is. Years ago he helped my kid, I owe him."

"Why bother me? That's a job for your guys."

Lilly looked to the side like what he had to say bothered him. "That's the thing. Cotter didn't offer and I didn't ask but, after talking with him, I got the feeling that if my guys find the safe first it might cause the barrister some embarrassment." He paused. "Maybe more than embarrassment, could put him in jail along with some others, all the way up to the mayor's office, hell, maybe even to Beacon Hill."

"The statehouse?"

"The feeling I got."

Lilly gave him a look like, See why I'm asking?

He said, "After the hit, Cotter hired a private investigator, the daughter of one of his rich clients." Shook his head. "She didn't pan out."

McCauley said, "You said this lawyer helped out your kid." Confusion sparked from his eyes. "But Sean's a good kid."

"People make mistakes," Lilly said, quietly, like he wanted to leave it at that. He dropped his cup into the bag, crumpling the whole thing into a tight white ball. "When Sean was thirteen he got popped tooling around in a hotbox." Let that sink in, then he snapped his fingers. "And Cotter was there for him. We've stayed in touch ever since."

McCauley said, "And because we're friends, you figured I'd help?" He took in a deep breath and stared at his sneakers, slowly releasing the air through his lips. Looked up and tried to be angry but his face wouldn't hold it. He lifted his hands to the "catch" position.

Now Lilly grinned. "I figured wouldn't hurt to ask. You were a great investigator, this should be easy for you."

He flipped the bag at McCauley.

"Ya, *easy*," McCauley said, catching it. "Isn't that usually something someone *else* does?" But Lilly could be right, what kind of moron breaks into a law office? Small-time burglar, a B&E artist, maybe a junkie?

He turned sideways and looked at himself, nodding at Lilly in the mirror. "I don't know, it's kinda hard to decide if I should," he said, bending his knees slightly, launching a one-handed set shot the length of the bar. The bag clipped the edge of a big gray barrel before going in.

He turned just his head and gave Lilly a wink.

"Two points," McCauley said, satisfied. "Looks like we talk."

SEVEN

E NFIELD HIGGINS WASN'T KNOWN for much and what little he was, was bad. Named for a rifle, he preferred using a knife — found it more personal — and, red-hot pissed, he was dying to use one on Dinny McLintock.

He'd been sitting inside Sullivan's Pub for more than an hour after sending McLintock, one of his boys — his boys, as if he could really control these louts — into the Old Colony Housing Project. Dinny was supposed to score some drugs: a little coke, some smack, so they could speedball their way through a short afternoon.

Dinny had left Sully's with a fist full of bills and specific instructions — where to go on Patterson Way and, if nothing was there, to another place on Pilsudski, where, if the guy wasn't too whacked out to answer the door, he could score.

The previous week, figuring they had something big, they'd ripped off a safe from a lawyer's office, some big shot down on the waterfront. But the *big* score amounted to shit, the usual these days. All they came out with was twenty-seven hundred, a half dozen photos of a naked blonde in curious positions — and a computer CD. And, after peeling bills for McLintock this morning, the wad a lot thinner, things didn't look good, the old familiar thought rattling around in his head like marbles in an old pressure cooker.

When this is all gone, where you gonna get more?

Resting his chin on his hand, Higgins gazed moodily into the empty longneck that he was tilting in front of his nose, like somehow the answer had mixed with the vapors inside the brown circle of glass. Looked down the bar to the jukebox in the corner. Fippa, the bartender was no where in sight.

He barely lifted his head when he reached for the *Herald* a few feet away, dragging it in front of his nose. Through half-closed eyes he read the headline about the state cop and the coke and chuckled to himself before laughing out loud, quieting down just as quick. "Cokehead fucking cop," he said softly. "Cokehead fucking cop," he repeated louder this time, like it felt good just to say it.

Still shaking his head, his chin tugging the skin on the back of his hand, he let his eyes drop to the photo at the bottom. Began reading the story. Suddenly, like on the hot end of a spinal, he jerked up in the seat, his eyes clicking between the photo of the bloody Beacon Hill crime scene and the name of the victim. Caleb Whitehead III.

Where had he seen it before?

He folded the top half of the newspaper towards him and stared at himself in the mirror. Momentarily distracted by the blank look on his face, Higgins snapped his fingers.

On the CD from the lawyer's safe.

He had taken a computer course during his last stretch in the can and got down the basics. Curious, he had scanned the disc on a buddy's computer. More naked pictures?

Disappointed. What he did find were names, eight altogether, some funny-sounding, like Caleb Whitehead III. Also funny, next to each name a huge dollar amount: $500,000 — twice — $780,000, $1,200,000, and dates next to them too, going back fourteen years.

Money, dates, names, places, and other weird shit like the weather those days jumped from the computer screen. What was the lawyer's connection to the rich boy Whitehead, and why the fuck was his name on the disc?

Higgins's mouth went dry as he pondered the questions, tried to piece things together.

Goddamn it, where's Fippa?

Everything pointed to payoffs, but to who? For what?

Maybe he'd just ask the lawyer.

He flipped to page three. Grinned at the photo of Whitehead. So, Daddy's got money, huh? Maybe he won't mind spreading the wealth? Tore out the story and photo, folded them into his wallet. His brief moment of triumph in the mirror cracking.

McLintock.

Never trust a junkie with money. The bum probably already holed up somewhere booting himself into Nirvana. His nostrils flared like they had washers inside them. Calm down, Ennie, have one more for the road. Then head into the OC and look for your *partner*.

Fippa came out of the kitchen carrying a stack of white porcelain sandwich-sized dishes that he stacked in three separate piles on a shelf. Just a quick peek at Higgins as he stuck a bar rag under the tap and turned on the water then wrung it. He remained there down at his end, singing softly to himself, and rubbed it in small circles on the bar's faded surface.

Higgins rapped the bar with his knuckles. "Hey, Flipper," he said, "how 'bout another beer, over *here*."

Fippa stopped making the circular passes and turned just his head, looked at Higgins. Squeezing one end, he threw the rest of the towel over his shoulder hard enough to let out a crack when it hit.

Now he was glaring. "Ain't *Flipper*, Higgins, the nickname's Fippa . . . *Fippa,* you got it, or say my real name, Phil," Fippa said, facing him with his whole body now. "Can't call me either, get your sorry ass outta here because I'm not takin' your shit."

"Sorry, Fip, forgot," Higgins said, nodding, staring ahead at the potato chip rack. "See, my associates are gettin' to me, just like your booze. What's that they say? Drink too much, first thing to go's the memory? Ever hear that — *Flipper?*"

Fippa yanked the towel from his shoulder, threw it in a clump on the bar. He tapped a fist, with an indefinite rhythm, into his palm. "They also say — for a pug — the last thing that goes is the punch," Fippa said. "I say I mix up a cute combination with the booze you've been drinkin' you'll be missin' more than your memory."

One hand playing with its neck, Higgins stared at the bottle.

Pulled the other one back and dropped it, casually, like it wasn't aware it was falling, onto his belt, which it followed along to the small of his back.

Fippa, up on his tiptoes now, leaning, catching the play, grinned knowingly.

"The knife, eh, Higgins?" Fippa said, settling back, reaching under the bar. "Like everyone in Southie, already know about *the knife*." Displayed a stainless-steel Bauer .25 automatic in the palm of his hand. He looped his finger around the trigger, resting the other hand on the receiver like he was itching to pull it back. Asked innocently, "Think I should throw a round in this thing?"

Higgins smirked and dropped his chin to his chest, and brought his hand back to the bar. He grabbed the empty and, tilting it towards him, squinting down its long neck briefly, he hauled it to his lips, downed the last drops. He said, "Ahh," as he pushed off the stool, flicked the hand towards Fippa he'd just used on his mouth.

"So, you're tellin' me, Fip, I'm really shut off? Hell, I'm not even fucked up — I'm just waitin' to be — and now your making that hard."

Higgins glanced at his watch, the knot in his stomach growing tighter. Where was McClintock, their fucking drugs?

Wasn't just Fippa making things hard.

Higgins pulled the wad from his pocket and waved it around like it was leaving a scent. "Hey, brother," he said, "know what this is? *Cash*. I ain't thinkin' about runnin' no tab today."

He faced the room and held out his arms like he was holding a beach ball, shrugged. "I ain't seein' no other customers, Fip, it's just us — hell, I'm the only one paying — and you're sayin' I still gotta *leave*?"

Fippa stood there frozen with his arms crossed, glaring. He nodded towards the door. "You get outta here now, maybe later I'll think about letting you back."

Pulling up on his belt, Higgins swaggered to the door, arms hanging loose by his side, and he pressed his forehead against the smooth, cool wood.

"Makin' a mistake, Fip," Higgins said near the hinge, "don't know what you got 'til it's gone"

"I ain't gonna miss ya."

"Ain't me, Fip," Higgins said, pulling back on the door. "I'm talkin' your *life*," he said, and stepped through it.

EIGHT

LILLY SAT UP ON THE BARSTOOL and stretched his neck, his eye on something rolled into a tube on the shelf directly in front of him. He shook his head at McCauley. "You're still reading *The National Enquirer*? You really got a thing for the dirt."

McCauley faked a pained expression. "C'mon, we're all destined to return to it, right? Just some do it sooner."

"But *The Enquirer*?"

"Why not?" McCauley said, sounding offended. "It's a habit I picked up in the can — feeling shitty about yourself? Turn a few pages of the lunatics they cover and it'll make you feel like a king."

He looked over his shoulder at Lilly as he reached up for the tabloid. "Be honest, you're dying to read it."

Lilly waved both hands, shook his head. "Forget it, I deal with enough dirtbags at work."

McCauley faced him and picked up his coffee, his eyes growing serious over the cup as he sipped, the lines in his forehead more prominent. He lowered the cup. "Talking about dirt, what's the problem, someone got a little on your lawyer?"

Lilly shifted his head and said, "First off, where is it?"

"What?"

"Your . . ." he held his hands up next to his temples, curling the middle and index fingers "coffee," he said. "It's called that legally if you make it from beans."

McCauley returned with a pot and filled a fresh cup that he handed to Lilly. Nodded at the cup. "Like living on the edge?"

Lilly took a sip, winced.

"Bad?"

"Hot," Lilly said. "*And* bad."

"Plenty more where that came from."

"I don't respond well to threats," Lilly said, sipping and wincing again.

"So, your lawyer friend, what's up?"

Lilly put the cup down but gripped it like he was afraid it might suddenly tip towards him.

"Like I said, someone hit his office last week and took the wall safe with them. I need to recover it." He waved the cup under his nose, frowned, sipped again.

"What was in it?"

"That's it, I don't know and don't need to," Lilly said.

"Maybe your guy's a weirdo," McCauley said, sticking his tongue out and grabbing his crotch. "A closet diddler. Maybe the safe held his personal porno, kiddy tapes, hell, maybe he dances with animals, goes to parties with politicos and they *all* dance with animals."

Lilly's eyes narrowed. "What kind of dancing you talking?"

"Tap," McCauley said. "And he's got a waterfront office? Business must be booming."

Lilly pulled at the knot in his tie, releasing the top button. "It is, and it runs in the family," he said. "His father was a big shot during the Kevin White days, one of his chief fund-raisers. Been told he was highly connected and had all the perks."

"The ones that can be spun into gold?" McCauley said

"Ya, and he did," Lilly said. "In the late sixties, the beginning of Boston's renaissance, Cotter's father, due to the position he held as chief counsel for American Goliath, was on the inside track."

"Construction?"

"You got it," Lilly said. "Legend has it he moved and grooved down city hall, anything he wanted he got: permits, zoning variances, *environmental* variances, and Goliath's bids were always right on the money. With his dance card filled to the limit with BHA bigwigs, the guy couldn't lose."

"Talk about dancing with animals."

"Well, the old man sure did," Lilly said. "With Fred Astaire's moves. Piloted American Goliath through an urban renewal minefield, made millions for the company, himself."

McCauley whistled softly. "Megabucks," he said.

"Amen," Lilly said. "But it came with a price. With all that money floating around, there were a lot of hands grabbing. The air was choked with rumors of kickbacks, rigged bids, and pay-offs. Combine that with a ton of shoddy construction and you've got a recipe for disaster — the feds came in like gangbusters. They ended up convicting a couple of the small fry, but never the guys at the top."

"The Big Dig's an instant replay," McCauley said.

"History repeats itself," Lilly said, raising his cup. He downed the last of the coffee and contorted his face, tugged his Adam's apple.

McCauley cackled. "Smooth, eh, Lilly? 'Course we make the *real* money on booze," he said as he took Lilly's cup.

"Before you go — and you *are* leaving because I have to set up the bar — I've got one last question. It's not your custom to bed down with attorneys, why are you helping out Cotter?"

Lilly whacked the bar with his fist. "I told you, my kid, Del," he said without blinking. "Cotter helped Sean. Sean's a good kid, but he screwed up years ago, my fault mostly, and Cotter was there to help him. At the time I was having problems with wife number one, Deanna, Sean's mum." Lilly scowled, shadowy memories clouding his eyes. "You met her.

"In those days I was just a young cop doing my job, but off the job I was bad, drinking too much, using coke. I was every-thing I detested in other guys, the ones I was putting in jail. Deanna was part of the problem, drinking, drugging, not coming home, screwing my best friend at the time. I was close to going over the edge, fighting to keep it together, and I lost track of my kid. He fell into trouble."

Lilly sat up in the seat, rested his forearms on the bar, and hunched towards McCauley.

"A street cop, I was in the district courts a lot back then — and that's where I met him. Cotter was a public defender fresh out of Harvard Law." Waved a finger at McCauley. "Del, I had my problems, but on the job I was a good cop, got you fair and square or you walked."

"Cotter liked that about me, I guess, so when my kid got

busted in the hotbox, the driver with stolen credit cards, he offered to help. I was broke back then, barely making the rent, and Cotter went balls to the wall for Sean and got him probation, dismissed in a year if no further problems. He asked for nothing in return."

"Until last week," McCauley said.

"Until last week."

"Why me?" McCauley said. "Why not hire a private dick?"

Lilly sighed. "Give me another coffee," he said, raising the cup and reaching.

McCauley grabbed the pot.

"Hell, never mind," Lilly said, flicking at his face like he was fanning away stink.

"He hired one," Lilly said, lightly tapping the cup on the bar. "I told ya, a broad, one of his rich client's daughters. She tried. Skulked around Southie for three or four days asking questions, but who's going to talk to her? Then I thought about you.

"You were a great investigator, Del, Southie born and raised, you know the worst of the lot over here, hell, on the job you were *chasing* half of 'em, at least the big ones. You've done time and, even though you were a cop, you've got a stand-up rep with the boys." He winked. "I know, I hear things. They'll talk to you over here, and if they're reluctant, well . . ." Gave him a broad wink. "You don't have to follow the rules. Maybe you could *convince* them to.

"Money's no object, Del, name your fee and brother, you decide to do this. The main thing to remember is Cotter's not asking — me, *I'm* asking your help."

McCauley rested his hands on his hips, looked out the window across Dorchester Street, the T bus stopped in front of Thornton's Flowers.

He said, "Guess I could do some snooping, but no guarantees." He pointed at Lilly. "I do this, you owe me, you bastard."

Lilly beamed, extended his hand, and grabbed hold of McCauley's. "Thanks, Del, I knew you'd come through."

"Don't get too excited," McCauley said, reaching for the pot. "Little more coffee?"

Lilly's face split into a grin as he pushed from the bar. "Naw," he said, "I'll take a rain check on that." He cupped a beefy hand next to an ear and said, "I think I just heard a big *thunk*."

"Thunk?"

"Ya," Lilly said, buttoning his shirt. "The sound of a body falling somewhere, used to work homicide, remember? Gotta go." Tugging his tie up he got halfway to the door, stopped. "I'm going to call Cotter," he said, turning, both hands working the knot, "and give him the news. I'll get back to you, Del, thanks."

"Something tells me I can't wait," McCauley said, refilling his own cup.

NINE

Esmond Cotter hung up the phone by dropping it the last few inches, and sank back into his well-padded leather chair. Nodding slightly every few seconds, after a moment, he got up, turned, and faced the glass wall behind him, the fine view overlooking the harbor.

He was not pleased with the conversation he'd just terminated. The good doctor implied that he could be considered an accessory to murder. He didn't see how since the victim was a former client of his — one who had been adjudicated *insane*.

But Durning had brought up a point. What about the others out there, former clients, the ones they referred to as *specials*? How might they react to Whitehead's murder? Especially after realizing he hadn't been simply murdered, but *butchered*. What if they became frightened and ran to the police?

But Cotter was getting ahead of himself.

He pulled a white cotton handkerchief out of a rear pocket and dabbed around the corners of his mouth. The damn CD, why had he kept it in the safe? The answer was obvious — it made sense at the time. With the federal probe continuing, a safety deposit box would have been out of the question.

Dabbing his lips again, he took a deep breath and ordered himself to relax. Once the disc was back in his possession, things would return to normal.

Gazing at the olive green harbor, Cotter barely noticed the huge LNG tanker sailing west past Castle Island. His fingers kneading his forehead, he closed his eyes; the sun felt warm on the back of his hand and he allowed himself to drift.

He was thirteen again, preparing to board one of the vans in front of the Buckingham, Browne & Nichols school, a day trip to Boston's Museum of Fine Arts. He was telling Jeff Aronson, his best friend at the time, how he'd decided to become a lawyer, like his father, and that Harvard, then Harvard Law School, was the route he would take.

Jeff agreed with him, thought it a splendid idea, said that he would become one too; they shook on it before boarding. Cotter remembered the animated conversation they had as they discussed their future that day all the way down Storrow Drive, even when they got to the Museum.

In the coming days it was different, though, it was mentioned perhaps only once, then never again. Cotter was thinking now how curious it was that Jeffrey Aronson ended up a veterinarian, not a lawyer, when the telephone rang on his desk.

Turning, half of him now covered in shadow, he picked up the phone. "Yes, Marie?" Cotter said tiredly. He nodded, looked at his watch. "Yes, Marie, put him through." Cotter looked at his watch again and grinned, almost painfully, like someone told him he ought to or they'd rip off an ear.

"Yesss, Mr. McCauley, thank you so much for calling," he said. He nodded deeply. "Yes, drop by anytime. Just call first to make sure that I'm in."

TEN

MIKE JANOWSKI EXITED MUL'S DINER rubbing his stomach. He checked both ends of the street. Coming out, stopping alongside him, Flippy Condon did the same thing before he burped and pulled a playing-card-sized advertisement from the pocket of the nylon jacket he wore, holding it in front of his face.

"Chip's Roofing," he read out loud, waving the card at Janowski. "Found it under my wiper this mornin'." His eyes widened. "Says here ol' Chip does rubber roofs, tile, slate, *metalwork* too, hmmm."

He looked at Janowksi.

"Man's got competition, Mike, 'cause we do metalwork, and wet work too. *Wet work*, hee-hee, ain't that what they call it in the spy movies, Mike?" Shook out his hands like he was snapping off water. "'Course, metal work turns wet *real* quick when you shoot 'em with itty bits of steel, then chop the fuckers up." He laughed again, stomped the sidewalk.

Janowski glared at him and said, "Shut the fuck up."

"Gotcha, Mike, just this card," Flippy said, losing his grin, waving the card by the corner. "Just these workin' stiffs, I can't figure 'em."

Flippy made like he was climbing a ladder. "'Course, it must be fun up there on the roof every day, fryin' your ass in the fucking sun, must get *real* dark." He angrily spit to the side, tore the card in half. "Think they call him chocolate?" he said, handing half to Janowski.

Janowski looked at him, tore his section in half, and picked his teeth with a corner. "What the fuck you talkin' about?"

Flippy shrugged, his grin frozen as he used his on his teeth too. "The guy's name's Chip — chocolate — Chip, get it?"

"Keep flappin' your gums, *you're* gonna get it," Janowski said, sticking the piece he used on his teeth to the side of Flippy's cheek. "C'mon, we got work to do," he said, stepping off the curb.

Flippy skittered sideways, furiously brushing as if it were two square inches of fire.

"C'mon, Janowski, that's disgustin'!" he screamed, dropping his card. "Know how many germs you got in your mouth?"

Flippy Condon picked his teeth with a fingernail as they headed east on West Broadway in a late-model emerald green Lincoln. "There's the boss, Mike," Flippy said, pointing.

Janowski said nothing, pulling the car to the curb on the corner of B Street in front of Street Lights tavern.

Jack "Wacko" Curran, current mob boss of Southie, stood with his back to the street talking to a man whose flattened nose, height, and width of shoulders gave him the appearance of a small bulldozer.

Two years before, following the murder of his predecessor, Marty Fallon, Wacko had forged alliances with the North End Italians and Chinatown gangs, slashing his way up through the ranks of the South Boston underworld before turning his eye to the untouched terrain of Roxbury, Mattapan, and Dorchester.

Then he did what no other Irish gangster had done before.

He reached out and had sit-downs with black representatives of the Humboldt and Castlegate gangs, and befriended the head of the Latin Kings. As Wacko expanded his empire, he rewarded his allies, maintaining an air of cautious optimism regarding his enemies — cautious as he stalled and stalked them, optimistic that in time they'd be eliminated.

The bulldozer, wearing a short-sleeved, aquamarine dress shirt he'd bought in Key West outside his crisply pressed faded blue jeans, nervously shifted his weight from one white cross-trainer to the other. As Wacko yelled something unintelligible, the big man tugged off his white-and-green Florida Marlins cap and sheepishly scratched at the top of his head.

"Sorry, Jack, know better, wasn't intentional," Butchie Limoli said. "Lots of things goin' on, kinda got caught up in the shit."

Wacko pressed closer, poked his chest with a finger.

"Naw, you only *thought* you were, Butchie. *Now* you're caught up in the shit." He glanced over his shoulder at Janowski, who gave him a wave, then leaned across Flippy, shaking both his head and a finger at Butchie.

Like someone had cut the supporting muscles, Butchie's shoulders slumped. He opened his mouth, but nothing came out.

As Janowski cracked the door to get out of the car, Wacko palmed him to a stop without turning.

"Remember, Butchie?" Wacko said. "*I* remember when the banks around here wouldn't give ya the gum off their shoes and still ya were hot to compete with all the other sports bars in Southie. Who'd ya come to? Me. Who helped ya — lent ya forty large. Now the renovations are over, ya gotta pay back — with interest — works for the banks, works for me."

Butchie grinned feebly, turning his palms up near his waist.

"Understand all that, Jack, I do, you saved my butt. I'm not sayin' I ain't payin'. It's just that business . . ." Butchie made little ascending circles with his hands. "Well, see, the bar's been a little slow. You gotta remember renovations — when you shut the place down — business sometimes takes a while to come back."

Nodding thoughtfully, Wacko cupped his chin in his hand. He said, "So, you're tellin' me business is slow?" Pointed up near the side of his head. "I think I'm startin' to get the picture," he said, and signaled Janowski to get out of the car.

"Ya know them spotters?" Wacko said. "The ones you hired from that security company to keep the peek on your bartenders, the ones you thought were stealin'?"

Butchie nodded, watched Flippy get out, shot Janowski a worried look as he rounded the front bumper of the car.

"Well, them spotters are workin' for *me*," Wacko said. "In an indirect kind of way."

Now Butchie shot Wacko a worried look.

Butchie said hoarsely, "But I hired those guys from Bernie, Jack."

Wacko slid even closer and growled, "Listen up — I *own* Bernie. He's into me for ten large, money I lent him to start up his company. Those spotters who've been reportin' to you . . . been reportin' to me too, tell me you're makin' a fortune."

Like he was checking for visual motor skills, Wacko slowly moved a finger side to side in front of Butchie's face.

Butchie blanched.

"So that makes Butchie a liar," he said softly, glancing at Janowski and jerking his head towards Butchie.

Janowski took two bouncing steps forward, launching an overhand right that caught Butchie Limoli square on the nose. The big man's knees straightened and his body collapsed back into the arms of Flippy Condon, who lowered him, with great effort, to the sidewalk.

The three standing men checked both ends of the street and looked at each other.

"No one seen nothin'," Wacko said, continuing to look up and down the street.

Janowski glared at Flippy. "Should have let him drop, bust open his head on the fucking sidewalk," he said.

"Naw, Flippy done good," Wacko said. "This fat prick cracks his coconut on the sidewalk and dies, how we supposed to collect?" He stared towards the police station a block down the street and said, "Get his wallet before one of them blue hornets flies out of the nest."

Janowski squatted down and rolled the half-conscious man from his side onto his stomach. Flippy straddled him and with both hands grabbed his rear pocket and, yanking back, tore the seat of the pants almost down to the knee. Over his shoulder he handed the wallet to Wacko.

Butchie groaned and rolled over. He sat up and felt under his butt as Wacko pulled bills from his wallet. Side-armed the wallet into Butchie's face, slapping the bills across the palm of his hand.

"Remember," Wacko said, walking in front of him. "How ya father used to slap ya, Butch, when he caught ya in a lie?"

With the back of his hand, Butchie swiped at the blood on his chin and nodded.

"I ain't your father, lie to me again I'll beat you to death," Wacko said, shoving the bills in his pocket. "Get this piece of shit off the sidewalk."

Janowski chortled as Flippy groaned and staggered sideways under the big man's weight.

Butchie swayed unsteadily, his eyes darting from man to man as he reached behind, tucked the torn length of pants into the top of his boxers.

Janowski shoved him, and the big man almost toppled again.

"You got off easy, Limoli," Janowski said to Butchie's back as the other man limped away. "I could have knocked out some teeth, fucking nose already was broken. Now," he screamed after him, "go back to your joint, and get us our *money*."

Flippy grabbed his crotch with a pained expression.

"Jesus, Jack, that fucker was heavy. I think liftin' him pulled me a nut."

"Be heavier dead," Janowski muttered.

Flippy winced and squeezed himself tighter.

Wacko opened the Lincoln's passenger side door. He said, "Gimme a lift down the Pen."

ELEVEN

JUST PAST THE LIBERTY BELL restaurant on West Broadway, Wacko told Janowski to pull over. "Collection day," he said with a snap, indicating the bar across the street with his thumb. "Get in there, Mike, get the *rent* from McGilvary."

Janowski looked out the window at Walsh's Tavern and tightened his grip on the wheel. He looked at Wacko.

"Ya, so what's up, what's the problem?" he said, opening his hands. Made a fist of the right and wrapped the left over it, rubbed the knuckles.

"What's up?" Wacko grinned. But the grin on his face said nothing was funny. "Nothing's *up*, unless *you* got a problem. You do, I'll send the kid in to get it."

Janowski snorted softly and turned off the ignition. His head moving slightly like the car was rocking; he stared through the driver's side glass. "I got a system, Jack, the same I've used for the past two years. I know *when* to collect, *who* to collect from."

He pinched the end of his nostrils together, examined the fingertips. "Funny, throw a hard punch, get a nosebleed sometimes." Wiped his fingers on a leg of his jeans.

Flippy sniggered, said, "Them they land on get one too."

Wacko turned his head to the side. "Anyone *talkin'* to you?"

Turning back, Janowski repeated how he had his own system. Always hit the Point area first, working his way down to the Lower End. Then he'd head to the South End, collect from the joints down on Shawmut Avenue, the ones up Columbus. Then on to Quincy, Weymouth, Braintree, down to the Cape. Twenty-two stops, he said, with everyone expecting him a certain time, the money waiting, right in right out, and he was on to the next.

Indicated with his head the bar across the street.

"These guys?" Janowski said, looking down at his watch. "*Won't* be ready 'cause I'm usually not 'round until noon. Got 'em trained, Jack. Don't like breakin' the pattern."

Wacko stared up the street, vacantly rubbing a finger in circles on the skin on the back of his hand. "Untrain 'em, *patterns* will get ya killed, fact," he said, slapping the dashboard as he said the word "fact."

He looked out the side window, scanning the flat roofs of the projects like he was expecting someone to be up there. Turned back to Janowski.

"Ain't *askin'* ya, Mike, go get the envelope."

Getting out of the Lincoln in front of the Pen Tavern, Wacko leaned back in, saying, "When you guys think you'll be back?"

"Around eight, why?" Janowski said, pulling the seat belt across his chest, fastening it.

Wacko raised his fist to the side of his head, extending the little finger and thumb. "Call me when you're close. You, me, that other kid, the boxer? Gonna head down Hap's tonight."

Janowski nodded. "Sounds about right," he said. "Hap's been dodgy with his payments lately, you're thinkin' maybe something's up?"

Wacko said, "Heard he's bettin' up a storm in some little stink-hole in Quincy. Bettin' *our* money. This cute little prick's hard to pin down, but his old girl still tends bar there, told me she'd call me as soon as he comes in. Wanna be ready."

"No problem," Janowski said, fingering the window button. "That it?"

"No, got some dry cleanin' at the Highland Cleaners. When you're heading down Dorchester Street, could you stop by, pick it up? See the guy Leo, he takes care of me good."

Janowski bit the inside of his cheek, winced, and barely said, "Ya." Slipped the car into gear. He struggled not to floor it as he pulled into traffic.

He suddenly ripped the wheel to the right, jumping on the brakes hard enough to toss Flippy from the rear seat to the floor. Janowski punched the roof and roared, "Fucking errand boy, huh?"

"Ain't no errand boy, Mike," Flippy said, pushing himself back onto the seat. "You're his number one guy." He blew at something in front of his face and slapped at his cheeks and eyes. "Christ, what do you got ridin' back here, a cat, fucking dog?"

Janowski yanked back on the steering wheel, inadvertently

hitting the horn. "Number one, huh? We'll see, motherfucker, we'll see."

Flippy picked his ball cap off the floor and whipped his knee with it.

Janowski's face darkened as he stared over the headrest. "Sometimes my sister takes the car, got a dog. Got a problem with *dogs,* motherfucker?"

Flippy shrugged, nervously u'ed the bill of his cap. "Huh? I like dogs, Mike, just could pass on the fur," he said.

"Dog rides in back, you a dog, Flippy? Maybe Wacko thinks *I'm* a dog."

Flippy turned around and looked out the rear window. "Jack . . . Jackie ain't like that," he said softly.

Janowski, biting his lower lip, nostrils flaring, nodded.

"He ain't?" Still nodding. "Good. Know what *I* ain't, Flippy?"

In the rearview Flippy shrugged his shoulders again.

"A fucking *chauffeur,*" Janowski said, turned back facing the windshield. "Now get your skinny ass up here," he said.

TWELVE

THERE WAS NOTHING FLASHY about T.K. O'Malley's. It was just your typical serious sports pub: not a lot of mirrors, a few thick-cushioned, black leather booths lining the walls, and small pedestal tables with long-legged, dark wooden chairs around them near the windows. There were seven flat-screen TVs in the place, including one in the john.

All night the TVs blared with a deafening din the Red Sox, Bruins, Celtics, or occasionally fights. Patrons screamed themselves hoarse over it, the main reason McCauley preferred to work days.

Today there were only three TVs on, all of them showing a golf game from somewhere in North Carolina. On a satellite radio Marvin Gaye's "Mercy, Mercy Me" blended smoothly with the boredom of the ten or so patrons who sipped their drinks, occasionally laughing and pointing at each other as they talked softly in small groups scattered around the place.

The thud of a fist at the end of the bar drew the attention of McCauley, focused on dumping his second bucket of ice for the day into an aluminum bin.

"Ya hear 'bout Kooky Keveaney?" Enis McGarrity shouted, readying the fist to come down again. "And yes, I *will* have another," he said, before McCauley could answer, pointing at his empty glass.

Backhanding a few stray ice cubes off the bar, McCauley came towards him, grabbed the empty, and swung it under the tap.

"A fresh glass, if you please," McGarrity said, frowning. "*Frosted.*"

McCauley blinked like someone had sprayed him with water, stared, turned over the glass in the dishwasher. He slid open the chiller and pulled out a frosted. "Customer's always right," he said, nodding, pulling the beer.

"'Specially ones who tip," McGarrity said, grinning, grabbing hold of the glass. Barely lifting it, he began sipping the suds.

Wiping his hand on a bar towel, McCauley threw a thumb over a shoulder at something behind him.

"Know what that is, McGarrity?"

McGarrity shifted his head to the side and looked under the other man's elbow. Took a sip of his beer, wiped his mouth with two fingers.

He said, "Looks like a fucking bell to me."

McCauley put his palms on the bar and leaned closer.

"It's a tip bell, McGarrity, you ring it when you're tipped — *if* the tip is more than a nickel, of course. Now, have you heard a bell today?"

McGarrity took another swig, wiped his mouth with the back of his hand, licked the foam off, and grinned. Pondering the answer he shook his head slowly.

"Can't say that I have, McCauley, 'less of course you count the one at the Gatey this mornin', callin' the faithful to Mass."

"And did you tip the nice priest at the Gate of Heaven?" McCauley said.

Now McGarrity shook his head faster.

"For the love of God, man, I'm never inside, why would I give him a tip?"

McCauley leaned even closer. "Maybe for the same reason when you're in this joint you never leave me one either."

"And that's?" McGarrity said, staring at him with watery eyes, using both hands to straighten his scally.

"You're a cheap fucking prick," McCauley said, pushing off.

"I'm offended," McGarrity said. "And here I was offerin' to give you some dirt,"

"Concerning Kooky Keaveney?"

"The same," McGarrity said, nodding deeply, like someone punched down hard on his chin.

"Rather the money," McCauley said.

McGarrity reached into his pocket, his eyes turning white as he rolled them. "Oh Keee-hrist, McCauley, my last two bucks, here, take 'em," he said, dropping the crumpled bills on the bar. "Now, will you ring the damn bell and shut the fuck up, let me tell you about Kooky Keaveney?"

McCauley looked at his watch, his eyes widening in mock concern. "Geez, almost four thirty," he said, pocketing the money, ringing the bell. "Be out of here in less than ten minutes."

McGarrity's eyes grinned along with his mouth. "Then I'll save the story for later, but I will have one more for *your* road, McCauley. That's if . . . you could put it on the cuff," he said, drumming the tips of his fingers together, smacking his lips.

McCauley pulled a beer into a frosted glass and set it down on the bar. "Because you're such a good tipper," he said sarcastically.

A woman's voice shouted from a booth behind them that she'd pick up the tab if McGarrity, in the future, would drink his beer elsewhere. Twisting around on the stool, McGarrity extended the middle finger towards the offending party, jerked it in increments towards the ceiling.

Turned back to McCauley. "An *asshole*," he said, satisfied. "So," using the knife-edge of his hand to awkwardly slice the air near his face, "where are you off to, your choppy-chop class?"

"Yup, to Quincy," McCauley said, "my regular workout."

McCauley had studied karate since the age of fourteen. Small for his age, he began it as a means of defense against schoolyard bullies, street corner punks. But as he progressed in rank, earning a black belt by the time he was twenty, he discovered karate was a lot more than just punching and kicking. Learned that it was a way of life that required discipline, dedication, and focus.

Like any recently released inmate, McCauley carried resentment, paranoia, and anxiety like cats in an oily sack with him. He was angry too; prison makes you that way, turns a man's sharp edges inward. But found that by going to the dojo and practicing his kata, working the heavy bag, he could leave most of the badness behind.

"Wish I'd done something like ka-ratty when I was a kid," McGarrity said sadly. He quickly brightened, dry-washed his hands, and wrapped them around his glass. He hauled it to his lips, closed his eyes as he swallowed. "You gotta have discipline," he said with a burp, wiping foam from his upper lip. "Lost mine years ago in Quincy, the Bargain Center, shoe section, I think. Oh, don't give me that look, McCauley, it was *easy* to lose things in that dump those days, the goddamn place was *filthy*."

"Imagine that," McCauley said, his face awash in wonder. "Lost your discipline in the Bargy, and *still* making it this far. Ought to buy you a drink for that."

McGarrity winked. He said, "You just *did*, McCauley," and took another slug.

THIRTEEN

B Y THE TIME MCCAULEY WALKED OUT of T.K. O'Malley's, huge gray clouds were blocking the sun and the temperature had dropped at least ten degrees, the quirky autumn weather. Outside of the Mexican restaurant, half a block down, a small, round-shouldered man in a white apron stood smoking a cigarette.

"Hey, Pepe," McCauley shouted to the Mexican cook, "your

salsa's hotter than that thing you're smoking." Pepe grinned, stuck the butt in his mouth, clapped once, and pointed at McCauley.

As McCauley crossed busy Dorchester Street towards the Mustang, in front of Thornton's Flowers, the cell phone on his hip rang. Snapping it open, "McCauley," he said brusquely, keeping an eye on the approaching eastbound traffic as he electronically keyed open the door.

On the other end a woman's voice said, "Yes, Mr. McCauley? My name's Kandy, the receptionist for the law firm of Cotter, McBride, & Cotter. How *are* you today?"

"I'm . . ."

"I have a phone number for you, a Ms. Wainwright's, the private investigator who worked for us."

McCauley didn't know the name, but knew who she was. He had spoken to Cotter earlier that day, the lawyer explaining how the firm, following the break-in and wanting to avoid the police, had hired a private investigator. A woman, he said, the daughter of one of his wealthy clients. She was new to the game but aggressive.

Apparently she'd made the rounds in Southie, made a couple of contacts, but McCauley surmised, because she was a woman and an outsider, she'd run into the inevitable brick wall. Not wanting to cover the same territory twice, McCauley had asked for her number.

"Thank you, Kandy," McCauley said sweetly, jotting it down in a small notebook. He hung up and dialed the number from behind the wheel and got a recording. He left a short message and a return number.

Nosing the Mustang into the Dorchester Street traffic, heading east, he had to slow down after a few blocks where people were crossing, joining others in a somber line outside of Casper's funeral home.

At the Eighth Street lights, he saw faces from the past, outside Sullivan's Pub standing around smoking. One of them, Moses Halloran, a notorious car thief, petty burglar, and gambling degenerate, stood tapping on a butt just beyond the doorway. He gave McCauley a wave, though he might have been shooing ashes.

McCauley warily nodded, partially lowering the window.

"Moses," McCauley said over the glass.

"Long way from the handball court, McCauley," Moses said, taking another drag, exhaling smoke through his nose. He shuffled ahead a few steps, stopped, tapped his toe on the sidewalk behind him, and glanced at the scratch ticket he held in his hand.

McCauley ran the back of his hand by the glass as he pulled away from the lights. Checked his watch, it was quarter to five. He'd pass by again, and if Moses was around, find a reason to stop.

The last time they had spoken was a year before, at a handball tournament in Norfolk prison. Both had been eliminated in the semi-finals. Prison sports are tough, played with a certain ferocity, and people often get hurt over "games." Moses took losing hard that day, and an argument had evolved into a fight. They lugged him back up the Hill, to maximum security, where he wrapped up his bid in the Essex block.

Moses couldn't have been out for more than a month, but Mc-Cauley knew that guys like him made their contacts quick. Probably already knew about the break-in. The trick would then be to get him to talk.

McCauley stopped at the Dunkin' Donuts in Andrew Square, got a large regular to go, and turned left after crossing the 93 bridge. A short distance down, in the narrow corridor between the South Bay Center and 93 South, a burly state trooper stopped traffic as a loader operator deftly realigned heavy Jersey barriers like matchsticks. As he waited, McCauley listened to Stevie Wonder's "Superstition" off a disc.

As the final barrier was being bulled into place, the trooper approached the car. McCauley recognized him as Lieutenant John Walsh.

Walsh grinned, made a cranking motion with his fist, and Mc-Cauley lowered the window. "How're you doing, brother?" Walsh said, grinning broadly, pumping McCauley's hand.

"I'm doing, Jack," McCauley said.

"Ya, me too," Walsh said, raising his palms, shrugging. "Two kids almost college age, with details I'm on seven days a week lately." Gave a wry chuckle. "Lately? Pretty much for the past goddamn year." Shrugged again. "Hey, whaddaya gonna do?"

"Still out in Framingham?" McCauley said.

Walsh shook his head, swept a rock aside with his foot. "Naw, outta there, did a year in the Lower Basin before transferring Milton, was working with Stevie Long, he just made captain."

McCauley remembered when Long had just made lieutenant.

"Stevie's a competent guy," McCauley said.

Walsh nodded, grinned. "Top notch," Walsh said, "but he's been sitting behind a desk too much," patted his stomach. "Been trying to get him to work out more." Grinned again just as the loader operator gave two short blasts of his horn. Walsh glanced at him, held up a finger.

"How are *you* doing?" Walsh said, looking concerned.

"Like I said, John, I'm doing, trying hard to get back in the groove."

"Listen, you need me," Walsh said, reaching behind, pulling a card from his wallet, "here, this is me you need anything, call, don't hesitate, all right?"

The loader operator hit the horn again. Tapping the roof twice, Walsh headed towards him.

"Stay sharp out there, John," McCauley shouted out after him.

Walsh waved without turning.

McCauley followed 93 South past a billboard advertising some new space movie. Then, after the Sunbeam Bread sign, took the Neponset exit.

Crossing over the river, bearing left onto Quincy Shore Drive, he kept his eyes peeled for a familiar face manning a state police speed trap, in an area notorious for them. Seeing no one, he pressed down on the accelerator, enjoying the burble of the dual exhausts, the pull of the Mustang's modified engine.

He passed two yacht clubs on the left along Wollaston Beach. The huge space behind them filled with bobbing sail and power boats. Across the bay and beyond the bridge at Long Island, the sky, which crushed a hard ribbon of yellow at the horizon, was grayer than Quincy granite.

Past the police station, through the lights after Quincy College, he made the loop around the granite church, turned onto Washington Street and pulled into a space in front of the post office. Grabbing a worn pair of red Super Bag gloves off the rear seat, he got out, went around and opened the trunk, pulled out a gym bag, and tossed the gloves in.

As he followed the sidewalk west up Maple Street towards Quincy Center, he reminisced about all the times he had thought about doing this, heading for a workout at the dojo, as he walked the dirt track in the Norfolk prison yard.

When you're behind the walls, it's like that. The good times are pulled up on a mental Rolodex, relived in a kind of detail he never would have considered when he was free. They're all you've got.

A warm rain began to fall as he turned left at Chestnut Street, entered the first doorway he came to, and climbed three steep flights of stairs

FOURTEEN

MCCAULEY HAD STUDIED OKINAWAN Uechi-Ryu karate since the age of fourteen, under the same two instructors, Forrest Sanborn and Carmine DiRamio. He held the rank of sandan black belt in the system.

Though Forrest and Carmine were both veteran cops, McCauley's ex-con status meant nothing to them. Both had been around long enough to know that, on "the job," sometimes shit happens, so in the dojo, when McCauley cinched the triangular knot in his belt, nothing else mattered except the matter at hand.

Students began every class with stretching exercises to loosen the ligaments, release the speed trapped within them. Kata was next. Kata, or forms, are an individualized, choreographed series of punches, kicks, and blocks.

When McCauley performed them with speed and a kind of animal ferocity, he focused on imaginary opponents, people who'd hurt him, future targets. Inevitably, however, as the workout progressed, he emptied his mind of all negative thoughts and connected with the chi, his inner power.

In his mind's eye, he envisioned glistening green harbors and bordering low-lying hills as he completed his kata and kumite, sparring with even more thrust to his kicks, snap to his punches. He reveled in the Kotickkite, where the students faced off and pounded each other's arms and legs in an attempt to better condition them to absorb the blows of opponents.

McCauley had added a whole other dimension to his fighting skills, learning to box in prison. He finished his karate training with rounds on the heavy bag.

After the final bow and clap at the end of the class, he removed his gi top, along with his belt, slipped on his Super Bag gloves, and began the first of six three-minute rounds using a windup egg timer to time them.

Feet diagonally splayed shoulder-width apart, McCauley circled to the right of the 150-pound bag with shuffling barefoot steps. He used his left hand like a fencer his foil, stepping solidly behind each jab — stick, stick, stick.

And move.

His two-hundred-pound frame skimming the floor's wooden surface, he feinted with the left hand, fired a short right hand, twisted his hips into a left hook to the head, sliding right, flicking the jab again to keep his imaginary opponent off guard.

Leaping hooks followed head feints. Lead right hands were chased by stabbing jabs that dented the bag as McCauley danced out of reach of his invisible adversary. He had awakened the bag, and now it was doing its best to drain him of his dwindling energy.

The last round ended with a left jab, straight right, left hook, right uppercut combination followed by a twelve-punch barrage. The final bell was followed by polite applause from a group of students who watched from the side. McCauley touched his right glove to his head, lowered it in a circular flurry, and wrapped his left arm around the still swinging bag. It tugged him slightly ahead before stopping.

"No one . . . beats the bag," McCauley said tiredly.

The students laughed because they could.

After showering, McCauley felt better. Nothing wrong with

being tired, it was how quickly you recovered. On the way out, he stopped outside the training hall. All the lights but one extinguished, its luminescence reflected off the hundred and fifty pounder, the ring of sweat beneath it.

He swore the bag grinned from the corner.

Outside, on Maple Street, next to a beauty shop, McCauley had dropped down to double-tie his shoes when someone behind him whistled. Rising, he saw his old friend and sensei, Forrest Sanborn, a fireplug with legs, with a quarter-mile grin, filled with a perfect set of choppers, coming towards him. Forrest had this never-off-balance rolling gait, and even with a bag over his head, McCauley would have known it was him.

"Hear the bell, Del," Forrest said, grinning broadly enough McCauley could barely see his eyes.

He said, "Knew I shouldn't have told you about me boxing in prison."

Grasping his hand in his enormous mitt, Forrest shook it into the shoulder joint.

"Relax, just kidding," Forrest said with what might have been a wink. "How's the slice-and-dice class going? Mario taking care of you?"

Forrest knew there were moments when quick hands weren't enough and had given McCauley an edge — literally. He introduced him to Doctor Mario.

According to Forrest, he first met the guy, a master of Philippine, Argentine, and Chinese knife-fighting techniques, in the service somewhere overseas during the waning days of the Vietnam War. It was said that Doctor Mario had given lessons to Diem, the president of South Vietnam himself, and that was good enough for McCauley. Since his mid-twenties, and again following his release, he made twice-monthly visits to Doctor Mario's Columbus Avenue studio to study the art of the blade.

"Going good," McCauley said. "With a knife in his hand the doc's got more arms than that goddess Kali. Be tough in a face-off with him."

Forrest's eyes disappeared again as he reached behind to the small of his back, and came out with a Smith & Wesson .38 Chief's Special.

"That's what these gizmos are for," he said. Then the grin softened and his eyes grew serious. "Anything new with the case?"

McCauley shook his head, picked up the gym bag, the Super Bag gloves extending out past the zipper.

"Nope. Still hoping that Matt Doyle, the agent, comes out of his coma. Docs say it could happen," McCauley said, shoving the gloves back down. "Been told he's showing signs, Forrest, the doctors are talking a miracle. I recently read about a firefighter down in New Jersey who, following an accident, was left comatose. The guy was brain damaged; mostly mute for almost ten years. Last week he came out of it and asked for his wife. Doctors don't know why, but sometimes people improve. If Doyle comes out of it and remembers what happened, my attorney thinks it could flip my conviction."

"Ya, three years too late, you already served your sentence."

"*Still* serving it, my friend," McCauley said as the phone rang in his bag. He fished it out and snapped it open.

It was Mackey Wainwright.

FIFTEEN

MICHAEL CIAMPA WALKED OUT THE DOOR of 40 Salem Street into the North End sunlight with a lot less bounce in his step than when he walked in.

"Hey fuckhead, where the fuck you think *you're* goin'?" the smoker's voice said behind him.

Like someone lassoed his neck, he jerked to a stop. Shifting weight to his heels, he looked warily past the huge steroid freak in the doorway, wearing a black tee, black jeans, cloddish squared-toed shoes, and into the dark eyes of Biaggio Vitale.

"Jesus, Mr. Vitale, no disrespect intended, thought . . . thought we were finished, we weren't?" Ciampa said, his throat contracting around barely enough air to squeeze out the words.

Biaggio Vitale, sockless in his tan Gucci loafers, wearing burnt-yellow slacks and a cream-colored Nat Nast shirt with beige stripe on the side, stopped twisting the diamond pinky on his plump right hand and signaled the steroid freak out of the way.

Curled an index finger towards his barrel chest twice.

"No, *I* was talkin'," Vitale said, "*you* was leavin', nothin' was settled, far as I know."

Ciampa held his hands out, palms up. "After you picked up the phone, you waved with your finger, I thought we were through."

Vitale looked at the floor, then to the side, made a face like somebody told him forty pounds less he'd look like Sinatra. "Naw, kid, not *wavin'*, the finger was pointin' — up — which means wait, pointin' down?" He chuckled. "Then *you* got a problem. Now get your gamblin' degenerate ass back in here before," he put his hand on the steroid freak's shoulder, "in front of Fredo here, I point at the floor."

In the center of the nearly empty room at the rear of 40 Salem Street, Ciampa shifted uncomfortably in the low-backed wooden chair. The only light was from two shadeless windows and an overhead bulb covered, oddly, by a green paper Chinese lantern.

In one corner of the dark-paneled room was what looked like a bar, with three wooden stools with red cushions in front. The sheen of the hardwood floor, brightest at its outermost edges, became veiled as it moved in towards the center — as if worn down by pacing.

Ciampa, thinking how, after climbing three flights, listening to Vitale wheeze close enough to part the hairs on his asshole, he had to sit and listen to this greaser, dressed like a can of Lemon Pledge, go on about who the fuck did he think he was not paying off his debts.

Vitale saying, You think because your father's a hotshot developer, friends with the boss, that because you're his kid you don't pay? Think again, Vitale said, leaning in close enough he could smell the garlic, anchovies, and cigarettes on his breath, Think *again*.

Spit flying, Vitale told him that when it comes to money, the boss had no friends, saying, "You owe us almost a hundred g's, now how you gonna pay?"

Ciampa listened, afraid to wipe his face, as Vitale ranted how

he'd better come up with a plan for the money — a plan he better believe — when Fredo stuck his head in the door saying there
was someone downstairs he should see.

The muscle-bound freak pulled the door closed behind him, but
the creaking outside it said he hadn't gone far. Ciampa stared at
the windows, with their spectacular view of a solid brick wall the
length of a ball bat away, and considered throwing himself out.

Sure he'd bet and occasionally — well, maybe more than occasionally — lost, but who the hell didn't? Loyal to the Celtics, he
bet them heavy. Up fifteen points in the fourth, they'd get sloppy
and win by three — when they were favored by four — and he'd
be out five grand. Same thing with the Sox, bet heavy when
Schilling was hot, say twenty-one and four, then watch him
kick dirt, have a bad day, and it was another ten grand down the
shitter.

Ciampa heard wheezing coming up the stairs, and Vitale came
into the room — with Fredo behind carrying duct tape in one
hand, pruning shears in the other.

"Just so you know," Vitale said, closing the door, "the boss
was downstairs, told him our problem. Said the *hell* with your
father, do what you gotta."

To the side, opening and closing the shears, Fredo stopped
squeezing, tucked them into his budge. Tore off some tape,
looked at Vitale. "Biaggio," he said, "tie the hands out front or
around back?"

Bending close enough to almost touch Ciampa's nose, Vitale
said, "Up to him, Fredo. The sight of blood — yours — bother
you, kid?"

Glanced up at Fredo. "We'll start with fingers," Vitale said,
straightening.

"Call my father!" Ciampa screamed, lurching out of the chair,
"he'll give you the money, he'll give you . . ."

Vitale threw a bear hug around him, and got dragged a few
feet before both crashed to the floor.

Ciampa thrashed like an eel and threw an elbow that caught
Vitale on the side of the neck, broke free, and managed to get to
his knees — only to be tackled by Fredo again who twisted him
onto his side.

Like he was sprinting, he pumped his legs, his shoes' edges scraping the floor, broke free flipping onto his stomach, and started to crawl towards the door. "Call my father!" he screamed as Fredo yanked on his the legs. "Call my father!" Fredo leaped onto his back, driving a huge forearm down into his neck, slamming Ciampa's face into the floor.

When Ciampa woke up from the dream, he had trouble breathing, and his arm was caught behind him in the sheets. It wasn't until he felt the pinch on his ear that he realized he wasn't in bed.

"Got the arm, boss," Fredo said, twisting, "you gonna lose him the ear?"

Ciampa marveled how the heavy palm on his cheek almost seemed comforting. Until someone poured hot lead in his ear.

Ciampa's scream was high pitched, feral, and quickly muffled.

"Fucking shit's amazin'," Fredo said, flattening the tape across his mouth, "'magine, stickin' through blood."

"Hit him with another piece, cover the lower lip better," Vitale said.

Ciampa inhaled blood, could only gurgle when the fire started again.

Upside down in front of his face, only inches from the floor now, Vitale's grinning face appeared.

"Amazin', huh?" Vitale said, his face appearing sideways now. "Only cut through it halfway and will ya *look* at the reaction. Oh, and kid, ya nose looks broke, wouldn't breathe too hard, might drown in your own fluids." The face disappeared.

"Pull off the tape, don't want the prick dead."

Fredo yanked off the tape, examined it as it dangled from his fingers.

"Some sticky shit," Fredo said thoughtfully, balling it, and underhand-tossed it onto the bar.

Ciampa was only vaguely aware of being hoisted from the floor, slammed down in the chair, and then the rasping tear, again and again, of duct tape circling his chest.

Vitale held out his open hand. "Now, where are them shears? The trouble this prick's caused us, instead of the pinky, gonna start with the thumb."

Ciampa's collar was glued to his neck and his nose felt like it was the size of an eggplant.

Fredo chuckled into Ciampa's ear, "Ear's like you, kid, barely hangin' on," he said, while Vitale stood in front of him clicking the shears.

"You righty or lefty?" Vitale said.

"Please," Ciampa said through swollen, stuck lips.

Vitale shrugged. "No matter, after today, lefty," he said, coming around, grabbing a hand.

"I can get ya the money," Ciampa shrieked. "Gimme a phone. Christ, gimme a phone, I'll get you the money." Started to sob.

Vitale tapped his head with the shears. "Ya? From *who*?" he said.

"My wallet, a card, number's written in red," Ciampa blubbered.

Vitale stuffed a twenty, three fives, some ones in his pocket, flipped the wallet back over his shoulder. Toed the small pile of debris on the floor. "Got a lot of shit in that wallet," Vitale said, stepping on Ciampa's driver's license, looking at Fredo. "How're we doin' there, Fredo?"

Squinting at a business card, Fredo punched numbers into a silver cell.

Vitale poked Ciampa's cheek with the shears, said, "Ain't better be games." Fredo looked at Vitale, nodded, and pressed the phone to Ciampa's ear.

"Yes, hello, it's me, Doctor, Michael Ciampa," Ciampa said, straightening, coughed. "Not so good, Doc, you said I need you, call."

Ciampa looked up at Vitale and rapidly blinked.

"Doctor, my father gave you over a million for me, I need a hundred thousand." As he turned away he closed his eyes, and tears ran down his cheeks. Shook his head.

"You don't understand," he said, raising his voice, "I'm not fucking asking, you pay me or I go to the cops. Just do it, you son-of-a-bitch, or the next call I make's to the D.A., the *Globe*, fucking *Newsweek* I have to."

Ciampa sank in the chair and nodded deeply a few times, like almost on the verge of falling asleep.

"Okay, Doc, that's the right decision, two days, no more."
Ciampa screwed up his face. "No, *I'll* decide where and let *you*
know, got it?" He pulled his ear away, looked at Vitale. "You're
getting your money," he said.

"Ya how, who the hell's he?" Vitale said.

"He's a doctor," Ciampa said, wiggling his fingers, rotating his
shoulders, his courage returning. "Hey, the fucking tape's cutting
my circulation."

Vitale got his eyes level with his. "How 'bout you convince me
or I cut off your *head*? Now, who the fuck is he?"

Ciampa tried to smirk, but it came out a grimace.

"Remember — a few years back, that kid I killed in the bar
fight in Cohasset?"

The other two nodded.

"Well, I got off, so to speak, because I was found, by a Norfolk County jury, not guilty by reason of insanity. Did all of my
time in Edgewater."

"Ya, so what?" Vitale said. "You were lucky then, ain't so
now, why you bringin' it up?"

Ciampa stared at him steadily. "Because this doctor's the guy
who runs the place."

"The same place you was?" Vitale said.

"Uh-huh."

Vitale looked at Fredo, shrugged. "So what, I'm missin' somethin' here?"

Fredo made little circles with his finger next to his head. "They
call it the Ranch, boss, fucking animals there, state hospital for
the criminal insane."

"I *know* what they call it," Vitale growled. Glared at Ciampa.
"Now what about this doctor?"

"My father bought the guy years ago."

Vitale said, "He *bought* this doctor, how you mean?"

Ciampa shuddered, quickly shook his head.

"I can't . . . can't tell you," he said, staring at the floor.

Vitale grabbed his chin, savagely twisted his head, stuck the
tips of the shears up his nose.

"You little prick, I oughta . . ."

"Go ahead, kill me, it won't get you paid."

"And what makes you think this doctor will pay?"

"He'll pay, guaranteed."

"Why?"

"Because he's more afraid than I am," Ciampa said.

SIXTEEN

WALKING DOWN MAPLE STREET, McCauley talked into his phone. "My connection to Cotter?" he said. "Can I call you Mackey, Ms. Wainwright?"

She told him he could.

"Actually," he said, "my connection's with Lilly. I worked with him in the past, been friends for years. Personally, I've never met Cotter." Then he explained why Lilly had contacted him.

Then it was her turn.

In a voice gushing energy, Mackey told him how her relationship with Cotter had begun with her father, who had been friends with the attorney for thirty years. Cotter had represented her father in his various business affairs and they had become friends, later golfing buddies. They sent greeting cards to each other's families at Christmas.

Because of Cotter, she said, as a young girl she had thought about becoming a lawyer. But while attending Northeastern, taking criminal justice courses, she had worked part-time for a private investigator who was employed by a large downtown law firm. It was then she was bitten by the *bug*.

She laughed after she said this, like it might not have been such a great idea, or maybe because it was. McCauley was unable to ask which, because Mackey's call waiting went off, and she put him on hold. She came back on seconds later, apologized, and told him she'd call him back later.

He was almost to his car when he hung up. He stood for a moment and thought about her voice, her words and laughter like a tuning fork still humming inside him. Probably only in her mid-twenties, she had the energy of a kid and reminded him of someone he knew about a thousand years before. He found himself wondering what she looked like.

Since his release from prison, less than three months before, he'd only been out on two dates. The first one had been Ida, a cousin of Walter's, the owner of T.K.'s, the bar where he worked. Take her out, Walter said, but don't dare bring her back after. Ida was sweet and divorced, with a couple of kids, and had the habit of repeating — coulda, shoulda, woulda — when she drank, which, apparently, was often and a *lot*.

The second was Rhonda, a girl from the projects, someone he had been in lust with since he was around twelve, she a few years younger. Now in her late thirties, McCauley had banged into her at the supermarket one day, a little small talk and they had agreed to go out. But when he went to meet her, she never showed up. Seemed she'd gone back to her old boyfriend who, she found out later, was gay.

In prison, the social workers had warned him, when he first got out, about getting involved in relationships. Told him you'll have enough on your mind. When the relationships go bad, they go bad fast, with all the years of pent-up anger, frustration, and anxiety exploding at once. He had taken their warning to heart.

Still, Mackey Wainwright, there was something about her — just her *voice*.

Tossing the gym bag into the trunk, he decided before talking to her again to first meet with Cotter. It wasn't professional discussing a case, in this case, with a relative stranger, before he had all the facts. But who was he kidding? This wasn't a *case*, he was doing a favor, and he certainly wasn't a *professional* anymore — unless you called tossing tequila and sour mix a profession.

Climbing into the Mustang, McCauley banged a Uey in front of the post office and stopped for the red light half a block up at the corner of Sea Street. As the turn signal clicked a mindless beat, he thought about the one person he did want to talk to.

If Wacko Curran would talk to him back.

Jack "Wacko" Curran was the boss of South Boston. Not the ward boss or the state rep from the district, the *boss* of it, and, most said, of points beyond too.

A few years older than Wacko, growing up in the Point in a comfortable house on Seventh Street near the corner of I, Mc-Cauley had known him since he was a kid. While Wacko grew up on Pilsudski Way, in the Old Colony Housing Project, where it hardly paid mornings to roll out of bed.

McCauley had hung with Jack's older brother, Mike, and both were active in South Boston sports. Baseball and football in the summer and fall, organized hockey at the MDC rink in winter. When everything bored them, they learned to box up The Muni.

Always tagging along behind his brother, Jack was more than tolerated. Everyone enjoyed his easy laugh and desire to please as he served the older kids ice water from the sidelines, or ran for Cokes after games.

But things changed.

In the seventh grade McCauley got into Latin while Mike went to Saint Augustine's, and he didn't see much of him after that.

And he never saw Jack again.

Never sure why it happened, perhaps just the way of most childhood relationships. But now, almost thirty years later, Mc-Cauley was certain about two things.

Mike's kid brother was now known as "Wacko," and he wasn't running for Coke anymore — he was selling it. He had become the city's preeminent drug dealer, a notorious killer and racketeer.

He wouldn't be hard to find. Word was the deceased mob boss Marty Fallon's empire fit him like a glove, and that Wacko ruthlessly ran it, with a grin and a gun, from a rear office in the Pen Tavern on West Broadway.

On the Boston side of the Neponset Bridge, McCauley pulled into a Shell station and stopped next to an air pump with a stump for a hose and a duct-taped sign on its face that read "not werking." He flipped open his cell and dialed the Pen's number.

As it rang, a gangly, olive-skinned attendant came out of the office and sullenly eyed him before returning inside. On the other end of the line, someone picked up.

"Ya?" the smoky voice said, then yelled something unintelligible to someone else there. In the background, glasses clinked and people talked. Above the din, Jimi Hendrix sang "All Along the Watchtower" with way too much bass.

"Hey, hello, *anyone?*" McCauley said, watching the same guy come out, but this time followed by a bigger guy, who pushed him aside and came towards McCauley.

The smoky voice came back on the line.

"Who'd ya want?"

"I'm looking for Jack Curran," McCauley said, nodding at the attendant, pointing at the phone.

"Jack who? Ain't no Jack here," the voice said. Then, like he was talking through a mitten, he said, "Put those fucking glasses over here. What I say, the guy's lookin' for Jackie?"

The big attendant stopped at the door, glared at McCauley, and fanned the air in front of his belt, like he just cut loose with a cloud of goat cheese and baba ganoush. Waving at him, McCauley pulled out of the station, heading towards 93 North.

At the top of the ramp merge, the background noise died, and another voice, not a smoker, could have been talking from inside a funeral parlor, came on.

"Who the fuck is this?"

And McCauley's stomach jumped like his cable had cut off during an episode of *Cops.*

"Delray McCauley, looking for Jack Curran."

McCauley's mind was on anything but traffic as soft, snorting laughter wafted like smoke from the other end of the line.

"McCauley? You got him, cop. Now, whadda ya want?" Wacko said.

"Long time, Jack," McCauley said at the top of the merge, cutting left around an MBTA van, accelerating. "Like to talk, if we could."

"Ya, and this *talk* is gonna benefit who?"

"If we could meet, I'll explain."

McCauley thinking for a moment that Wacko would hang up, but he didn't. There was just stony silence before he said to someone else there, "What time we meetin' the other guy?" and it must have been signaled.

"You're lucky, McCauley, cancelled my meeting with the *Cardinal* today, ya might get his slot. I'll call you back."

And the line went dead.

Traffic was slow up ahead, flashing blue lights, after the Morrissey Boulevard exit, the reason for the bumper-to-bumper. As he passed the NSTAR gas tank, with Sister Corita's painting on the side, McCauley told himself lies. That he wasn't nervous, that he was just meeting the brother of the Pop Warner quarterback. But time had passed and the quarterback was dead, killed in a car accident in his teens, and the kid brother had been murdering people for years.

But Wacko wasn't the only killer.

To protect himself, McCauley had also killed in the line of duty. He wondered, as he passed the Dorchester Yacht Club, if Wacko, in a perverse twist, could present the same defense: that his victims were merely a consequence of defending *his* life?

He also wondered what Wacko knew of his investigations in the mid-eighties, when Wacko and another brother Kevin were robbing banks all over New England and he was on the bank robbery task force. How close they were to catching them? At least until McCauley's gangster/informant, an Old Colony boy by the name of Terry Ahern, who had run with the Currans for years, was gunned down early one morning, as he stepped out the door of the L Street Diner with a bellyful of blueberry pancakes.

McCauley's every instinct said that he did.

The *Boston Globe* had just slipped past the passenger-side window when his cell phone rang again.

"Where are you?" Wacko said.

Taking the Columbia Road exit, McCauley told him.

"Meet me, fifteen minutes out the Island, front of Sully's — alone," Wacko said, and hung up.

As McCauley spun out of the top of the rotary heading north towards the state police barracks, he thought about all the friends he had there, men who'd still put their skin on the line for him, and he wanted to stop, to tell them where he was going, who he was meeting — if anything happened.

And then he was past it, and the ocean was ahead on the right, and the sunlight was finding cracks in the dun-colored sky, the L Street Bathhouse crowding the beach in the distance.

Pushing the gangster out of his mind, he filled it instead with memories of the L when he was a kid: of swimming lessons, doing chin-ups to impress the girls, how it felt after a steam, exiting through those huge front doors in winter.

As he passed the L he tapped the horn, brought the Mustang up to forty; the dual exhausts hummed with a throaty resonance. Wacko said fifteen minutes. He'd be out the Island in less than one — plenty of time to check the parking lot in front of Sully's before the gangster arrived.

The phone rang again.

"McCauley," he said.

"Del? It's Mackey, sorry it took so long to get back, is it still a good time to talk?"

SEVENTEEN

WHEN HE ENTERED THE PARKING LOT at Castle Island, McCauley barely had to feather the brakes. Didn't need much, it was nearly empty.

There were only three vehicles: a blue van with commercial lettering just to the right of the entrance, and two late-model, full-sized cars parked twenty feet apart in front of Sullivan's restaurant. On the hill behind Sully's was nothing besides a few young trees and the castle itself, the granite block colossus, Fort Independence.

Sully's was a seasonal joint, an assembly-line takeout selling hot dogs, cheeseburgers, clams, and fries to the masses who jammed the lot seven days a week, beginning early March when it opened. Along with each order, the employees served up a side dish of bored indifference. The indifference came free.

By mid-October, winter had confirmed its reservation and Sully's was closed. For the most part all that remained were seagulls circling high above the fort in a sky where sunlight grew more precious with each passing day.

As McCauley circled past the two cars, he looked inside. In one of them, two people faced each other, their backs to the doors, a woman pointing angrily at a middle-aged man behind the wheel. He looked down, nodding his head slowly when maybe he should have been pointing back. In the other car, a couple of kids were behind the wheel, two heads, one set of shoulders.

McCauley came back around to the entrance and pulled alongside the van. The lettering on its side read PETER'S EXPERT PLUMBING and had little painted wrenches on either side. Below that read: *I can do anything!* McCauley looked at the guy, figured he probably could, but he was asleep. His mouth was open; a newspaper flopped over the steering wheel. Either Wacko was a master of disguise, or he had yet to arrive.

McCauley shifted the car into reverse, backed up, and stopped it in gear. Checked the area around Sully's again. The car on the left, the fighting O'Reillys, was in the process of leaving and was backing out of the spot. The other car remained where it was, the two heads together.

McCauley checked his watch. Exactly fifteen minutes since Wacko had called. McCauley, always punctual, was thinking maybe that Wacko wasn't, or maybe that the gangster was jerking his chain.

He glanced down to check the time again and when he looked up, Wacko was there, standing at the rear of the car, framed in the side-view mirror, like he'd just beamed down from the mother ship, and McCauley wondered how in the name of God — or something else — he got there.

A rap on the roof was followed quickly by the sound of drumming fingers, and Wacko's face appeared in the passenger window. In a weird kind of salute he touched the inside edge of his open right hand above his unblinking eyes and the drumming stopped. His nostrils flared ever so slightly, like a wolf taking in the scent of his surroundings, before he straightened and pointed at the lock.

McCauley still pressed on the brakes when Wacko squatted a little and stared. The eyes were without a hint of emotion, as if he were staring at something a thousand miles away to a corner of the world where it was already night.

McCauley hit the lock-release button and Wacko got in, closed the door, examined the palms of his hands.

"Fuckin' car's filthy, oughta clean it," he said, wiping his fingertips on the dash.

Nothing clever or smart came to McCauley's mind, so that's what he said. He was more interested in examining the man to see if he could detect the changes. Like maybe the things that had shaped him, created the creature he allegedly was, would be there forming, like drops of water, on the Gor-Tex surface of the blue L.L. Bean jacket he wore.

But McCauley was disappointed.

He expected a monster, but all that sat next to him was a memory. Still relatively young, Wacko was just an older version of the boy he used to know who chased footballs on cool leaf-swept days down at Columbia Park.

Leaning left, he shifted his gaze to McCauley's feet.

"Won't be movin' like that," Wacko said, sinking back in the seat, staring ahead. Nodded towards the other end of the lot. "Head up that way, park to the right facing the Sugar Bowl."

McCauley did what he told him.

"Now what?" McCauley said.

"Now what? We walk," Wacko said, getting out of the car.

The two men followed the sidewalk along in a southerly direction. "Nice day," McCauley said, and immediately regretted it.

Wacko looked at the sky, squinted.

"Ain't bad," he said "How's Mum?" He looked over his shoulder towards the parking lot and the Mustang.

McCauley looked back over his. "No one's hidden in the trunk, Jack," he said softly.

Wacko gave him a strange grin like he was clenching something between his teeth and quickly looked over the opposite shoulder.

"Ain't worried, Del-boy, fact," Wacko said, flicking at his nose. "So, Mum, how is she?"

"Ma's great," McCauley said, "been living in Braintree. After Da passed she got rid of the house on Seventh. Too many memories, took years to stop the longing for Southie. And yours?"

Wacko bit his lip, laughed dryly.

"Oh Christ, I hear ya. Ma's good, I guess. After Kevin . . . well, after Kevin I finally got her outta the projects. She *let* me get her outta the projects; moved her into a nice little place in

Quincy. Remember, when we were kids, they used to call Quincy the Irish Riviera? Been there lately? Goin' to hell. Be movin' her outta *there* pretty soon, probably this time with a fucking towtruck. She's not keen on movin', Mum."

McCauley tapped Wacko's forearm with the back of his hand. He said, "Sorry to hear about, Kevin, Jack. Was behind the walls when it happened."

Wacko hooked a finger inside his elbow and stopped him. In his eyes, McCauley could see sadness bleeding into anger.

He said, "How *sorry*, cop? Sorry it wasn't the state cops that got him, or sorry he didn't get it sooner? What the fuck do you know, *sorry*?"

For the second time in minutes, McCauley had no response. The wind was freshening and, off to his right, there were small crests forming on the surface of the gray Atlantic contained in the area known as the Sugar Bowl.

Wacko pulled the zipper tight to his neck, picked up the pace. McCauley had to jog to catch him.

"Look, Jack," McCauley said. "Sorry about your brother, but I'm not apologizing for something I had nothing to do with."

As Wacko lengthened his stride he alternated between staring ahead and glaring at McCauley.

"Who's askin' you to?" he said. "What are you lookin' for, cop? Why'd you call the meet? How 'bout we shitcan the pleasantries, all right? Talk about what you really want. *You* want." He threw his hands over his head. "Son-of-a-bitch, why'd I come out here?"

McCauley knew he was losing him. Wanted to grab him by the coat and slow him down, but he was afraid to touch him, afraid if he did, Wacko would pull away swinging, and McCauley wouldn't take that from any man.

Wacko abruptly stopped, carried slightly ahead by momentum, turned and faced him. McCauley's hands began to subtlety rise, and Wacko caught the motion and gave him that same weird grin.

"Hands?" he snarled derisively. "I don't fight with my fucking hands."

Behind them, on a hill near the fort, a mist of starlings descended into a leafless maple with branches like twisted wires.

McCauley, on the verge of losing any chance he had of connecting with the gangster, had to do something quick.

He screamed, "What the hell's wrong with you? I didn't come out here to fight."

With a look like someone had touched off a sparkler in front of his face, Wacko stepped towards him, growled, "Don't bark at me, motherfucker."

"Not barking, Jack, talking," McCauley said "I came out here to talk.

"Ya? So far you've been talkin' a lot but you haven't said shit," Wacko said, balling his fists on his hips. Stared across the harbor at Spectacle Island and slowly shook his head.

"Rule number one, don't talk to cops . . . ever. I'm outta here," he said, turning. He looked up towards the fort like he was searching for something. As he started to walk, the starlings rose with a whirr and broke cries.

"I'm not a cop," McCauley shouted at his back "I held my water, did my time just like you did, Jack. So if you think I'm still a cop, what they say about you's true."

Wacko turned and came back at McCauley, stopping only inches away. His eyes were penetrating and dark. His entire symmetry seemed to suck into itself like he was coiling, getting ready to spring.

"And that's?" Wacko said.

"You're fucking *wacko*," McCauley said.

Wacko's mouth was a grim line as his face contorted into dark, red folds. His eyebrows rose like a pair of helium balloons, to a height McCauley didn't think possible. He looked towards the parking lot, then back at McCauley, raised his right fist shoulder height, and threw it down hard enough that the material of the sleeve zipped and cracked from the effort.

When he raised it again, it held what looked like a .25 automatic that he pressed to his hip. Tilted it down at McCauley's groin, shot another glance over his shoulder, stepped even closer, shoved the gun into McCauley there.

"Watch *The Sopranos*, McCauley? Blink, you're gonna be one. *Now*, what was that you called me?" Wacko said.

EIGHTEEN

WITH ONLY A MASTER'S DEGREE in psychology, Noah Durning wasn't really a doctor. People just called him that — and it was something he never discouraged. Whether it was done out of respect or something else, didn't matter. What mattered was that he was director of forensics at Edgewater State Hospital, the marshal of this here crr-aazy town, and whatever he decreed was law.

He sat behind a huge oaken desk facing an apartment-sized window. The desk, according to the antiques dealer he bought it from, had belonged to the doctor who, in the middle of the nineteenth century, discovered anesthesia in Boston. He'd brought them into the modern age, much like Durning was doing now, and if the desk was good enough for him . . . well.

The window overlooked an expansive yard — a prison yard — though Edgewater wasn't a prison in the traditional sense.

Oh, there was certainly the twenty-foot outer security fence, as well as a twenty-foot inner. And between the fences, swathed in miles of razor-edged concertina, was a dead zone where a man could be shot just for walking. Armed guards watched from towers, patrolled the fences twenty-four/seven with dogs.

Still, Edgewater was officially known as a *hospital*. If a defendant was proven mentally incompetent to face a criminal trial, no matter how heinous the crime, he would end up in Edgewater State Hospital, where there were doctors and nurses, and the inmates were referred to as *patients*.

Elbows on the desk, fingertips forming a bridge under his nose, Durning focused outside the window across to a spot where a small marble statue of a naked nymphet with a dove on her arm stood. On a pedestal, across an expanse of lush, neatly trimmed lawn, beyond a cement walkway — patients *must* remain on the walkways — she kicked her leg out gaily beforeher, frolicking in the middle of a twenty-foot ring of manicured, low-lying shrubs, its core thick with geraniums, marigolds, and impatiens.

He stared without blinking, thinking how he hadn't been left with a choice, the degenerate had dug his own grave.

Said to himself, lie in it you troublesome son-of-a-bitch, lie in it. Pulled open a drawer, shuffled some papers aside, looked down at his Remington 51, .380 automatic. Would have liked to have killed the bastard himself.

Jolted by the telephone's ring, he closed the drawer and his eyes as he lifted the receiver.

"Doctor Durning," he said tiredly.

"You're mad, you know that."

Durning smiled, got up from the desk, and crossed to the window, where he put on his glasses. There was more than the usual madness in the yard.

A gray-uniformed patient, windmilling his arms, had just run out the door of the B-1 block. Three guards were in pursuit, one losing his hat as he ran; the patient was making a beeline for the statue.

"I don't *know* any such thing," Durning said, touching his glasses, "other than you could accurately say that to anyone here, except for one of the staff. I'll have to ask you to trust me, Cotter, try to understand my position."

On the other end, it sounded like someone was choking.

"Your position? Your *position* will put us in jail. People aren't stupid. Good Christ, man, you're unable to see it? We could hardly afford the first one."

The lunatic tugged at his belt as he leaped over the ring of low-lying shrubs. The guard nearest him tripping on shrubs, going down, face-first, through the geraniums.

"I thought I made it clear," Durning said, watching the other two guards run past him, "he's extorting money from me today, he'll be ringing *you* up tomorrow."

The patient scurried like a crab up the pedestal, ripped down his pants, and started humping the nymph.

"I've made the arrangements," Durning said, like he didn't care to explain it. "*Arrangements* can be stopped."

"The messenger's already out on the street. I won't see him again until the package is delivered."

Durning stared through the glass and readjusted his glasses.

Two guards pulled on the patient's legs while the other, geraniums dropping off of his chest, leaped up and grabbed hold of the back of his shirt, They wrestled him down, rolled about, flowers kicking into the air, a tangle of legs, open mouths, and arms.

"There's something else," Cotter said softly, "something we haven't discussed but have to. Something's happened, and if the wrong person finds it . . . God, man, the names are on it, *those* names. Understand what I'm saying, any more, there'll be *problems*."

Durning turned from the window and ripped off his glasses.

"What are you telling me?" Probably best not to talk on the phone.

He gazed at the ceiling, dropping the phone to his chest. Shook both his head and the fist he'd made of his free hand before lifting it back to his ear.

As calmly as he could, he said, "Where are you now?"

Looked out the window. Order was being restored.

"I'm here, in the office all day. You have to do something to stop it. You must."

"Listen to me, Cotter," Durning said, watching.

Hands cuffed behind his back, two guards on his arms, one at the ankles, they carried the attacker of nymphs, facedown, bare butt in the air, back towards B-1.

"Yes . . . What?"

Durning threw his glasses on the desk.

"Not to worry, Cotter, I'll be there shortly; we'll talk about it then."

NINETEEN

CIAMPA HAD SEVEN HOURS TO WASTE and used two of them up at the Village Steak House. Less than a mile from his new apartment, he had only eaten there one time before. He didn't go anywhere regular these days, he owed too many people. And the next thing you know, someone's telling someone else, yeah, he's always hanging at so-and-so, and then there's a problem.

He had moved, beating the landlord out of nearly two month's back rent, from a nice little two-bedroom apartment in Winthrop, on the beach near Deer Island, to a studio in the Gaslight Village complex off Route 18 in Weymouth. Some called it "downsizing."

Ciampa called it healthy.

When Biaggio Vitale said, Don't think about hiding, kid, we know where you live — nice little view of the ocean, huh? Like that was supposed to *scare* him. He'd neglected to tell him, really, that he didn't *know* shit. That he'd been in Weymouth for over a week.

As he eyed the beautiful blonde, Ciampa spun a toothpick around next to a canine and hooked a thumb in a front pocket. Standing next to the hostess stand, she gave him the eye. Still spinning the toothpick, he moved a few inches closer and said, "Maybe you should let me take you to Vegas sometime, a pretty girl belongs where there's lights."

Taller than Ciampa, no problem there, she was holding a clipboard, wearing a cream-colored blouse that allowed a fair amount of the creamy inside tops of her breasts to show; tight-fitting, straight-leg black pants; and black sandals, the last four toes of each foot wrapped by a thin strap.

She smiled and looked down, made an exaggerated check on the clipboard. Stuck the end of the pencil in her mouth, tugged down a little on the lip. Made it obvious she checked out the hand with the toothpick.

Little bat of the lashes. She said, twiddling the pencil between a finger and thumb, "Ain't married, huh? Hate the way married guys are always hitting on me."

Ciampa's eyes widened. Sharp little number.

"No, I'm not, haven't had the pleasure. Doesn't stop me from hoping, though, you know, that someday I'll find her."

"And take her to Vegas?" she said, blinking, sticking the pencil back in her mouth.

"What happened?" she said, pouting, pointing at his bandaged ear, the bruises on his face.

"This?" Ciampa said, touching the ear, wrinkling his nose a

little. "I'm a bouncer see, got into a fight at work. Ought to see the other guy."

Like a flashbulb, the smile. "You can really handle yourself, huh?"

"In all the *good* ways," Ciampa said.

From out of a side door behind her, a cheap tan suit and red tie approached, eyeballing Ciampa across her shoulder. Kept his eyes on him as he straightened the knot.

"Marlene," the man said, switching his gaze to the clipboard.

Marlene stared at Ciampa, jerked up her eyebrows, and made like she was going to cry.

"How're we doing with the lunch crowd?" he said, glancing up at Ciampa again.

Marlene held the clipboard in front of her face. "Pretty good, Arnie, tables one through eight are already filled. Sixteen through twenty *were* filled for a while, but they already ate and left."

The suit and tie looked over Ciampa's head into the room behind him. Checked his watch.

"Only tables one through eight? We've got twenty-four. Could you please try to spread out the customers?" He looked at Ciampa and said, *please*, like he was tired of saying it again. "You don't, and when the other waitresses complain, I'll just have to send them to you."

The hostess frowned.

"Arnie, people don't want to sit in the back, everyone asks for up front by the windows."

"Like me," Ciampa said, "because sunlight's good for the digestion."

"And you are?" the suit said. Smart little prick.

"Like I told you, a customer."

Arnie gave Ciampa a pleasant look that made him feel less than.

And that made him mad.

"Personally, I think she's doing a wonderful job," Ciampa said, leaving the toothpick in his mouth, rising a bit on his toes.

Arnie stepped away from Marlene, pressing his palms together in front of his chest. "Can I help you somehow?"

Staring. "Didn't ask for none, *Arnie*, but the food here sure's great." Ciampa nodded at Marlene. "Just like the staff."

Ciampa took the toothpick from his mouth and pointed it over his shoulder. "Maybe you should check on the waitresses who aren't busy, figure the areas you could cut back on the help," he said, flicking the toothpick past him.

Struggling not to laugh, Marlene bit her lip and without turning, looked back at Arnie. Arnie's chin quivered.

Well . . . thank you," Arnie said, glancing back, "about the food and the service I mean, but I . . ."

Ciampa said, "See, know a little about the business myself, my dad owns a restaurant. When I come back — and I plan to — we can talk if you'd like."

Arnie's face flushed a deep shade of red. He looked past Ciampa again.

"Sounds good, probably best to try and keep the other girls busy," he said, walking past him.

Marlene hugged the clipboard and beamed. My hero.

Ciampa gave her the oh shucks, ma'am, tweren't nothin' look, and her smile notched a crease in her earlobes.

"Like I was saying," Ciampa said, looking into her eyes, "I'm always on the look out for the perfect girl."

"And how will you know when you've found her?"

"That's where Vegas comes in. It's all in the way they handle the light, if they absorb it or reflect it. And there's a hellava lot of light in Las Vegas."

"And if they *handle* it well?"

"Well, if they handle it perfectly, and I almost don't believe it could happen, lot of disappointments, you know? But Vegas's got almost as many wedding chapels as it does neon lights. If I find the right girl, who knows? Might return one day, use one."

Still smiling, she played with the end of one of her waves, tilting her head to the side.

He had her.

"You're crazy, you know that?"

Really had her.

"It's the searching that does it," Ciampa said. Give me the chance, baby doll, you get a full-body search.

Ciampa checked his watch. Only one thirty. He was supposed to get the dough from the doctor at seven — in the middle of the South Shore Plaza.

Safety first, with a million eyes watching.

Figured he'd give the old greaser — really, he should just tell him to go fuck himself after what he did to his ear and the rest of his face — ninety-five, no, make that ninety dimes, tell him the doc needed time to round up the rest. The Sox were playing New York tonight and, with Schilling playing like shit, he was betting the Yankees hard. And with any luck he'd be at a card game at the Tremont Hotel, killing the suckers at blackjack. In one fast night he could make up the difference of what he owed Vitale.

Ciampa patted himself on the shoulder, must be psychopathic, he thought, the way he could see into the future. And so as not to waste his trip to the Plaza, he'd pick up something sparkly for the baby doll here to help grease the rails to his bed.

Ciampa shrugged, said, "Hate to say it, doll, but I gotta scoot." Lowered his voice, leaned towards her conspiratorially. "If there isn't a significant other, any chance of me giving you a call?"

Keeping her eyes on him, Marlene grabbed a napkin off of a shelf. Her blouse opening further when she leaned over to write. Her breasts hanging firm, round, and loose in the light cotton bra, Ciampa fighting the urge to rise up on his toes.

Pursing her lips as she straightened, folded it, handed it over. "Best time's after six," she said, arching her back, hugging the clipboard again.

With this babe, Ciampa thought, how could anything *before* six be worse?

He closed his eyes, held the paper to his forehead. "The letters are forming; I see . . . a name . . . *Marlene?*" Triumphantly opened his eyes.

Marlene giggled, playfully swung the clipboard at him, "You're such a brat. You heard it from Arnie already."

Covering his head, he took exaggerated steps past her, gave the front door a push, and winced as a spasm of heat hit his face.

"Still hot out there?" Marlene asked coyly.

Turning, Ciampa winked at her, said, "After meeting you, doll, it feels like AC."

TWENTY

TO BE ON THE SAFE SIDE, Ciampa had gotten to the Plaza around six. Grabbed a coffee near the information booth, then flirted with a Brazilian girl at a kiosk outside the doorway of a sneaker joint. She was selling toy helicopters that came back around when you threw them. Got her number, too.

At another kiosk he bought a cheap radio that he plugged into his ears. Listened to the game as he waited. The doctor said seven. Bad enough at seven thirty-five he still hadn't shown, but the Red Sox were handing the Yankees their ass.

And the other thing.

People seemed to be staring. It wasn't obvious enough he could say, Hey, you know me? No? Then what the fuck are you *looking* at? Just every once in a while he'd see a face looking, then turning away. Natural curiosity? Maybe. Natural fucking nosiness, probably. Made him uneasy. The only thing that relaxed him was that none of them looked eye-talian. Hoping that guys like Vitale rarely went out of their circle.

He got a call from the doctor a little past eight. Had been an emergency, he said. In the chow hall a patient had used a fork on his throat, tore himself up pretty good. When the guards responded, about a dozen other patients attacked them. A hostage was taken, the place was locked down. Had been impossible to get to a phone.

He said, Can I meet you tomorrow? The earlier the better, how about eight? You name the place; I'll be there on time with the money.

Ciampa agreed and gave him a location closer to his place. Closing the phone, he found himself grinning, shaking his head.

Out of control, under control, just like that, Ciampa thought.

Scowling, he pressed fingers into the earphones. Son of a fucking . . . the bottom of the sixth, the Sox up by five and Damon had just blasted a three-run homer into the bleachers. Then something that screamed inside of his head almost transferred to his mouth. He jumped to his feet and ripped out the earphones, speed-dialed a number on his cell.

"Good evening, Tremont Hotel, how may I direct your call?"

"Ya, hello, room . . ." Ciampa said, scanning a paper scrap he tugged from his pocket. "Four sixty-five, please."

"Connecting."

"Ya."

Ciampa said, "Stingy, it's me, who's up there tonight?"

"We got a full house, all guys who *pay*, what you want?"

"What you mean, what do I want?" Ciampa said, looked at his watch. Could be there in less than a half an hour.

"Said we got a full house, don't got any room unless you're comin' to pay off your marker."

"Yeah, the marker, yeah, I was going to pay off on that tonight, told that to Stevie today."

"Stevie ain't here."

"He's not?" Slow down, he'll pick up you're desperate. "Gee, that's funny, he told me the game was tonight, he'd be there, he's not?"

"What don't you understand about no?"

Ciampa stuck an earphone in. The Fenway crowd was one big roar. Shut the fuck up, shut up, who the hell scored?

"Stingy, thing is, Stevie knew I was coming into money today."

"And the money you came into, you bringin' it here?"

Home run, Manny Ramirez? Drove in another? I'm fucked. *Fucked*.

"Well . . ." Calm down, or the prick will hang up. "That's the thing, it didn't happen tonight, tomorrow, first thing, guaranteed. On my mother. Stingy, I need in this game tonight."

"Increase your marker."

"Yeah, if I lose, but I won't, I'm due, Stingy, I'm due."

"The fact you wanna increase your marker tells me you've *decreased* what's left of your brains. You want them to stay in your head, Mikey boy, pay your marker."

"That an okay, Stinge? Mean that I'm in? Stingy? Stingy?" Ciampa stared at the phone, screamed, "You son-of-a-bitch."

Started to throw it, dropped his chin to his chest, the phone to his lap. Fuck the card game, doesn't mean shit, for all I care Stingy's dick can fall off.

Got everything under control.

Cautious, he took the back roads from the Plaza, followed Washington Street south through Braintree. Just before Holbrook he took a left on Plain Street over the tracks and followed it until he turned right on Route 18 in Weymouth.

Nothing to worry about, really. Vitale wouldn't dare make a move until he was certain he wasn't getting his money. Ciampa giggled, stamped his feet on the floor — he had just decided he wasn't.

In the morning, after the doc dropped the dough, he'd head over to Logan. Or rent a car. Might take longer to reach New York but, with the heat at the airports, he wouldn't have to worry about the hundred dimes in his pocket.

Or maybe just head to Chicago.

Turn the cash into bank checks, hop on a flight. In no time at all he'd connect with a sports book and, with just a little more, he'd be rolling in dough. Wasn't planning on mushing Vitale. When he got home he'd take care of the guy. Throw in a bonus, a little extra cake in the box to smooth out the hairs on his back.

He stopped for the lights at the hospital, pulled out the steakhouse girl's number, swung it up over the dash. Under the street lamp's glare the black ink jumped from the napkin, the writing in an identifiable feminine script — Marlene O'Mara, with a number beneath.

Ciampa whispered her name. The napkin was soft, but he imagined, compared to her skin, like sandpaper. She was Irish and beautiful, and dying for this stallion — 100 percent eye-*talian* — to give her a call. Pulled on the wheel. Yeah baby, yeaaah.

When the light turned green, he had the napkin to his nose, the guy behind him leaned on the horn. As the guy roared past, Ciampa gave him the finger. Let him go, Ciampa thought, accelerating slowly, still holding it up to his nose.

Less than a mile, after a Friendly's, he turned left off 18, passed between a pair of brick pillars. On one was a sign, gold print on a green background: Gaslight Village. Surrounded by acres of woods, the apartment complex had street lamps set on fancy square poles every hundred feet along the narrow, two-lane road leading in.

Passed the first of a cluster of four-story buildings: their white stucco fronts set off by empty black balconies, the parking lot across from them filled. Drove past another block of apartments at the rear of the complex, turned right just before a swimming pool, headed up a small hill. The parking area behind it also seemed full.

Following what had become his nighttime parking routine, wanting to hear what was coming, Ciampa shut off the radio and lowered the windows.

Traveling slowly along the rows of parked cars, past a space that resembled a mouth, he noticed backup lights flaring at the end of the lot that looked like they belonged to a van. The space, under a street lamp, was next to a Dumpster, what looked like an SUV on the right. Ciampa liked parking under a light.

Tiny drops were just beginning to collect on the windshield when he shut off the engine and looked at his watch. It was almost nine thirty. He checked the side mirror, the rearview, then over his shoulder. Nothing but cars, and now fucking rain. Over the dashboard, under the light he looked at the napkin, said her name, Marlene O'Mara.

Thinking he should call her, tell her he's leaving — leavin' on a jet plane, don't know when I'll be back again — that kind of bullshit, get the longing for him in her heart, how he misses her already. Opened his cell phone. Maybe she'd come? No, but sure as hell set the stage for the return engagement. Ciampa thumped the steering wheel. Yeah, *baby*.

The drops were thicker now, heavy like mercury with less space in between, the impact on the roof growing louder. Through the rear window the lights in the apartments seemingly Vaseline-smeared. Closed the phone, thinking, my luck be pouring like hell when I'm through. He'd call from inside.

Outside, above him, the street lamp flickered and almost went out. What the? Ciampa pulled himself close to the windshield, looking up. Its dull, diminishing glow illuminated a small cloud of vapor above it. Grabbing the napkin, he got out of the car, walked underneath, and squinted up in the rain.

Above him the halogen lamp crackled as something inside writhed like an iridescent snake. A blue electrical charge arced from a small hole in the front.

"Think it will pass?" a voice said behind him.

Startled, Ciampa spun.

"What?"

To the left of the rear bumper, silhouetted in the lights from the apartments behind, stood a huge figure.

"Meant the rain," the giant said, looking up without squinting. He lowered his gaze and took a step towards him. "The name's Jarvis . . . *Reems*. Do you think it will pass?"

Ciampa's bandage was getting wet now.

The street lamp crackled, the iridescent snake writhed.

Ciampa's eyes widened as he took in the guy. Certainly no guinea, looked more like Doc Savage. Definitely time for exit stage left, but he couldn't climb over the Dumpster, sure as hell wasn't running through briars. The guy was a nut? Good, get the bull on the nut, be the aggressor, Ciampa barked, "Hey, who the fuck are you — the Weather Channel?" And took a step towards him.

Big mistake. The giant moved two steps closer, stopped at the gas cap. Ciampa could see he wore some kind of vest over a dark long-sleeved tee, black sneakers or shoes on his feet. His dark pants appeared to be tied at the ankles.

Ciampa watched as he took a short length of broom handle, from a large pocket on the side of his leg, and laid it on the trunk. Dropped next to it what looked like a poker chip that he pulled from another.

In his left hand, held close to his hip, was what looked like a *pipe*? Used just the wrist to swing it up, point its center mass at Ciampa.

"Hey, man that's . . ." Ciampa said, pointing, the rain now soaking the napkin, "you're holding a piece on me and telling me your name?"

Reems smiled pleasantly. "Walther PPS, with attached sound suppressor. What you'd call a silencer," he said. "Except in movies, they don't exist. Still, you heard nothing when I shot out the light."

Ciampa looked up over his shoulder. "You shot out the . . . *why*?"

Reems nudged up the barrel. "Move back towards the front."

"You picked the wrong guy, I ain't got a dime," Ciampa said, taking a quick glance at the Dumpster. No place for a foothold, everything's wet. Now his ear was beginning to sting. *Fucking Stingy keeping me out of the game, that son-of-a-bitch behind this?*

"Drop your pants."

What? "Hey man, you're some kind of faggot, you've got the . . ."

On him that fast, he couldn't tell if the guy leaped or slid, pressed into his chest with the silencer.

Ciampa looked down, his lower lip trembling. "Hey, man," he whimpered.

"Pants. Won't ask you again," Reems said, raising the gun to his throat.

Ciampa unbuckled, let them drop to his ankles.

Another jab in the throat. "The underwear too." Gave him wiggle room, then straightened him back up.

Ciampa, afraid to move now, if he did he'd fall over. *This was out of control, man, out of con-trol. Wondering this guy going to kill me? Rape me? Had his ball bag shrunk from the rain or from fear?*

"Hey, please, if it's money you want, Christ, give me a chance I..."

"Shut up."

Reems dropped the barrel back to Ciampa's chest, tilted to the side, reaching down. Straightening, he kept his right arm close to his body.

Ciampa was afraid to look down.

Reems smiled. The rain ran in rivulets through his Marine-style haircut, down his cheeks, off the edge of his jaw.

"You got a question?" Ciampa said, fighting hard to maintain his composure. "Well, I got the answer to any you got — money, you hear that? A hundred fucking dimes in the morning."

Like it was all understood, the giant nodded and took a step back. The rain was falling harder now, seemed to explode off his nearly shaven skull.

"So, we got a deal?"

Like he had a joke he was dying to tell, Reems jerked his eyebrows up twice.

"So, do we have a . . ."

"Question," Reems said, "the biggest man-killer in Africa, what is it?"

He's giving me *trivia*? Fuck it, gotta keep his mind on the money. "Listen, Reems, know what you can do with a hundred dimes?"

Reems made a face, disappointed, shoved him with the gun.

"Final answer?" he said, the voice deep, weighted with doom. "Your life depends on it."

"My life?" I'll play this fucking game. "Man-killers in fucking Africa?" Ciampa said. "How 'bout hundred-thousand-dollar lions?" Smirked. "*Final* answer."

After the Walthers 9mm's two muffled pops pulverized his heart, Ciampa had just enough air left in his lungs to gasp. Pressing in close enough to kiss him, Reems drove the foot-long, serrated black blade under his chin, through the roof of his mouth into his brain. The napkin hit the ground, the blood and ink mixing together

"Wrong," Reems said, jerking up twisting the handle. "*Hippopotamus*," he said.

TWENTY-ONE

THE SAME DAY, after his meeting with Wacko, McCauley had called Cotter as he followed Day Boulevard along the Sugar Bowl's curve away from Castle Island. A very protective secretary picked up.

Cotter was in a meeting, Kandy said, and then she seemed to change her mind. Did I say meeting? No, he had gone out to lunch. McCauley told her good, he had a good idea where he ate, that he'd meet him there. He thanked her abruptly and hung up the same way. Turning right at the Farragut statue, heading towards L Street, he went over the meeting with Wacko in his head.

He had explained to the gangster how he was looking for sources: B&E guys, burglars, even junkies, the names of anyone local who might be involved in the trade. Made it clear that they weren't going to be busted or turned over to the cops. What was important to him was getting the safe.

Not surprisingly, Wacko had some questions of his own for McCauley, like, Bad enough you want to help out this cop but why should *I*? And while we're at it, who was the broad sniffing around here last week? And ya, what's *in* the safe and what's in it for you? McCauley didn't know much, but told him what he knew.

Finally, Wacko had said, as they rounded the rear of the fort, near the Clipper Ship monument, I'll give you some names, guys who might be involved, then *you* do the legwork, keep *me* informed, and the safe, if anything's in it worth havin' — he stabbed himself in the chest with a finger — me, *I'm* gettin' an end of it, see?

McCauley made it clear that he did. "Good," Wacko said, "call ya later."

They didn't shake hands when they parted.

*   *   *

On Summer Street, after the old Fargo Building, McCauley turned right at the lights heading towards Northern Avenue and the Seaport district. Once simply known as the Waterfront, a bustling triangle of fish-processing plants, honky-tonk bars, and night clubs with violent reputations on one side of Northern Avenue, and blocks of empty warehouses on the other, was an area that, even before sunset, always seemed dark.

Then things got worse.

In the late seventies, with the depletion of New England's once-rich fishing grounds off George's Bank, the Waterfront fell on hard times. The fishing industries folded and, outside of the barrooms, there were few signs of activity.

Legitimate activity.

Where fishing boats once docked, smugglers now unloaded tons of high-grade Colombian weed, taken from mother ships miles outside of the harbor, and a new use was found for the warehouses.

In the nineties things changed. Big developers came in and turned everything into towering glass-and-steel high-rises and the

Waterfront morphed into the Seaport district.

Half a block up from the World Trade Center Boston, Mc-Cauley found a metered space across from the twenty-story Seaport Building. He got out of the Mustang and checked his pockets: two dimes, three ones, and a ten.

The meter only took quarters.

Looking down the road in a northwest direction, he spotted a state trooper writing a ticket at the rear of a Lexus. Slipping it under the wiper, he headed in McCauley's direction.

As the cop checked the meter next to a late-model Caddy and started to write a ticket, McCauley tried to make out his face. Thought it might be someone he knew from the old days but it wasn't, the trooper was young. Wanted to tell him he had ten years on the job while he was still skipping classes in high school, but didn't. Decided to wait in the car until he passed.

When he opened the door he heard someone shout, "Sneaky bastard, McCauley." And McCauley looked up. Half a block north, South Boston resident artist Norman Crump stood in the doorway of his newly opened Crump/McCole Gallery waving a finger. "*Know* what you're doin', Del, you're hoping he'll pass." Norman shook his head. "Won't, he's a prick," he said and started towards him.

The last time McCauley had seen Norman Crump was three years before, when they both attended a play written by a Southie kid whose father had been killed by the mob.

With the door still ajar, McCauley said, "Shouldn't you be off selling a painting or something?"

Norman continued to shout even as he got closer. "Enough time for paintin', Del, and I do hate to preach, but I'd stick a few coins in the meter."

McCauley shook Norman's hand and said, "Seems I'm fresh out of quarters, you got any change?"

As he fished in his pockets, Norm shook his head sadly. "Friggin' shame, Del. All those years on the force fighting bad guys and now having to deal with a rookie's tickets?" Jerked his head towards the trooper. "Just the battle of the empty meters for him, probably never been out on the road. "Kid's name's Alberino, daddy's the East Boston state rep. Kid's got the life of Reilly down here, writes a few tickets, busts a few balls, then he goes off and flirts with the chippies who flock out of yonder office building for lunch," Norman said, nodding at the Seaport Building. He scowled. "Shit, almost jealous," he said.

McCauley looked past him towards the gallery.

"Heard the store's doing well, been meaning to stop in."

Norman looked amused. "*You*, visit the gallery? Like years ago when you told me, after we went to the McGrail kid's play, we gotta hook up for drinks?"

McCauley said. "Think I can blame the D.A.'s office, Norm, for the missing time."

Norman's eyes softened and his grin melted like frost from the windshield of an east facing car.

"Sorry, Del, everyone knows you got screwed. Didn't mean to imply . . ."

McCauley put his hand on his shoulder. "Forget it. Got what I got, didn't deserve it, but I did my time and it's done. Now, like everyone else, I'm out here dodging *parking* tickets. But after what I've been through," McCauley held out his arms, "it ain't hard to take."

Norman chuckled and said, "Hear you, brother." He separated some quarters from the change in his palm. "'Least you won't get one today," he said, handing them over. McCauley offered a dollar but he waved it away, pointing a chunky finger. "And next time you're down here, get your butt in the store. We'll have a coffee and talk up old times."

When McCauley first got out of the can he wondered how people would view him, especially "civilian" friends like Norman. It wasn't like he was searching for approval, holding his breath hoping. Figuring if people couldn't handle his past, they could stay in it, while he moved ahead.

But the reaction from Norman couldn't have been warmer. All he got from his old friend was genuine joy, a little sadness, and encouragement to visit him again.

Slipping the quarters into the meter, McCauley thought about how he would have liked to have talked to Norm longer, but the Seaport Building was across the street and Cotter was in there. He needed to talk with him more.

TWENTY-TWO

WHEN HE ENTERED THE CATHEDRAL-LIKE LOBBY of the Seaport building, McCauley immediately got the feeling that he didn't belong. Like everything in it was designed to intimidate, from the magnificently columned sixty-foot ceilings to the pink marble floors, and the walls of the same material where brass was affixed to every spot where they ran out of marble. The entire lobby gleamed impossibly, with an energy that drove you back towards the door.

Following a narrow blue carpet the length of a tennis court, he turned left at a fountain: lots of fish and mermaids vomiting water at each other. McCauley headed towards a bank of elevators facing one another, behind an elevated security desk.

Two security types in blue blazers, gray pants, white shirts, and black clip-on ties eyed him coolly and tapped walkie-talkies against their legs as McCauley passed by them heading towards the security desk. He stared at the building directory on the wall behind it.

As he studied it, the man behind the desk stood up. Tall and gaunt, with an elongated neck, he reminded McCauley of one of those toy curiosity birds that dipped forever when you put water in front of them.

Lifting his nose, he said, "Sir, can I help you?"

And as McCauley looked at him, the guy dipped.

Looking for water, McCauley rose on his toes. "Thank you, but unless you could spot me a C-note, no," he said pleasantly, turning his attention back to the wall.

The security man straightened like someone had poured ice down his back.

"Ex-*cuse* me?"

McCauley pointed. "Found my guy, Esmond Cotter, ninth floor, thanks."

The security guy's eyes narrowed and he dipped again.

"I'll need a *picture* ID."

Checking the top of the desk again, McCauley pulled out his license.

"Looking for something?" the security man said, looking at the license, at McCauley, at the license again.

"Water," McCauley said.

Birdman made a face like he smelled something rotten and handed McCauley a credit-card-sized piece of white plastic. "While in the building, please keep that on you. When you've finished your business, turn it back for your license. There's no *water* in the lobby. I suggest you ask your *lawyer* for some."

The elevator doors opened at the ninth floor and McCauley got out, read the room numbers sign, and followed the red arrow right. Advancing down the empty corridor, which smelled of new carpet and fresh latex paint, he was barely aware of the hush of the elevator closing behind him. At the end of the corridor was a floor-to-ceiling wall of glass with two doors in the middle, each with a thick brass handle shaped like a palm leaf. On the other side of it, a pretty young woman sat at a desk.

Resting her forearms on the clear Lucite surface, she talked into a microphone the size of a pencil eraser attached to a thin wire that disappeared behind her ear. She had a look like she could see who she spoke to.

McCauley approached her directly, stopping in front of her desk, but, talking to someone else, she couldn't see him. She continued talking as McCauley walked over and admired a Monet lithograph on a wall. It featured a young Victorian-era woman in a billowy white dress. She was seated on a promontory overlooking the ocean where, below, a fleet of tiny sailboats skipped across whitecapped waves.

"Can I help you?" McCauley heard the receptionist say.

Turning, he said, "Yes, I'm here to..." She held up a finger, looked at someone else.

"Cotter, McBride, and Cotter," she said. "No, I'm sorry he isn't." Looked back at McCauley, then away again. "Yes, that won't be a problem," she said to the ghost. Typed something on the keypad, hit the last key hard. "You're welcome sir," she said brightly. "I'll be certain to give him the message."

She refocused on McCauley. "And who . . ."

Staring at her, McCauley said, "How can you tell which one?"

"Excuse me?"

"The two Cotters, you know when somebody calls looking, how can you tell which one?"

"One of them's *deceased.*"

McCauley nodded thoughtfully. "That makes it easy. Is Esmond in?"

"And you're?"

"Delray McCauley," gave a little bow, "he knows who I am."

She held up a finger and looked at someone else. "Cotter, McBride, and Cotter," she said. Her eyebrows arched up into her bangs and she put a hand on her chin, giggled high enough for dogs to respond. She nodded deeply and said, "Oh yes, I *told* you that, Mrs. Hasselbeck. I think he's in, please let me check."

She looked at McCauley like it was for the last time that day. "Mr. McBride won't be returning from court at least until after three," she said curtly.

Putting his hands on the desk, McCauley swung his chin over it.

"Works for me, sweetie, I'm here to see Cotter, remember?" He shoved off, heading down a long corridor on the right line with doors on either side.

He made it past the first one before she shrieked, "You . . . you're not allowed to go down there!"

McCauley turned and faced her and held up a finger, and said in a singsong voice, "Cotter, McBride, and Cotter. One Cotter's deceased, and McBride's in court, where's the other Cotter?" He opened a door and looked in. "Where the hell's Cotter?"

Moving faster now, he opened the next door. A closet. Then the next, found a man behind a desk: mid-twenties, white shirt, red suspenders, matching tie, open-mouthed like he was expecting a spoonful of ice cream.

Behind him McCauley could hear Kandy's voice, "Yes, District Six? We have an intruder, in our law office. The Seaport Building, ninth floor. No, he isn't a *client.*"

At the far end of the corridor a door swung open and a tall, slender figure stepped through it. "That will be all, Kandy," Esmond Cotter said in a strong, clear voice, shoving the remains of what looked like French fries in his mouth. Wiped his lips with a napkin. Between chews, he said, "Tell the officer everything's fine . . . there's been a mistake. Mr. McCauley's a . . . *friend* of mine."

As she spoke quietly into her wire, lowering herself slowly into her seat, Kandy appeared puzzled.

Like he was directing traffic, Cotter motioned to McCauley and said, "Come . . . come into my office, Mr. McCauley," and went in before him.

McCauley gave Kandy a wave. He said, "*Told* you I know where he eats."

Kandy looked at him dismissively before her eyes blanked, and she looked at someone else. "Cotter, McBride, and Cotter," she said.

TWENTY-THREE

COTTER WAS STARING OUT THE WINDOW, his back to him, when McCauley walked in. The office was large. Everything about the place said money, but in subdued, subtle tones, like it was all right to let the clients know, but not to rub their faces in it.

The wooden floor, beneath the intricately woven Persian rug in the center, was a highly polished, hand-inlaid parquet job that breathlessly met the twelve-foot walls, which were covered in a pale, ropey-looking paper that, though certainly expensive, looked more like the insides of bleached-out flour sacks. There was the requisite red leather couch and chairs and fireproof files and costly lamps that, McCauley imagined, must also cast an understated glow.

Cotter's desk was heavy, expensive, and looked like walnut or mahogany, with a thick slab of green marble on top. On the edge facing out was an elaborate Swift Instrument barometer set-up that would have baffled an MIT student. Next to it a photograph of a mid-thirtyish blonde with shoulder-length hair and two small children in front. Her smile looked strained, almost air-brushed in.

To the right, near a door, in the place where almost certainly the sun streamed first thing in the morning, was the trophy wall. Where Cotter went, what he learned, and what he was qualified to do with the indecipherability of the scribble on the fancily framed diplomas proportionate to the amount he had paid to secure them.

On other walls there were the requisite prints, nothing too busy or bright, lots of red, and an assortment of framed photos of Cotter with the mayor, Cotter with the governor, Cotter rubbing elbows with a compilation of local political windbags. Cotter even had one with the maître d' at Anthony's, demonstrating he had no problem mixing with the proletariat as well.

Curiously, a battle-ax was mounted on the wall to McCauley's left, taking up space near a thin closet door. Cotter noticed him noticing.

"Family heirloom," he said proudly, approaching it. "Are you familiar with English history, Mr. McCauley, the War of the Roses?"

McCauley nodded, told him he'd read something about it.

Running his fingers along the three-foot shaft, Cotter said, "My grandfather — five, maybe six times removed — fought for the Lancastrians. In 1464 he used this ax at the Battle of Hedgeley Moor. It's been in the family ever since." He winked. "A little secret. There's an armory museum, the Higgins, out in Worcester, that's been after it for years."

"The war, your grandfather's side win?" McCauley said, coming closer, admiring the blade.

Cotter shrugged. "I think they did, though I'm not sure." He shrugged. "Either way, didn't matter much for Lord Cotter. The very same year, at the Battle of Hexham, the old man caught an arrow in the eye."

Compressing the napkin between his hands, he returned to the window, gazing out, he spoke.

"I was eating lunch, Mr. McCauley . . ." He turned just his head slightly. "Sorry, rude of me, would you care for a drink?"

"Not when I'm working, thanks."

"Good," Cotter said, nodding, "I feel the same way . . . usually. Anyways, we were talking . . .?"

"Lunch, I believe."

"Yes, I got a scallop plate to go from Jimmy's, absolutely the best coleslaw — have you heard that they're closing?"

Turning, Cotter faced him, dropped his arms to his sides. He continued squeezing the napkin with one hand. He said, "Sorry about Kandy, can be a pit bull; she's *very* protective when it comes to the partners."

Doing the guy a favor, no need to hold back. "Too bad she wasn't chained to the desk at night," McCauley said, "might have saved you a safe. Speaking of which, counselor, mind telling me what's in it?"

Despite the fact the room was awash in crisp sunlight, Cotter's eyes darkened, like suddenly an oily lamp had flicked off within. The thin line of his lips curled into a smile, but his eyes weren't getting the message.

"You're certainly direct, Mr. McCauley. Did they teach that at the academy or . . ."

McCauley scowled. "Sorry my asking offends you, but an hour ago, while I was out *there* trying to help you, I had a guy stick a gun in my balls." Grabbed himself. "See, they're something I'm used to having around. If you'd like to continue having *me* around, I suggest you tell me or you can find it yourself."

Cotter plopped the bag into the bucket next to the desk, and lowered himself into the black, heavily padded chair behind it. He leaned back and studied McCauley.

Nodding towards one of the two red cushioned chairs in front, he casually checked his watch and said, "I've got a meeting here shortly, but please have a seat." Pulled the cuff down over the watch. "Don't think me ungrateful, Mr. McCauley; of course I'm indebted to you for helping me."

McCauley sat down, shook his head, waved a finger at the lawyer.

"Got it wrong, Counselor, not you, I'm helping out Lilly. And I've got people to meet too, now what's in the safe?"

Cotter stared for a moment before he turned in the chair, facing a painting next to a huge bookshelf filled with volumes of maritime and Massachusetts general law.

The painting was that of a stern-faced older man who closely resembled Cotter. Dressed in a dark, three-piece suit, grasping a massive book in his hands, he looked like a banker or lawyer, someone used to spending large amounts of other people's money. McCauley pointed his chin at the painting.

"Your father?"

Cotter nodded. "Yes, it is," he said, returning his gaze to McCauley. "Regarding the safe, you want the *facts*, Mr. McCauley? Here's the truncated version.

"The safe contained a few thousand in cash, and some paperwork that was important but replaceable. What was irreplaceable was the *CD*."

"A computer disc."

"Yes," Cotter said, placing his palms on the desk standing.

"On it is an account, the day-to-day records of various business arrangements between a well-known real estate developer and the mayor's office that, regretfully, both my father and I were an integral part of about five years ago. The material is of a highly personal, sensitive nature. If the wrong person were to access that disc, and knew what he was looking at, it could cause a great deal of embarrassment, to myself and the firm — or worse. It could also tarnish the reputation, even imperil the careers, of some of the most powerful political figures in this city, including that of the sitting mayor."

McCauley said, "How does your father tie into this?"

Cotter blinked and got up from the desk. He was looking more tired now than when McCauley first entered. "My father was very politically connected," he said, "as was his father, dating back to the days of James Michael Curley." He pressed just the tips of his fingers together, forming a triangle in front of his chest. As he moved from behind the desk he gazed into it like he was viewing a prompter.

"I'm certain since you were 'born and raised,' as they say, in South Boston, you're aware you have to play ball with the people in power if you're planning to do business in the city. It's a game, Mr. McCauley, played from time immemorial, nothing has changed."

McCauley held up a hand and pressed the palm towards him. "You're short on time, Counselor, and that works for me. There's no need to review ancient history. If, years ago, you and Daddy were involved in something crooked, as long as those activities didn't include murder, mayhem, or snatching kids off the street, I'm probably okay with it, not here to assess your guilt or innocence."

"Understood," Cotter said, "but there's certainly nothing like that on the disc. My father and I were involved in some delicate . . . *negotiations* between the current mayor and two large developers of real estate. The disc contains financial records for my own . . . reassurance, shall we say, that would preclude anyone from forgetting, if they were inclined to, who their primary benefactors were."

"You two were middlemen," McCauley said.

Cotter's voice developed an edge and his cheeks noticeably flushed when he said, "Yes, if you must. The negotiations dealt with a large parcel of land, the very land upon which this building was built, and another huge tract in Charlestown that's currently under development."

McCauley made a time-out sign with his hands. "I'm getting the drift; everything needed to bury your associates is recorded on the disc. Again, it's none of my business and I could care less." He looked around the room. "Now, where was the safe taken from?"

Cotter pointed to a door in the corner near the windows. "From out of my private conference room."

"Are there any other entrances?"

"None, like I said, it's *private*. We have two other conference rooms that are available to the partners and associates. This room's used so rarely, I believed it was secure enough for a safe." He walked over and opened the door. McCauley came in behind him.

The office was smaller than Cotter's but there was still a lot of glass for one room. In the middle was an oversized table, a big twenty-footer, surrounded by a dozen chairs. Below the bank of windows a shorter, narrower table hugged the wall. It was loaded down with an assortment of late-model flat-screen monitors and keyboards. On an open shelf below it were a half dozen computers, new fax machines in boxes, and printer/scanner/

copiers. This stuff was expensive. McCauley gave Cotter a look.

"Yes, Mr. McCauley, there *is* a lot of equipment here." Nodded towards the back wall, where a sixty-inch LCD HDTV was mounted in the center above a cherry wood armoire. "For visual presentations," he said, guiding McCauley towards the rear of the room, pointing out speakers above them in the ceiling. "With the most up-to-date acoustic support."

"Of course," McCauley said.

Stopping in front of the armoire, Cotter pulled open the door on the right. The shelves inside were filled with new laptop computers and a half dozen PalmPilots still in boxes.

Odd, McCauley thought, all this equipment just lying around. Reminded him of the lair of a fence, the type of place he used to raid. Cotter picked up on it.

"Mr. McCauley, everything here was *legally* purchased. You must understand, we're a fairly large firm. Presently two partners — in the process of interviewing for a third — we have seven associates, a paralegal, two legal secretaries, and Kandy, whom you've met. This room doubles as a repository for the company's computer and accompanying electronic needs. Time is money. If a piece of equipment fails, we can ill afford the time it takes to run to a store to replace it."

"An impressive collection," McCauley said, staring, not knowing what else to say. But seconds later, he did, and said, "So, where was the safe?"

Cotter gave him a look like he was standing inches away from a land mine and he was waiting for him to step. Reaching across McCauley's chest he tugged open the other door.

There were no shelves on this side, and whatever had been there, was gone. All that remained was a smoothly cut gaping hole in the wall. Three naked wood hangers dangled from a length of chrome tubing above it.

Cotter had made his point. "You're telling me whoever did this," McCauley said, tapping one of the hangers, watching it swing, "took none of this other stuff with them?"

Cotter nodded gravely. "Exactly, not even a pen."

Leaning in, examining the hole, McCauley's voice reverberated, "What kind of safe was it?"

Cotter looked pensive, tapped his lips with a finger. "Can't recall the name, but it wasn't expensive." He was shaking the finger like he hoped the answer might fly from the tip, and said suddenly, "Gardall, that's it, we purchased it from a small shop in Weymouth."

Gardall. McCauley recognized the name, it was a workhorse brand, sturdy enough, you weren't going to smash in its face in with a hammer, but not hard to remove from a partitioning wall. It could be torn or cut out without a lot of effort, with a crowbar or a SawzAll, tools available to anyone. Any amateur could have grabbed it, but how the hell did they know it was there? In the other room the phone rang too loudly.

"Excuse me," Cotter said, turning, hurrying out of the room.

McCauley heard him pick up and say something before sticking his head back in through the door, the face redder now than the last time he saw it. Cotter held up a finger and closed the door.

McCauley stood at the window. The early afternoon sun had reached its highest peak and begun its slow descent to the west. Across the street, beyond the row of commercial buildings, a white, twin-hulled ferry, carrying passengers towards Long Wharf and Logan, raced across the harbor from its port at the shipyard in Quincy. Its hulls sliced prettily through the jade green water, smudged in places by overhead clouds.

A block south on Northern Avenue, a state trooper, working a detail, stood at the rear of his cruiser, the lights flashing from every corner like the ceiling of a North Shore strip joint. Raising a hand he put a hold on the traffic while behind him an excavator, its yellow lights blinking, slowly backed into the street. There were ten or twelve cars stopped in a row, but the last, a small foreign job, either didn't see the cop or decided he couldn't mean *him* and, kicking up a funnel of dust, cut down the side of the road.

Throwing his hands in the air, the trooper stomped at an angle towards the foreign job that skidded briefly in a line before stopping. McCauley could only see the top half of the trooper, over an SUV's roof, as he berated the driver, who probably wished he could only see half of him too.

In the other room Cotter slammed down the receiver. He came back through the door and stared at McCauley. "There was a man on the phone, I didn't recognize the voice. He boldly told me that he's got what I want. Naturally, I was stunned but before I could respond he laughed and said — Cotter's voice developed a street tone — 'Got a lot of expensive equipment up there, what are ya, some kind of fence?' "

"And what did you say?" McCauley said.

Like he didn't hear him, Cotter threw up his arms and followed the table to the rear of the room. "Wha . . . what would *you* say?" he said, turning. "I responded. I said, 'Who the hell is this?' And the voice said, 'Call me the solution to your problems.'"

Like someone who had something to barter would say.

"Anything else?" McCauley said, watching Cotter lose it, slam the door of the armoire shut. He turned and faced him again, rested his hands on the back of a chair. "He said, 'I . . . have your disc . . . and I know what's on it.' " Cotter shook a fist at McCauley. "The son-of-a-bitch laughed after he said it." Cotter paused, seemed to think about it more. "And then he said, 'You don't want me going to the authorities, we should talk about money, you buying it back.' " Cotter's shoulders sank. "That's all he said."

McCauley thought maybe Cotter was making it up. A thug referring to cops as *authorities*? "And he said nothing else."

Cotter chewed his lip before speaking, said disgustedly, "No . . . 'I have your disc and I know what's on it.' "

His face darkening, he hammered his palm with a fist. "That *bastard's* got nerve, something to sell — to *me*?" Shook the fist, slammed the chair into the table. His eyes slowly rising to meet McCauley's. "I want my disc back, Mr. McCauley, whatever it takes."

The office phone rang again.

Cotter unclenched his hand, shifting his head as he straightened his tie. "The son-of-a-bitch," he said hoarsely, and walked from the room, McCauley following behind.

Cotter picked up, said hello, kept his eyes on McCauley. "Yes, Kandy," he said, pressing a thumb and finger into a spot just above the right eyebrow. "I'm finishing up with him now, the doctor's due here any minute." He turned his back to McCauley. "The last person who called, Kandy, anything come up on the caller ID?" He scratched at his cheek, nodded. "Blocked, I see. It's okay, yes, he was an old friend. I just wanted to see if his number had changed."

Balls, McCauley thought. It took balls to rip the guy off, then call and tell him he'd sell back what he stole. The guy wasn't stupid, he knew what he had . . . or did he? Obviously knew he had something, but how? *Simple* case. He thought about Lilly.

You owe me, you bastard.

As Cotter went on in velvet tones, McCauley crossed to the window and stared diagonally across the boulevard-sized avenue at the Crump/McCole Gallery. He didn't see Norman out front. He was probably inside, showing some beautiful woman his sketches.

To the right of the gallery, a few blocks up, just before a Chinese restaurant, McCauley could see the young state trooper, hands clasped behind the small of his back, standing in the "at ease" position, talking to a couple of women. From here he couldn't tell if they were pretty.

TWENTY-FOUR

A S WALTER COLLINS FIDDLED with the dishwasher behind the bar, McCauley leaned over it and stared at him. He said, "Isn't that thing under some kind of warranty?"

Walter used a ratchet wrench on something inside it, gave something else a yank, and pulled out a length of white plastic hose. "Damn recirculator's always developing leaks," he said, rising, examining the hose. Tossed it aside. "Ya, it's under warranty, the dishwasher's a year old, but by the time the repair guy comes out to fix it, the *glasses* are piled up to the roof. Bartenders nowadays" — he glared at McCauley — "don't like gettin' their little hands wet."

Walter pulled his hands close to his shoulders and started to flap them. In a girlish voice, the big man said, "Walter, the dish-washer's broke, the dishwasher's broke," and pranced around in a circle. He growled, shook a fist, and snapped a wrench off the bar.

McCauley said, "Don't hear me complaining."

Walter's voice echoed up through the machine. "Ain't sayin' *you*. What time you meetin' the broad?"

"Meeting her here about four."

"How 'bout a burger, you got time," Walter said, banging on something with the end of the ratchet.

McCauley took a sip of soda water and lime. "Thanks, but I was thinking, mind you just thinking, about seeing if she'd like to get something to eat after we stop at the Pen."

Walter stopped banging, and got up on his knees. He wiped his forehead with the back of his hand. "We? You're takin' a *girl* down the Pen, what for, you crazy?"

McCauley squeezed the lime into the glass, folded it into a napkin next to it. "Told her when we spoke, I had plans to go down there, and she told me that she had been in there before, only last week, asking questions. She was telling the truth, Wacko brought her up out the island. Got a kick out of it, I think."

Walter laid the wrench on top of the dishwasher and wiped his hands, then the wrench with greasy bar towel.

"Snoopin' around the Pen askin' questions ain't healthy. Usu-ally the only *kick* Wacko Curran gets is when he's doing it to your head."

With the wrench he made little circles next to his own.

"Bad enough ya gotta go down there, but to compound the problem? I'd keep away from her, Del — snoopin' down the Pen — she's a looney or a dyke, keep *a-way*," he sang, lying down on his side, cranking the ratchet on something else.

McCauley swirled the remnants of the liquid in the glass and downed it. "Don't know if I want to, Wally. Only talked with her twice, but, I don't know, there's something about her."

"Ya, that *somethin'* will get ya killed. Now, what I tell ya about callin' me Wally?" Walter's head popped over the edge of the bar. "And you got that Stuffa callin' me that too, I'll fire *his* ass." The head disappeared.

McCauley grabbed the napkin and lime, leaned over, and tossed them into the trash, settled back on the stool. In a loud voice he said, "That machine almost ready? Got a glass here to wash," just as a figure passed by the front window, backed up, took off her sunglasses, shielded the sun from her eyes, and looked in.

She paused, after passing through both sets of doors, allowing time for her eyes to adjust. She wore a white cotton, short-sleeved blouse, khaki pants, and brown leather, closed-toe sandals. She carried a small valise or a large pocketbook, Mc-Cauley couldn't tell which, attached to a strap running over her shoulder.

Her thick auburn hair was wavy and pulled tight into a pony-tail, and did little to outline her face. But the lady had a face that didn't need framing. She looked like a girl on a Camel poster, but McCauley couldn't imagine her with a butt in her mouth.

She pulled a white handkerchief out of her pocket, daintily dabbing around the base of her throat. The girl hadn't blinked once since she entered. "Mr. McCauley?" she said softly.

Forcing himself not to sit up too quick, McCauley nodded and signaled with a finger he was. Behind him Walter was up on his knees, forearms resting on top of the bar. He whispered, "That her, McCauley? Get me her handkerchief, Christ she's a knockout."

"Get back under the dishwasher, Wally," McCauley said under his breath, watching him sink, "or I'll tell her you called her a dyke."

The Camel girl crossed the floor still dabbing. "Mr. Mc-Cauley," she said smiling, quickly shifting the handkerchief to the left hand, extending the right. "Mackey Wainwright, my God it's hot out there today, isn't Indian summer a joy."

McCauley took the hand. The skin was soft, the grip strong, and lingered to show him it was.

McCauley threw a thumb over his shoulder. "Behind me, my friend Walter Collins, the owner of T.K.'s, got a second career in dishwasher repair."

Without surfacing, Walter waved a hand over the top of the bar. Mackey went up on her toes. "Hi, Walter," she said, flash-ing a palm near the shoulder.

"Whatever you do, Mackey, don't call him Wally."

Walter's voice echoed up from inside the machine. "The *lady* can call me anything she wants, that only applies to bums like you."

Mackey shrugged and smiled, displaying a set of perfect white teeth.

She said, "So, where can we talk?"

At a table near the window but out of the sun, Mackey told Mc-Cauley how, while on the case and doing her legwork in Southie, she had pretended to be an insurance investigator. How she told whoever she spoke with that there was a reward for the return of the safe and its contents, excluding the cash, and made it clear they could keep the cash. When people asked her what else was in it, she told them papers, you know, legal stuff, original copies that would take tons of work to replace.

Her green almond-shaped eyes sparkled, like rain forest pools.

She told McCauley how she had gone down into the few remaining waterfront gin joints and talked to the bartenders, some of the customers and left behind a number where she could be reached. She giggled and leaned closer to him, telling him how she'd even changed the message on her answering machine to something that said they had contacted an insurance investigator. McCauley took it all in, her breath smelled like strawberries. It was easy to laugh along with her.

McCauley asked how she ended up down the Pen.

The next day, she told him, she went up to West Broadway and stopped at the places the bartenders suggested: Triple O's, Street Lights, the Tunnel Café, with always the same spiel, emphasizing the reward, but never a figure. McCauley listened as she explained how she'd just jerk up her eyebrows when somebody asked. And yes, she said, actually, they were nice down the Pen. But no, she'd never heard of Wacko Curran.

McCauley said, "The people you spoke to, you get any call-backs?"

She told him, though she believed some knew more than they were willing to discuss, only one called her back. Some guy called the Worm.

The name rang a bell with McCauley. The Worm was a son of

the Old Harbor project, also a Southie legend. The jockey-sized burglar was known for his ability to squeeze into spaces that would have strangled a ferret. He had enjoyed a prolific career, with the requisite stops in the pokey in between, spanning decades. The guy had to be close to seventy.

Mackey continued, saying when she got back to the office, the Worm called, said he had something to talk about. Meet me in an hour at Sal & Betty's, he said, and maybe I'll let you buy me a sandwich. She was excited but when she showed up with her tape recorder the Worm closed up like a clam. From that point he'd only talk about the Red Sox and how the L Street Bathhouse was going to hell.

McCauley patiently explained how, in Southie, you can't walk around with a recorder and expect to maintain your ability to chew. Mackey responded, "But if you record what they say, aren't they less apt to lie?"

"Yeah, if they're *citizens*," McCauley said, "but these guys are criminals, most pathological liars. Record them and they think what they're saying's important. He shrugged. "Just makes them lie more creatively."

Mackey frowned. "Didn't the Mad Hatter have something to say about that? That up is down and down is up, and sideway's all around?"

McCauley leaned closer, he wanted more strawberries. "In Southie the Mad Hatter would have been mayor," he said.

TWENTY-FIVE

GOT NICE HANDS, Mackey was thinking when McCauley returned to the table with two soda waters with lime. As he put hers in front of her, his cell phone rang. Mackey glanced down at her pocketbook.

"Mine," McCauley said, snatching the phone from his hip, "might be the *man*."

Mackey silently mouthed the word "Wacko" as McCauley opened it, nodded.

"Ya?" he said, looking at Mackey.

On the other end the male voice had a chiding tone. "This you, McCauley?" She watched him nod again and point at the phone.

"Ya."

"Jack says come down the Pen. He's got somethin' for ya."

"And who's this?"

The response was quick. "Ask a *lot* of questions."

"I recall only one."

"I watched you out the island, pig, ya, I was out there on the hill watchin'. You and your fucking questions. Jack, up close stickin' that piece in your . . ." There was a sprinkle of dry laughter. "Looked like two fucking queers. Said, that cop ain't gonna be queer for long."

"And you're not going to tell me your name?"

The same dry laughter.

McCauley said, "You seem mighty focused on this gay stuff. Maybe you've got latent tendencies we could discuss."

There was a long pause and his ear grew hot like the other was sending it through.

"Discuss, with you? You cop fuck. I don't think so. I wouldn't give you the sweat off my ass, but Jack says call, I call. Now, you comin'?"

"Ya,"

"The Pen, ten minutes."

And he hung up.

Pulling his lips to his teeth, McCauley stared out the window. "I'm sorry," he said, "but I have to cut this short." He reached for her glass. "But you can take this with you, I'll put it in a cup."

Mackey shook her head, took a sip, and pressed a napkin to her lips. "Nope, I'm fine, thank you, mind telling me who called?"

"Sounded like Mike Janowski," McCauley said, staring through the window up the street. He turned his head and looked at Mackey. "Me and him — well, let's say we *don't* get along."

Mackey had never heard the name. "Is Janowski one of Wacko's men?"

McCauley looked out the window again, then at his watch. "Ya, one of the worst, a real psycho, a cop hater. Recall a few years back, in the North End, the holdup where a cop lost his arm in a shoot-out?"

Mackey made a face like she was trying to recall, then she brightened and nodded.

"I remember," she said, rapping the table with her knuckles, "the police thinking it was a Mafia thing first. They later surmised the gang came from Southie. Never caught anyone, if I remember correctly."

"You've got a good memory, and yes, the bad guys are still on the loose. Janowski's a prime suspect."

"And you're meeting *him* at the Pen?"

McCauley shook his head and picked up his glass.

"Meeting Wacko," he said, swirling the ice, eyeing the crushed lime at the bottom. "Janowski's his butt boy, plays in the same sandbox."

"I'd like to go with you."

He looked at her. "I thought about taking you, but no."

She slid the chair back, stood up, and faced him. At five eight, she was only a few inches shorter.

Mackey batted her eyes. "C'mon, I told you they treated me nice, better than they'll probably treat you. A woman can have a calming effect."

McCauley was thinking Mackey had a good point. A pretty girl might put the guys on their best behavior but, then again, it could backfire.

She said, "Look, think of the time I'll save you because you won't have to hit the places I've already canvassed."

"You're saying I *owe* you."

"Yes, I tag along and we're even."

McCauley looked over at Walter, who leaned on the bar, and shook his head slowly.

"All right, we're even. But you stay behind me, and I do the talking. Any questions so far?"

Big smile. "No questions, you do the talking," she said.

"Good," McCauley said, "I like a quick learn."

TWENTY-SIX

A LITTLE AFTER FIVE, the crust of the city's rush hour, Mc-Cauley and Mackey ran, like broken field tailbacks across busy West Broadway towards the Pen Tavern. Located between a locksmith and a Chinese takeout, everything about the Pen, from its single grimy window to its beige brick, exhaust-stained facade, warned you away.

"Remember," McCauley said, squeezing in between two cars parked out front, stopping on the sidewalk, "we're dealing with *lunatics* here, only one of us talks."

He didn't turn to see Mackey nod and pull her fingers across her lips like a zipper.

The spotter behind the window eyed them blankly when they came in through the door. McCauley looked around.

Inside, the citywide smoking ban ignored, the air was blue in layers. Along the wall on the left, men sat in dark booths playing cards; a couple turned and stared. On the right the patrons at the bar were more genteel, nobody turned; instead, eyed them coldly in the mirror behind the double rows of half-filled bottles reflecting a kind of urine-colored light. From somewhere in the ceiling, like from inside a can, Sammy Davis, Jr., belted out "The Candy Man."

Suddenly, from the back someone yelled, "Hey, who's the fucking broad?"

And every eye in the place was on them.

"Hey, honey," someone else shouted, "last week you seen somethin' you *liked*?"

The room erupted in laughter.

Mackey, edgy now, glanced at McCauley, removed the strap from her shoulder. Now she held the bulky pocketbook from the top with both hands, in front of her waist, like a shield.

The movement wasn't lost on the spotter.

Lugging his skinny ass off the stool, he sauntered over behind them, hopped alongside her, put his hands on his hips. Bending over he leered at her waist. "What ya got in the *bag*, baby doll, a little .22?" he said, and winked at his audience. Mackey squatted to meet his eyes, bringing his head back up as she straightened.

At her full height, an angry crimson flush began to grow in her cheeks and she batted her eyes sensuously, looking down into his. "That's better now, isn't it?" she said. "Regarding your question? Actually I'm carrying a Smith & Wesson 642CT six-shot revolver, hot loaded with Hornady 140 grain bullets. Had the trigger machined to lighten the drag, want to see it?"

McCauley glanced at her, dropped his eyes to the floor. Girl's got a *gun*? He glared at the spotter and said, "The lady's licensed, what about you?"

The spotter smirked at McCauley, turned his head, double-eyebrowed the bartender and, tugging on the bottom of his T-shirt, swaggered back to his chair.

As he scanned the room for Wacko, McCauley recalled another time, when he was younger and found himself in another kind of den where every eye was on him.

He had gone to the Oktoberfest with his older brother, Bob, and a friend. After drinking his fill one day, he decided to visit the zoo.

At the Siberian wolf exhibit he had attempted to spot them, without any luck, through the towering twenty-foot fence. Shoving the camera into his pocket, he scaled it and, after passing through a stand of young firs and walking over an outcrop of rock, he spotted them, less than a hundred yards away, resting beneath some cedars.

There were seven in all, staring. And then two curious males began to lope towards him. He ran for his life for the fence.

Now, inside of the Pen, two males approached from the back of the room, but these weren't curious wolves. These wolves knew exactly who he was.

Mike Janowski had on a black Polo shirt with the collar turned up, black nylon warm-up pants, white sneakers. As he came towards them, he turned his head to the side like he wanted to spit, then looked at his watch and grinned at his sidekick.

The other guy was older, the far edge of thirty, wearing a black pocket tee, sharply creased blue jeans, and the same type of sneakers. The huge brass buckle on his belt had an Indian's face on it. Around his neck was a flat, gold chain, worn outside his shirt, attached to a pair of tiny gold boxing gloves.

Janowski stopped a few feet away, stared hard at McCauley's face, like he wanted to memorize every detail. He held out his left hand, palm up, to the side, and said, "What I tell ya, Joey, cop's right on time, knew he'd show up, where's my sawbuck?" Joey reached into his pocket, pulled out a roll, peeled off a ten, and slapped it into Janowski's palm.

"You're the shit, Mike, knew for a fact."

Now Janowski memorized Mackey's face, and he seemed to be enjoying the task.

"I knew because this guy and his tart want somethin' from us, and it's gotta be somethin' important." Got closer to Mackey, made it obvious he was taking in her scent. "Believe it? Five years ago this maggot's tryin' to put Jackie away, now he's askin' for *help*?"

"Head's up, Mike," the spotter said, "the bitch might be packin'." His tinny laughter ended in a snort.

Joey jumped back, faking a horrified look. "*Manos arriba*," he shouted, and threw up his hands. Waving them overhead as he leered at her waist, he swung his own like he was sunk in a Hula-Hoop. As he dragged his eyes up her body, Mackey stiffened, shifting her hands to the side of the bag.

Joey said, "Yup, she's packin', all right. Got a nice pair of tits, 34Bs *minimum*."

Struggling for control, McCauley said hoarsely, "Jack Curran sent for me, where the hell is he?"

Janowski's jaw dropped. "Where the hell . . . *what*?" Looked to the side. "He's at it again, Joey, askin' questions that no one can answer." Tilted his head. "Who the fuck are you, the *Riddla*, you punk?"

Shoving his thumbs behind his belt, Joey swaggered to within inches of Mackey, stared at her breasts, inspecting her like prey, like his very first shot deer.

A smoldering in his stomach ignited in McCauley's throat. With no attempt at deception he shifted his weight, pivoted to the side. Joey mirror-imaged his movement, took his eyes off her chest, and popped McCauley a look.

"I'm thinkin' this is gonna get interestin', Mike," Joey said, shifting his head slightly off center, locking his eyes on Mc-Cauley's. "Go ahead, Mike, whaddaya guess? 34Bs? Bigger? 38s? I say," sniffing the air around her, "closest one takes her, *everything*, whaddaya say Mike, huh?"

Leaning to within inches of Mackey's face, he licked his lower lip, his voice dropping an octave. "So, Tootsie Roll, what are *you* sayin', gonna cooperate, help set us straight?"

"That's enough, boyo," McCauley growled, twisting his hips behind an open palm strike landing on Joey's chin. The thug was barely stunned, but it lifted his head.

McCauley slid sideways and caught Joey, who was stepping in with an overhead right, with a picture-perfect left hook to the chin.

Joey staggered into Janowski, knocking him sideways over a chair, just as McCauley caught him again, clean on the cheek, with a vicious right cross. Out on his feet, he was tumbling towards Queer Street when McCauley landed a final, crushing left hook, and Joey bounced off the floor like oversized hail.

There was no time to gloat.

Behind him he heard Mackey scream just as a pair of spindly arms wrapped around his head, pulled him back towards the door.

Twisting, McCauley rolled with the energy, swinging his right elbow, the bony hatchet landing on the spotter's neck with a sickening thud. Turning, circle-blocking the arms, he snap-kicked him in the solar plexus, and the spotter collapsed like a convertible top, rolled onto his side, and puked.

Facing the room again, McCauley found Janowski directly in front of him coming in low, reaching into his pocket. With a crazy grin he pulled out a knife, snapped his arm sideways, locking the five-inch blade into place. Crouching, jigging the knife in his hand, he confidently closed on McCauley.

The pocketbook's leather strap brushed McCauley's cheek as it rocketed past his shoulder; hit Janowski square in the face. Staggering backwards, he slashed it away, his countenance an incoming storm tide of rage.

Janowski roared, "You bitch, after I do him, I'm gonna do you. I'll open you up like a Saturday night whore."

Then, like someone had ripped the plug from the wall, Janowski froze in position.

From the corner of his eye, McCauley could see Mackey's arms were extended, and both hands were gripping a gun.

Joey rolled over and said from the floor, "It's only a little two-incher."

"Two inches more than *you* got," Mackey said, keeping her eyes on her target.

Tilting his head, the grin now even crazier, Janowski said, "The bitch got a *piece*?" Looking down at the red dot on his chest, losing sight of it as it rose towards his throat.

"It's a laser sight and between your eyes now," Mackey said, "take one more step I'll put a hole where it was."

Janowski's eyes bulged as he began to push off from the balls of his feet, then two large caliber gunshots thundered from the back of the room.

"That's *enough*," a voice barked a few decibels louder.

Like someone had hit "pause" on a VCR, everyone in the room froze — then three guys on barstools dove for the floor.

Holding a gun shoulder height, pointed at the ceiling, Wacko stood at the rear of the room, silhouetted in light from the open door behind him. In the booth next to him, card players brushed plaster from their hair, checked their hands, then turned and looked back towards the front.

Wacko gave Mackey a look like she was a kid riding a mechanical horse at a mall. He said gently, "Hey, girly, put the gun away, please?" and stuck his in his belt. Following a nod from McCauley, she lowered the gun.

Coming towards them, Wacko said, "Know something, Del, I've been told and I believe that life is in the details." He swept Janowski with a venomous glare, ignoring Joey as he pulled himself from the floor.

"It's the little things," he said malevolently. "Like doin' what the fuck you're told."

And then McCauley swore if tigers purred, Wacko did, and wrapped an arm around Janowski's shoulders and pulled him in close.

"Seems you already know my friend Mike," he said, and his eyebrows floated up. "To say this guy hates cops . . . well, let's just say he *hates* cops."

Shook a finger at Janowski. "Bet you didn't even *try* to play nice," he said as he shook his head sadly. "What am I gonna do with you?"

Wacko looked at McCauley, winked. "But that's just a detail, see?" Jerked his head towards McCauley. "Michael, give the man what I told you to."

Janowski averted his eyes, yanked a folded paper from his pocket, then, like a fire hose, turned them back on McCauley.

"I'll only *give* him one thing, Jack, and that's a piece of steel," Janowski said, handing it to Wacko. He turned and walked to the bar.

Wacko smirked. He shrugged his shoulders.

He said, "See, Del, like I told ya, another *detail*, manners."

Keeping his eyes on Janowski's back, McCauley said, "So, what do you have for me, Jack?"

Wacko unfolded the paper and held it up to the light like he never had seen it before.

"Couple of phone numbers, guys you could call: burglars, professional B&E men, even a few junkies — shitbags who steal for their habit. Word's out, anyone who operates 'round here gotta talk to you — within reason, of course."

Wacko refolded the list.

McCauley said, "Thank you, Jack, this means a lot."

Wacko waved the paper under his nose, inhaled, shut his eyes, and grinned.

"Means a lot, huh? How much is that, money-wise, Del? See, the way I'm figurin' it, this *client* of yours musta got hit pretty hard for something important, maybe kinda touchy important, ya know, since he can't go to the heat." He glared at McCauley. "And that's why he hired you and the broad. Must be payin' ya's good, huh? I mean, gotta be good to get your ex-cop ass down here to the Pen to beg a dirty gangster for help. How am I doin', gettin' warm?"

"Didn't know I was begging."

Like he was staring into a stiletto of light, Wacko's eyes narrowed.

"Details," Wacko said. "And if I told you, you ain't gettin' the numbers, what then?"

"And I didn't beg?" McCauley said. "We'd both be disappointed."

Wacko gave him a lingering stare, then, like someone had dropped a punch line on him, suddenly broke out into laugher. Like it was okay now, snickers rippled around the room.

Wacko handed McCauley the paper, and when he reached, let it drop.

The mirth was gone from Wacko's face, and he stared at McCauley with the dark dull earnestness of men who have killed.

"Don't much like cops either," he said, turned, and walked away.

TWENTY-SEVEN

HOW 'BOUT PASSIN' THE KETCHUP," Enfield Higgins said, staring down the length of the table. Cheeks distended like he was chewing on golf balls, Billy Sims, without looking, grabbed the bottle on his left, wiggled it, and shook his head.

"Fucking thing's empty," he said, dropping it onto its side.

Higgins hammered his fist on the table and looked over his shoulder. A corrections officer was standing there, giving him the eye. Turning back, he glared across the table at Catchy Davis. He said, "Fucking screw, like to bury this fork in his face."

Catchy, like Higgins, loved to use knives; it was the basis of the bond between them.

With an open hand, Catchy patted the air a few inches above the table.

"Relax, Ennie, I'd like to gut him too, but do it, they'll-get-ya." He tapped Higgin's forearm. "Relax, I'll get you some ketchup, re-laax."

As Catchy called out for ketchup behind him, Higgins angrily stuffed bread in his mouth. He still couldn't believe he'd been lugged back to Norfolk, and all because of that moron, Dinny McLintock.

Only last week they were partying hearty with money they'd

got from a score. It had only taken them minutes, at one in the morning, to break into and liberate the Liberty Bell restaurant of three hundred bucks from the register, and five hundred more from the manager's desk.

Later, as they pounded down beers up West Broadway at Street Lights, Dinny gave him a bump with the shoulder. Says, "Ya know my cousin, Scully, from Charlestown just moved into the D? Him and his girlfriend are moving the yak. She'd been living there for years, he said, and because too many Townie cokeheads had guns, Scully had been using her place in the projects to store his stash."

Higgins looked at him, "Ya?" McClintock said, "Ya, Scully had been living at 65 Polk Street, moving the shit in the Bunker Hill projects, but someone had ratted him out. When the cops hit him, they found a digital scale, cut for the coke, but no drugs. Charged with paraphernalia, the BHA tossed his butt out of Charlestown."

Higgins was listening, but not good enough, when McClintock had told him how, the very next day, his cousin set up shop down the D. That alone should have been a stoplight for Higgins — big, bright, and red — but it wasn't. That was his problem, when chasing the coke he couldn't see stripe on a skunk. But he remembered one thing that he did tell McLintock — cops don't forget.

Later the same night, after leaving her place, the cops were on them like flies. Seems she'd been under surveillance for weeks. Carrying the package, McLintock got busted for felony possession. On parole, Higgins was urined. When it came up dirty, his PO violated him, lugged his ass back to Norfolk.

As they walked the dirt track in Norfolk's east field, Higgins suddenly hauled off and swung a fist through the air. He threw up his arms and did a three-sixty. "You're shittin' me, right? Thought I was finished with this *shit hole* forever." Kicking a rock into the infield, he continued to rant.

"Fourteen fucking counts a day, five of 'em standin'. You can't sleep until ten because you gotta be on your feet when they count? Fucking insanity."

"Joint's just the same as you left, only worse," Catchy said.

"And there I was eatin' *good* on the street."

Catchy let his eyes roam, frowned. "You was *eatin'*? Good wind comes up, have to tie string to your leg."

"So I lost weight, so what, don't matter, was eatin' good when I ate — nothin' like this shit. Turkey salami, turkey bologna," he said, counting each finger, "turkey ham, turkey hot dogs, Christ, they'd make turkey tuna fish, they could, and they won't give you *ketchup* to drown out the taste?"

Catchy patted his shoulder. "Still talkin' ketchup? Re-lax. You'll be seein' the parole board in another six months."

"Easy for you to say, you're gettin' out."

"Ya, after six years, six years for stabbin' someone tryin' to stab me, go figure. But I sure as shit learned something from it."

"Not to get caught?"

Catchy stopped walking, eyeballed the guard watching him in the tower. "Somethin' concernin' *how* not to get caught."

The twin modular units to their backs, they sat on a backless bench along the third base line of a well-used softball field. Pretending like he was following a butterfly's path, Catchy glanced at the tower over his shoulder. "Even with a parabolic," he said, swinging his head back around, "be tough pickin' up what we talk about here."

Higgins continued to stare at his feet. "What the fuck are you talkin' about, paregoric?"

"Bolic . . . para-*bolic*," Catchy said. "Shotgun mikes, that's what they call 'em. With 'em these bums can pick up your voice clear as a bell the length of a football field away. Been usin' 'em here, up the Hill, OCCC, Souza-Baranowski for over a year after you left. When you're walkin' the Quad, the IPS point 'em at ya from inside the Ad Building. Better be talkin' about sports."

Higgins threw a glance back at the tower. "So, what you got?'

Catchy's eyes brightened, he lowered his voice. "My thing for not gettin' caught?"

Higgins rolled his and said, "Ya."

"Know anything about flying saucers?" Catchy said. Then he made this ooooo-weeee noise and fluttered his fingers. Higgins rolled his eyes again and started to get up.

"Not so fast, Speed Racer," Catchy said, grabbing his arm,

"I'm tellin' ya, they're *real*. They're whippin' people off the streets; they'll get ya, sittin' on your toilet, from outta your car. Worst thing is, the government *knows* it." Stared into Higgins's eyes without blinking. "People are leavin' the planet, Ennie." And he gave him a knowing nod.

"So, E.T.'s your alibi," Higgins said with a serious face.

Catchy looked Higgins dead in the eye.

"I know about E.T., you know anything about cattle mutilations?"

Higgins's mug said he didn't know nothing.

Higgins listened as Catchy told him how out west, they'd been finding dead cattle, with body parts missing. How ranchers were seeing black helicopters hovering and strange lights over the prairie at night.

Next day they'd find cows, even bulls, big guys with horns, ain't talking no kitty cats here, stretched out stiff as museum wax dummies, missing eyes, lower jaws, sex organs, entire rectums cut out. All of it done surgically, hardly no blood. There's no footprints or tire marks anywhere, Catchy said, everyone's blaming the aliens.

Higgins said, "Ya know, around Southie they been findin' *people* like that. Think the aliens are franchisin'?"

Catchy held up a finger, nodded before beaming. "You're a smart man, Ennie, *knew* you'd catch on." He looked over his shoulder at the tower again, lowered his voice.

"They're *franchisin'*, you're right. Next guy I carve up, *I'm* doin' it."

"What?"

"Cuttin' out their eyeballs, maybe their asshole, lower jaw, extra-sharp knife, real fucking clean." He wrinkled is nose. "Won't fuck with the dick, though, gotta have standards."

Higgins bit his lower lip, bobbed his head gently. "And they'll blame it on — *aliens*."

Catchy beamed again, held up his hand in the high-five position. "Exactly," he said, as the other man gave him a weak one.

TWENTY-EIGHT

THINKING ABOUT THE CLASS he had just taken, Mc-Cauley shoulder-opened the door into the Columbus Avenue sunlight. He had studied the knife-fighting science, rooted in Malay/Filipino tribal arts, in the same South End studio above Charlie's Sandwich Shop, for almost ten years, not counting the three he was away.

During each ninety-minute class, students practiced attacking and counterattacking, strikes, fakes, and parries. They learned the importance of tactical footwork, how not to telegraph movement, proper pacing, and proper breathing technique.

The energy of the class was always high but would almost become frenetic when the students, utilizing various combat scenarios, sparred with each other. During these times, two, sometimes three, students, armed with rubber knives, would attack a single student. The "victim" had to fight for his life, using his training weapon to slash or stab hard enough to shock or disrupt the attack. Doctor Mario would watch from the sidelines, offering criticism and tips, sometimes even adding to the fray by attacking himself.

Taught that a true knifer makes the art a part of his life, McCauley had continued his study following his release from prison. Still, he was hesitant to carry a knife knowing that three years in prison had made him angry and bitter, and anger and weapons don't mix.

But now he had problems — problems that wouldn't be settled with hands. Since the incident at the Pen he had begun carrying, always one, sometimes two, Benchmade Access folding knives, both clipped to the inside of his front pockets.

Dropping the small gym bag containing his knives — a titanium bowie, two folders, a rubber six-inch double-edged — on the sidewalk in front of a parking meter, McCauley squatted and loosened his cross-trainer laces. He'd developed the habit of tightening them before classes; it didn't pay to be swimming in your shoes when someone was lunging with a knife.

Looking behind him over his shoulder through the window of Charlie's Sandwich Shop, he noticed someone waving inside. Coming in through the door, McCauley said, "Arthur, how's tricks?" Sat down on stool at the counter, dropped the bag between his feet.

Sauntering over, without asking, Arthur put a cup on the counter in front of him, filling it from the pot he held in his hand. "How're you doin', McCauley?" he said. "Cut anyone to ribbons today?" And locked his eyebrows in the upright position.

McCauley took a sip and winced.

"What's a matter, no good?"

"Hot," McCauley said.

The other man grinned. "Good thing, McCauley, you said, no good be *needin'* those knife-fightin' lessons. How 'bout somethin' to eat?"

"Just coffee for now, Arthur, thanks."

"Been workin' much?"

McCauley shrugged. "Depends what you mean. Are you talking the kind you get paid for, or the other?"

Arthur looked at him, puzzled.

"Whatever 'the other' is, I ain't askin'," he said.

McCauley sipped and held up the cup. "Get past the heat, the coffee ain't bad."

"One thing, McCauley, heat you can handle," Arthur said, walking away. He held up the pot. "Now, who wants more coffee?"

As McCauley watched the traffic go by on busy Columbus, he thought about Mackey; how after leaving the Pen, her complexion was only a shade darker than Lenox china. He remembered asking if she was okay, and her bitter reply, "Yes, I'm okay . . . it's that *sewer* that isn't." Then how she'd hooked her arm through his and hurried him across West Broadway.

As they walked into the Burger King lot, where they parked, Mackey said, "It almost seemed choreographed, like it was some kind of game."

McCauley wanted to tell her that nothing that happened surprised him. That guys like them never played nice, but rolled out of bed playing hardball each morning. But he didn't, he just let her vent. He was surprised when she agreed to go with him to get something to eat, but somewhere out of South Boston, she said.

At the Fat Belly Deli, in Dorchester's Adams Corner, they sat at a back table next to a tall window with a view to the street. Mackey ordered a crab cake appetizer, soda water and lemon, McCauley a salad, chicken Caesar.

While they waited, they talked, mostly about her. Where she grew up, Wellesley, went to school, Wellesley High, and, afterwards, how she almost went to her father's alma mater, Boston College. She said, "It was mostly because Dad was a 'Triple Eagle': Boston College High, Boston College, and Boston College Law School. Her smile seemed strained when she told him that maybe a son would have been better suited for the legacy trip. Considering a career in law enforcement, she ended up attending Northeastern.

McCauley said, "You're pretty good with a gun. Mind me asking how come?" Mackey replied that her father was a gun nut and had taught her to shoot as a kid. She practiced weekly at the Braintree gun club, and usually carried when out.

Then, as she sipped the lemon and water, it was Mackey's turn for questions, which were mostly generic: Have you lived in Southie all of your life, any kids, ever married? For a while she seemed to purposely avoid touching on his conviction, incarceration, or his law enforcement past, except for some basic questions concerning surveillance: the proper distance to remain back on a tail, what to do when you're spotted. It seemed almost like she was afraid that if she didn't control the conversation, he might start talking about prison — which he had no intention of.

Then, right after the waitress delivered the rolls and butter, without warning, Mackey said, "I've been told, by Esmond Cotter and some others, that you really got screwed by the system. Can you tell me what happened?"

McCauley didn't mind. People who got screwed rarely did. He told her how he had been working with a joint state police/DEA task force, which had been monitoring a methamphetamine lab for over a month. Located in an abandoned factory complex on the east side of Brockton, the lab belonged to the Devil's Disciples, a notorious motorcycle gang. The DDs weren't part of your new breed of weekend, dying-to-look-bad guys driving Harleys, McCauley said; they weren't lawyers, construction workers, or accountant types out for a good time. The DDs were the real deal, most were ex-cons, they were ruthless, organized, and not afraid of cops.

"The night of the raid, we surrounded the building. Then we hit it, from every angle. Shots were fired, and people were hit — both cops and Disciples. Some of the Disciples escaped from the building."

Mackey said, "In all the confusion."

"*Chaos*, is more like it," McCauley said. "You plan these things as best you can, but when the starting gun's fired . . ." He shook his head.

"Seems there were tunnels leading out of the building, and I spotted my guy popping out from behind an old chimney fifty yards from the building; took off like a rabbit, with me right behind him. In almost complete darkness, both of us running through the grounds of this former shoe factory, and me without backup."

Mackey looked confused. "But the radio, you must have had one?"

McCauley grimaced. "I did, but thirty seconds into the chase, I hit a chuckhole and went flying, almost broke my ankle, did the damn radio."

"Where was everyone else?" Mackey said.

McCauley said, "The rest, not directly involved with detainment? Fanning out through the complex. I found *that* out later.

"So the rabbit's running, seemed always at least fifty yards ahead, but still I'm behind him. I'd see him, lose him, then, in the moonlight, spot him again. At one point I lost him completely then *heard* him, his footsteps, like a sonic scent trail coming from between these two huge buildings, both the length of a football field. I got to the entrance of the alleyway between them and there was a break in the clouds. In the moonlight I could see all the way down to the other end, *knew* he couldn't have made it that far."

Looking past her now, McCauley shifted in his seat. "The moon went behind the clouds as I entered the alley, couldn't see a thing. I'm feeling myself along — it's filled with debris: fifty-gallon drums, wooden reels on their sides, trash, then the moon comes out and I see him again, thirty yards down, stepping away from the wall."

"He was hiding," Mackey said.

McCauley nodded. "And he sees me too. I'm a couple of hundred feet in, but he's a hundred away, right near the end." McCauley leaned closer. "He turns and faces me, strokes his hair back behind his ears, casual, like he's standing in front of a mirror and, I swear, the guy grins."

"Taunting you?" Mackey said incredulously.

McCauley shrugged, made a fist of his right hand, cupped it with his left, raised it. "I pointed my weapon at him, wanted to yell freeze, but maybe it was the drain following the adrenaline rush, all that came out was a halfhearted *hey* — and he bolted the last fifty feet, rounded the corner, and was gone."

"You never caught him?" Mackey said.

McCauley lowered his hands and looked out the window, then back at Mackey. "He was *caught*, all right, but not by me.

"Seconds after he rounded the corner there was this blinding white light, and I hear men screaming through bullhorns. I start to run towards it, but trip on a wire, something, and I'm back on the ground."

"The bullhorns, they were your men," Mackey said.

McCauley nodded. "They were, and it quickly turned into a nightmare," he said. "Turning the corner, I found, up ahead, a bank of klieg lights and a gaggle of angry troopers holding riot batons and flashlights, standing over a body."

"The Disciple?"

"That's the trouble, he *wasn't*," McCauley said, shaking his head. "Turns out the *Disciple* was actually a guy named Matt Doyle. Two years before he'd infiltrated the gang, he was deep undercover for the DEA."

Folding her hands like she was about to pray, Mackey said gently, "So far, Del, I haven't heard that *you* did anything."

"I didn't. Didn't *see* anything either. That was the problem."

Mackey gave him a look, how?

"The agent almost died from the beating, and it turns out Matt Doyle wasn't just an agent. Here was a guy who had done irreparable damage to the gang, who was the cornerstone of the lab bust that night. Was to have been a corroborative witness in the upcoming trial of two Disciples accused of executing a meth dealer employed by the rival Hells Angels. He was on the verge of discarding his 'colors,' and rejoining the good guys, and *this* happened."

"How many cops went to jail?" Mackey said, breaking a roll, opening butter.

"*Prison*, not jail, there's a difference," McCauley said, tapping his chest with a finger. "Just me."

"But what about the men who actually did it," Mackey said, straightening.

"Three were forced to resign," McCauley said. "Me? I was the *fall* guy, convicted of perjury and obstruction of justice. I got three years because I testified that I never saw anything."

"But you didn't."

"Not a thing, I got there too late."

"And the agent, Matt Doyle?"

"Still in a coma," McCauley said, shook his head as he looked out the window, and slowly returned his attention to Mackey. "Want my perspective? *Two* good cops were lost that night."

"I don't know what to say," Mackey said, breaking a piece off a roll, pressing it between a finger and thumb.

"I do," McCauley said, shaking out his napkin, spreading it across his lap. "That's ancient history, let's talk about now. For starters, your line of work, how did a Wellesley girl get involved in private investigations?"

McCauley was content to sit and listen to the voice that had so intrigued him go on about how she got into the work, the agency she worked for downtown, how interesting she found it. She complained, though, that because of the sometimes odd hours, there wasn't much left for a social life.

Mackey told him how she dated a cop, a Watertown detective who worked similar hours, and though the arrangement had worked for a while, it turned out that he lied, he was married. When she said that, her eyelids fluttered, and she looked down at her bread, and something in McCauley's gut twisted. Then it lifted, and she was smiling again, and whatever had done it was gone.

When she finished they went over Wacko's list. A few of the names had phone numbers next to them, while others had just an address. Mackey recognized one of the names, a guy called Flabo. Next to Flabo was a number and a Quincy address.

She told McCauley how she'd already met Flabo at a tavern called Street Lights on West Broadway. He was sitting at the bar when she came in and said something she didn't quite get.

McCauley said, "What did he look like, was he young, old, a boozer, what?"

"I'd say early thirties," Mackey said, looking up, trying to picture the guy. "Kind of heavy, I'm guessing six feet or more but I'm not really sure, he never got off the bar stool." She checked the image again. "And no, he didn't look like a drunk, but his eyes were glassy, he'd had a few.

"Soon as I came in he made some kind of remark, wiseguy crap, and I stopped and came right up in his face." She grinned. "I prefer to be proactive," she said.

"How'd he react?"

Demonstrating, Mackey turned in the chair, hooking her arm around towards her. "First off, grabs his Budweiser off the bar, pulls it to his chest, and denies he said anything. He was embarrassed, I knew it and capitalized on it. I gave him a chance to play nice and make up." Winked "So I hit him with a couple of questions, real quick, told him I wasn't a cop when he asked."

"Get any answers?"

Mackey batted her lashes. "Sure, pretty much. You know, guys like to talk to us ladies. Use what you've got, right?"

The waitress put Mackey's order in front of her. "Like your gun?" McCauley said, nodding at the waitress as she put down his salad. Her mouth opened slightly and she glanced at Mackey.

"Yes, my weapon if I have to, but I prefer using my wits and," Mackey batted the lashes again, "my *wiles*, if you will." She shook out her napkin. "Crab cake? There's three, I'll never eat three."

McCauley allowed her to put one on his bread dish.

"So, I'm asking questions and Flabo's coming on to me — getting his confidence back — and I'm going along with it, I'm not offended, see, and maybe I might be interested a little if only he'd help me out.

"He's playing the role, sure he knows lots of people around here, yes he knows guys who do B&E's, let me ask around he says, and what are you doing later tonight?"

She ate some crab cake, closed her eyes, and lifted her chin. "Crab cake's delicious," she said, squeezing some lemon on the piece on deck.

"So, I gave him my phone number, my *office* phone number, asked him for his in case, wink, wink, I came up with any more *questions*."

"And he gave it to you?"

Mackey nodded and popped in another piece. "Got it with me," she said happily chewing. She pulled a small notepad from her pocketbook. Flipping it open she wrote the number on a napkin and handed it to McCauley.

"Your first name, like mine, is odd," Mackey said as the waitress cleared away a few empty dishes. He told her he was conceived in Delray Beach, Florida, during a trip his parents had taken. Mum took a piece of it home with her.

When he asked about hers, she told him her father, a Marine major and a Vietnam vet, had greatly admired his commanding officer, a gung-ho colonel by the name of McArthur Lantini, affectionately known as "Mac" to the troops. Then how, during the waning days of the war, after Lantini was killed in a rocket attack, he swore his first son would be named after him.

"I was his firstborn, mother was unable to have any more." Mackey said, and shrugged. "Daddy always kept his word."

In the parking lot across from the Fat Belly, as he walked her to her car, he asked if he could call her sometime, adding quickly, "You know, if something comes up. . . on the case, might need your input."

She gave him a lingering, slightly curious look.

"You could do that," she said, pointing the remote device, unlocking the red Audi RS4. She opened the door and got in.

He said, "Thanks again for the backup today."

"You're welcome, thank *you* for the meal," she said over her shoulder before closing the door.

On the way back to the Mustang it struck McCauley how Mackey never asked about the contents of the safe. Either she already knew, or was too professional to inquire. He was glad that she didn't; he didn't want to lie and tell her he didn't know either.

TWENTY-NINE

As he headed down Gallivan Boulevard towards the ramp at Neponset, McCauley thought about Mackey, impressed she was tough, had a good head on her shoulders, a hard combination to find even in cops. It didn't hurt either that she had a face like a doll.

By giving him Flabo's number, she had saved him a trip, maybe a lot of trips, since guys like him tended to move around a lot. He dialed Flabo's number as he sat at the lights at Neponset Circle, under the 93 overpass.

Flabo picked up on the seventh ring and McCauley took a minute to explain why he called. "That so?" Flabo said, like he would love to have said something to Wacko about it. Instead he said, "So, how's Jack?"

McCauley said good.

"You and him friends?"

"Why don't you call him and ask?"

"Just strikes me as strange, him havin' me talkin' to you, bein' a stranger."

"It beats being struck," McCauley said.

McCauley heard Flabo wheeze, before he switched to speaker-phone.

"Hey, I'm cooperatin'," he said, like he was talking from inside a toilet, "don't tell the big guy I ain't, just sayin' strikes me strange, is all."

McCauley could hear water running and the clink of dishes, and the squeak of a sponge on porcelain.

"I interrupt dinner?"

"Just washin' dishes, what does it sound like, that what you called me to ask?"

When he performed interrogations, McCauley liked to start his subjects off easy, pitch a few simple questions, no curve balls or fast balls, nothing confusing, but to every question, Flabo's response time was slow, like his brain was encased in molasses.

McCauley got to the point.

"So tell me, Flab, heard anything lately about a break-in in a law office?"

Flabo cleared his throat and there was a rustling sound like he was tugging his collar away from his neck. "Strange gettin' hit with the same question twice. Take it you and the little broad work together."

"Which *little broad* are we talking about?"

"The pretty one last week who came down to . . . the place I hang out at . . . snoopin' 'round askin' about a safe bein' stole from some lawyer's office."

"Not working with her, but I know who she is."

"If she ain't your partner, then what's the connection?" Flabo seemed to have second thoughts. "Ah, the hell with it, Wacko says you're okay, you're okay. She ain't your wife or girlfriend is she?"

McCauley told him she wasn't.

"Good," Flabo said. Sounded like he was rubbing his palms together.

"Tell ya the truth, McCauley, she's a hot little number, tight little butt, but got them blank Betty Boop eyes, teeny walls in 'em, see, like you're not supposed to know what's inside her." Flabo chuckled. "But like you, I'm a guy, can tell when I'm hittin' a chord in a broad. Hell, didn't she give me her number? Not that I called yet." He laughed. "I believe it's better to make 'em wait, to build up the yearnin', before ya move in for the kill, we agree?" He chuckled again.

"So I did some askin' around 'bout this lawyer thing, got something might get a rise from her nipples." It sounded like he was squeezing a sponge. "But why should I give it to you?"

McCauley said, "Let me call Wacko, you can give it to him. Or maybe I'll ask him to send down Mike Janowski, you can whisper it into his ear."

Flabo coughed, and the same sound came across like he was

tugging his collar. "Uh, can't see no need to get those guys involved. This ain't a big deal. Christ, all we're talkin' is some legal beagle gettin' broken into down the Waterfront, right?"

Flabo sighed and McCauley imagined him rubbing his forehead.

"I'll tell ya, McCauley, no one I know breaks in a law office, what you gonna get, some stick-em pads, a few lousy pens? Unless, of course, maybe that lawyer fucked them. My advice, good chance you'll find your man when you look for the guy who got fucked by this lawyer."

McCauley said, "And that's the *something* you believed might get you laid?" Now it was McCauley's turn to sigh. "You're not narrowing it down for me, Flab."

"Can't argue the point," Flabo said finally.

He told McCauley that since the guys he ran with didn't do offices, the fact he heard nothing meant just about as much. He was a fence, he said, dealt in high-end stuff: furs, appliances, convection ovens, Sub-Zero refrigerators, jewelry, then he went on about the pitfalls of "the trade." Southie was "gentrifrying," he said, and the "yuffies" (young, urban, fucking fools, he explained) were flooding its streets. Killing him, he complained, cheap, wouldn't part with a buck, even for top of-the-line shit, but what about McCauley? Would he be interested in something nice for his own apartment?

It was fast becoming just conversation when Flabo wheezed, 'cause you're a friend of Jack's, and he gave him a name and number not on the list. He said the guy was a fence of big stuff and small, and went by the name of Jimmy Quarters.

The phone rang four times and a small voice picked up.

"He-llo?"

It was a kid, probably a girl, and even though it was early evening, she sounded like she had just rolled out of bed.

In the background a television blared, some talking head on a news channel droning on monotonously about a three-car accident, with fatality, up on 93 North with traffic backed up to Andover.

McCauley said, "Is your daddy there?"

She didn't respond, but the TV chatter in the room had switched to a story about a dog-fighting den that was raided up in Lowell, resulting in twenty arrests.

"Hello?"

McCauley said, "Ya, honey, could you get your daddy or anyone there named Jimmy?"

As he waited, he stared at the number on the Burger King napkin, wondering if he dialed the wrong one, when the little girl shouted,

"Mom-my, someone wants to talk to Jimmy Quart-ers."

And, somewhere in the house, an extension picked up.

A male voice said, "I got it," and there was a click and the voice said, "Who the fuck's this?"

"The name is Delray McCauley and Flabo gave me your number."

The voice on the other end became muffled and said to someone else there, "Will you please give me a minute here?"

A woman's voice, which sounded like she was talking from the bottom of a teapot, said, "*Told* you, I don't want you doin' your damn business in my house. Who gave him the number?"

"The guy says Flabo now, please, give me a minute, okay?"

The male voice was loud again. "Fucking Flabo got no right givin' out this number. Told him a dozen times. This is my girl's house, you understand, Mister, ain't no office. Now, who the *fuck* is this again?"

McCauley told him.

"Don't know ya, and you say you're a friend of Flabo's?"

McCauley told him he wasn't and gave him a brief rundown of how he got the number, what he was looking for. When he was finished, Jimmy Quarters said angrily, "So, let me get this straight. You're not a friend of Flabo's, but he gave you this number here, knowing he shouldn't, because he was afraid of what Wacko would do if he didn't?"

"Something like that," McCauley said, "but I think maybe more because he wanted to help."

"And you're thinkin' . . . *hopin'* that maybe I will too? Because believe me, Del-ray, and what kind of fucking name is that, I ain't *afraid* of Jackie Curran, known him since he was a kid."

McCauley said calmly, "I'm glad you're friends, and yes, I did hope you'd help me. Regarding your question, I was conceived in Florida, and was named after a beach. Don't think Mum wanted to come back to Boston but had to, my father his job."

Jimmy Quarters chuckled.

"So, Ma took a piece of the sunshine state back with her, huh? Women, they're beautiful. Okay, Delray . . ."

"Del's fine."

"All right, Del, let's get this straight. You tellin' me Jackie C says you're okay, and I'm checkin' it out, and Flabo never laid eyes on ya and still gave you my number?"

"Correct."

"And you know Jackie from . . . ?"

"Since we were kids."

"You from Southie?"

"Born and raised, K and Seventh."

"Really? I was M Street near Sixth."

McCauley said, "M and Sixth, you must know Stooey Wallace?"

"Knew him, ya, but I gotta have a few years on you, Del, I ran with Wedgy, his older brother."

McCauley said, "Ya, I remember Wedgy, he was big, always scowling, not nearly as cute as his sister, Maggie. Me and her dated in high school."

Jimmy Quarters gasped. He said, "Maggie? Geeee-zus-fucking-Christ. You dated Maggie? I was in love . . . she was a fucking bombshell. What was she like, Del? Naw, forgetaboutit, sound like some fucking pervert."

And then Jimmy Quarters didn't seem to care if he sounded like a pervert.

He said, "Ya know, as a kid, musta been eighteen, nineteen, I remember stoppin' by the house to pick up Wedgy, a bunch of us used to go to the Broon's games and Maggie, bein' no more than thirteen or so then and I swear woulda married her. Christ, here I go soundin' like a pervert again, but it's the God awful truth. You dated her, huh?"

There was a pause and McCauley thought they had disconnected or maybe that Jimmy had dropped the phone dreaming about Maggie. But he hadn't. Then he heard the woman's voice in the background again, and this time Jimmy Quarters wasn't so polite.

He said irately, "Get the fuck out of here, it's business, get out." And she screamed something about how he'd be the one who was out, and when she slammed the door it sounded like someone slapped a pillow with a tennis racket, and Jimmy was back on the line.

"Geee-zus Christ. What I gotta deal with, all of us, huh, women. You think Maggie's still out there runnin' around?"

They both laughed out loud, then Jimmy Quarters said, "Okay, Del, who the fuck am I to argue, you sound like a good guy, maybe better than me bangin' . . . excuse me, *datin'* Maggie Wallace, I'm so fucking jealous, you prick."

"I'd tell you more about it, Jimmy, but I never kiss and tell," McCauley said.

"All the more reason to respect ya. I'm supposed to say that, see?"

And the two of them laughed again.

"To get back to the point of this phone call, though. You're talkin' about a break-in at the Seaport Building, a lawyer's office, correct? That in itself's kinda strange, amateurish, somethin' kids would do or maybe a pissed-off client."

"That's what Flabo thought too, but these guys tore out the safe."

Jimmy Quarters softly whistled. "Don't sound like kids then, and nothin' else stolen, nothin' vandalized?'

"Far as I know, no."

McCauley visualized him scratching his head.

He said, "Who'd break into a lawyer's office? Did he know about the safe, or just get lucky and find it? I'd be lyin', Del, I told you I could think like a burglar. Never so much as broke a pane, climbed through a frame in my life," he said rhythmically. "What I do starts when those guys finish but, for obvious reasons, no one's ever come with a safe."

"No, I don't think kids did your lawyer. Ain't pros breakin' into offices either. My guess, junkies, and, at the moment, I only know one crew trying to palm off the gartsy stuff to me, you know: calculators, used laptops, even electric pencil sharpeners, for chrissakes."

When McCauley said, "How about a name?" he heard the click of an extension pick up and the same little voice came on.

"He-llo?"

"Marisa, honey, hang up the phone," Jimmy Quarters said softly.

"Jim-my, you gonna read to me, I'm gettin' ti-red again."

"I'm gonna read to you, honey. Soon as you hang up the phone, the big bear's comin' to read." And there was a barely audible click, like from a thermostat when the heat comes on.

Jimmy Quarters laughed.

"What I tell ya, women? If the big ones don't get you with the left, the little ones do with the right. Let me sniff around, okay? Got an idea who, but ain't sayin' no names on the phone tonight that already haven't been said, and one more thing. This is between us, the cops, the fucking cops get nothin', understand?"

"You have my word, Jimmy."

"Good. Meet me tomorrow morning down Mul's, say quarter of nine, grab somethin' to eat. Anything I come up with I'll give to you then."

THIRTY

TEN MINUTES AFTER THE STREETLIGHTS blinked on, Wacko Curran walked out through the open door of the High Hat bar in Quincy. As he got into the passenger side of the green Lincoln parked out front he felt the ghost of the warm bar air leaving his clothes, giving itself up to the night. Turning his head he looked back into the bar, catching the flash of glass that streaked past the entrance, exploding against a wall.

A voice inside roared, "*He* ain't gonna protect ya, you're dealin' with *me* now."

Wacko stuck his arm out the window, slapped the door panel, and shouted, "C'mon, Mike, I said, let's *go*."

Turning back to the windshield, he grinned as Leppy Mullen came out of the bar, tilting a beer to his lips. Stopping at the edge of the step, he eyeballed Wacko and nodded. Behind him a chair sailed across the room, and there was the sound of heavy glass, like a mirror breaking, falling in sections. A voice strained with fear screamed, "Jesus, Mike, no please, it isn't my . . ."

Leppy smashed the bottle in the doorway and grinned, shrugged his shoulders. He stepped down to the sidewalk and stretched his arms overhead.

Mike Janowski filled the doorway next, shoulder muscles straining against the straps of his tank top as he ran the fingertips of both hands through the close-cropped hair on the side of his head. He shrugged his shoulders, jerked his eyebrows up twice, and approached Wacko. Tucking his thumbs behind his belt, he said softly, "Now what?"

Flippy Condon backed out the door behind him. Remained facing it as worried faces popped from the door frame on either side looked out and pulled back.

"Now what?" Wacko said, turning his head, staring back through the windshield, "Ya, get back in there and do what we came here to do."

Janowski looked up the street, shook his head. "Still think shoulda done it right the *first* time, Jack."

Leppy checked both ends of Water Street, said, "Hey Mike, street's clear, don't see no heat in sight."

Resigned, Janowski nodded, muttered, "Trunk open?"

"Is now," Wacko said, leaning across the armrest, hitting a button on the driver's side door.

After a click-whoomph sound at the rear of the car, Janowski flipped up the rear deck, then slammed it shut, tossing an aluminum ball bat to Flippy, slapping his own palm with an iron window counterweight. He came alongside the passenger side door, said to the counterweight, "Whatever I hit with this breaks."

Wacko looked at him.

"Good, but remember the guy *owes* us, keep it below the neck."

As Janowski gunned the green Lincoln off Furnace Brook Parkway, merged with traffic on 93 North, Wacko turned and glared behind him at Leppy.

"*You*, it happens again, it's comin' out of *your* pocket, got it? Got better things to do than kick the shit outta your slow-payin' customers."

Leppy frowned at his lap, looked out the window. High-beams from an oncoming truck slashed his face when he spoke.

"Jack, Lefty's a good mover, never been late, well almost never been, figured I'd give him a chance."

Janowski growled at the rearview. "Ya, you gave him a chance with *our* money, motherfucker."

Moments earlier, when Janowski went into the High Hat for the second time that night, he was only inside for a couple of minutes. That's all it took to put Lefty Ahern under a table with a fractured collar bone, broken ulna — right side since he was a lefty — it could have been worse. While this was happening, Flippy had waved his bat like a laser sword and the rest of the patrons had remained glued to the walls.

"When a good mover like Lefty's a week late, it's okay you cut him some slack," Wacko said, "but you *tell* us you are. You don't let him run, get six weeks behind."

Back to the door, foot on the seat, Flippy was staring steadily at Leppy.

"Into us for five large, and the guy's sittin' in a bar, smokin' our coke? Makes us look bad." Wacko faced front, nodding at the mirror. He glared at the redhead. "And we look bad, Lep, gonna find out whether you're allergic to pain."

At the bottom of the Morrissey Boulevard exit off 93 North, Janowski looked at Wacko as he braked near the merge.

Wacko said, "What?"

"So, how come Jack, twice? Why didn't we just kick the shit out of Ahern the first time we went in? Second time, our luck, the cops coulda drove by."

"More *bang* for the buck," Wacko said, eyeing the lights of the Savin Hill Yacht Club. He shifted his body, checked the speedometer, settled back in the seat. "Keep it under fifty, staties been campin' out at the war memorial lately, don't give 'em a reason to stop us."

"Fifty feels like twenty in a Conty," Janowski said. "So how come?"

Wacko stared ahead like he was watching a screen.

"When we walked into the High Hat, Lefty was shittin' himself. *Knew* you were dyin' to swat him."

"But you stopped me."

"Did because word on the street is Jackie Curran's tough but fair, he'll give ya a chance. Naturally, everyone's expectin' a bloodbath, instead we throw 'em a curve. I say to Lefty, pay what you owe us or *next* time, my man here's gonna tear off your head. I split and he sees you still chompin' at the bit, dyin' to hurt him. You break a few glasses, toss a chair through the mirror, and when you leave, it's one big ex-hale, them thinkin' it's over — but it ain't.

"Not only are they terrified of me, our organization, but when you and Flippy came back through that door, now they're literally shittin' their pants knowin', though I tried to, even *I* can't control you." Wacko grinned. "The devil just got *bigger* — and news like that got little red wings. Tonight they'll be talkin' about it in every joint in Quincy, by tomorrow it will be down on the Cape. Next time a coke dealer thinks about mushin' us, guaranteed he'll think a lot harder."

"Think we should have just clipped him," Janowski said. "*That* sends a message."

"Too much of a message," Wacko said, waving a finger. "Scare 'em like that, others might run to the cops."

"Hey," Flippy said from the back, "since you guys are devils, that make me a *demon*?"

"Want to meet one, keep runnin' your mouth," Wacko said without turning.

Looked at Janowski. "I know what I'm doing here, trust me."

"You're fucking with their heads," Janowski said.

Wacko nodded.

"Can do anything we want to their bodies," he said.

"On the McCauley thing, you doing your homework?" Wacko said as they entered the rotary near the Old Colony Projects.

"Got feelers out, Jack, gettin' some feedback," Janowski said, turning right onto Dorchester Street. Nodding at the windshield, staring at Bell's Market half a block up. "Just about now might be gettin' some more," he said, slowing down after East Ninth Street.

"There he is, Jack," he said, briefly accelerating, then braking to a stop. "Think the bum sleeps in the doorway," he said, throwing the car into park

The way he used his nickel on the Mountains of Cash scratch ticket, Moses Halloran, sockless in his high-top black sneakers, gray hooded sweatshirt that hung past his balls, wouldn't have noticed flames sprouting from the crotch of his hot BVDs. He pulled the ticket close to his face, blew on it, frowned, and flicked it like a baseball card into the street . . . where it landed on the hood of the Conty.

Wacko lowered the window. "Get your ass over here, Moses," he said, staring at the spot near the wiper.

Moses tugged at his sweatshirt, took a step back, nodded like he had stepped into a hole. Looked at Wacko, past him to Janowski, waved like he was cleaning a mirror.

"Ain't a winna," he said, his crazy grin exposing a couple of busted front teeth.

"Neither are you, fuckhead," Janowski said. "Losin's contagious, get it the fuck off of my car." Watched as he did what he said.

"Lookin' like shit, Moses," Janowski observed. "Used to be in tremendous shape. You one of them guys can't handle the street?"

Leaning on the roof, lowering his head to the window, Moses said, "Little too much partyin', gotta get my butt down the L."

"Them arms you're leanin' on, got track marks on 'em?" Flippy said.

Moses straightened up, offended.

"Never *shot* nothin'," he said, and jabbed a finger at Flippy. "And someone who's always smokin' that shit oughta watch what comes out of their mouth."

"Smokin' *what* shit?" Wacko said turning, eyeballing Flippy.

Flippy lunged through the window at Moses. "Fucking junkbag, watch what you're sayin' I'll . . ."

Wacko pounded the dash, "All of ya's, *everyone*," he shouted, "calm the fuck down."

Leppy snapped open a knife and kicked open the back door. He snarled at Moses, "Get into the *car*."

Janowski looked over the seat and laughed. "Ain't reelin' him in with *that* kind of bait."

Wacko threw a backhand at Flippy, missed. "You givin' orders, *you*?" Turning, he glared at Moses as he backed up towards the market. "And *you*, stay put." He said to Janowski, "You ask him about it?"

Leaning across him, Janowski said, "Moses, few days ago what we discussed, you come up with anything yet?"

Cupping the sides of his mouth with both hands, Moses said, "You're talkin' the safe?"

"Ya what'd you find?"

Moses toe-tapped a cigarette butt into the gutter. "Heard it was Higgins and McLintock, Dinny not Arnie, Arnie's in Raybrook, that done it."

"You sure?" Janowski said.

Moses nodded.

"Last week him and the other guy was hangin' around Sullivan's Pub, buyin' everyone drinks. Got pretty fucked up for four or five days, then . . ." shrugged, "whatever they had must have run out."

Wacko folded a fifty length-wise, inserted it the same way between his middle and index fingers, and waved it at Moses.

"Know if anything was in it besides money?"

Moses licked his lips. "Naw, wish I did, but didn't hear nothin' . . . thanks, Jack." He plucked the bill like he was pulling a splinter, shoved it into his pocket, pulled out a tissue. 'Scuse me, Jack." Blew his nose. "Allergies," he said, dabbing the end.

"Ya, the *injectable* type," Flippy said from the back.

"Here, might wanna use this to clean up your *own* act," Moses said, tossing the snot rag at Flippy.

"You motherfucker!" Flippy shrieked, brushed at it, tried to stand up, fell back onto Leppy. It stuck to his crotch, then his leg. "Ahh, ahhh, get the fuck off," Flippy screamed. He kicked open the back door and was lunging at Moses as Janowski accelerated away from the curb.

"Tryin' to give me AIDS, you fuck, you *fuck*!" Flippy screamed out the window.

Wacko ignored him, "Where do we find Higgins?" he said to Janowski.

"Was out on parole," Janowski said, watching the rearview, slowing down after Telegraph Street, "he got violated, and they lugged his ass back."

"Back?" Flippy said, waving the tissue on the tip of his knife, flicking it out the window. "Head back, I'll shove *this* down his throat."

"Shut the fuck up," Wacko said, "What about his partner?"

Janowski said, "McLintock? Got pinched on a coke beef but he's out on bail."

Now stopped in traffic, a half block from the lights at the West Broadway merge, Janowski indicated with his head a bar on the right. "McCauley works there."

Wacko looked at T.K. O'Malley's. "Sure it ain't all you know about the guy?"

Janowski smirked. "Where he lives, what he drives, what he eats, where he hangs," he said, taking a slow left at the lights.

Wacko nodded, looked at him. "Ya? This kid McLintock, do the same thing. Anything else in that safe, I wanna know."

THIRTY-ONE

T WAS OVERCAST, the sun trying to break through the clouds, when McCauley pulled open the door to Mul's diner. He hadn't gotten ten feet inside when Beate Viglione, one of the owners, greeted him from behind the counter, with a voice like someone practicing riot control without the benefit of a bullhorn.

"OOOP! Del-ray Mc-goddamn-Cauley, where you *been*, honey?"

And every eye in the joint was on him.

At the counter he slid in next to a man in a brown construction-type jumpsuit picking up some coffees to go, and stretched over the counter and embraced the huge woman. "Jesus, Del, how are ya?" she said still at the same volume.

"Where's Frank?" McCauley said, looking.

"My ol' man? Hates it when I call him that, he's back in the kitchen batterin' chicken for the lunch crowd."

"Got the best fried around."

"Thanks, honey, you're lookin' great, Del, but," she patted herself around the waist and gave him a banker's frown, "you lose some *weight*?"

McCauley leaned closer. "When I came out of the . . . *other* place, B, I was thin as a rail. I ate like a pig the first couple of months, packed on twenty pounds fast." Pinched his waist.

"Had to lose it, get back into fighting trim, so I cut out breakfast . . . *your* breakfasts."

Beate sternly waggled a finger. "You're talking extremes here, Del. A man's gotta eat, maybe not breakfast, always, but a man's gotta eat. Now, why don't cha let ol' Bee-bee whip you up some home fries, some eggs over lightly with a side of Canadian." Threw a thumb over her shoulder at a skinny man, a nose long enough to hang coats off of, cooking behind her. Bent over the griddle, he furiously chopped at strips of sizzling bacon with a long steel spatula.

"Lou's cookin' up a fresh batch now — get to work, Lou," Beate barked at the room, winking at McCauley.

She peeked over his undulating shoulders as Lou waved the spatula dismissively.

"Damn it, Lou, don't crisp it too much, ain't got beavers here gnawin' damn wood."

Lou nodded, waved the spatula again.

McCauley took in the room. They were two deep at the counter and every table filled. In the far corner a guy in a red sweatshirt, with B.U. on the back, sat at a table with an open *Herald* in front of him. Next to him, draped over a chair, an expensive-looking oversized parka, the kind a scalper might wear outside the Fleet Center in winter.

He turned and gave McCauley a look.

From the sound of his voice, McCauley had pictured Jimmy Quarters to be older, but the face, beneath the bushy head of brown, unkempt hair, put him somewhere in his mid-forties. The guy gave McCauley a nod and, as Beate handed him a steaming cup, McCauley did the same back.

Beate hooked a thumb towards herself. "Change your mind about breakfast, Del, give the lady a holla."

Coming up alongside the table, McCauley said, "You Jimmy?"

With some effort Quarters took his eyes off the paper and looked at McCauley, then shifted his gaze towards Beate, who was two feet from Lou and still screaming orders.

Quarters said, "Loudest damn door chime I ever heard. Beate couldn't sneak into Texas."

Noticing their attention, Beate put her hands on her hips, comically glared at them both, and said, "Hey, what's that som-bitch sayin' about me, Del?"

And laughter broke out across the room.

McCauley took the chair opposite, nodded at the parka. "Expecting the temperature to drop?"

Quarters grinned and patted the jacket. "Beauty, huh? Got it this morning, and a dozen more like it." He said, "I grab when I can, no matter what time of year." Resting his arm on the coat, McCauley watching the elbow sink into the down. Quarters was just staring now like he was trying to get a read.

McCauley met his gaze, then dropped his eyes to the table.

In front of the other man, an empty coffee cup and a plate scraped clean of home fries and eggs. A thin paper napkin was balled in the middle.

"Been here long?" McCauley asked, lifting his eyes, Quarters still staring.

He said, "Only beat you by a minute. You eatin'?" And laid the *Herald* on top of the plate.

"I didn't come here to eat," McCauley said, "was hoping you had something for me."

Quarters reached under the paper and came out with the cup, swung it into the aisle. He raised it up once, lowered it, and gave little nods and continued to stare as the waitress refilled it.

"Fucking cop, huh?" he said finally. "You ever try the pastry here, *cop*?"

Caught off guard, McCauley's lips involuntarily retreated against his teeth. "I'm not a cop," he replied tightly, hoping the burn in his neck wouldn't flash into his cheeks.

Jimmy Quarters chuckled.

"Oh, that's right, you ain't *now*, are ya? But even an *ex*-cop should like pastry, think of it like *doughnuts,* though it's fresh from the North End." He dabbed at his lips with a napkin. "My advice, so your trip won't be wasted, try some before you head out."

Now there was something new in his eyes, it wasn't quite smugness, more of what a man projects when he thinks he's in control. McCauley leaned closer. Quarters didn't realize it, but he was getting slammed with the same look back.

McCauley said calmly, "That's pretty astute, you've done your homework, but now that detail's out of the way, can we get to the point? Last night you promised to look into something. I'll ask you this once, you find anything out?"

Quarters eyelids fluttered. He tightened his grip on the mug and tried to stare through McCauley — but only got as far as the tip of his nose.

McCauley returned it. His was punching through the other man's head.

Now the hand delivering the cup to Quarter's lips shook.

McCauley said, "I'm not asking for state secrets."

Quarters looked down at the coat, and a smile, like a ghost in a window, flickered briefly across his lips. Instantly McCauley was out of the seat, now close enough to count the pores on the other man's nose. Quarters's smile melted like wax.

Struggling for control, McCauley said, "You act like a tough guy, are you? Because *I'm* a tough guy too."

Quarters looked into his eyes "No one's sayin you ain't," he said hoarsely.

"They ain't? So tell me, Jimmy, what *are* they saying?" Sitting down again.

Quarters clenched his jaw, yanking his head to the side, like someone had cracked an ammonia vial under it. He turned back and faced him. "Ain't sayin'," he said.

"You're not?" McCauley said, the veins in his neck thickening. He looked out the window. "You know, getting tired of running into the same kind of bullshit I did back in the can." He looked back at Quarters. He was searching for something. "You done any time?" Feigning surprise. "No? Well, I have, and here's how it works. When you're new behind the walls you don't talk to strangers. Good guys introduce other good guys to each other. That's how you avoid the rats, the skinners and diddlers, and all the other scumbags you find in the system.

"But, more often than not, for me, after I'd been introduced to someone, inevitably the same guy would approach me, maybe a day or two later, and say, usually kind of nervously, hey, I heard you were a cop. And my standard response? Got a problem with it? And if he didn't, which they *never* did, I'd say now you go and tell that paper gangster piece of shit who told you that, that if *he's* got a problem to come and see me.

"And you know what, Jimmy, after I punched the living shit out a few guys early on in the bid, no one ever did. Now I ask you, do *you* have a problem with it? Because you do, I'm betting I could kick your ass all the way up West Broadway until it cuts east. What'd ya think, Jimmy, want to try me?"

"Ain't no fighter," Quarters whined, "don't want no trouble. Don't need this kinda shit." He started to get up.

McCauley put a foot in the aisle and rose with him, said, "Sit the fuck down."

Like he was hit behind the knees with a sock filled with soap, Quarters dropped back in the seat.

McCauley said, "Up to you, you want out of here. We're all through with the preliminaries: born down on A Street, raised up on B Street, Southie is my hometown, horseshit. I'm here looking for a guy who likes to steal safes, and you're going to tell me who."

Quarters kept his eyes on McCauley as he folded the *Herald* and signaled the waitress.

"Hey, Murla," he said weakly, "breakfast is over." He looked out the window at the St. Peter and Paul church. He visibly shook. "I ain't tellin' you nothin'," he said. His voice suddenly rising: "I ain't a rat."

"That's funny," McCauley said, rising, "because you're sure as hell starting to *sound* like one."

Murla tore off the check and waved it.

"*I'll* take that, dear," McCauley said, keeping his eyes locked on Quarters.

"Pl-easse," Quarters whined.

McCauley handed over some bills with the check.

"No, Jimmy, I *insist*, you paid the last time, this one's on me. Keep the change, Murla."

McCauley came around to Quarter's side of the table and put his hand on the back of the other man's neck. He said gently, "I *understand*, Jimmy, how maybe you don't want to tell me a name." Quarters gave him a look like he'd just paid his bar tab at the Quiet Man Pub.

McCauley pulled a pen from his pocket, dragged a clean napkin in front of Quarters, and dropped the pen on it.

"So, that's why I'm going to allow you to *write* it," he said, tightening his grip just a little bit more, and Jimmy Quarters began to write.

THIRTY-TWO

MCCAULEY DIDN'T FEEL GOOD after he put the napkin with the name and number into his pocket. Not physically sick; it was more the empty feeling a man gets when he knows he's taken advantage of someone weaker. Not that he felt sorry for Quarters, the guy had asked . . . *begged* for it. He had made his own bed, forced McCauley to rip off the covers.

Still, the guy he'd spoken to the night before wasn't the same Jimmy Quarters. The way he'd handled that little girl, the easy way he loved her, he could feel it through the phone, showed he had substance. But the guy sitting across from him the next morning had none of that. All he knew was that he hated cops, and his hatred made everything hard.

After firing up the Mustang in Amrhein's lot, McCauley banged a U-turn and headed east on West Broadway. A couple of blocks down, across from Sonny & Whitey's, he pulled to the curb. Glancing at the old-timers outside of the gin joint, smoking, itching to get back to their beers, he took out the napkin and silently mouthed the name with the crease running through it.

It was an odd name, sure, but McCauley was certain that he

had heard it before. Pleased now that only yesterday he had followed up with Moses Halloran when he found the ex-con standing outside Bell's Market, a sandwich in one hand, enough scratch tickets in the other to play fifty-two pickup.

Prison associates, not friends, they had shared the minimum small talk. What you been up to? Seen any of the guys around? Who'd gotten out, who's heading back in, with McCauley slowly working his way down to the part that always got their attention — so, how are you doing for money?

"I'm doin'," Moses said, taking a bite of the sandwich. Chewing fast, he gave him a squirrelly look and said, "Okay, maybe I could use a few bucks, what ya got?"

Forty bucks got McCauley a name. And it was the same name he just got from Quarters.

Figuring it was as good a reason as any to talk, as he pulled from the curb he called Mackey.

"Hi, Del," she said, sounding busy.

"You busy?"

"Kinda, what's up?"

"Where are you?"

"In Weymouth, heading south on Route 18, trying to keep this cheating husband in sight. Oh-ohh, oh-ohh, hold on, Del, gotta make this light, make it, make it. Yes! *Yes!* So what's up? Oh, oh, don't-pull-over . . . pp-llease don't pull . . . thank you, thank you."

"Had a fast question, but I can call you back later."

There was a moment of silence then. "No, no, you got me, go ahead. Slow down, you, slowww-dowwwn."

"Ever heard of a guy named Enfield Higgins?"

"No I haven't, Del, who is he?"

McCauley explained. When he finished, he added, "And I got his name from two different sources, both of them said he's an addict. Makes sense, stealing's what an addict does best."

"Junkies can be dangerous, Del," Mackey said like she was quoting from Narcotics 101.

"Anyways," McCauley said, "just figured I'd ask, thought you might have heard it before and forgot."

"Forgot?" Mackey said, "A name like that?" Sounded like she

had dropped the phone, her voice now distant. "My guy pulled over, went into a store, and now he's coming back out carrying two coffees. Okay, Vinnie, baby, who's the other one for?"

McCauley heard a camera rapidly firing, then an engine start up.

"I'm back . . . soon as I can pull into traffic . . . there. Sorry, Del. Like I said, doesn't ring a bell, think a name like Enfield would stick in your head. Just be careful, when I think junkie, I also think desperate, know what I mean?"

McCauley did. He'd dealt with some in the past but had never viewed them as dangerous. Remembering it was a different game then, he'd had a gun and a shield.

A badge is a powerful thing. Not because the guy wearing it's a badass, in McCauley's experience, that was rarely the case, but because of the enormous resources and backup behind it. Most cops like to think of themselves as trained professionals, able to handle whatever comes up. But without the badge — and they don't call it a "shield" for nothing — a cop is like anyone else, out there alone, and, right now, McCauley hadn't felt more alone in his life.

Mackey said, "Del, I've got the feeling he knows I'm behind him, I have to hang up."

Timing's right. McCauley blurted, "How about grabbing a bite tonight, maybe we could discuss investigative technique?" Then punched the ceiling. Damn. Sounded like a jerk.

Like she hadn't heard him, Mackey said, "I see you up there, you're taking a left, you drive like an asshole, but you're taking a left. Sure, I'd love to, Del. He did, Del, took the left, all over the road and still takes the left. When?"

"Supper tonight, or would tomorrow be easier?"

"Marigold Drive," she said like she was writing.

"What?"

"The guy's stopping in front of a big colonial, Marigold Drive, I'd say the girlfriend's got dough. Hold on a second, I'm passing him now."

Now Store 24 was coming up on his right, him noticing a guy standing out front, a cup to his lips. He looked in McCauley's direction and waved.

"Mackey," he said, "I'm pulling over, a guy's waving me down. How about I call you later this morning?"

"Sure, but let me call you. I'm now in a strip mall, a few blocks down from the house. Marigold's a one-way. Valentino will have to pass me after his tryst."

McCauley pulled over, double-parked alongside a van with an advertisement on the side offering physical therapists who'd come to your home. He watched the guy with the cup approach stopping outside the front fender. Taking a sip he looked over his shoulder back up the street. He turned back and stared at McCauley.

The same age as McCauley but something other than time had carved deep crevises into his cheeks and forehead. His thinning hair was unstylishly long and covered the collar of his blue windbreaker. He took a jerky sip from his cup and looked back again towards Dorchester Street before he came alongside and used the back of his hand to rap on the passenger-side glass.

Who the hell is he? Trying to place the guy, McCauley hit the door-lock release and the guy got in quick and sunk in the seat. He glanced at McCauley and pulled down the visor. He smelled of cigarettes, stale coffee, and some kind of cleaning agent like ammoniated wax stripper that McCauley had used a lot of in prison.

"Take it you're not looking for a taxi?"

The other man gulped down the last of his coffee, dropped the cup to the floor, turned around quick, and glanced out the rear window.

"You was the ex-statey, right? Can't sit here," he said, "drive." Bending over, he grabbed the cup off the floor. He looked at McCauley. "Sorry," he said and slid the cup in behind him. "Drive, please — but not straight, they're hangin' in front of the Black Rose, they see me with you, I'm fucked. Bang a Uey."

Heading back the way he'd just come, McCauley watched his passenger stretch his neck and looked over the top of the dash. "Don't turn down D Street," he said, "they hang in front of the Teamsters too, this damn no-smoking-in-bars-anymore bullshit."

The Pen Tavern came quick on the left and the Styrofoam coffee cup crinkled and popped as his passenger sunk down even further.

"Seem to know me, who the hell are you?" McCauley said, eyeing two enforcer types hanging out in front of the Pen.

The coffee guy covered his eyes with his hands, shook his head. "Oh, Jesus, please, wait a sec, after . . . after we get out of this fucking area," he said, folding his knees even further under the dash.

McCauley took a right at A Street, then right again on West Third, stopping about a block down in the shadow of the Cliflex Bellows building. He shut off the engine as the cell phone started to ring and kept his eyes on the unfolding form of his passenger as he opened it.

"Del?"

"Ya, Mackey?"

"You at work yet?"

The guy was now pulling pieces of Styrofoam cup from under his ass. Tossing them out the window, he sheepishly showed Mc-Cauley his coffee-stained hands.

"Not yet," McCauley said, "my shift at T.K.'s doesn't start until ten, we're currently taking a tour." Reaching under the seat he passed the guy a napkin. "So when will you see Valentino again?"

"Hasn't come by yet, but concerning us, how about meeting after four at the bar?"

"Perfect."

"You said, '*we're*,' mind me asking who's we?

"I'm trying to figure that out."

"Del?"

McCauley said, "Good luck with your guy. I'll tell you about mine when I meet you tonight."

THIRTY-THREE

McCAULEY RESTED HIS HANDS on the wheel as he stared at the nervous wreck next to him. He said, "So?" and watched the guy ball up the napkin and flip that out the window. McCauley hated litterers.

He said, "You're making a hellava a mess."

The guy rubbed his palms on his windbreaker like he was working in mink oil and said, "Never been into fuckin' trees."

"Mean *hugging* trees?" McCauley said.

The other man scowled.

"Ain't into it *whatever* they're callin' it these days. I've got problems enough of my own. The name's Donovan, McCauley, Jim Donovan, though the guys down the Pen call me Stinky — but that's only because of my job. Twenty years working for a cleaning outfit — ain't complainin' — least the stink's honest."

And he held out his hand.

After they shook, McCauley said, "So tell me, you're afraid Wacko's boys might see you with me, why?"

Donovan looked over his shoulder out the rear window, came back around, started to say something, stopped. He took in a deep breath and stared at his lap.

McCauley said, "You act like the boogeyman's chasing you."

Turning his head, staring, Donovan gave him a wry smile. "What, like he don't *exist*? Let me tell you, McCauley, the boogeyman's real, and he owns the fucking Pen Tavern. I seen you in there a few days ago sparrin' with *Michael* Janowski," he said with a hint of a brogue. Then shuddered like a splinter of arctic wind had lodged in his spine.

"Ain't tellin' you your business, but that was a mistake."

"Maybe for him too."

Donovan nodded hard like he was head-butting a wall, chuckled. "Wouldn't know nothin' about that, McCauley, what I do know is Mike's a mean motherfucker — a *mean motherfucker*, and-he-don't-like-you."

With the back of his fingers, McCauley brushed the key ring that hung from the ignition. Donovan watched it swing, and click against the column.

McCauley reached under and wrapped his fist around it. "You didn't flag me down to sit here and bullshit, and if they sent you to scare me, you don't, but I have some advice. End of the month's Halloween, you should head out to Spooky World and get a job, work on the basics and go from there." He turned the engine over.

"Now, you walking, or you want me to drop you somewhere?"

Donovan's eyes bugged.

"Not so fast, McCauley, you'll want to hear what I gotta say."

Stretched a hand towards the key ring, but stopped before touching it. "Mind?" he said, staring into his eyes.

"This better be good," McCauley said, and Donovan turned the key towards him.

Grabbing the cell off the console, McCauley held up a finger and said, "Before you say anything."

As he dialed, he studied his passenger's face. The nose was thin, had been broken before, and there was a bushel of small scars around the lips and the cheeks.

On the other end, Stuffa picked up.

"Stuffa, Del, going to be late fifteen minutes." Closed his eyes. "What do you mean puke's all over the place?" He opened them, nodded. "Just the bathroom, you said all over the place. The door to the stall got torn off?" McCauley closed his eyes again. "I'll take care of it when I get there, ya, and be careful with the glass, use a shovel. See you in fifteen." He closed the phone.

Donovan's face was a question.

"Bachelor party last night in the bar where I work," McCauley said. "Rugby team came in for last call, their adrenaline pumping, after hitting a strip joint on Washington Street. The new place, Scores?" Frowned. "Couldn't have nothing on the old Combat Zone. Cut my teeth as a bouncer there, the old Downtown Lounge, remember?"

Donovan grinned, nodded, scratched at the back of his hand.

"Knew it well," he said, wiggling in the seat. "Never quite figured it out, but sure as hell there's something about strippers that makes a man want to fight." He dreamily stared through the windshield. "Not me though, just *loved* bein' around 'em."

The spell broke and he shook out his hand, made a fist. Opened it and stared at the palm. "Got something to trade, McCauley," he said, looking at him. "Could work it so one hand washes the other. You was an ex-statey, right? Heard you was a hotshot until you went down, did some wall time." The eyes were unblinking as he focused on McCauley.

He leaned a little bit closer. "Also heard that the beef was bogus, beyond that don't know a hellava lot more 'cept you still got connections. That true?"

"Maybe, I've still got friends on the job," McCauley said. "What's it to you?"

Donovan's grin chameleoned into a grimace. "Ain't for me, my son," Donovan said, and stared at the radio. "He's a good kid, McCauley, a little wild is all."

"So, what's your wild child done that might involve me?"

Donovan shook his head sadly, rubbed his eyes with his palms, tilted his head back, and laughed. "The fucking draft — the Bruin's, McCauley, and my kid with a head full of crazy ideas."

He slapped his knee and stared, bobbing his head. "Ya know what this little *shithead* did? The day of the draft he puts on his suit, an expensive three-piece job, and pulls a brand new Bruins cap onto his oversized head. Drives his ass out to Stardust Jeweler's on Route 9 in Framingham, you know, across from that big fucking mall? Then, with his brass balls swingin' between his legs, he walks in lays a line of bull on the salesgirl.

" 'How're ya doin'?' my genius says and flashes his hundred-watt smile. 'My name's so and so and I'm from Winnipeg, and I got drafted by the Bruins today,' and he waits for the expected reaction.

"Naturally the girl behind the counter's impressed and she does that little push thing that girls do to their hair and tilts her hips just so. Now you gotta realize this kid's six one, eighteen years old, got movie-star looks. Don't look at me, McCauley, he got 'em from his Ma.

"He tells the salesgirl how he'd like to buy his parents a token. You know for all the sacrifices they made getting him where he is today: Scrimpin' money to buy him equipment, drivin' him to hockey practice at three in the mornin'." Donovan shook his fist, "and that part's *real*, the little son-of-a-bitch."

McCauley said, "So, what'd he do, rob them?"

Donovan made a noise like he had a hair in his throat, he coughed and wiped an eye.

"Ya, in a way, ya. Lets this little broad convince him what he needs for this 'token' was matching Rolexes, his and hers. She lays out six different sets: stainless steel, gold and stainless, gold, gold and diamonds, and, of course, the little prick can't make up his mind, 'cept, of course, in reality, he already had — he wanted 'em *all*."

"Then he tells her he'd like to see some kinda watch that I never heard of, and her eyes light up, seein' the sale of the century. She gushes, I'll be right back, but by the time she does, this 'Bruin's skated out the door with her watches. Another clerk chases him, but *Cam Neely* had a *partner* waitin' in a burner outside. They got away clean — so they thought."

"How'd they catch him?"

Donovan shook his head again. "Got the moron on *camera*. The damn thing close enough to whack with a hockey stick, he had one. Should have sent it to America's funniest videos to get back some of the bail money I put up for the bum."

McCauley said, "Then somebody recognized him, who?"

"Oh, he was recognized, all right. Seems afta the score they showed the video up the Framingham barracks, which you could hit with a rock from the scene. Seems one of the troopers happened also to be an assistant hockey coach at St. John's Prep. My kid was a hockey all-star at B.C. High, last year cocaptained the team *before* he got the hockey scholarship, a full goddamned ride to B.U. Right off the bat this cop/coach recognizes my kid, calls me at home. I confront the kid and after a little bit of a go-around, which includes me battin' him upside the head in front of his poor mother, the kid fesses up. Bright and early the next day, we drive out to Framingham District Court, and he gives himself up.

The thing is, McCauley, they got back their watches, the kid got no record, give it a rest, huh? He takes a felony pinch on this bullshit beef and it's curtains for the scholarship. I'm a workin' stiff, nine–ten hours every night, polishin' floors, doin' windows in office buildings. Most of it goes to the family, the little I got left, I enjoy losin' down the Pen, cards. That's how I seen you."

"So, how can I help you?"

"You were a statey, put in a word for the kid, he's a good kid, McCauley, crazy but good. Scared shitless, knows he ain't goin' to jail, ain't got a record, but the scholarship, loses that, he'll end up down Gillette, on the assembly line, he's lucky."

McCauley had been stationed for years at A Troop headquarters, Framingham, had been a fixture in the Framingham court, knew most of the prosecutors. He also knew that larceny of over one hundred was a felony, there was no way the kid was going to walk away unscathed.

He said, "The best you could hope for, considering his record, would be to have the case continued without a finding for a few years, probation, to be dismissed if there's no further trouble. I could talk to some people, might get some results, but why should I help you?"

Donovan gave him a long dull stare.

"Because I can help you?"

The uneasiness that had been festering in McCauley's stomach instantly sprouted an arm. He started to wish he'd never seen Donovan, that when he'd got near him he was checking the floor for loose change, or looking across the street at some leggy girl.

He said quickly, "Spit it out, it's worthwhile maybe I'll help, if it isn't, I want you out of my car."

Donovan licked his lips and pinched his nostrils together like he was equalizing his ears to the pressure.

"Okay," he said finally. "But remember, can't tell this to no one, they find out we talked, they'll find *me* in a Dumpster."

Donovan took in a deep breath, rested his forearms on his knees, and talked to a face on the floormat.

"After you left the Pen that day, I heard, plain as the smell of stripper on these clothes, Janowski say he was gonna kill ya — and the sooner the better."

Inhaling quietly, McCauley held it before releasing. Now it was his turn to look out the rear window.

"And then Wacko, er, Jack, said somethin' about — and it ain't like I care about the business between youse two because I don't — findin' out about what was inside the safe, he kept mentionin' *the safe*, and how if this lawyer had you lookin' for it, hadda be somethin' important. Got the feeling he intended to do his own snoopin'."

Staring at each other, Donovan looked like he had just finished with a barf bag, the dark rings around his eyes even darker now, like his eyebrows were bleeding down into them.

Nodding vaguely, McCauley said, "I'll make the calls."

And like a pebble dropped into a pool of dark water, the sliver of light that began in Donovan's eyes ringed out across his face.

McCauley pulled a pad and pen from the glove box and dropped it in his lap.

"Give me the kid's name, first, last, and middle initial, date of the offense, name of the prosecutor, the judge, if you know him. Not making promises, but if I can connect with the right people, your son might get to skate a little longer."

Donovan finished, tore off the sheet and handed it back.

His eyes sparkled as he held out his hand. "Jimmy Donovan thanks you, McCauley." Held it firm a few extra seconds and stared into McCauley's eyes. Nodding once, he opened the door.

"I'll give you a lift," McCauley said.

One foot on the street, Donovan twisted and said, "You've done enough, thanks, besides, I think I'll enjoy me some air." Closing the door, he gave a little salute before heading south on A Street, swinging his arms like the Munchkins did when they learned the witch was dead.

McCauley pulled out from the shadow of the Cliflex Bellows building and as he passed, on either side, blocks of newly renovated row houses, he thought about Janowski and his threat. It was serious. Even as a cop, it would be, but as a civilian, an ex-con/civilian, the threat was deeper. He wanted to be ready, but how could he be with no gun, nothing but his hands and a few knife-fighting skills?

Near F Street the long, gray granite Saint Vincent De Paul parish house came up on his left and he tried to remember the last time he had attended Mass. Figured it had to be close to eleven years, about the same time Carolyn, his fiancée, broke off their marriage by getting herself killed in a Storrow Drive car crash.

Nothing was ever the same after that. It was, for the next two years, like he had sailed off the edge of a trampoline and continued to fall. He had to push Carolyn from his mind to survive.

But when he passed Saint Vincent De Paul that day, for some reason, Carolyn popped back into his head and he thought about Mike Janowski, and his plans for him to meet her again.

THIRTY-FOUR

J UST BEYOND BOSTON'S FINANCIAL DISTRICT, across the street from city hall, on the corner of Congress and North, is a long, spare park. On one end, contained within the same strip of land that juts like a finger between Congress and Union, is the New England Holocaust Memorial, with its impressive glass-tower construction; on the other, the Curley Memorial Plaza. The statues representing James Michael Curley, the larger-than-life former mayor of Boston, are, as they should be, closer to city hall.

One life-sized figure, stomach jutting like he's set to burst from a gate, stands in the middle of the small red-brick plaza, eyes up-raised like he's searching for something.

The other occupies a bench, one of four ringing the plaza. This Curley is more contemplative, casually sitting, right leg over left, left elbow resting on the back of the sturdy bronze bench, as if he were telling a good story, or waiting to hear one.

Farmsworth Cotter sat at the end of the bench. He was wait-ing for someone and looked it. A dry seventy-six degrees, suit coat was draped across Curley's knee, he straightened the knot in his tie.

Growing irritated as the minutes passed by, he glanced over his left shoulder and smirked at the super-sized customers drift-ing out of McDonald's on the corner of Union and North. To the right, behind him, he scanned the facades of the Purple Sham-rock, the Blackstone Grill, the Tap, and Hennessey's, in a row in that order, then looked at his watch.

He had been waiting long enough to have had a Chivas, rocks, in every single one, instead of sitting here listening to the Chinese girl sitting across from him shriek and giggle into her phone.

A middle-aged man with bushy red hair sat on the bench di-rectly opposite, facing the standing Curley. Dressed in tan cargo shorts and raggedy sandals, he lazily answered his cell phone with its *Addams Family* tone-riff. He chuckled through his handlebar mustache and nodded at Cotter, or someone ten miles behind him. Cotter, thinking that he looked odd with the phone, like instead he should have been holding a cup filled with change.

On the front of his dingy gray T-shirt, in faded black letters, was the message, "Where in the World Have You Been?" Funny, because Cotter was thinking the same about Durning when he spotted him, finally, up the street, in his tan three-piece suit, crisp as a Cape Cod shingle, descending the back steps of City Hall Plaza.

Twenty feet away now, Durning began speaking and kept his sunglasses on as he did.

"Sorry I kept you waiting," he said. "This heat, seventy-six, in October? Feels like *eighty-six*, you ask me."

Cotter looked at his watch, or his wrist, he knew exactly the time.

"You're twenty minutes late," he said. "I got here an hour early. A good habit to be early, just in case."

"In case I was too?" Durning took off the glasses, folded them over, and put them inside his jacket.

"Or on time . . . please, have a seat," Cotter said, sliding towards Curley so the arm was now over his shoulder.

Durning squinted at the bench, wiping something off it before he sat down. He crossed his legs and grinned like something funny had struck him.

"This heat reminds me of Darius Crux," he said, staring at the back of the standing James Michael Curley.

Turning towards Cotter, he said, "Darius was an Edgewater patient of mine. He was committed some years ago for torching his rooming house in the Grove Hall section of Roxbury." Made such a pity face. "It seems that," Durning flexed the first two fingers of each hand near his head, "*demons* lived on the floor above him." He chuckled softly as his hands spiraled downward. "Sent them all straight to hell."

He carefully wiped the side of his nose with a finger, absently rubbing his thumb in circles against it.

He pulled at the cloth of the knee that was on top. "He approached me one day, it was mid-July, in the hospital yard. I'd just left F Ward — in the facility's maximum end — and was heading towards B block in the minimum. Darius stopped me in front of the chow hall.

"My guard escort steps in to brush him away, but I stop him. I said, 'Let the man talk.'

"Darius says, not complaining, but matter-of-factly, 'Doctor Durning, it's hot.'

"I said, 'Yes, Darius, it is, it's the middle of summer.' He thought about that for a moment, then gave me a look like he'd figured it out.

" 'What they say, Doc? Ain't the heat, it's the humility,' he says."

Durning dropped his leg to the ground, grabbed both his knees, and gave Cotter a "can you believe it?" look. "When he said, 'The *humility*? I didn't correct him.' "

Like he couldn't care less, Cotter said, "And what happened to dear Darius?"

"He's dead," Durning said, like it was an effort to say it. Picked something off the front of his vest, snapped his fingers to dislodge it.

"Stuffed a sock down his throat." Durning made a sad face and shrugged. "You know, we can only give them so much protection. Like our 'specials,' we can only give them so much."

"So, who's next in line, me?" Cotter said bitterly.

Pressing closer to Curley, wishing deeply he had taken that drink.

"Why, have you done something *wrong*?" Durning said calmly, staring into his eyes. "I mean, aside from that fact you kept *records* on us."

Cotter met his gaze coolly. *I don't have to explain it to you.*

"The others," he said, "six 'specials' remain, they're all out on the street, what do you propose to do about them? Have your *creature* destroy them?"

Durning clapped once and rocked back in the seat. "Creature?" he said, chuckling, shaking a finger. "Ohh, I don't think Jarvis would like to hear that. No, noo, he's not your standard deviant.

"He's a professional," he said sternly, "and if it wasn't for him, we'd be sitting in a jail, staring into a stainless-steel mirror."

"And if he's caught?"

The squintlines around Durning's eyes relaxed. "Caught? It's highly improbable I never told you about Jarvis, did I?"

"It's not something I wanted to know," Cotter said.

A man with a camera approached and said something to Cotter in German. Pointing at a pretty young woman and a boy about ten standing by the statue of Curley, he smiled as he moved his finger between them and the camera.

"Oh, you want me to take your picture? Glad to," Cotter said, glaring at Durning.

"You waited for me, I'll wait for you," Durning said, raising his chin, throwing his arms over the back of the bench.

When Cotter sat down, Durning said, "Operation Phoenix, during the Vietnam War, you recall it?"

Cotter thought for a moment. "I think so. Wasn't it an unsanctioned outlaw affair? Elements of the CIA, working with special ops units: Green Berets, Navy SEALS. Vietnamese informers supplying them with names. They descended on villages, usually at night to add to the terror, executing anyone they considered sympathetic to the communists. What about it?"

Durning leaned towards him, nodding gravely. "The same thing was done in the first Iraq war."

"Reems, as a member of SEAL Team Six, was assigned to the Sunni Triangle. Along with CIA operatives, they utilized information, supplied by agents of the Mossad, to locate and eliminate elements loyal to Saddam Hussein," Durning smirked, "with extreme prejudice, as they say, sometimes entire villages. Jarvis was, how should I say it, extremely . . . *proficient*." He gave Cotter a wink, and a he's-*our*-boy-now look.

"With the war winding down, the number of suspected sympathizers diminished to nothing. Suddenly it was the Mossad agents they were finding without heads."

Durning crossed his legs again, picked at the crease. "Nothing was ever proven, of course. Maybe too efficient, Jarvis was shipped back to the States, and relocated to a loft in Manhattan's Lower East Side. Seems they were trying to give him a chance to *unwind*."

Durning closed his eyes, inhaled deeply like he was trying to catch just a hint of the scent of the image before him.

"Again, nothing was ever proven, but, in the first four months the murder rate, in a twenty-block radius of where he'd been housed, quadrupled."

"And Reems was never charged with a criminal offense?"

"No, never," Durning said, removing his suit coat, folding it in the middle, draping it over his knee. He dabbed at his brow with a handkerchief he kept folding.

"One day I looked up from my desk and he was just *there,* whisked out of New York and committed to Edgewater by federal officials. I had nothing to say, I was briefed on his background, and ordered to treat him."

Durning stood up, stretched his arms overhead, looked down at his stomach, and gave it a pat. "Been meaning to order one of those TV sit-up machines. Think they're as easy to use as they make it?"

"So he was treated, what then?" Cotter said.

"Periodically *they'd* call, check on his status." He sighed, "Will he ever be fit to return to society?" Durning grinned; like a shark he had too many teeth. "Certainly hope so, I'd tell them, the man's showing signs of marked improvement. What with the counseling — individual — I took great personal interest in him, and of course, especially in the later stages, the use of certain psychotropic medications.

"Actually, Jarvis has come a long way. As a matter of fact, as we speak, he's right in the middle of the *reintegration* process." Winking at Cotter. "But I gather you figured that out."

He smiled and tapped Cotter's knee, saying cheerfully, "Coming soon to a neighborhood near you."

A horrified look spread across Cotter's face.

"You mean he's back out here . . . *now?*"

"Been out for two weeks. It's the longest he's been."

"But where do you house him?" Cotter said, and nervously glanced over his shoulder, like he might see Reems leaving McDonald's.

Durning shuddered. "Housing could have been a logistical nightmare," his eyebrows jerked up, "*if* I didn't own a few rental units, and some other property, in Quincy. I own a small boatyard that's been closed for years. In back of it there's a small apartment. He remains there until called.

"When I need him," Durning pulled out a cell phone and tapped on the keys, "I send a text message, everything pertinent he needs: name, description, address. I rate the urgency too — using stars — he likes that, must be the patriot thing."

Cotter mocked him. "And how did you rate Caleb White-head?"

"Our Beacon Hill boy?" Durning said, easing a finger through his thinning gray hair, scratching the top of the skull. "He was a five out of five. When he got out of Edgewater, he should have been happy just to spend Daddy's money, instead, he found *God*." He folded the finger and looked at the nail, "Too bad . . . it led him to something much *darker*."

"And God got him killed?"

Durning gave him a look like, You really don't know?

"The Swedenborgians, Cotter, their Beacon Hill church. Whitehead *joined* them."

Palms pressed together under his chin, he lifted it, caught glimpses of blue through the gold-and-red canopy above him.

"Good Christians all, they couldn't have cared less that he murdered his girlfriend. In front of the entire congregation he gave his confession, and such avid listeners all of them were, as he went on about the murder — oh, how he loved her — the rapacious lawyer, the unholy doctor, and the deal they cut, with his extremely wealthy father, who paid them handsomely to put him back on the streets.

"Lucky for us, most paid little attention to him, more interested in healing his soul than his mind, but one person did," Durning pinched the end of his chin, "thankfully he was a colleague of mine. A psychologist friend, and an active practitioner of the religion. After listening to Whitehead, he got on the phone right away."

"I can't imagine how you reacted, you must have been shocked."

"I was but, of course, didn't show it, agreeing it was the nature of the business, we both had a good laugh." He narrowed his eyes. "I had the last one, I made certain."

"But he *wasn't* the last one."

Durning's eyebrows drifted up. "Ciampa?"

He shook his head slowly, threw a leg, like Curley, over his knee.

"Even if no one had ever stolen your disc, we still would have had problems with Ciampa.

"The boy was *born* with problems, refused to address them and, unfortunately, seemed to *water* them daily. Oh, yes," Durning said, nodding, "Ciampa was a problem." He leaned closer and whispered, "He's not anymore."

Cotter looked at him wild-eyed. "Good, God, man, this . . . this," now he didn't care who was watching, and covered his mouth with his hand, "what in the name of God have we done?"

"Enlighten me, counselor," Durning said coldly, "the blessed or the desperate, which invokes the name of God more?"

Cotter almost flew out of the seat. "But the way he was killed, it was ghastly, ritualistic."

"Your voice," Durning hissed. Like he was counting drops of sweat on the other man's face, his eyeballs clicked back and forth in his head. "Cotter, sometimes you talk like you're wearing a wire. Tell me you're not."

Cotter leaped to his feet.

"I don't have to listen to this."

He snapped up his coat and began walking away.

"Oh, Cotter, please, I was *joking*," Durning said, putting both feet on the ground. He rose from the bench, shouting, "Besides, we're not *finished*."

Almost to the street, Cotter stopped. His shoulders sagged. "I think you're mistaken," he said.

Coming up behind him, Durning put his hand on his shoulder and gently guided him towards the corner of Union and Congress. He said, "No, Cotter, *you* were mistaken when you created that disc." They stopped on the corner. "When your man Mc-Cauley comes up with a name, I'll need it, understand?"

Cotter's look said he did.

"Good."

Durning looked at his watch, pulled on his jacket, and pressed the button on the pedestrian light. "Well, have to be back to the office by four, meetings. You?"

Cotter tugged at the knot in his tie, popped the top button. With his head he motioned behind him. "I'm going back to the Tap, for a Chivas, rocks."

Traffic stopped on the yellow and red, and Durning stepped

from the curb. Without turning, he said, "Good, sounds perfect, have two — one for me."

Later, the blinds pulled tight, Durning, illuminated by the light of a single lamp, sat at his desk, made checks with a pen inside small boxes, to the left of a column of paragraphs.

The telephone rang. He looked at his watch, it was seven o'clock, the meeting had lasted longer than planned.

"Doctor Durning," he said.

It was Cotter.

"Are you bus-zhee?" he said, the voice thick with alcohol.

"Catching up on patient evaluations, is there a problem?" Durning said, sitting up, dropping the pen. He checked the time on his wrist again.

"No, problem, Doc-tor we've got a name." Soft laughter.

Durning picked up the pen, tapped the end on a small yellow sticky pad.

There was the sound of liquid being poured into a glass.

"You're not still in the bar?"

"Was when he called me. What, information received in a tavern's not valid?"

"I'm not saying that," Durning said, irritated. "Where are you, home?"

"Yes, not my choice," more soft laughter. "After six, the Tap got too crowded. Investment types from the Financial District, along with their floozies, could barely hear McCauley over the din."

Durning pressed the tip into the pad.

"What did he say?"

"He's a local, not surprising, named Enfield Higgins, a god-damned junkie."

"How do we find Mr. Higgins?" Durning said, scribbling.

A swallow and cough. "McCauley's trying, along with my po-lice officer friend, to get something on him: an address, phone number, where he buys gas, something to pinpoint him. For *Egor*, of course. Been a few days since the last one, huh? Must be hungry as hell, dying to give someone else a good *talking* to."

More laughter. Durning heard the clink of a bottle on glass.

He said, "Cotter, you've had enough whiskey."

"Know what?" Cotter said. "I had *your* drink, then couldn't remember if I had mine first. Didn't think about it for long, though, they teach you in law school to go with your gut, so I had *mine*, then another for you. Might have had another before I left."

"And you're *still* drinking."

"Am I? Can't recall. Don't you think memory's overrated?"

Durning underlined Higgins's name until he cut through the paper.

"Go to bed, Cotter, sleep it off, we'll talk more tomorrow."

He thought he heard sobs.

"Tomorrow? Yes," Cotter said, barely coming through now, "I *remember* tomorrow, it's supposed to be better, isn't that what they say?"

"Go to bed, Cotter," Durning said coolly, "go to *bed*."

THIRTY-FIVE

LILLY WASN'T IN WHEN McCAULEY called him from T.K.'s. Left a voice message, asked him to BOP Higgins, pull up his record, find what kind of rap sheet he had. Was he a junkie? Any drug arrests? Dealing, using, what? Had he ever taken a B&E pinch, if so, how recent? And, most importantly, have an address for him?

Business at T.K's was slow at lunch, then picked up until two, dying shortly after. Around three, two construction types: work-boots, worn jeans, sweatshirts, and a girl dressed the same way, looking freshly washed from whatever coating had covered them that day, came in and ordered some beers, a few bags of chips, took a booth along the wall.

Right behind them came in a middle-management type, took a seat at the end of the bar. Sat there pounding VOs and water, quenching the fire in his belly — or the one in his head — white sleeves rolled up to the forearms, half watching the flat screen in the corner. A tennis match from Australia. McCauley never got tennis.

Downing the last of his beer, Ennis McGarrity at the bar, center, watching McCauley, behind the bar, tearing open cases of Heineken. The way McCauley kept glancing at the door, been doing it for most of the day. Ennis burped and lowered the glass, lining it up perfectly with the wet ring on the bar.

"Them cold?" Ennis said.

"Cold ya," McCauley said, loading the green bottles sideways into the cooler on top of each other. "Why?"

Ennis wrinkled his nose. "No need to chill 'em, you could put 'em in warm, no one *I* know drinks German," he said, frowning. He lifted the glass. "When you're finished consortin' with the enemy, McCauley, could ya pull me another good *American* beer?"

McCauley clinked the last two into place, closed the cooler. "Its Belgian, not German," he said, tossing the empty case under the bar. He tilted a fresh glass under the Budweiser tap, pulled foam, dumped it, pulled amber he filled to the top. Laid a napkin on the ring, the glass on it, straightened up, wiped his hands with a bar towel.

Like he was trying to dislodge something from its tip, McGarrity motioned him away with a finger.

"You'll get your money," he said, taking a slug, pinching the excess off his lips with two fingers, "when the *festivities* end."

McCauley snapped the bar towel over his shoulder, blew Ennis a kiss. "Good-bye, bar tab," he said, shaking his head. The telephone on the wall rang. "T.K's," McCauley said into it, scowling at McGarrity.

It was Lilly. McCauley glanced at his watch. "Called you six hours ago, you shacking up with the commissioner, can't call me back?"

Lilly telling him how, the night before, some kids had kicked a homeless man to death behind the cemetery of Saint Augustine's chapel. Following the initial investigation, he had to return to the scene, to address the concerns of a neighborhood group. Public relations, he told McCauley, you know how it goes.

Holding his palm in front of his face, McGarrity focused on it as best as he could, pretending to write, and mumbled, "The check, if you please."

Phone to his ear, McCauley turned from him and walked into the kitchen. Thinking, when he offered to help Lilly, he didn't foresee that, like a clam digger on the flats of Wollaston Beach, he'd be up to his knees in muck before he got to the meat. And the muck's name, Janowski, was clinging and deadly, and he wanted to give Lilly a heads-up.

Lilly said, "We can roust him, you like, make his life miserable."

McCauley picked a carving knife off a cutting board, slapped the flat of the blade on his thigh. "It already is," he said, "and they'd lay it on me if that happened. Remember, I have to live in this town."

"The operative word being *live*," Lilly said. "This lowlife isn't hurting a cop."

McCauley chuckled. "Don't think he intends to *hurt* me, Lil. Besides, not a cop anymore, just an ex-con trying to survive. When you get the information on Higgins, get it back to me quick?"

"You got it. Should have something today before I leave. Got a fax there?"

McCauley pushed back through the swinging door into the bar. Raising his voice, he said, "We would have a fax machine if the fucking *bar* tabs were paid." Glared at McGarrity.

McGarrity perked up in his seat and grimaced.

"Just call me, Lil, I'm good with a pencil," McCauley said as he hung up, noticing a man in a ball cap pass slowly by the front window, and stop past its edge. As he watched him, McCauley fingered the clip of the knife on his pocket's exterior.

Waving his money, McGarrity said, "I thought I was leaving." Wetting a finger and thumb, carefully laid the bills on the bar in a row. "And was payin' my tab, but this waitin' for you got me *longin'* for another . . . Budweiser," he said, smacking his lips, "frosted glass, if you please."

Outside, at the edge of the window McCauley caught the flash of elbow as the man turned his ball cap backwards. A head peeked in, pulled back just as fast.

McGarrity offered a feeble, "Hey," as McCauley slid under the end of the bar and followed the wall out of sight of the window. Thinking he was bringing a knife to what could be a gunfight.

Now at the front door, looking east up the street, anxious to see if the guy had a friend. With the exception of an old man walking his dog, the sidewalk was empty. Across the street was empty too, except for a heavyset black woman waiting for the bus, frowning fatigue in a hospital outfit.

Pressing his cheek to the glass, looking west, McCauley could see a dark half-silhouette crowding the wall. Had to get to him before he could pull out the gun — if he had one. McCauley snapped his wrist to the side, gravity yanking the blade from its cradle. Now the sidewalk was empty.

Reversing the blade against the inside of his wrist, he checked his target again, took in a deep breath and slowly exhaled. Make it good, boyo, make it good.

He burst from the door.

Outside the door to T.K. O'Malley's, Mackey Wainwright stood wide-eyed, staring at the two men twenty feet away. She said, "Have an accident, McCauley, or are you two just playing?" McCauley picking up the guy, workboots, dungarees, faded black sweatshirt, off the sidewalk.

"Sorry, Ace," McCauley said, slipping the knife into his back pocket. As he dusted the guy off, looking like he was patting him down.

McCauley said, "I was looking across the street when I ran out the door for a customer who wanted hot sauce." Nodded at the Mexican restaurant. "You okay?"

"Jesus, mister," the other guy said, on his feet now he swayed into the wall. "Knocked me for a fucking loop. I was supposed to meet my girl here and thought she was inside, ain't. I was enjoin' a smoke out here waitin', and the lights went out." He gingerly pushed McCauley away. "Hey, enough with the dustin', Jesus-H-Christ, these are my work clothes."

Sitting on the back patio of the Eastern Pier restaurant, facing the harbor, they watched the petite Chinese waitress place brown paper bags, stapled shut at the top, into a white five-gallon pail. By means of a thin yellow cord she lowered it over the railing to three men bobbing in a thirty-foot Sea Ray in the rolling green harbor below. Reeling back the bucket, she counted the money inside as they roared away through ridges of olive-tinged foam.

Mackey's eyes widened, and her face lit up. "Chinese take-out, ocean style? Incredible," she said, and sunk into the seat, the lapels of her robin's-egg-blue blazer folding under her chin. Glancing down, she pulled at the coat flat, then smiled at McCauley.

"Such a beautiful day," she said, looking up at the sky. "Though the way I spent it was sordid, chasing that *lothario*," frowning, "and he's got such a beautiful wife," she folded an eyebrow into a point, "soon to be *ex*-wife."

McCauley told her about Jimmy Donovan, his son, and the smile returned briefly, then faded when she heard about Janowski. She asked him what his plan was.

He told her about Lilly, how he was not only checking on Higgins, he'd keep an eye on Janowski — if anything happened to him — at least Lilly would know where to look first.

Mackey's eyes said it wasn't enough.

They shared crab Rangoon, and he had a Sam Adams draft, Mackey a glass of pinot noir. He listened to her, watched her mouth, the perfect symmetry of her lips, forming the words that she used to describe her father. Retired now for years, he'd been in the computer business, worked for a large defense contractor. He specialized in something called Infosec, a kind of computer security, and how beyond that, she didn't know much what he did.

Growing up, he'd be away for months, with assignments all over the world. Her only contact were brief phone conversations, usually Thursdays at seven. An only child, and it seemed that nothing else mattered except hearing his voice. His traveling eventually took its toll on her mother, who wanted for nothing that money could buy, but was devoid everything else. How she left them both when she was sixteen.

A few months after she left, Mackey said, she learned that her father, since his graduation from Harvard, had been employed by the CIA. She shrugged and stared silently across the harbor towards East Boston for a moment, sipped, put the glass down, then absently dabbed at a spot of lipstick on its rim with a napkin.

Lowering her chin, her eyes taking him in at an angle, she said, "So, a Southie boy, huh?" Studied him intently, almost imperceptibly shifting her head, as if she were looking for something. Finally, she said, "Tell me, exactly what does that mean? Is this neighborhood the same one you grew up in?"

McCauley told her.

About a mostly blue-collar neighborhood, where everyone knew just about everyone else, and watched out for each other. How his father, a Boston cop, never rose above the rank of patrolman. A conscious decision to keep his life simple so he could spend time with is wife and two boys.

About the great Southie athletes, the ice hockey players, the fighters, how his father had played for the Chippewas, Southie's now defunct semipro football team. The yacht clubs and how, as a kid on special summer nights, he'd sit on a bench and watch his parents dance on the outside deck in the moonlight.

He explained about "times," the fund-raisers, Southie people helping each other. Whether it was for down-and-out families, or defense-lawyer money for friends who'd been caught. How the "times" were held almost weekly, it seemed, at the social club on Eighth Street, the Lithuanian Club or the Vets Post on West Broadway.

The neighborhood was rapidly changing, he said, as the waitress put down a steaming platter of chicken with black bean sauce, white rice on the side. Ever since he was a kid, in the early seventies, during the era of forced busing, Southie had suffered from "white flight." Mackey told him she had read about it, watched a show on it on the History Channel, the public school system in chaos, longtime residents leaving in droves, property values plummeting. How it took twenty years for it to slowly come back.

McCauley separated the onions from the chicken and black bean sauce. "Too many onions," he said, winced, and patted his stomach. "They're good, but . . ."

"Heartburn, don't tell me," Mackey said. Then she said, "Why don't you tell them no, when you order?" Using chopsticks to shovel snow peas with oyster sauce into her mouth.

"I forget to, and there's no one around to remind me," he said, grinning, glancing up at her as he munched some chicken, then rice.

"Anyways, for the past decade, Southie has been selling out to developers, just grabbing the money and running." He looked at the harbor. "Maybe I can't blame them, but nowadays, everything's condos. Great for property values, the city tax base, but for the neighborhood, no. Southie's no longer tight-knit, and, though it's still safer than most urban neighborhoods, there's more crime."

Mackey dabbed her mouth with a napkin. Bent her arm, looked at her wrist, worried. "It get me?" she asked.

He looked at her cuff, shook his head. "You're good . . . lucky, oyster sauce's tough to get out."

She pulled back her sleeve and used a fork to stir the vermicelli. "You mentioned crime. I remember a few years back reading in the papers about the Irish mob in South Boston. It all coming out when this big gangster was killed. That's crime, *major* crime."

Dipping a chicken chunk into black bean sauce, then into his mouth, McCauley chewed thoughtfully for a moment before answering.

"The Irish mob, under Marty Fallon — the guy who was killed — had Southie in a death grip for years. But that was *organized* crime, gangsters dealing with others of their ilk."

"You're not saying that's okay?" Mackey said.

"Of course not. I was a cop, remember? I was assigned to track those guys down, did my best to get them." He held his thumb and finger a half-inch apart. "Came this close to getting Wacko, his brother, Kevin, *and* Mike Janowski, but our case went south when our informant got killed."

"You think it was Curran?"

McCauley's look said maybe, he shoveled some chicken.

"The thing is, ya, there were gangsters in those days, same as today on a lesser scale. But those guys never bothered the average citizen. On the contrary, if Mrs. Kinneally, on M Street's up all night because of rowdy kids on the corner, she'd make a phone call. She might not know anyone direct but, in those days, everyone knew someone who knew 'the boyos,' the hard men you call gangsters. Next thing you know, a car pulls up and a few of the *real* tough guys get out and *talk* to the lads, end of the problem. Believe me.

"After Fallon's murdered, there was a scramble for power, guys were being dumped in the doorways, left where they fell."

Mackey stopped eating. "I was a sophomore at Northeastern, I remember the war, that's what the papers called it, a war.

"The mob violence brought heat, and the feds came in put a lid on the pot, things quieted down on that end of the spectrum." He tapped his fork on the plate. "But they sure as hell picked up on the other.

"Now you were dealing with things over here that would have been incomprehensible before," McCauley said, his face growing darker. "Old ladies being mugged, hit on the head with half bricks up the Heights." The lines in his brow more pronounced. "Sexual assaults down Marine Park. Heroin junkies climbing through windows. Crack dealers dealing to ten-year-old kids." He looked to the side like he wanted to spit.

"The old gangsters were bad, but they *knew* heroin was and had nothing to do with it, and wouldn't." Now McCauley's hands grabbed the edge of the table, leaning in closer, his eyes narrowing. "*Wouldn't* have allowed this to happen." He leaned back in the seat, picked up the fork, began to angrily cut chicken with the edge.

"Which brings us to Higgins," Mackey said, bobbing a ball of vermicelli on the end of her fork.

"Which brings us to Higgins."

The phone rang on his hip. It was Lilly.

McCauley said, "Go ahead, Lilly," nodding at Mackey, dragging a fresh napkin in front of him. "Pen's out, I'm ready," he said.

THIRTY-SIX

FIPPA WHIPPED UP TWO KAMIKAZES, *extra* vodka, placed them on the end of the bar. Hand alongside his mouth, he shouted good-naturedly, "Hey, Catchy, look like a waiter? Get over here and get 'em yourself."

Signaling from a booth in the corner, Catchy looked back at Dinny McLintock. "See, what I tell ya, two more on deck, and the whole ride's on me. Now, we were talkin' about . . . oh ya, Ennie, how he telling me, back in Norfolk, about the score you guys made, you guys pretendin' to be painters."

Dinny scowled and held it a little too long. "Weren't pretendin', we *are* painters, union, Local 577." Through bloodshot eyes, looked over at Fippa.

"Hey, Fippa say we're up again?" Dinny nodded, drove a finger into his chest. "*I'll* make the run." Caught the corner of the table as he got up, almost went over, and weaved his way through the crowd to the bar.

Catchy watched him, shook his head in a way, to someone else watching, might have looked like he was just loosening his neck. Goddamn drunk, Catchy thought, worse, a chemical garbage pail, put it in front of him, he'd drink it, snort it, or smoke up a cloud, certainly not the kind of partner he would have picked. But Ennie?

Too much a horse of the same color.

In Catchy's mind you had to be able to trust a partner, it wasn't just about taking down scores. How's the guy behaving after? Will he turn up the heat by buying a Caddy? Worse, load up on drugs? Oxys? Jesus. Coke? Run around tellin' anyone who'd listen how clever he was, how clever *they* were?

Dinny came back, put the drinks on the table. Licking the tips of his fingers, he said, "You got anything left for the head?" Threw a glance at the bathroom over his shoulder.

Catchy had to lock his eyes not to roll them, said, "Sure, Din," and reached into a pocket and pulled out some bills he dropped on the table. Patted the other, squeezed it, reached into it, coming out with a package. Palmed it to Dinny, pretending to shake.

"Always a pleasure to see ya again, Mr. McLintock," he said, sweeping the room with his eyes. "And how's the missus? Good a fuck as the last time I had her?"

Dinny grinned. "Thank you, she's doin' much better, been paying for lessons."

Catchy thinking, as Dinny walked towards the bathroom like the floor suddenly tilted, With a nose like a Hoover, he won't bring back a flake. Pissed, he was under no delusions that he'd have to re-up.

But not until after they left.

Hey, kid. Come on now, you ain't talking about quitting? The night's young, we're just *startin'* to drink.

At least something was working in his favor. During his seven years in the pokey, the price of coke dropped. A two-fifty eightball now went for a hundred. Had he done a dime, would the price be, say, fifty? Wasn't itching to find out. When they left here he'd grab another eight-ball at the Dominican store.

A huge man at the bar, not tall, wide, black shorts, red tank top, Red Sox cap backwards, eyeballed Catchy, him catching the action. Following the time it took for their eyes to connect, he didn't so much slide from the chair as, like cement off a shovel, pour in a clump. Sauntered towards Catchy, sawing under his nose with a finger.

Catchy tried to ignore him by closing his eyes as he sipped on his drink. Felt the burn in his throat, the thickness growing around his eyes. Gotta slow down, Catchy boy, start dumping the drinks in one of them fake fucking ferns, gotta chance here, be sharp.

Talk about sharp.

Reaching behind to the small of his back, fingers searching beneath his Hawaiian shirt, fingering the handle of the double-edge blade in the sheath he had tucked into his pants. Got the shirt from his ma when he first got out. Telling him it was about softening that dreadful prison pallor. Charles, girls want to see the real you. Red palm trees, blue flamingoes the *real* me? Charles? Shit.

Now at the table, the big man offering a hamhock with fingers, saying, "Catchy, how's tricks?" Catchy taking the hand without looking. Grown man, fucking mook, wearing a baseball cap backwards.

"Hey, Steama, ya," Catchy said. "Ask ya to sit down, but only got one booth, what's up?"

Steama, more comfortable now, edging closer, his belly absorbing the edge of the table.

"Seen ya with Dinny, him hittin' the head, don't think me forward but could use some for mine . . . if you're sellin', that is. Not askin' for freebies, a cuff, I got cash."

Catchy looked at his face for the first time. Cool in here and the guy's sweaty, shiny, a blasting AC and he's wet like he went through a car wash — the final-rinse soup. Doubted nothing these days. Catchy telling him, back away from the table, you got sweat in my drink. Steama retreating an inch, wiggling the ham hocks, the fingers like puppets, moving in every direction. He said, "Was high, Catch, *am* high, see, but I'm comin' down, need just a little bit more for the head, you holdin'?" Shoulder hair sticking up like he just had a fright.

Catchy watched Dinny come out of the men's room, wiping his nose with the back of his hand. Stopping, talking to Moses Halloran at the end of the bar, trying to score, probably cuff. There's never enough for these bums. Look at him patting his back, yakking it up, uh, Dinny roaring, Moses *that* funny? Stopping too quick. A put on, ya, you're funny — now got anything for the head? Guess not, stopped laughing, coming this way, getting lost behind Steama.

Up close, Dinny inspected the big man, said, "Steama, them shorts would be loose on a barrel." Shook Catchy's hand. Catchy making a fist inside his, slipping the package — nothing but paper — under his leg.

Steama catching the play.

"How 'bout I buy just a line?" he said, reaching into his pocket, squinting at Catchy.

Catchy said, "Tell ya what, Steama, stick the other hand in your pocket." Watching him do it. "Good. Now grab hold of your dick, if you can find it, and pull yourself back to the bar. Or maybe you'd like me to cut the thing off? Your choice."

Steama hoisted his hands to his shoulders. "Hey, Catch, no need to get frantic, just askin' is all."

Starting to rise, Catchy said, "Figure you used up your quota of asks."

Sliding in opposite, Dinny patted the table. "Hey, Catch, give Steama the package, can't help he's a fat fuck. Besides, all that's left is a line . . . maybe." Giggle, sniff. Catchy stared without blinking. *Tellin'* me I'm buyin' him more? Little prick.

"Lucky day, Steama, my buddy here likes you," Catchy said, fisting the package.

Steama reached his hand out to shake.

At six o'clock it was still almost seventy degrees. The orange sky growing dark in the west, some of the cars passing Sullivan's burning headlamps. Leaning against a street sign, Dinny McLintock littered the sidewalk around him with butts that kept missing his mouth. Walking out through the doorway of Sullivan's behind him, Catchy shouting to everyone over his shoulder, "Before I head home, I'm droppin' Dinny at Street Lights, lucky prick, *he* got a date." Hoots and cheers followed.

Dinny, still glued to the pole, was trying to pick up the butts without falling. Catchy hooking his arm just before. "C'mon, I'll buy you some more," Catchy said, leading him around the corner down Eighth Street.

Standing behind a card table at the end of a couch, Catchy, cutting up coke into lines, said, "Got a cat?" Brushed at his face, blew, slap-brushed it again. "Jesus, do you?" He looked at Dinny, down the other end. The bum, half out of it now, nodding.

Dinny curled onto his side, giggling. "Me, cats? Naw, Ennie's aunt had a bunch. When the old lady died, she left him the house. Got rid of the kitties, but the fuckin' fur's everywhere. Whatsamatta, allergic?" More giggles.

Catchy stopped cutting and stared. Funny, huh, *really*? Mark it down, Catch, collect on it later. Rounding third, comin' into home plate . . . *slidin'*.

Catchy bent down and sucked up a fat one, straightened, almost gagged, felt the burn in the back of his throat. Nodded, fucking shit's *good*. He walked behind Dinny, dropped the straw next to him. He said, "I'm getting a drink, want one?"

Coming out of the kitchen holding a beer in each hand, he put Dinny's on the arm of the couch, paced back and forth behind him. "We're switchin' to beer, both of us," Catchy said, swinging the can to his lips. "Keep drinkin' the hard stuff, it'll ruin the night. I say we each have another brew, do a few zippers, then head out again, all right?" Patting Dinny on the shoulder. I'm your friend, pal, I've got your back. "Maybe hit one of those new joints downtown, near The Crossing?"

"Fucking yuppie scum," Dinny said, sitting up, pressing the side of his nostril. Sniff. "Wow, the shit's good, really pickin' me up," he said, reaching out, grabbing hold of his beer.

"Them joints downtown pack 'em in like cordwood, actually lie the yuppies on top of each other. They can't carry cash — nooooo — takes up too much *space*, only *plastic's* allowed." He cracked his beer and took a long swallow. He looked at the ceiling. "Plastic people, plastic money, gotta be some kind of meanin' there, huh?" Sniffing, reaching down, fumbling between the dirty red cushions. "Hey, you got the straw?"

"Don't worry about it, cut you another," Catchy said

Talk about cutting.

"So, the thing you guys grabbed from the lawyer, the disc, heard the guy's nervous you got it. 'Least accordin' to Ennie. He seems to think it will make ya's money, *lots* of money, you?"

"Found it," Dinny said, and held up the straw. He looked over his shoulder at Catchy. "Ennie says with it, we got a license to print money. Don't know much more, know shit about computers."

Catchy stopped at the end where the card table was, so high now, almost ejecting out of his skin. Struggling just to keep his voice even. "Funny, a few minutes ago you were talking about plastic, how it's the same thing as money. With that disc, it sounds like you got the same thing. Ever wonder what's on it?"

Like it was infinitely more interesting, he returned to the coke, picked up Dinny's license, and started to chop. Don't have to tell me you don't want to.

Stretching, Dinny sat up, eyeballed the table at the end of the couch. Catchy over it now focused, chopping, separating long lines. God, looked like monsters. A tingling in his balls rocketed into his stomach. He took a hit of the beer, stuck the straw in his nose, sunk his head back into the cushion. He said, "One more blast, we're outta here, okay?" Closing his eyes.

No answer from Catchy, just the chop, chop, dragging sound from the table. Oh, what the hell, just tell him.

Closing his eyes tighter, visualizing, Dinny said, "On the disc were big money numbers. Had a doctor's name, and a lawyer's too, Ennie said both of 'em bigshots. And there were other names. Ennie found out most of them rich kids said, looks like someone was shaking somebody else down."

Dinny opened his eyes and stared at the ceiling. Maybe one more beer, another line, and stay home. Maybe he was getting old, felt it, he said, "Funny, recently in the paper? One of them guys got himself killed."

Eyes brightening, he pointed the straw at Catchy. "See, that's how Ennie found out, recognized the name. The murdered kid, same one as on the disc.

"Made him curious, but Ennie's that way, always sniffing around. Got this cousin who works at the BMC, probation department, got him to run the other guys' names. Don't know what he told him, but he got happier and happier the more he found out.

"I'm standing right there when he calls up this lawyer — a big shot — he says something to him, then covers the mouthpiece, this shyster's face, love to see it, he says. After, keeps tellin' me how we're partners, how we're gonna be rich. Ennie's a genius. Fucking genius." Dinny closed his eyes, took a sip of the beer. "You almost ready with them lines?"

"Just about." Catchy said. "So, mind me askin' what you did with the disc?" Chop, chop-chop, drag.

Dinny chuckled, he shrugged. "Got it here in the house, where else would it be?" Threw an air ball at the corner. He said, "In the *rabbit*, over there."

Catchy looked where he threw.

In the corner, near a window with the curtains pulled tight, was a huge, carnival-type Bugs Bunny, crumpled, head tucked between its knees like it was getting ready to crash, in the hollow of an orange beanbag chair.

Chop-chop. "In the rabbit?" Drag.

"Ya, up its butt." Dinny dropped his head back, closed his eyes, laughed. "I mean, who'd ever think of lookin'?"

"Done yet?" he said, pulling the straw from his nose.

Catchy stopped chopping. "We're finished," he said. "It was hid in the foot, you might have been luckier."

Tilting his head back even further, Dinny opened his eyes, Catchy's face now only inches above him. "Hate wastin' good coke on an asshole," he said.

Dinny started to say, hey, what the fuck, but all that came out, from the center of his neck, was a noise that sounded like a fart. He clutched at his throat. Something was moving under his fingers, sawing, something else yanking his hair. Looking up, like through a pipe, Catchy's face getting smaller, the tinny voice saying, "Dinny, what's that you're sayin'? Didn't quite get it."

Catchy kept sawing until the blade bit the spine.

THIRTY-SEVEN

TAKING IN MORE THAN A GRAND every week, Flippy Condon was grateful. And, according to Mike, it was just the start. Not bad for a tenth-grade drop-out.

He remembered a Southie High math teacher, an old fart named Lyons, calling his mother, telling her, your kid don't belong here, be much better off in the trades. Funny thing, the old fart was right, had a trade now — hurting people.

And he tried, every day, to have a learning experience.

As a kid, action figures never did diddly for him. Transformers? Forget it. Early on, the signs were there that he'd be the one doing the transforming. Starting with ants. With short legs like him, they couldn't run fast. Little gas down the anthole, flip a match on it, whoomph.

But he couldn't see enough of the damage.

When he got older and was able to run fast, it was hornets and bees, glass jars and matches. Look at 'em squirm, see-how-they-melt.

On to cats.

But they made a racket, then dogs, a few strays, not many, they'd put up a fight, have to punch them silly with hockey gloves on. Lousy at hockey — weak ankles — he'd douse 'em with thinner, burned hotter than gas.

Then Flippy discovered people.

From behind. "Open the trunk."

Flippy jerked up in the seat and looked in the mirror, he fingered the trunk-lock release. After the rear deck was sprung and blocked the rear window, he lost sight of Janowski hugging two cases of Becks. A big thunk and the car sunk an inch, Janowski slammed the lid and got in.

In the rearview, Flippy watched the two men watching them closely from the window of Rotary Liquors. He looked at Janowski.

"Take it, it's a donation," he said, pulling into the street, stopping before entering the rotary.

"A donation, ya," Janowski said. "Jackie's thinkin' about makin' them *partners*, they know it too. They'd give me the store to delay it."

"Delay it, like it ain't gonna happen?" Flippy said, following the circle back up Old Colony.

"Gonna happen, all right, when Jackie says when — turn onto Dorchester — I ain't in no rush, got enough shit to handle." Nodding at a bum who waved from a bench in front of the projects.

"Kenefick," he said, with a jerk of his head.

Flippy's eyes bugged like his head was expanding. "Can't be," he said, and looked at Janowski, swinging his eyes back to the road.

"Is."

Slowing down in front of Bell's Market. "We ain't lookin' for Moses?"

Janowski shook his head, pointed. "No, just head up the Point."

"So it was him, Kenefick?" Flippy said, checking the rearview again.

"Ya, what don't you get?"

Flippy gave him a what, I'm an idiot look. He said, "I just re-member when he was worth tons, one of Marty Fallon's *golden* boys." He grinned, shook his head.

"Then Fallon got whacked and his crew got sloppy. Haven't seen him since we," he jabbed the guns he made of his hands to-wards the windshield, making kuu-kuu sounds, "*cleaned* up the mess. Hee-hee, Kenefick, I thought he was dead."

"Might as well be," Janowski said, glaring as they passed T.K. O'Malley's, "like someone I know."

Passing a tanning salon, pizza parlor, and nail joint, they headed east up the Broadway hill, Janowski watching both sides of the street. He said, "After Fallon got clipped," popped a palm with a fist, "there was nothin' but chaos, I'm talkin' right afta. The head's blown off, but the snake won't stop wiggling. It was no easy matter makin' it stop.

"We left some of his boys right where they fell, while the oth-ers with money, like Kenefick, were snatched off the street and taken to basements. We lit up the cuttin' torches. 'Now, where's the money, you fuck?'

"We grabbed Kenefick early. Believe me, we didn't have to so much as strike up a Bic to get him to roll over, throw his legs in the air. He gave us a half a refrigerator box full of cash, then took off to Florida."

Janowski waved a finger. "Wasn't like we needed the money, had enough of our own, but used Fallon's to put his own outfit to sleep." He patted Flippy's shoulder. "Used it to bring in mus-cle like you."

"Would have come in for nothin'," Flippy said, grinning.

Few more pats on the shoulder. "You would've, I know, you got talent, not just capable, *creative,* and the best thing . . ." He jabbed the air with his finger, "you listen."

Flippy said, pulling around a truck turning right onto G Street, "But Kenefick came back from Florida, how come?"

"A degenerate gambler, he got into the coke. Lost everything he had on Jai Alai, the ponies. When he was into the shys down Miami for thousands, *then* he comes scurrying back to Southie."

Janowski softly snorted, pinched the end of his nose, checked his fingers. "Look at 'im now, put the fork in, he's done, hangs on the bench bummin' quarters, I'm told. Pull over."

Flippy stopped the Cadillac in front of South Boston District Court. Leppy Mullins, in a blue windbreaker, gray oversized shorts, more pockets than fabric, brown Sperrys, leaned up against a mailbox, smoking facing the street. Janowski powered the window down.

Leppy took a hit on the butt, flicked it behind him, came over, and leaned on the roof. "Gentlemens," he said.

"What's hap-penin'?" Flippy said, giving a little salute.

"Ain't healthy for you where you're hangin'" Janowski said, "in front of the courthouse. You never heard of Black Holes?"

Leppy's look told him he hadn't.

With a finger, Janowski made little circles over the dash. "Black Holes are in space, see, like you Lep — in space — but *these* things are dangerous. Get your ass near them, they'll suck ya right in. Turn you inside out like a fucking cartoon. My experience, courthouses are like that. A guy gets too close . . ." He pinched his lips, shrugged.

Leppy pushed away from the car and peered over his shoulder like maybe the building had suddenly crept up behind him.

"Mike, I'm waitin' for Arnie, my brother. He's in there appealin' a speedin' ticket he got near the yacht clubs, fucking statey." Looked over his shoulder again, shuddered. "Hate courthouses too, feels like I swallowed raw eggs just smokin' out front. Leppy glanced down the hill, we ain't talking a courtesy call here. "So, how can I help ya?" he said.

"Halloween," Janowski said.

Leppy pursed his lips, nodded, thinking. He stepped back, bugged his eyes as he threw out his hands. "Okay, I give up, what are we *talkin'*?" he said.

Crooking a finger, Janowski motioned him closer. "Fucking mook, you're dealin', correct? I'm talkin' how you holdin' for Halloween? It's almost a holiday, remember? People party on Halloween, and you take care of the people who do. It'll be here in three weeks" he leaned out the window and whispered, "So, how're you holdin'? The last time you picked up was two weeks ago, a lousy few ounces, whatsamatter, business slow?"

Janowski's eyes narrowed. "Or maybe you hooked up with another supplier?"

Like the curbstone carried a current, Leppy jumped back. "Jesus, Mike, on my mother, ain't buyin' from no one 'cept you."

Arms flailing, Janowski launched himself half out the window. He said hoarsely, "Fucking moron, you know where you are? Shut the *fuck* up."

Leppy blinked a few times, scratched at his balls, nodded. "Ya, Mike, cool, sorry, I remember, the *black hole*, it's just that . . ."

Janowski cracked the door and started to get out. "I told you, shut the fuck up." Yanked it shut, whispered, "I'm expectin' an order — *we're* — expectin' an order. Something in line with a big weekend, what you think, double the usual?" Janowski looked at Flippy, nodding, Flippy nodding back. "Yeah, double, sounds about right."

Looking up at Leppy, Janowski said softly, "Place your orders early and often, isn't that what James Michael Curley once said?"

Leppy scratched an elbow, looked down the street. "Think Curley was talkin' about votin'," he said, "when he was runnin' for office?"

"Votes? Got it wrong, Lep," Janowski said, turning away, staring out the windshield. "*You* ain't got one. Place the order, you'll thank me."

Staring at the tips of his shoes, Leppy murmured, "Ya, Mike . . . thanks."

"You're welcome," Janowski said.

At Broadway and I Street, they stopped for the light, U2's "In the Name of Love" blaring from all six speakers. Flippy singing along, "Once more in the naaaame of love," Janowski looked at him, saying, "Hey, know what I'd like?" Flippy looked at him, "What?" " Smash that fucking radio's what. I'm tryin' to figure this out, do you mind?"

"Nothin' to figure," Flippy said, killing the radio. "Leppy'll buy what you told him."

Shaking his fist in front of the dash, Janowski said, "I'm not talking about Leppy," he said, "I'm talkin' about Dinny McLintock."

"Think McLintock will be there."

"Ennie Higgins is back in the can, word's McLintock's watchin' his crib. He'll be there, all right," Janowski said.

"You seem awfully certain."

Janowski said, "Few days ago, Moses was telling he saw Dinny and Catchy Davis hangin' out down at Sully's. He said that Catchy was doin' all of the buyin': coke, booze, crystal, which was strange since them two ain't known to hang out together."

"Maybe Catchy was lookin' for somethin'," Flippy said.

His eyes on the road ahead, Janowski was grinning now, tapping his fingertips together. "Ya, Catchy and Ennie were pals all right. Ennie's celly up the Hill, his work-out partner in Norfolk." He stopped tapping, turned his head and stared at Flippy. "Maybe Ennie whispered a secret before he got out." Folding the fingers now into fists. "Maybe he *knows* what they got."

As they passed M Street park, Janowski said, "Guys like McLintock are nothing but vampires, they're out all night looking for scores, sleep all day. Dinny will be there, trust me."

They took a left at N Street, a right on East Third, after passing a block of two- and three-family homes, crossed O Street, pulling over, stopping at the edge of a cinderblock building, the doorway to Teamsters Local 122 covered by a rolled-metal grate. The Lincoln the only car parked on this side of the street. On the other side, every space filled as far as they could see.

The Lincoln was across from a large, overgrown field with fenced-in backyards lining its northernmost border. Beyond the houses, in the distance, the stacks of the Edison plant rose in the cool morning air. At its easternmost edge, a wobbly, unpainted fence separated the field from the yard of a yellow two-family house. Both men stared silently at the house for a moment before Flippy looked at Janowski.

"Dunno, they got street sweepers comin' this mornin', Mike. We'll get tagged we park on this side of the street."

Janowski turned and looked out the rear window. "Ya, and go where? You see any spaces? Maybe double-park and attract snoopy cops? I don't think so. We're stayin' put, it ain't gonna take long."

The guy ain't getting it, tell him straight out.

"I'm not second-guessin' ya, Mike," Flippy said, "but we're in there and somethin' goes wrong, the Lincoln's registered to you. A parkin' ticket puts us here, got the time on it, everything."

"Re-lax, nothin's happenin'," Janowski said, keeping his eyes on the house. "We're *talkin'* to Dinny, nothin' else. He gives us a hard time, which he won't, or we don't get what we want — whatever *that* is — we'll take care of him later. Believe me, he won't see it comin', nor will anyone else. Now, where's the pad?"

Bending, almost touching his ear to the wheel, Flippy pulled a yellow legal pad out from under the seat and handed it to Janowski. Janwoski took a pen from the glove box. He said, "When we ring the bell, he don't answer the door, he's probably sleeping. We'll hike around back. Remember, because of this field the whole area's open, some nosey prick might be watchin' us over the fence. If we have to go back there, as we walk down the side, I want you to stop every few feet and point up at the siding, point down at the foundation, don't give two shits, you point at your prick. While you're doin' it, I'll pretend to be writing."

He tapped the dash with the pad. "This little yellow pad professionalizes us, see. We're insurance guys, contractors givin' an estimate. So much construction in Southie these days, no one will look at us twice."

The men separated after they got out of the car, Janowski diagonally crossing the street stopping in front of 782 East Third, its first-floor bay window covered by blinds. The building's foundation under a blanket of ivy, climbing, encircling the window, the one above it spreading like a locust cloud as it rose toward the roof.

Flippy had walked to the other end of the block before he casually crossed over, headed back. Like he'd been out for a stroll and spotted Janowski.

Nobody's answering, he heard Janowski say to the door, pressed his palm to it like he could hear inside through it. Flippy sat on the steps, watching the Lincoln, didn't need no meter maid putting them there. Janowski turning, pointing up at a pigeon, checking the windows of the row of houses behind them, saying, think it's a hawk?

Knowing that they were the only hawks on the street.

Following the alleyway down the side of the house, Flippy pointing, Janowski writing, Flippy suddenly stopping, pointing over the fence, complaining about a guy in the lot over there allowing his dog to drop shit. Janowski saying, so what, dog's gotta shit, wouldn't catch me with a bag behind one.

Flippy relating how it was personal, see, how he snuck through a window of a house one night with shit on his foot, waiting for a guy who owed him money to come home. How he used the guy's toothbrush to scrub it all off. But the guy had no dog, and when he came home, got a whiff of the shit, got scared, and ran out. Took another two weeks to catch up with this bum, and all because some jerk-off didn't pick up after his mutt.

At the back of the house, they looked at each other. At the top of the stairs the storm door was wide open. Climbing the steps, Flippy still pointing, Janowski still writing, entering an enclosed porch. To the right, a jumble of cheap plastic pots filled with talcum-dry earth and dried yellow plants, in a tilting tower beside them, empty pizza boxes. Directly in front a chocolate brown door, its single tiny window covered on the inside by a red calico cloth.

The door was unlocked, and they entered the kitchen and found the air inside dense and reeking of garbage.

And something much sweeter.

Through a doorway in the corner flies dive-bombed in and out in an almost continuous flow. On the counter some had collected on the rim of a coverless pickle jar with no juice inside. Beside it, on a plate, a half-eaten sandwich, some kind of meat, from the sides black flesh curling upwards, dots of green and white mold filling where the bite marks had been.

In the next room a strange light barely flickered, like sunlight through branches and leaves. They entered a place where a ceiling fan turned, and flies followed the blade in a circle. Blocking the small room's only window, in front of a dirty red couch, Roman armies soundlessly marched on a huge flat-screen TV. Now the huge head of a Roman senator–type, with the hair plastered down, arm jutting, shouting something that looked like, hail, Caesar.

The sweet smell getting stronger, the overhead blades driving the stench through their skulls, the roof of their mouths, the knowledge there was nothing alive in this house except flies.

Janowski leaned in through the doorway, turned his head, and froze. Wiping his palms, he turned, looked at Flippy, the eyes cold then vacant like he was erasing a vision, before he moved on. Flippy glanced at the TV, wanting to push it aside, throw open the window, and jump the hell out.

Especially when Janowski said, "*Found* him."

Flippy had seen dead people before, but not like the kid in the movie — he killed them himself — but this guy. Straddled over the back of a couch, pants rolled down to his ankles, butt in the air. The black specks covering him rising in a cloud, resettling, rising again. Maggots boiling from a gaping hole where his rectum had been, like someone had used an auger. Holding his nose, Flippy said, looks like he got fucked by Godzilla and gagged, took in putrid air and a fly, almost puked. On the floor, face-down in front of the couch was a giant, carnival-type Bugs Bunny. Someone had also carved Bugs a new asshole.

Weird.

Lying in a small pile of coke, on a card table next to the couch, McLintock's license. Janowski checked the photo, bending to examine the face, the neck at a right angle, the remains of a cheek pushed into a cushion, a pool of frozen black blood. Even swollen like this, the lower jaw missing midway to the throat, it looked like McLintock.

The open eyes did it.

Flippy looked in the rearview as he started the car. "No ticket today, fucking lucky," he said, and pulled from the curb. Neither man looked at the house when they passed. After they turned onto Broadway, Flippy pulled up the front of his shirt to his nose, made a face. "Christ, smells like that *thing.*"

Janowski sniffed his own shirt, the back of his hand, wrinkled his nose. "It's on the skin too, and I didn't lay a hand on the fucker." Leaned forward, flicked up the blower on max. He said, "Head down the Pen."

As they passed the park at the top of the hill, he said, "Do that to a man hadda want something bad. Jack ain't gonna like it."

"That McLintock got done?" Flippy said. "He know him, they pals?"

They passed the Beer Garden. On the other side of its huge front windows, people sat at tables, munching buffalo wings, laughing. Pretty girls half-watching the traffic, who's looking at me?

"Don't think he knew him," Janowski said. "I wonder if he knows Catchy Davis?"

Flippy looked at him. "He's gonna now, right?"

Janowski nodded, looked out the side window, coming up now on a bank, a guy out front selling T-shirts. "He's gonna, all right, but not before *we* introduce ourselves first. Here, pull this rig over and grab us some shirts."

THIRTY-EIGHT

S O, THAT'S WHAT HE'D LOOK LIKE with a quarter-sized liver mark, color gold, under his eye. McCauley's hands bubbled the cutting cape as they went from his lap to the arms of the chair. He shifted his head, now the liver spot hung from an ear. "Hey, Charlie," he said, "you going to replace this damn mirror? Makes me look forty years older."

Charlie stopped cutting, looked at himself. The two on his face, detracting from the real ones he had. "Fifty years, almost, I got in this shop," snip-snip, snip-snip, "the mirror's my friend." With his head he indicated the barber chair next to McCauley's. "Next time, we'll cut in the other, ain't as bad."

"You've been cutting me twenty-five years," McCauley said, "you ask me, both mirrors have the same Momma."

Snip-snip, shrug, snip-snip. "Everyone's complainin' 'cept for old Charlie, and at eight bucks a cut, *I* should be the one howlin'. You want spiffy mirrors, go down Newbury Street, charge you sixty bucks to look at yourself."

Charlie spritzed him with water, ran a comb through the top, pulled out the hair on the sides, measuring length. "'Course you might get it cut by some young floozy smells better than me," sniffed his armpit, "not much." Snip-snip. "Or better looking," he said, checking himself in the mirror, moving his head to the side, "not much." Snip-snip. "But you ain't gonna get," pointed his scissors at the corner, "a thirty-year-old color console TV that don't work, an air conditioner that only works sometimes *and*," walking to the front of the shop, jabbing the scissors with a Zorro-like flourish, "the best goddamn come-on in Southie." In the Charlie's front window, the large cardboard sign read:

SHOP HOURS
Open most days about 9 or 10. Occasionally as early as 7.
But sometimes as late as 12 or 1.
We close about 5 or 6. Occasionally about 4 or 5.
But sometimes as late as 11 or 12.
Somedays we aren't here at all.
And lately I've been here about all the time.
Except when I'm someplace else.
(Charlie)

"Don't hear me complaining," McCauley said, "about the sign, I mean." Snip.

Charlie's hands dropped and he glared at him over his shoulder. "Smart that ya don't, wouldn't matter ya did, 'cause *I* know it draws 'em like flies." Nod. Snip-snip, snip-snip. "Everyone worryin' 'bout heppy-titis these days. Back of your neck shaved, or no?"

Fingering loose hair from his ears, McCauley pushed himself out of the chair. A haircut usually made him feel better, and he needed to feel better today. At the Eastern Pier, he had found out from Lilly that Enfield Higgins was on parole and had recently been violated. The charges had something to do with the possession of coke, and a B&E investigation, a sandwich joint down on Big Broadway.

Lilly said he would wrap up his old bid, the original one, in another six months. But by then he should be tried and convicted on the coke beef. Apparently, because he was an addict, there was a good chance that he wouldn't be looking at any additional time when he wrapped up. Probably just a suspended sentence with probation.

McCauley understood.

He'd been around long enough to know if you put every guy caught with a little coke, pot, a couple of Percs, in the can, there'd be no room left for the real bad guys. Higgins was a career small-timer: B&E's, receiving stolen goods, his own worst enemy and the courts knew it too.

Lilly also informed him that he lived up on Third Street, along with his partner, another small-timer by the name of Dinny McLintock. Both men, heavy drug users supporting their habit, were identified as "persons of interest," regarding a recent wave of B&Es in Southie.

That night at the Eastern Pier after Lilly had called, with the shadows beginning to deepen, McCauley had asked Mackey, Have you ever been out to Castle Island? She told him she hadn't, but that her parents had been there in '76 to watch the parade of tall ships. She saw pictures of the Island when she was a child. McCauley saying, In '76? That's when the Island was discovered. "Discovered?" Mackey said.

Explaining that, outside of having your own boat, the best place to view the tall ships was the Island. That year, thousands of people, from all over New England, poured through South Boston to Castle Island. Word got around about the beauty of the place. It was the beginning of the end of a wonderful secret.

That night, McCauley made sure Mackey discovered it. The huge granite fort to their backs, they sat on a bench near the boathouse and talked. Later, on the ocean side, they followed the path to the pier, in front of the clipper ship monument, where, out of sequence, fishermen, aligned in a row, hauled back with their poles and threw with their shoulders. Hunched over the railing, staring across the flat green, island-pocked expanse, nodding whispers, waiting for the strike.

Later that night, when McCauley got home around nine, he was thinking about Mackey, and wondered, Any chance she was thinking about him too? It didn't seem possible. Maybe, if he were ten years younger, and still on the job, with a promising future, maybe. Not a lousy, forty-year-old ex-con. He viewed himself, at most, as an irregular role model, someone to learn from. That he might do the same in her position.

Still, he couldn't put her out of his mind, didn't want to, and *that* bothered him. He remembered growing up when he was a kid, the lilies his mother always had in the house, their stamens covered in a beautiful yellow-gold pollen. And his mother's warning, Stay away, once it got on you it was hard to get off. Had he gotten too close to the flower?

He convinced himself briefly he was just filling a gap. A hole that had been left, unfilled for years, after Carolyn died. How long after before he dated again? Though his eyes still followed beautiful women, any real interest was gone. When he tried to imagine himself dating: drawing them in, trying to get close, the small talk, re-learning to listen, the effort of trying to know them, it all seemed too much. There was no way he could do it and not think of Carolyn.

With Carolyn gone, he had buried himself in his job. Maybe too much. There was nothing beyond it, and he was blind to everything else. Maybe part of the reason he fell?

From the time he got out of prison, he tried to keep himself busy, afraid to look back, or to even acknowledge the anger he carried. Between the bar, the dojo, the occasional disastrous date, and now the investigation for Lilly, something he thought would be easy. And now this distraction.

He couldn't control what was happening, though, his feelings towards Mackey — the girl *was* different. Not only beautiful, she was intelligent, funny, aggressive, Christ, how would *that* translate?

The way she talked with her hands. She had beautiful hands. And tapped on his arm to drive home a point. The hand lingering once, before pulling away quickly, like blue flame had suddenly flared from his arm. The eyes averting, then looking past him, down, slowly rising, meeting his, the what-happened-there look.

She wore tiny, beautiful lizard-shoes. Antiques, she said, that belonged to her grandmother. Saying, I would never buy anything like this today, the poor animals. He asked her shoe size.

Size six-and-a-half, why? Tiny. She had beautiful feet. Beautiful hands and feet, for McCauley, important attributes in a woman. Your sneakers must look like erasers, he said. And she laughed. He had made her laugh other times that night too, it was easy. Not as easy later, in front of Sully's, holding open the door to her car, his mind racing, say it, tell her he wanted to see her again.

The door almost closed now, her face, turned looking at him over her shoulder, the eyes curious, meeting his, smiling up through the long rectangular gap, saying, Thank you, wouldn't have known it's so lovely out here. Standing, until the curve in Day Boulevard, along the Lagoon, absorbed the glow of her tail lights. He got into his car.

Had gotten too close to the flower. Damn.

McCauley had planned to head to Higgins's house the next morning, but decided, in the neighborhood, why not swing by it now.

Following Broadway to O Street, he turned off onto Third and pulled over. He got out of the Mustang and walked towards the house. There were stars overhead and a sliver of moon, and a freshening breeze was blowing in from the east, like maybe a storm was approaching. He stood at the edge of the field and examined the house, just your basic two-family, not a light on, everything dark.

Walked into the field and noticed the open storm door at the rear of the building, made a note — where McLintock might run through if someone knocked on the front. He headed back to his car and sat there thinking after he turned over the engine, the Mustang quietly rumbling just beyond the luminescent cone of the street lamp. He stared at the house, his cop sense for the most part dormant for years, now kicking in.

There wasn't any doubt he was involved in some kind of chase. He closed his eyes and let the feeling flush through him. But who was the prey? Higgins? McLintock? Maybe himself? And what about Janowski? True, the gangster had plans for him, but he knew what they were. Rolling down the window, he leaned out his face and took a deep breath, like he was trying to catch a hint of something before the wind changed.

That night he slept fitfully and got up late the next morning, went to work, after work to the dojo. It was more than a work-out, the way he punched and kicked and went through the katas, like he was preparing for something. But what?

The next morning, the phone jarred him awake around six. No introductions, no you awake yet? Sorry I called you this early. Just Lilly inquiring, Have you been to Higgins's house lately? And if the answer is yes, did anyone see you?

McCauley sat up on the edge of his bed, scratched his scalp, left his hand there, pressing the hair as he explained that he'd been there two nights before and done some surveillance, but hadn't attempted contact, why?

"Yesterday," Lilly said, "someone called in a report, one of the neighbors on O Street. Seems she saw a couple of men, said they looked like building inspectors, walking around Higgins's house with clipboards. Then she watches them enter the house through the back. She thought it was strange. Of course the old biddy's got nothing better to do, so she just sits there and waits. Tells the desk officer when the pair came out again through the back door, they come walking right down her side of the street, see her house is right on the corner. Told the desk officer it was the faces that got her."

"What do you mean, *faces*?" McCauley said.

Lilly seemed aggravated. "Let me finish, I'll tell you. The *faces*, the way the guys looked, in particular one, like he'd seen a damn ghost. Both of them in a hellava hurry to leave there."

"She get the reg?"

"Couldn't, said an old maple was blocking the plate, but it was a big fancy thing, a Caddy or a Lincoln, green."

"What your boys find?" McCauley said, dropping bread in the toaster.

"That's the kicker," Lilly said. "They went in, found a guy who won't be anymore, stretched over the back of the living room couch. The kid's name, McLintock, ring a bell? At least we figure it's him, won't know for sure until the M.E. gets through. It's one hellava mess." As he put a pan of water on the stove for coffee, McCauley asked him to explain, then almost wished that he hadn't.

Lilly telling him seems the back door was open. Inside, along with the dizzying stench and a black cloud of flies, was a body. Lilly wouldn't go into detail here, inferring more than the heat had done a job on the thing. He did say he had never seen anything like it before. The body was multilated, and that's why they weren't sure.

It seems that Higgins, *known* for his fondness for knives, had nothing to do with it, but they checked on him anyways and found he was still up at Norfolk. Detectives were heading out there later today, to ask him some questions, Lilly said. If Higgins would talk, which was unlikely.

"Thing is," Lilly said, "he just might be pissed off enough to. The boys will try to fire him up first, using the details as fuel. They'll tell him your pal's been butchered, knife boy, like a veal calf, in your auntie's house — *your* house. We're talking major disrespect here. Hit him hard with the disrespect angle. It's big in the joint. Disrespect a man, he might kill you, or piss him off enough, he might even talk."

Later, as McCauley washed the sleep from his face and brushed the crappy taste from his mouth — a reaction to the images Lilly described? — he decided to call Cotter.

As it rang, Hi, Esmond — and just between us, who gave you that name? — I've got a lead on this case I'm not making a dime on. The bad news is that he's dead, and remember Higgins, the other guy I told you about? He's in prison, one of my homeys, a Norfolk boy, ya.

Seven rings later Cotter's voice mail picked up. Waiting for the beep, McCauley took the pan off the stove, poured the water into a cup. Identifying himself, he said, "Yesterday the Boston police found our best lead to date, a kid named McLintock, murdered." He said nothing about how he had planned to see him this morning. McCauley said, "I'm working on another lead, when I learn something else I'll call you back." Knew he was full of it as he closed up the phone. Besides putting two teaspoons of instant in a cup, he wasn't working on anything.

Besides, he was thinking he was wasting his time. He didn't

have to report in, wasn't working *for* Cotter, wasn't working for anyone. Why should he care? Bringing the cup to his lips, the coffee losing some of its sting.

He was helping out Lilly.

McCauley walked out of Charlie's barbershop and stood on the landing slapping his shoulders. He said to the street, "See you in two weeks."

Charlie looked up from sweeping behind him.

"Can hardly wait," he said, and resumed pulling the broom.

Taking a step down, McCauley said, "And maybe I won't pick on your mirrors."

"Hardly wait."

Across Dorchester Street a man in a ball cap was keeping his head down but actually watching him from under the bill. He leaned up against the pole of a street sign that read Reverend Burke Street. As McCauley brushed at his forearms, he said over his shoulder, "Charlie, that Moses Halloran waiting in line?"

Charlie stopped sweeping and came to the door. Pushing down the top of the broom, he squinted. A long nod. "Another customer — who doesn't *complain* — have a nice day, McCauley."

With a curious hand movement, like something had just buzzed his ear, Moses signaled to McCauley, began heading west towards Old Colony Avenue Walked a short distance, looked back at him, You coming? McCauley followed the sidewalk in Moses's direction, watched him cross the street dodging traffic before disappearing through the doorway of Coyne's tavern.

From the outside, Coyne's didn't look like a bar. More like one of those joints in Kabul they sold guns out of. It was a squat, red-brick building, black grillwork covered its single window, there was no sign above it, or anywhere else, to indicate what the place was.

McCauley walked in through the windowless door.

THIRTY-NINE

WHEN MCCAULEY CAME IN, Moses was sitting at the end of the bar near the door. Down the other end, a flock of noisy old-timers, probably there from the time the place opened, were drinking their fill.

McCauley watched himself in the mirror as he pulled out a chair, settled in next to Moses. He said, "Buy you a beer?"

Moses took off his ball cap, ran a hand across his crew cut as he stared at himself in the mirror. "Little early, don'tcha think?" And tilted his head towards the other end crew. "You think I'm like them?"

"Wouldn't make you if you did," McCauley said. "Moderation, Moses, it's the secret to life."

Moses looked down at the bar. He said, "Naw, just a Coke, that's okay. Just have a Coke."

McCauley ordering two, putting a ten on the bar.

Moses pulled his ball cap back on, said, "So, how long you been going to Charlie's?"

"Twenty-five years."

"Really, same here, since I was five been going to him." Moses looked out the window. "Who'd figure twenty-five years later I'd be in the same place?" The bartender put down the Cokes. "Got a lime?" Moses said, burned up a little, the guy made a face.

"Two, please," McCauley said, using just the tips of two fingers to shove the ten towards him.

Moses took a sip of his Coke. Looked at McCauley and the bartender. "You do understand, McCauley, people get out. Get outta the projects." He looked out the window before turning back. He said, "Tell me I'm wrong. Look at that kid Brian Goodman, done good for himself, fucking Hollywood star, probably bangin' Lindsay Lohan. And, and Pete McGonnigal. His brother, Andy, the bank robber? Remember when everyone knew what he did? Those were the days, geez, the projects were jumpin'. Then Andy got shot on that Somerville job and sent up the Hill. He still in?" Moses took a sip and shook his head.

"But Peter? Peter's a cop. One of Boston's finest, 'magine that shit, see, it *can* be done," pointing at the mirror, sticking a finger in his own face, "*you're* a fucking loser, but it can be done."

The bartender stuck a lime on each glass, plucked the ten, and turned towards the register.

"Keep the change," McCauley said to his back. The bartender turned back and gave him the look. You whacked?

"We're in the same business, keep it," McCauley said.

Big grin, someone else in the trenches. The bartender said, "Thanks, the name's Jim, need a refill, give a holler."

Moses, pushing back now from the bar, the chair balancing on just the rear legs. "Wasn't waitin' for you out there, really, wasn't," he said, coming in, with a thud, for a landing, grinning. He squeezed the lime, dropped it back, circled the straw in the glass.

McCauley did the same, pulled out the straw, laid it down next to the glass. "Wasn't thinking you were," he said, sipping. "But you *did* lead me down here."

Moses speared the lime with the straw, pulled it out, examined it like he was looking for eyes. He smirked, began talking to the mirror-McCauley. "McCauley, you came into the system a cop, and never really lost the stink, nothing personal," he said.

Nothing personal? McCauley could feel the heat building in the base of his neck. Calm down, McCauley, hear the man out. The problem's *his* problem, he's nothing more than a two-punch combo waiting to drop.

"Your point," McCauley said, giving away nothing, bringing the glass to his lips, sipping, the drink mostly ice now, the lime in the way, he should have taken it out.

"Few nights ago, in Sullivan's Pub, Dinny McLintock, Ennie's partner, was there."

"So?" And McCauley gave Moses an I-followed-you-down-here-for-*that* kind of look.

Moses volleyed back with a hold-on-man-I-ain't-finished look, saying, "Remember a while back you asked me about Higgins? Well, about the same time, someone else was asking me too." He gave him a broad wink. "Wacko Curran," he said finally, turning back to the mirror-McCauley. "In particular, Mike Janowski and Flippy Condon, the little psycho piece of shit he runs with.

You give me a few bucks, McCauley, and they do the same, neither side knowing nothing until now." He chuckled to himself and stared into the glass and said, "Pretty smooth, huh?" Then the face became serious and scowled. "Ya, real smooth," he said sadly, "Moses, you *moron*."

McCauley looked up the bar and held up his glass, and the bartender nodded.

"So," McCauley said, "how's it feel working both sides of the street?" The other man locked his eyes on the mirror.

Scared, Moses was scared. Moses gripping the glass with both hands, McCauley watched him stare into it like he was seeing his future. Moses shrugged, closed his eyes, dropped his head for a moment.

The bartender put down two more Coke and limes. Moses tiredly squeezed in his lime, but this time he didn't stir. "He was partying with Catchy Davis," he said, "and he got ol' Dinny really *messed* up. They had a grand time, then they left together."

"Where'd they go, to Higgins's house?"

Moses jaw dropped. He turned his head and looked at McCauley.

Gotcha.

"You know, huh?" Moses said.

McCauley nodded. "The question's who did it, Catchy?"

Moses fished out an ice cube he stuck in his mouth. Crunching, he said, "Naw, not Catchy." He crunched on the ice. "You'd seen 'em together, you'd never think that, they were partyin' like friends." He continued to stare. "I told you there were others around asking questions about the kid."

"Janowski."

Moses nodded, made a gun of his hand that he put to his temple, and shot.

"I'll tell ya, McCauley, they did it, I'm finished too." He patted his chest. "Moses Halloran turned them on to the kid. Never asked them what for . . . those kind of guys you just don't. Figure the less I know, ya know?" He shifted nervously in his seat. "But if I'm the link, linkin' 'em, I hope you got cable, 'cause I'm next up on the History Channel." He hoisted the glass and sucked water through ice, put the glass down, and stared at it. The eyes rose and went back to the mirror.

McCauley wasn't thirsty now, and slid his Coke in front of Moses. He said, "Why are you telling me all this?"

Moses scooped a couple of cubes from the top and popped one into his mouth. Looked like he was doing his best not to laugh as he jiggled the other around in his hand. He said, "'Cause you were a cop, right? Got a lotta cop friends. Something happens to me, you got no problem droppin' a dime, it's kinda your duty. You're gonna help me pull 'em down from the grave." He palmed the other cube into his mouth and grinned at McCauley. "The other kid, Catchy? Should be warned too, these guys are bad news. The last one who seen poor Dinny alive? He could be next."

Moses took a hit of McCauley's Coke and spit the ice back in the glass. He shook his head and said, "Me? I ain't ending up like Dinny, cut up like Alvin Wonder used to do dogs."

Talks like he's high.

"Who's Alvin Wonder?"

"Don't know Alvin Wonder?" Like he was trying to figure out why. "He was a project rat when I was a kid, a big, scary dude. Ever hear of a dog called a dingo? Got 'em someplace — Australia?" He shrugged, trying to place it. "Anyways, they don't bark and Alvin had a pit bull but wanted a dingo . . . cut its throat." Moses's eyebrows popped up. "Didn't bark anymore, or anything else. Didn't stop ol' Alvin from tryin' though — all through the neighborhood — 'til he cut the wrong dog and the owner shot him . . . in the neck. I think." Picturing it, still a little amazed. "Never heard of Alvin, huh?"

Looking uncomfortable, gently tugging the skin of his neck, Moses leaned forward and studied the backs of the hands he pressed to the bar. Turned just his head and looked at McCauley. He said, "Know something, McCauley, think I will have that beer."

CHAPTER FORTY

T
HE SAME WAY YOU FOUND OUT," Moses said, now on
his fourth beer, "from the cops." McCauley had switched
from Coke to soda and lime, had to piss like a racehorse but
remained glued to the seat. Moses, head bobbing lightly, trying
to focus his eyes on McCauley's hairline, said, "How 'bout a
chaser? Just one," his thumb and index finger a pencil-width
apart, "small one to take off the edge."

With an I-understand grin, McCauley lifted his hand and signaled Danny, saying to Moses, "Jack, Moses?"

Moses nodded, he said, "J.D.'s ma man," and took another
hard pull on the longneck.

McCauley said, "Danny, shot of J.D., straight up in a rock
glass, my friend here."

Moses wiped his mouth and tilted the bottle, checked the
wedge of beer at the bottom. McCauley turning, looking back up
the bar, "And another Budweiser too."

Moses gave him a nod, thanks. "Fucking cops," he said.
"Wasn't like they pulled up and told me, I got it from Fippa," he
said.

McCauley had passed it a thousand times but had ever gone
into Sullivan's. Never much hung out in bars.

He said. "Fippa's a bartender at Sullivan's?"

Moses held up the bottle, yes, and chugged the remainder.

Moses ignored him as Danny put the Jack down along with a
Bud, took the empty away. He said, "Bobby Marr, know him?
Works outta six." He eyeballed the drinks and winked at Mc-
Cauley as he pulled the Bud towards him

"Seems it was cops from six that found Dinny's body." Started
to peel off the label. "Bobby's a regular, Fippa's old pal, got his
own barstool down there. He don't like that cop bar, Foley's,
over the South End, too many cops, he says." Moses waved a finger at the mirror and said, "*One's* too many for me." Took a hit
of the beer.

"Bobby Marr knows McClintock used to hang out at Sully's

so he gives 'em a courtesy call — figuring he didn't, Fippa would spit in his drinks — and gives Fippa a heads-up telling him the cops might come down there askin' some questions." Moses held up the J.D. and gave the mirror a nod. He said, "Cheers."

McCauley watched him toss back his head with the drink — make a face like he had his nuts in a vise — chase it with beer. Moses wiped his mouth with his forearm.

Christ.

McCauley asking how close was Catchy to Dinny McLintock.

Moses telling him Dinny and Catchy were both friends of Ennie's, but *those* two weren't close. He shook his head crazily and sunk into the chair. "Naw, never ever seen 'em together," he said, "until that night."

"So, it was strange them being together?"

Moses shook his head, said, "Figured Catchy, him being fresh out of the can, was lookin' to celebrate and he spotted ol' Dinny, you know, a *union* brother."

"What union?"

Moses gave McCauley another I-can't-believe-you-don't-know-that look, lowered his chin to the bar and extended his arms. "The painters union," he said. "Local 577, them three are in it." He pushed the empty rock glass to the edge of the bar and tilted it back with his fingers.

McCauley said, "You ready for another?" starting to lift up his hand.

Moses turned his head and looked at him, the eyes trying to focus, almost losing the glass doing the finger-and-thumb thing. "Okay, just a little one," he said.

McCauley knew something about paint. Less than six months before, assigned to the maintenance crew at the Shirley minimum, he'd been ordered to paint the interiors of some of the "cottages." He knew the difference between oil base and latex and remembered the odor of latex when he visited Cotter.

Moses had narrowed it down. If union painters painted the Seaport Building, there was a good chance they came out of Local 577, and he was lucky to have a contact there.

Denny Huffington, aka "Huffy," was the business agent for 577, and he was also McCauley's cousin. One of those relatives he'd see growing up rarely, maybe twice a year — at Christmas and Saint Patrick's Day — but through him he could get the information he needed, the phone number and address of any dues-paying member.

A track mechanic for the T when he was younger, Huffy cement-waterproofed on the side. About the time he started his own company he got a book in the painters union — all before the first shovelfuls of dirt from the Big Dig were flung.

With ten million cubic yards of concrete eventually poured, and all that water around it, Huffington had made a fortune. Selling the company, after his final contract on the Zakim/Bunker Hill Bridge was completed, he successfully ran for business agent.

He invested the score from the sale into a variety of enterprises. Some legal, some not. One acquisition was the Teamsters Pub, on the corner of D and West Second, that he bought from relatives of its former owner, the late gangster Marty Fallon.

The Teamsters catered to union types: painters, laborers from local 223, iron workers from 7, sandhogs from 88. The place could be rough — the average patron sucked beer through a gap usually filled by a dental plate — if you didn't carry a union book. But if you did and needed information on work coming up, or the best time to take a layoff, you could bet on the Teamsters. Ever frugal, Huffy kept a tight hand on the till and worked the bar days.

Esmond Cotter sat at his desk in the sun, twisting his college ring, Harvard. He had already seen two clients this morning. One was a drug dealer who got nailed with his stash. The stateys only found police a few pounds of pot when they busted in the door to his big house in Braintree. It was a more painful when they found the two hundred large he kept in his bureau.

Then it got worse.

Handcuffed in the living room, the head cop came over and shoved a key in his face. He said, "When's the last time you visited your storage facility?" A few hours later, the state police did and found another two million in cash.

His client was . . . distraught?

His other client, a wealthy regular — he'd handled the divorce from his first wife, the prenup then legal separation from the second — in the neighborhood had stopped in to pay his respects.

Cotter had recently represented his son, hit by a bogus sexual harassment complaint by the board of the prominent university he attended. When they tried to expel him, Cotter had leaked the story to the press, *accidentally* exposing the name of the victim, who it seems had a *history*. The woman recanted. Don't get mad, get even, and they did, with a fat out-of-court settlement.

But Cotter wasn't feeling very successful now, more like a badger backed into its hole. According to McCauley's message, this hoodlum McLintock, Higgins's partner, was found murdered, and Cotter wondered if Reems was involved. But if McLintock had the disc, how did Reems know? Unless Hagsworth had someone else out here tracking them too? Tracking *him*?

Cotter stopped twisting the ring and pressed his palm to the desk, tapping it now on its marble surface. Click-click. Maybe the doctor was out of control and . . . if he was . . . would he see him as a threat? He tried to force a grin, absurd, how could he? He hadn't given him a reason to, right? Click-click. Besides, they were friends . . . if not *friends*, long-time partners. Click-click-click.

Cotter shifted uncomfortably in the seat. Once this state cop/ex-convict got back his disc, things would return to normal. Click. Normal? He pulled a bottle of whiskey from a lower drawer and took out a glass he put on his desk. He unscrewed the cap quickly and started to pour, wishing he had ice, when the telephone rang.

Startled, he put down the bottle and straightened up in the chair. Collecting himself, he rested one hand on the knot of his tie as he picked up with the other. Nodded. He said, "Yes, Mr. McCauley, I did get your message. No, it wasn't good news. What?" Scanning the walls. "Yes, my office . . . the entire building *was* recently painted — yes, after hours. Why do you ask?"

McCauley explained how Higgins and McLintock were both union painters. They must have found it while they were in there, he said.

Cotter said, "It was *painters* who stole it?"

"Beginning to look that way," McCauley said, "but they couldn't have taken it while working that floor, would have looked suspicious. I figure they came back a couple of nights later, while working the next, carted it out with them when they left in the morning."

"Okay," Cotter said, "we've determined it was this Higgins who stole the damn safe, and we know how ... what do you plan to do next?" he said.

"Ever hear of a guy called Catchy Davis?"

Cotter's head dropped, and he closed his eyes tight, his fingers kneading his forehead. "No, Mr. McCauley, I don't think ... I have."

"I've got the feeling, counselor, that he may have the disc. I'm working on an address. When I get it, I'll give you a call, fill you in more."

"Thank you, Mr. McCauley."

When McCauley hung up, Cotter's eyes remained closed, the phone remained pressed to his ear.

FORTY-ONE

McCAULEY WALKED INTO THE TEAMSTERS PUB and stopped beside the cigarette machine next to the door. A cardboard sign on the machine's window read: Cigarettes $2.25 **Customers Only!** Out on the street, cigarettes were selling for four-eighty a pack. McCauley figured Huffington had bought them hot, by the case, for nickels on the dollar, a come-on to get customers into the bar.

Wasn't working today.

Huffington, who stood in the middle of the bar polishing a glass with what looked like a cut-down white hand towel, was tall, early forties, built like a basketball player whose knees had gone bad and had since developed a small belly. Dressed in blue jeans and a black collared short-sleeve, with Teamsters in white letters across the chest, he was talking to a little old guy in a black windbreaker that said MDC on the back, a ball cap on his head. There was no one else in the bar.

The old guy's cap was cocked off-center, like he was afraid it might interfere with the twenty-two-ounce draft he brought to his lips every couple of seconds.

McCauley just stood there until his cousin looked up, stretched his neck, and gave him a look like he was trying to pick him out in a crowd. Huffy chuckled and said, "Jesus, Delray? Long time no see. What's it been, more than a month and now you come by when I'm *busy*?" Grinned.

Rapping his knuckles on the machine, McCauley took the two steps down to the floor and headed for the bar, saying, "Huffy, I heard smokes were cheap in this joint, had to see for myself."

Huffington's eyebrows jerked up like someone poked them with pencils.

"Since when do you smoke?" he said, flipping the towel over his shoulder. He turned and slid the glass onto the shelf behind him.

"Don't," McCauley said, now almost to the bar, "but figured with these prices I'd be able to start."

Huffington chortled and whipped the towel over his head a few times before letting it fly at McCauley.

McCauley head-feinted right, quick-stepped left, caught it in front of a table. Side-arming it back, he reached over the bar and shook Huffington's hand. Watching the scene in the mirror, the old man put his glass down in the puddle below it, moved it around slowly in figure eights. He straightened his hat, turned, gave McCauley a look, and said softly, "Afternoon to ya, Del. See, I can say that now you ain't a cop no more." He turned back to the mirror and gave the hat a tug right, nodded, and brought the glass to his lips.

"Afternoon, Mr. Kiley," McCauley said, looking at Huffington, back at Kiley. He hadn't spoken to Bobby Kiley in over twelve years.

The last time, McCauley was holding the handle of the twelve-pound sledgehammer he had used, seconds before, to bust down the door of a business Kiley owned, the Coachman tavern, on East Broadway.

One of Southie's biggest bookmakers, a multimillionaire, Kiley had been a major earner for Marty Fallon, Southie's former gangster chief. McCauley, part of an MSP organized crime strike force working with a similar unit of the Boston police, had hit the Coachman at four in the morning, with all the ferocity of a usual raid. Within seconds the door was off its hinges and the place was secure — or so they thought — with four perps hand-cuffed on the floor.

Bobby Kiley burst from a closet that night, moving like a freight train towards the table full of betting slips at the back of the room. In one hand was a large open container of gas, in the other a lighter he kept striking with his thumb. He got some gas on the slips, the rest of it splashing on the three cops who tackled him. Bobby would have burned the joint down, all of them in it, to prevent them from getting the slips.

McCauley remembered how Kiley had asked him that night, as he lay hog-tied on the floor, to loosen his cuffs since they were cutting his wrists. McCauley did it and carried the stench of gas with him the rest of the night.

"Care for a beer, Del?" Huffington said, flattening the edge of the folded towel on the bar. "Got something new here called Stella Artois, comes from Belgium, supposed to be good, take a taste." He grabbed a rock glass from a shelf behind him, grabbed the center draft arm from a stand of five, pulled it towards him.

It burped once and spit white foam, followed by a stream of golden liquid. He filled the glass and put it down on the bar. Resting his hands on his hips, he rocked back on his heels, winked, came back the other way and, with a finger, tapped the glass a few inches closer. "G'wan, try it," he said, "the *kids* say it's good."

McCauley picked up the glass and said, "Stella," in his best Marlon Brando, "I coulda been a contenda."

Huffington gave him a look. He said, "You're mixing your movies." Glanced at Kiley, back at McCauley, rested his palms on the bar, leaning closer. "Don't matter . . . what *does* is, you *were* a contender," he said softly. "Can't say you won't be again, salud."

McCauley raised the glass a few inches more. "Salud," he said, and drained it. Nice taste. "Not bad," he said. Huffington beamed.

"Knew you'd like it. Next time you come in — unless you want one now, but you don't look like you're interested in beer — I'll give you a twenty-two ouncer like Kiley's over there."

Kiley glared dark daggers at Huffington, pointed a finger at him and McCauley. "For the record, McCauley, I ain't drinkin' no foreign shit," Kiley said. "And you," folded the finger into a fist and shook it, "when you're mixin' my name with the other bullshit you're spitting, get your facts straight." He held up the nearly empty glass in front of his face, swirling the last half-inch in the bottom. Winked at the glass. "Budweiser, McCauley, it's *American*, like me. Won't catch Kiley drinkin' no Bel-*chun* piss." And he downed the rest of the beer.

Huffington snorted and shook his head. "Geez, Bobby, why don't you just tell us how you *really* feel? You want another draft?" Kiley gave Huffington a look like the other guy's face was decaying, falling in pieces before him.

"Huffy, how many fingers ya got?" he said.

Huffington looked at McCauley, back at Kiley. "Even you know the answer to that one, Bobby."

"Damn right I do," Kiley said with a nod, "and I'll give you another. You just keep pullin' those drafts until you run out of fingers. Then *I'll* decide if we'll move on to toes."

Huffington pulled another Bud draft, threw a napkin on the bar, and carefully centered the glass on it. He said over his shoulder as he head back towards McCauley, "Keep your shoes on, Bobby, and wipe the foam off your nose." Kiley gave it a brush and flicked his fingers at Huffington's back.

Without asking, Huffington put an empty glass down in front of McCauley, filled it with soda water from a gun, stuck a lime on the edge, and said, "If you're not having a beer, Del, what can I do you for?" He leaned closer, said conspiratorially, "If there's something I can."

McCauley sipped from the glass and said, "Ever heard of a guy named Enfield Higgins?"

Huffington pushed up from his forearms and leaned on his palms. He stared hard at the bar, then raised his eyes slowly until they were level with McCauley's. "He's one of us," he said bitterly, "but a shit bag, sad to say."

"He's a painter."

Huffington gave him a wry smile. "No, he's a junkie, a petty thief who happens to have a book in our local. The guy works when it suits him and, from what I can tell, it's only when," counting fingers, "he's out of jail, when he's desperate, when there's nothing 'round left to steal. Why're you asking?"

McCauley said, "Trying to help a friend get something back that was stolen."

"Higgins?"

McCauley nodded. "Higgins and *company*. What about Dinny McLintock, what do you know about him?"

Huffington folded his fists alongside his temples, bobbed and weaved like a fighter, while he barked like an announcer. "There it is, folks, today the big man's landing a plethora of vicious combos on his cousin, double hooks, uppercuts, all solid, but the cuz is still on his feet." He cupped his mouth and made the crowd sound, stopped, and dropped his hands. He exaggerated slumping his shoulders. "Ya got me, Del, geez, it's embarrassing, but McLintock is one of us too."

"Catchy Davis?"

Huffington glanced at Kiley, rested his forearms on the bar, hunching over closer to McCauley. "Him too. What the hell's going on here?" he said.

"Like I told you, I'm helping a friend get his property back. You got an address for the guy?"

"Higgins?"

"No, he's up in MCI Norfolk, Catchy."

Huffington slapped the bar, said, "I can help you there. Heard he just got out of the can, he should be looking for work. I can ring up the hall for his last known address, see if he might have a new one. Since he just got out, he'd have to reregister with us, you know, for mailing purposes: notices of union elections, the monthly magazine, that type of stuff."

McCauley looked down the bar at Kiley as Huffington turned and grabbed the phone off the wall. Kiley, both hands wrapped around his glass, watched him in the mirror.

"Junkies are nothin' but trouble," he muttered, picked the glass up an inch, put it back down. He stared at McCauley. He said, "They can say what they want about Marty Fallon, but in the old days, maggots like them wouldn't have been heard from or seen." He took a hit from the glass and nodded. "Bet your *arse* on that." Shook his head. He said, "Junkies in *Southie*, Jesus H. Christ."

Huffington hung up the phone, finished scribbling on the small yellow pad.

"Here, Catchy's got a Quincy address, think he lives with his girlfriend," he said, placing the sticky on the back of McCauley's hand.

"Taylor Street," McCauley said, holding it out, studying it. "Think it's off Beale, had a girlfriend once who lived around there." He slipped it into his pocket.

Huffington rubbed his hands together like he was working in soap. "Now the bull work is done." He bent over slightly, slid open the top to the cooler, pulled out a frosted glass, wiggled it.

"Sure you won't join me?" he said, turning and pulling himself a sixteen-ounce Sam Adams. Kiley groaned, pushed away from the bar, with the screech of chair legs on hardwood. He pinched up his face like he'd sucked an old lemon.

He said, "Owww! Would it be accurate to say, Huffy, you ain't pulling *yourself* a bel-chun, because you're savin' it all for the *kids*?" Turning, he headed for the men's room.

Huffington stared at his back, sipped his beer, wiped his mouth with the back of his hand. "About as accurate as you are when you piss, Kiley. Try to get some in the toilet this time."

Kiley flipped him the bird over his shoulder before yanking the handle of the creaky door in the corner. Huffington shook his head as it slammed.

"That old son-of-a-bitch's worth a fortune, could buy and sell me a dozen times over. Got three bars of his own, yet he's a regular down here. He comes in almost every day, just to piss me off." He grinned. "I don't mind, he's just a character, Del, not a bad sort, though you might differ with me on that point."

McCauley shook his head. "Nope," he said, "I've got nothing against Kiley. Did his time just like me. Besides, Kiley was just a bookie, not a leg breaker. Heard he rarely used them. He was never into the violent stuff."

As a cop, McCauley wouldn't have messed with the guy, if

someone above him hadn't given the order. But they had because, for some, it was just about headlines, how far a big bust can push you up the ladder.

Huffington seemed to get it, but McCauley drove the point home.

McCauley snapped open an imaginary newspaper. "Front page *Boston Globe* reads, 'Mob Bookie Tied to Irish Gang Chief Marty Fallon Busted!" Fluttered his open hands alongside his head. "Oooowwwoooo," Like he'd seen a ghost.

"As soon as you mention the word 'mob,' John Q. Citizen gets the chills, then he gets a woody, either for it or against it, though without him, the mob couldn't exist. It's Johnny Boy who places his bets with the wiseguys, borrows money, plays their numbers, buys their dope, their women, hot merchandise. It's one big happy circle jerk.

"No, Kiley wasn't a gangster, bookies rarely are. Just a successful pencil pusher with a head for numbers." McCauley tossed up his hands. "The damn *lottery* replaced him. All they did was pass a few laws, now the state's taking the money instead of guys like him. Seen your taxes gone down?" McCauley snorted.

Huffington stared at him sadly like he was reading a memoriam for an old friend off an obituary page. Before speaking, he swiped his mouth with his fingers.

"The old days are gone," he said sadly.

McCauley lifted his glass. "To the old days, the good guys and bad." Gave a nod. "They're gone," he said, and took a sip.

Huffington sighed. His shoulders heaved, he belched, put his beer down on the bar. Pressing his palms flat on it, he lowered his voice and said, "Not everything from the old days was good," subtly nodding, eyes tracking past the front window to the door.

Behind him, McCauley heard the door open and two sets of shoes shuffle in, leaving the door open. Nicotine addicts searching for an inexpensive fix? He subtly dropped one hand to his pocket cupping something, brought it back up to the bar.

On the street outside, one of those low-riding clown cars went past, the bottomless base of some hip-hop song throbbing from it rattling things loose. In the distance the diminishing sound of a siren when somebody finally spoke.

"Hey, tough guy, seen your little Mustang outside. Little early to be drinkin', ain't it? Or maybe you need it to get up your balls."

Huffington blinked like he'd just used Visine. Pressed down on the bar to stop his arms from shaking.

Like his lungs were clawing for air, he said, "We don't want any trouble here, Mike." McCauley turned in the chair and stared towards the front.

Mike Janowski stared back. "Ya's don't, huh? Tell ya somethin', fuck face . . . *we* already got it," he said.

FORTY-TWO

MIKE JANOWSKI, DRESSED IN A WHITE Polo long-sleeve, the collar turned up, outside his designer jeans, a pair of black suede high-tops, stood facing the cigarette machine. He made it obvious he was reading the sign. Next to him, Flippy Condon with a grin like he had searched for his car keys and found them.

McCauley's eye went from their eyes to their hands. Relieved, at this point, they were empty.

"Sellin' 'em cheap," Janowski said, turning his head, staring. "Picked 'em up hot, Huffy, where?"

Huffington straightened. "Uh," he said, scratching his forearm, "no disrespect, Mike, but its kinda my business, I'm not known as a rat." He glanced at the back of McCauley's head.

Janowski and Flippy smirked at each other. "Good," Janowski said, nodding. "Ain't a rat, huh? Gonna *call* you on that later," he said. Wink.

McCauley was half turned in the seat, arm on the bar, facing Janowski. Had slipped the knife from his pocket under the bar towel.

Like he caught something, Janowski tilted his head to the side.

"Under the bar rag, cop, whaddaya got, a piece?" he said mockingly. Looked at his partner. "Naw, couldn't have, Flippy, wanna know why?" He pointed at McCauley. "Because the bum don't got a *license*. No license — poor-little-cop." Pouted, then grinned.

Pressing his palms together, Huffington said, "Maybe get you guys something to drink? How 'bout a cold beer. Got some new stuff here . . . think you'll like . . . *all* the young guys seem to." He slid back the cooler top, reached down for a glass.

In one quick motion Janowski pushed off the machine and, dropping his hand to his belt, he lifted his shirt and rested his hand on the butt of the gun there. "Huffy," he snarled, "fucking hands . . . where I can *see* 'em . . . now!"

Like he had grabbed a lit fuse, Huffington jerked his hands towards his chest. "Jesus, Mike, no guns, please. Whaddaya? Dough? I already kicked into Jackie — the new guy, Touchy? Touchy picked up Jackie's kiss a day, day and a half ago. I never been late, never." He gave McCauley a can-you-back-me-up look.

The two gangsters walked farther into the room. Janowski looking right then left, bending, looking under the tables, then focusing again on the bar. He said matter-of-factly, "Imagine that, Flip. Huffy's never been late. And ya know why's that?"

Flippy locked his gaze on McCauley, pulled a spring-loaded blackjack from his pocket and shrugged.

"Because if Huffy was late . . . he'd be *the* late. And ya know that, Huffy, don't ya?" The gangsters looked at each other and cackled. The break McCauley needed to use his thumb to half-open the blade.

Keeping his hand on the rubber grip of the gun jutting out above his right pocket, Janowski covered the room with his gaze, lingering on the drop ceiling like he was counting the squares. Twisting his lips into a crooked grin, he said dreamily, "Hear that, Flippy?"

Flippy responded with two slow nods. "Bet I can, Mike."

Janowski lowered his gaze to McCauley.

"What about you, McCauley, can you?"

McCauley couldn't hear a thing, but apparently neither could Janowski, as he clicked the knife open.

Huffington choked, "Mike, please, I . . ."

Janowski slashed the air with the edge of his hand and growled, "You, shut the fuck up," then, softer, "you're ruinin' the song." His eyes grew glassy as he focused on nothing, rolled his head listening.

"Yep, she's singin', all right," Janowski said with grim certainty. Pursing his lips, he pulled the gun from his pants. "Not a great voice, no Celine, what's her face, but distinct — the fat lady, McCauley — I'm surprised you can't hear."

The phone on McCauley's hip rang. Janowski jerked up the gun, pointed it at McCauley's head, and waved a finger.

"No, no, noooo, don't answer it," he said, cupping the gun butt with the other hand now. Frowned. "Anyways, you're all out of answers, McCauley."

The phone rang twice more before it was silent, but the distraction allowed McCauley to get both feet on the floor. In his head he could hear Doctor Mario's voice — get within fifteen feet of a target, even a guy with a gun, he was dead. He was still too far away. He had to get Janowski closer.

Janowski dropped the gun to his side with a disappointed face. He said, "Huffy, why the long face? I ain't gonna kill *you* — I'm gonna kill *him*. You'll just catch a beatin' for consorting kind of."

Flippy gave Janowski's shoulder a pat, then turned and walked back towards the door. Closing it, he stood there blocking the entrance, glancing over his shoulder through the window every couple of seconds.

McCauley said, "You're tough with a gun, Janowski, but it's the only thing that makes you."

Janowski's features contorted, his entire face darkened. "You fucking punk," he roared, lashing out at a chair with his foot. It skittered across the floor, ricocheted off the bar, and crashed onto its side. He edged himself closer. "Spent a lifetime taking apart maggots like you."

Just a little bit closer.

Glancing over his shoulder at Flippy, he said, "He's acting like this because of back at the Pen." Glared at McCauley. "Takin' *kindness* for weakness . . . aren't ya, *tough* guy." Swung the gun level with McCauley's face. "You got lucky at the Pen, you *ain't* lucky now." He cocked back the hammer.

Huffington covered his head with his hands and crouched. "Oh, Jesus, Mike, no don't — pp-lease," he moaned to the floor.

An eerie light flickered in Janowski's eyes, like eels were fighting within them. He spoke to the others in a calm, clear voice, like he was ordering a cold beer in August. "Put the blackjack away, Flippy, I changed my mind. I'm killin' them *both*."

Huffington peeked over the top of the bar. He pleaded, "Michael, please, you don't have to do this." Janowski pulled his teeth to his lips and shook his head sadly. "You're wrong, Huf, I *do*." Sighed, took a step closer, jerked the gun towards the ceiling. "Now please, do me a favor and stand?"

The men's room door suddenly swung back on its hinges and Kiley came out tugging up on his fly. Janowski crouched and jerked the gun towards him. He gave a disgusted look and lowered it.

"Kiley? Jesus, Bobby what the fuck are you *doin'*?"

Kiley, indignant, put his hands on his hips. "Pissin'. I'm old, takes *forever* to come out." He glared at Huffington. "Even with good *American* beer." Refocused on Janowski, screwed up his face. "I could ask you the same thing, Michael," he said, shifting his head. Clicking noises came from his disappointed face. "You and your *gun*."

Janowski swung the gun back in McCauley's direction. "It's got nothing to do with you, old man. I'll give you a chance, get out of here now."

Behind him, twitching like a ferret on espresso, Flippy said, "Mike, you said comin' in we'd only do one. There's three of 'em now, I don't like . . ."

"*You*, don't like?" Janowski snarled, trying to look back but keeping his eyes on McCauley. "Who the fuck — like you got *options*? I'll make it four, you keep runnin' your mouth."

Kiley started towards the end of the bar.

"Old man, I told ya to get outta here," Janowski growled. Doubling his grip on the gun, he edged even closer.

Waving him off like he was shooing a fly, Kiley sneered, "Who the hell you think you are, ya pup, you and your bloody *gun*?"

Scooping change and bills off the bar in front of his empty glass. As he stuffed his pockets, he glared at Janowski. "It's your lucky day, Janowski. If I hadn't left all of me back in the toilet, I'd be sprinklin' a few drops on yer shoe."

Continuing down the bar, he stopped in front of where Huffington crouched and said over his shoulder, "And I ain't goin' nowhere, your *majesty*, 'til I get all of my money out of his dump." He tossed two slips on the bar that he pulled from his pocket. He said to the bartender, "Keno, Huffington, winning numbers, you'll cash 'em out now," he said with a nod. He jumped his eyes towards McCauley and winked.

"Last time, you old coot, get outta the way," Janowski raged behind him. Lunging forwards, he grabbed the old man by the shoulder.

Kiley cried, "Jesus, Mary," and threw himself down, pulling Janowski's arm with him.

Everything next happened in seconds.

Rocketing forward, McCauley yanked on the gangster's forearm, swinging the knife in an arc. The blade buried itself deep in the meat of his shoulder and Janowski roared like Godzilla, tried to angle the gun at McCauley's head.

Pull back, get shot, there's no where to go but straight in.

Grabbing the other shoulder, McCauley yanked himself in, driving his forehead into the gangster's face. Janowski's nose made the same sound a turkey wing does when it's wrenched from the bird, and the .380 barked twice, close enough for McCauley to feel the blast in his hair, the rounds penetrating the register, shattering the mirror.

Bending his knees, McCauley dropped a few inches before straightening, twisting into a left uppercut that lifted the gangster's head. Janowski's knees buckled, and the gun hit the floor.

Flippy charged toward them. "You motherfucker!" he screamed, blackjack held high.

Spinning Janowski, McCauley held him locked in a chokehold. Elevating his chin he pressed the knife to his throat while Janowski cursed him wetly through his loosened front teeth.

"Not another step," McCauley barked, stretching Janowski's neck. Flippy squeaked to a stop and lowered the weapon, his dark eyes dancing towards the gun on the floor. McCauley pressed on the blade. "You go for the gun, you'll leave with his head."

Flippy giggled as he jigged the spring-loaded jack in his hand, eyes bouncing from Kiley to Huffington, back to McCauley. "You're talkin' a lot of cutting," he said. Eyes dusting the gun again, he took a step towards it. "Don't think you're up to it."

Lifting the gangster's chin higher, McCauley shoved the tip of the blade in. Janowski shuddered and made gurgling sounds as a stream of claret coursed towards a spreading patch in his collar.

McCauley barked, "Back away, maggot. Any deeper, he talks through a voice box."

"Bck-aaawyy," Janowski bawled, frantically waving his hands.

McCauley never found out what Flippy planned to say next because an empty, long-necked bottle hummed through the air and disintegrated against the side of his face, opening a cut, from hairline to eye, as deep as a Badlands gulley.

Flippy howled and brought his hands to his face, blood gushing between his fingers. He took two steps to the side and went over a chair that splintered beneath him as he crashed to the floor. Pushing up from the floor, Janowski lashed out with his feet but McCauley restrained him, shifting the blade from his neck to a new spot under his eye.

He picked at the lower lid and said into his ear, "How'd you like it cut out on the floor?" And Janowski stopped moving.

Grasping a table, almost tipping it, Flippy pulled himself up just in time to catch another full long-necked Bud off the back of the head. Beer foam mixing with blood, Flippy groaned, took two staggering steps before he dropped to his knees and fell on his face.

Glancing back over his shoulder, McCauley watched Huffington gleefully rubbing his hands together. He blew on his fingertips with a look of amazement. "Gee, Cuz," he said, "thought the fast pitch was gone."

He nervously giggled as he vaulted the bar, picked up the gun, and coolly said to Janowski, "I'm keepin' it, Mike."

Janowski's eyes narrowed into flinty slits. "I'll be back for it . . . and *you*," he said hoarsely.

"Ya," McCauley said, "I'll get you and your little *dog* too."

Loosening his grip on Janowski's neck, McCauley slid the knife to his temple and said, "Speaking of which, I know diddly about dogs, but a little something about licenses." Tightened his grip. "You mentioned before how I don't have one? Remember this."

Sliding his arm from under his chin, he shoved the head savagely forward, tugging back with the knife. The serrated blade carved a bloody channel through skin and hair, severing the top of Janowski's ear.

Falling into a crouch, the wounded man shrieked, "Motherfucker!" as the piece bounced from his shoulder to the floor. "You *mother*-fucker," he said, pulling the hand from his ear, checking the blood on the palm.

Kiley bent down and picked up the cartilage casual, like the other one had just dropped some change. Offered it back. "They say you should keep it on ice," he said softly. Janowski glared as he silently took it. Huffington reached over the bar and grabbed a fistful of ice, turned and offered it to Janowski.

"Move quick enough," McCauley said, "they'll reattach it at Boston Medical."

Janowski spit a bloody lunga on the floor, and grinned at McCauley like he had the knife. Wincing, skidding slightly in his own blood, he helped Flippy off the floor.

He limped towards the door, pushing Flippy in front of him, stopping just before it. Kept his back to the room when he spoke. "You told me, McCauley, I'd be *rememberin'* somethin'." Wiggled the severed piece between a bloody finger and thumb. He said, "*This* what you meant?" and laughed softly.

"No," McCauley said. "This — I don't need a *license* to kill you."

Janowski choked off the laugher. The dead arm hanging by his side like a rope, he twisted around like he was tossing a Frisbee, back-armed the scrap of ear at the bar.

"Neither do I," he said and walked through the door.

FORTY-THREE

McCAULEY HAD TO TALK TO LILLY, needed him in his corner if anything happened. Heading west on Broadway, crossing B Street, he pulled the Mustang over and double-parked next to an empty cab in front of Rondo's sub shop. As he looked for a space, he thought about the conversation he'd just had with Cotter. Told him, after meeting with Lilly, that he'd be heading to the guy's house who he thought had the disc. Before hanging up, in one of those almost-forgot-to-tell-ya moments, mentioned the Teamsters and Mike Janowski. Left out the part where he cut the guy up.

Half a block up, just before Amrhein's parking lot, he watched a battered Chevy pickup, its bed loaded with thick, sheared hunks of electrical cable, their copper cores reflecting the sun, pull out of a space. He pulled up and backed in.

Crossing West Broadway he went through the main door of the squat, fortress-like District Six police building. Inside the lobby, to the left, a young guy sat on a bench filling out a form using a pen attached by a string to the clipboard he held.

He gave McCauley a disgusted look, wiped his nose with the back of his hand, and continued to write. He spoke to the wiggling top of the pen. "Mister, better hope *your* house is alarmed."

McCauley turned from the empty front desk and looked at him over his shoulder. The talker stopped writing and stared at him. Seemed to be glad for the contact.

"I just came back from vacation," he said, "a few days up Winnipesaukee? I walked into the house and found the stove, brand-new, refrigerator, compactor, also brand-new, gone." Looked angrily to the side. "Moved from Brighton to Southie because I was told it was safe." He slapped the pen on the clipboard.

"Junkies. Southie's no safer than Roxbury, from what I can tell." He shook his head and picked up the pen, started to point it, the string snapped taut and it jumped from his hand. He snatched it as it swung by his leg, saying, "Get an alarm is what I can tell ya, get an alarm."

"I'm sorry to hear it," McCauley said, empathizing. "It's not the same Southie I knew as a kid."

A voice behind the desk said, "Sir, can I help you?"

McCauley turned and faced a woman in a Boston police uniform. Thick build, only a little bit shorter than him, her haircut severe, too close on the sides, but her eyes were kind, like she might have taught grade school.

"Well, *I'm* moving to Roxbury," the voice said behind him. "At least there's more *cops* on the street."

The woman cop leaned and peeked over McCauley's shoulder, jumped her eyebrows at him. She said, "When you're finished with the form, Mr. Hogan, I'll have you talk to Detective McKenna, he handles street crime."

"Oh, great," the clipboard guy said. "You're talking opposed to the ones that occur in the *air*?" Then, in a deep voice, "Detective McKenna, where were you yesterday, the day before, *whenever* these rip-off bastards cleaned me out?"

McCauley told the desk officer he was here to see Lilly, was the good captain in? She answered him yes, and you'd like to see him regarding? Lousy coffee, McCauley told her, tell him it's about the coffee. Eyebrows rising, she dialed up the desk phone, kept her eyes on McCauley. Name? When he told her, she said it and stiffened, then a smile graced her face, gaining inches as she nodded, pointed at a door in the corner that buzzed when he got there. She said to his back, up a flight turn right, first door on the left.

McCauley found Lilly sitting behind a big wooden desk. With one hand he sorted papers that were scattered behind his name plate, while the other one rested on a Rolodex filled with photos. He was gazing at one of them. Lilly's oldest son and him, graduation day, Boston College, one year before. The kid had no interest in becoming a cop, got a business degree, wanted to be a millionaire and that was okay with him. These days, between college incentives, overtime, and paid details, you could only become *half* a millionaire being a cop. Lilly could live with it.

He slapped the desk and said, "I've been sucked in. You come by empty-handed, where's the damn coffee?"

"Didn't want to get your nerve endings tingling," McCauley answered, pulling a cheap metal chair from the wall to his desk, dropping in it. "Figured after hearing what I came here to tell you, your nerves would be jiggy enough."

Lilly rolled his eyes.

McCauley told him about the Teamster's, focusing on why he had gone there and what he hoped to find out. Then he told him about Janowski walking in on the party.

When he finished, Lilly threw up his hands. He said, "Why're you telling me this, Del?" turning his head towards a wall filled with badges, police patches, plaques of appreciation from community groups, the feds, FBI and DEA. He returned his attention to McCauley and leaned back in the chair.

"Janowski's a maggot, and it's true you're my friend, but, brother," he looked at the wall, "what you did to him's *mayhem*." Now Lilly extended his arms, palms up towards the ceiling, looked ready to explode but didn't. "Damnit Del, you can't go around *disfiguring* people." As he sat up and straightened his tie, he shifted a framed photo to his left on the desk, his father in a Boston police uniform. He pulled a pen from a mug that said BRAINTREE POLICE and tapped it once on the desk before pointing it at McCauley.

"Christ, mayhem's a twenty-year felony, Del . . . but I'm not going to book you." He shook his head vigorously. "Noooo, I'll pretend I didn't hear it," pointing again, "and you never told me, you got it?"

McCauley nodded, saying all right, he got it, but that he was just sending a message, that he really had wanted to kill Janowski but couldn't. He put his forearms on the desk hunching forward, bugged out his eyes "Because that would be *murder*, Lil, and you just can't go around *murdering* people. Even the ones planning to *kill* you."

He pushed off the desk. "Come *on*," he said wearily, and spread out in the chair. "Janowski sent a message, so I sent one back." He winked at Lilly, "So I slapped on some extra postage, so what?"

Lilly started to rise, dropped back in the seat, muttered, "*Extra postage*, Christ . . . what have I gotten myself into?" He stared at a large color photo on the opposite wall, his father pinning a badge on a much younger, thinner version of himself.

McCauley jumped up. "Gotten *yourself* into? How about me? What the hell have you gotten *me* into?" He planted his palms and leaned on the desk. "I'm minding my business working the bar, then you come along and ask for a favor. Fine, we're friends, fine, I'll always help when I can — but when it comes to defending my life, don't direct me." He shoved off and turned for the door.

"I'm *not* directing," Lilly said to his back. "I just don't want to see your ass in a jam. With a record like yours, Janowski files a complaint — which he won't — but he does, you'll be *lucky* to get another five years."

Lilly stood up, shoved his hands in his pockets, and came around in front of the desk.

"This whole thing's a mess, Del. Maybe it's time to call it a day." He looked at the trophy wall again, intermittently tapping an index finger against a thumb like he was sending a distress code. He looked at McCauley, his hand on the knob, watching him over his shoulder return to his seat. He sat down heavily. "I'll tell Cotter we're attacking this thing from some other way."

McCauley let go of the doorknob and turned, holding up his hand like a student in class. "*Attack?* I can relate to that — I'm *under* one, Lilly." He waved a finger. "And it's not only me, your boy Cotter? A little bird's telling me same the goes for him too."

Lilly looked at him weird. He said, "Cotter's in danger? From who? All right, McCauley, what the hell's going on?"

McCauley walked over to the white board on the wall, grabbed a black marker from a tray at the bottom, and pulled off the top. He printed two names — Higgins and McLintock — and replaced the cap on the marker. He turned and faced Lilly. "Those are your thieves," he said matter-of-factly.

It was clear to McCauley that Lilly recognized the names. He looked disgusted and said, "Drug addicts, Del, both of 'em . . . shitty nickel-and-dimers. But when those guys take a pinch they get public defenders. How'd they know the safe was there?"

"They were part of the crew that painted the building," Mc-Cauley said, "stumbled across it while they were there. Way I figure, a couple of nights later, while working the next floor, they came back and took the safe with them. Probably peeled it, froze it . . ."

"*Froze* it, what're you talking?"

"Small safe like that," McCauley said, "they'll freeze it by emptying one of those big CO_2 fire extinguishers on it. Right after they whack it with a twelve-pound sledge, thing cracks into pieces like pottery." McCauley smirked. "Surprised you don't know about freezing, Lilly, how long you been a cop?"

Lilly frowned and made a masturbation sign with his hand. He said, "Tell me more, Sherlock."

"That's about it," McCauley said. "After peeling the safe, they split up the spoils, which, money-wise, was chump change." He rubbed his hands together. "But there was just one more thing."

"Ya?" Lilly now motioning give-it-to-me with his hands.

Touching a finger and thumb together McCauley made a circle. "A CD," he said.

Lilly squinted, at him. "A CD?" he said, like that's all there was?

"And your buddy-boy, Cotter, told me what's on it."

"*And*?" The hands motioned McCauley again. "I'm not your dentist, McCauley, I don't like to pull teeth."

"A record," McCauley said, "a record of what Cotter wants no one to see: dates, times, people, places, amounts of money exchanged."

Lilly slapped the top of the desk and said, "A record of *what*, between who?"

"Seems a while back, Cotter, his daddy, and a gaggle of city hall hacks, bigshots, some of them still holding office, climbed into the sack with some shady developers."

"Remember back a few years down on the waterfront? The big mixed use — you know, high-priced condos, health clubs — retail complexes going in? Believe me, these guys do too. It seems Cotter and company fast-tracked those big jobs by doing an end run around the rules."

"How?"

McCauley jabbed with his finger. "By ignoring environmental impact studies and altering engineering reports. And once the jobs were up and running, by using substandard materials: watery concrete, number eight re-bar when the specs call for three, pressed-wood paneling instead of the real stuff. You want me to keep going?"

Lilly said, "They got away with it how? The jobs were all union, someone had to see something."

"The unions?" McCauley rolled his eyes. "They took *care* of the unions, the BA's who controlled the big locals. Each got a kiss, a fat envelope, twice a year in the mail. When it came to the pit bulls at Inspectional Services, the developers utilized their clout to rein them in. The projects were completed on time and under budget, which gave them tens of millions in gravy. The money ran in rivers and everyone was happy . . . until now."

Lilly pressed his knuckles into his eyes, dropped his chin to his chest. He said, "Knew I should have gone to Aruba. I've got a friend with a time-share. For the cost of the plane fare I could have gone with the wife. But she told me nooooo, no one goes to Aruba in October. Noooooo . . . Christ, I wish I went to Aruba."

"Sure it's too late?"

"Too late for that, but not for this," Lilly said, his fingertips now kneading the bridge of his nose.

McCauley looked at him, puzzled. He said, "What do you mean, *this*? You're losing me."

Lilly continued squeezing, kept his eyes closed as he talked. "I was worried there might be something about me on the disc."

McCauley's gut jumped. "About *you*?"

Lilly opened his eyes, dug a thumb into his chest, nodded, and said, "Me."

He turned just his head, stared at the blank TV on the wall. His eyes drifted back to McCauley's.

"When Cotter told me there was something in that safe that, if it saw daylight, would create major problems . . . it started me thinking." Lilly looked at his lap, the eyes slowly rising. He said, "I could be part of that crowd."

The blood seemed to drain from McCauley's legs and he had to sit down. Christ, what's he planning to drop on me now?

Lilly continued. "I mentioned my kid, how he got into trouble years ago and Cotter helped him?" Pulling himself closer to the desk, he reached around and faced the Rolodex towards Mc-Cauley and tapped a photo.

McCauley leaned towards it, his fingertips steadying the edge of the picture, a handsome kid in a maroon robe, black mortarboard hat, standing next to a grinning guy in a suit. "Me and my son, Sean," Lilly said, "graduation day from Boston College last year. He's got a great job in New York now. And if it wasn't for Cotter . . ." Lilly lowered his voice. "If it wasn't for Cotter . . . well, what can I tell you, Del, I owed the guy."

"But you're *paying* him back," McCauley said. "You're helping him now, what's the problem?" Scrutinized the other man's face, swore it grew paler as he watched him anxiously pinching the webbing between his finger and thumb.

"I helped him once before." Lilly said, and gave him a look like there, I've said it, then folded his hands on the desk.

McCauley said, "If you've got something to say, say it."

The hands remained folded as Lilly told him about a Beacon Hill murder nine years before. A socialite shot dead in a Mt. Vernon street apartment. The chief suspect? The boyfriend, Caleb Whitehead III, Lilly said, a rich kid from the North Shore, Manchester-by-the-Sea.

McCauley listened as Lilly explained how, though just a patrolman then and not involved in the case, he got lucky — watched him frown, maybe not so he said — and managed to capture the suspect a week-and-a-half later.

"I'd been assigned to District Four, the South End," Lilly said, settling back in the seat, like the memory relaxed him a little. "Working the three-to-eleven, I had just completed my shift. It was eleven thirty or so when I pulled up to the lights, the corner of Tremont and Dartmouth, in my little Dodge Spirit, remember that car?" McCauley nodded once.

Lilly seemed to think of the car for a moment. "Anyways, next to me, behind the wheel of this old black Mercedes, was a kid, all dreamy-eyed, staring up at the lining, singing to himself. Didn't think it odd, with all the nightclubs around there those days. Figured he'd probably just left one, little buzz on, singing a tune — then it hits me, the face. How I'd seen it before, on the stationhouse wall."

"The Beacon Hill shooter," McCauley said.

Lilly gave a deep nod, straightened against the back of the chair, put his hand on his gun, and pretended to pull it.

"Before he looked over, I'm out of the car." Lilly's eyebrows arched, he made his eyes bigger. "I came around the back of the Dodge and up the side of his car, real low, tapped the business end of my .38 on the glass near his head." He shook his head at the memory. "The way the kid looked at me, Del, like I'd come up to the window to serve him a drink. He's still got that dreamy-stoned mug, and he's talking to me through the glass, but I can't hear him because I'm *screaming* — Put your hands on the wheel! Put your hands on the wheel!" He nodded. "Good thing he did."

Lilly suddenly jerked in the seat, snatched air towards his chest. "I get the door open and yank the guy out, throw him face-down on the street and snap on the bracelets. Cars are passing me, people are slowing down, scared, staring. I ended up flagging a cabby, yelling, call it in for me, will ya?" Lilly grinned. "Cruisers screamed to the scene for the next fifteen minutes."

He turned his head and blankly stared out the window, a skyline of three- and four-story buildings that rolled towards the ocean, said to the glass, "You know they put me in for the Hannah Award? Some guy that saved three kids in a fire, bumped me the last minute." Shrugged.

McCauley said gently, "Hey Lil, that's a great story, but what's the tie-in with Cotter?"

Without turning his head, Lilly held up his hand like it was coming, hold on.

He turned back to McCauley. "Three days later, I get a call at the station house. Seems the kid's father had retained Cotter to defend him." Grabbed the arms of the chair and shifted position.

"I thought it unusual, ya, I mean the fact he had wanted to talk with me. Normally, something like that occurs, I'd refer them to the D.A., but it was Cotter . . . hey, the guy helped my kid."

"You agreed to meet him."

Lilly nodded. "I did and met him at a little place called the Penguin Café, near Brigham Circle, you know, near the hospital?" Lilly made circles with his finger near his temple. "Over a slice of pizza, he's telling me he's preparing an *insanity* defense, wants to know what my observations were that night."

"Observations? But everything was in your report."

Lilly nodded, agreeing. "Of course it was, Whitehead was either high or drunk and singing to the roof when I saw him. Cotter read it."

"They blood-test Whitehead after the bust?"

Lilly shook his head. "That's the thing, no. He was asked if he'd been drinking or under the influence of drugs, but Whitehead was a smart kid, as *well* as a rich kid, and would only give us his name, then he waited for counsel."

"So, Cotter's angle, what was it?"

"He asked me, instead of singing, do you think Whitehead might have been *talking* — to himself, you know, like delusional?"

Lilly told McCauley that the kid looked high, drunk, whatever, and was definitely singing. But Cotter said there was no proof he was either.

"If he wasn't singing," McCauley said, "chatting it up alone in a car late at night might lead a reasonable person to believe he was nuts."

Lilly extended his arms over the desk and lifted his palms towards the ceiling. "Exactly," he said.

Forearms on the desk now, Lilly hunched over them. "He didn't ask me directly to lie for him, Del — which I wouldn't have — but did ask if there was a *possibility* I'd made a mistake, saying, You had just finished your shift. Had made an arrest earlier that day, a suspect in an attempted armed robbery at the Upton Spa. You interviewed witnesses, completed hours of paperwork, it was late, you were tired. At the lights, when you looked over at Whitehead, wasn't it possible he was talking and not singing to himself?

Lilly sank back in the seat, absently played with the end of his tie.

"Knew exactly what he was looking for, Del. Didn't say I would, but, in the end, when it came time for trial, I gave in."

Shook his head. "Turns out, even if I hadn't, there's good chance he still would have won."

"Cotter's that good?"

Lilly threw up the tie, then his hands. "I don't know, I can't figure it. Defense psychiatrists testified that Whitehead was looney, *gone* then, which came as a complete surprise, the state prosecution shrinks agreed. Me testifying that he *could have* been sitting there talking to himself just kind of clinched it."

McCauley got up and went over to a wall with two diplomas on it framed in black plastic. Lilly's criminal justice degrees from Northeastern. McCauley said, "I read recently in the *Herald* that Whitehead's been murdered," turning slightly to look back over his shoulder.

Lilly nodded as the phone on the desk rang. He picked it up and said, "Lilly," and looked at his watch. "Headquarters at two, I'll be there," he said, "but tell him *he's* buying the coffee." He hung up and looked at McCauley.

"I'm aware of it, yes, but he's not the only one. A guy named Ciampa, Michael P., formerly of Nahant, got himself shot and hacked to death a few days ago in a parking lot in Weymouth." Lilly picked up a pencil and tapped the eraser end on the desk.

"There's a connection to Whitehead?"

"Could be. Four, maybe five years ago, Ciampa, another rich kid, his dad's in construction, was found not guilty by reason of insanity for a murder he committed in Cohasset."

"There's the connection."

Lilly dropped the pencil, fluttered his hand over it. "At this point, I don't know. Maybe it's karma, what goes around comes around?" He shrugged, picked up the pencil again. "Maybe it's more."

"More, like maybe Cotter defended them *both*?"

Lilly kept his eyes on McCauley as he picked up the phone. "You never know . . . it's something I could check."

Holding a thumb and finger to his ear, McCauley said, "You find anything, give me a buzz." Walked to the door, opened it. Turning, he said, "In the meantime, I'm catching up with Catchy."

"Yeah, what's with Catchy?" Lilly said, cradling the phone on his shoulder.

"I want to talk to him."

"*Talk* to him."

"Ya, he's got the disc, I'll talk to him *good.*"

Lilly got up and came around the front of the desk. He folded his arms, resting his butt on the edge. Said, looking up like he was reading off a sheet in his head, "Ernest 'Catchy' Davis, a local *boyo* known to us, Ya. Basic pond scum: small-time coke hustler, credit card fraud, uttering, got a history of tail-gating trucks. He's a real psycho who loves using knives, but when he does, usually gets caught. Done a couple of state bids because of his violent propensity." He focused on McCauley again. "If he's got the disc, how did he get it?"

"Ennie Higgins may be a dirt bag, but he isn't a dummy," McCauley said. "After scanning the disc, I figure he knew he had something, so he tested the waters and gave Cotter a call to get his reaction — I was there when he did. You should have *seen* his reaction."

"But his big blackmail plan went kaput when Higgins screwed up his parole and got his ass lugged to Norfolk. While there, he banged into Davis and gave him the whole skinny."

Lilly shook his head and reached behind him, moved papers around the desk. "I've got some paperwork on Davis," he said, making a face, "*somewhere*, fucking desk's a mess."

He turned back to McCauley. "Anyways, last report a couple of stoolies, bar flies down at Sullivan's Pub, put him with McLintock the night he was killed. Maybe the last one who saw him alive, we'd *love* to talk to him too." He pointed at McCauley. "It's a homicide, Del, you know where he is, you gotta tell me."

McCauley grinned and made the time-out sign with his hands. He said, "Hold on, there, gunpowder, you're moving too fast. I know where he is, got an address at least, and I'll give it to you, *after* I talk to him."

"The disc, you think he's still got it?"

McCauley nodded and said, "It's looking that way. After Davis got out of the can, McLintock was the first one he hooked up with. How come? When little birds told me they weren't exactly friends."

He walked over to the second-floor window, gazed down on

West Broadway, following the road in-town until his head touched the glass. Focused on a building on the corner diagonally up the street. "I hear they're doing a gut job on Amrhein's. Any word when it opens?"

Lilly came over and stood alongside him and looked where he was. "They're saying sometime in November." Looked at McCauley. "You're thinking Higgins gave Catchy the scoop on the disc?"

McCauley nodded and faced him. "Ya, and Catchy liked what he heard and knew it was worth something. Hell, he's a guy coming out after doing a seven-year bid, seemed like easy money, far as he was concerned."

"But to kill a guy over something when you're not certain of its value?" Lilly said. "It doesn't make sense."

McCauley returned his attention outside, watched a pair of gulls riding the currents in an almost cloudless sky. He said, "That's only because you're using your own morality as a barometer to measure a guy's from another dimension. You're a cop, and cops think they know about prison because that's where they send guys." Still watching the birds, figuring they had to be over the Postal Annex now. He waved a finger back at Lilly. "But you're fooling yourself."

"When you're in that world, the outside world stops, your priorities become twisted like a Gordian knot. The old rule book's been tossed, you're reduced to a number, and the first rule you learn is, your life is worth nothing."

"For years, Catchy Davis lived in places like MCI Walpole, OCCC, Gardner, and Norfolk, working some lousy walks and grounds job for a dollar-fifty a day. He put up with the monotony, the constant noise, the harassment from screws and other inmates, until finally he wrapped up his bid. When he walked out the door, I guarantee he was angry . . . and broke."

"It wouldn't take much to make a guy like him happy. He must have taken Higgins's word the disc was worth something, how much or how little, he hadn't a clue, and hooked up with McLintock and became his best buddy — if for only one night. He gets McLintock whacked out on drugs, lures him back to his place, and when he got what he wanted, he clipped him."

Lilly nodded. "Must have done it without warning, there was no sign of a struggle."

"Guys like Janowski and Davis generally don't give any," McCauley said. "These days, neither will I."

There was a smear of worry on Lilly's face. "Here's a suggestion," he said, "back away from it, Del, you've done enough. Let me have Davis's address and I'll grab him and the disc if he's got it."

McCauley was thinking, What don't you get? "Walk away?" he said. "Now? It's a little too late, don't you think? I walk away now, think Janowski will too? When you asked me to help, you knew I was in for a penny." He shook his head grimly. "Now, it looks like I'm in for a pound. Besides there could be others out there looking for this, what if Cotter lied about its contents? What if you're *on* it?"

Lilly stared at him. "You said *others*, like who?"

"Moses Halloran told me that Janowski and Flippy Condon were down Sullivan's asking about McLintock just before he was killed. How come? They knew he had something but, like wolves on a blood trail, didn't know what they'd find. You said the men leaving McLintock's house got into a green car. Janowski drives a green Lincoln, guaranteed it was them."

Lilly stared at him. "Think they killed him?"

McCauley shook his head. "No. They went there to get something — bust him up they had to — but, my guess, he was already dead. Will this stop them from looking?" He shook his head. "No more games, I'm taking the offensive."

"You already cut off a guy's ear, you got other plans, don't tell me."

"That was a warm-up," McCauley said, tugging the door towards him. "See, I learned some things in the can. One, got a problem with someone? Hunt them down *first*. Two, never give anyone your game plan."

He stepped through it and turned. He said, "I'm off to catch Catchy. You come up with something that connects Cotter to the dead NGIs, give me a call."

"You got it," Lilly said, lifting the phone from his shoulder, tapping the keypad. He pointed over his desk at McCauley's back and shouted, "Just *talk* to him, Del, hear? Nothing more. Then call me, because we're next up at bat."

CHAPTER FORTY-FOUR

A S HE WALKED FROM THE STORE, Catchy Davis hugged the brown paper bag close to his chest thinking the nerve fucking chinks, looking at him like that. His girlfriend, Leda, telling him before that they weren't chinks, fucking Korreans, she said.

The store, Suzy's Market in Quincy, the corner of Beale Street and Safford, used to be Louie's Variety, belonged to a little Jew named Daitch. Catchy grew up in that store, bought comic books there, *Treasure Hunter's Monthly*, penny candy from a big glass display case, the old man patiently handing you choices, mixing vanilla Cokes with a long silver spoon.

About the time he sprouted hair on his face, Lebanese took it over, and lasted until he graduated high school. Then the Koreans came in.

Catchy didn't like the way they gave him the look, suspicious, like he was stealing. Caught him only once before. Boy steal, boy no come back. Ya? Boy come back after doing a seven-year bid.

And the little slanty-eyed bastards recognized him.

Catchy switched the bag to the other arm and reached under the shirt he wore outside his pants. Tuna cans, tucked in at the underwear line left red rings on the stomach. Plopped the Bumblebees into the bag. Fuck them chinks, he spit out his gum.

Following Beale west, he turned right at the school, half a block down he came in through the front door of 182 Taylor, a charcoal-gray single-family across from a playground. Leda in the kitchen in the back of the house, water running, dishes clinking. Her voice, "That you, Catch?" coming up the hall.

Catchy walked to the front window and looked up the street, down it, dropped the bag on a rust-colored armchair, fabric tape covering the tears in the back, saying, "No, it's the *Cuban* you used to go out with."

"Never went oo-ut with no Cuu-ban," Leda sang from the kitchen, the water turning on and off, the pipes banging inside of the walls.

"Spoke Spanish like a spic," Catchy said, looking through the window again, north now towards Brooks Street.

At the end of the hall in the doorway of the kitchen Leda stood drying a dish, said, "Spics ain't Cuban, they're spics. *Carlos* was from Spain."

"Long as it wasn't a chink," Catchy said, coming towards her, pulling out a white-and-blue bread bag with balloons all over it and a large bag of chips from the bag.

Putting them down on the kitchen table, he said, "I'm hungry, how 'bout some tuna? Got everything we need."

Leda passed him in the hall, Catchy slapping her ass after she swatted him with the towel. "You're *fresh*, you know that?" Leda said over her shoulder.

"Hungry too, want tuna or no?" Catchy said, turning, watching her disappear through a square in the wall. He opened the chips.

"Gonna make tuna, gonna need mayo," Leda's voice said from the bedroom.

"When I was out," crunching some chips in his mouth, "anyone call?"

"Ya, like who?" Leda said, the sound of pillows being fluffed from the bedroom, "no one on the planet knows that you're here."

"Right answer, that's why I love ya," Catchy said, tugging open the fridge. Making a face. "Ain't shitting, ain't got any mayo." Counting his fingers. "Lots of beer, though, bologna, rotten lettuce . . . *cat food*?" He looked around. "You gotta . . . where's it at?" Frowned. "Macaroni in an open plastic bowl? Hey, ain't you supposed to *cover* this shit?"

Leda, behind him in the doorway now, folded her arms and tapped her foot. "*You're* worried about covers? How 'bout fresh outta the joint I'm coverin' your ass . . . with a *roof*."

Catchy grinned and held up a finger. "Point taken," he said. Fresh little bitch, one good score, never see me again.

"Hon," he said calmly, closing the door, "think maybe you run to the store, get us some mayo?"

With her hands on her hips and a tiny stamp of the foot, Leda said, "Hey, I ain't your maid. Those things . . . growin' outta your waist? Use 'em to drag you back where you were."

Catchy waved the tuna. "Honey, look, already spent every dime I had, think this shit's cheap? Besides, them slant-eyes don't like me up there. They make some crack I can't understand, have to demonstrate kung-fu don't stand up to a knife. You *want* that, I'll go back for the mayo — may-*be* go back to the can." He stared at her doggy-eyed. "You really want that, baby?"

Leda, melting, coming over, sliding her arms under his, pulling him close, nuzzling his neck, pulling his arms up around her. "You're right, Catchy, you stay here, I'll get the mayo. Besides, I'm all outta of ciggys." She pulled her head back, scowled at him. "Wouldn't be if you wasn't stealin' my butts . . . and you talked about quitting."

Catchy nodded. "I'm gonna," he said. "When I get me some dough, I'll make an appointment to see the Mad Russian."

Leda looked at him, confused.

With his fingers Catchy made circles in front of his eyes. "He's a hypnotist, up in Brookline, I think, stops ya from smokin'. Waves a watch in your face, abracadabra — zoom, bing — ain't stealin' your butts anymore."

Leda, amazed, pushing an arm's length away, staring into his eyes. "A hypnotist, yeah? Seen them on the telly, they put you in a trance, make you do things you don't want to, like barkin' or walking like a chicken. Think it will work?"

Catchy solemnly nodded. "Has for some guys," he said, brightened. "It don't, could still pick up some tricks while I'm there."

Leda stepped closer, narrowing her eyes, she said, "What kind of *tricks*?"

Catchy grinned slyly. "You said a hypnotist can make you do things you don't want to? Maybe I'll have him teach *me* how to get *you* to take off your clothes." Making an oooo-weee noise, and circling her face with his fingers again.

Leda covered her mouth in mock horror, shook a finger at him as she backed up the hall. "Figures, same thing that's on every guy's mind." She changed her expression, began to walk towards him, accentuating the swing of her hips. "By the way, what makes you think I don't *want* to?"

Tilting his head, leering, Catchy rushed towards her. She squealed as he scooped her up in his arms, spun her in circles.

"Please Catchy, all right, all right, I'll take off my clothes," she said, laughing. "Don't need no Mad Russian for that."

He pressed his face to her neck, growled, kissing her there, put her down facing the door. "Honey, go get the butts and the mayo, okay?" he said, little slap on the ass. "I'll grind the tuna and after we eat, you can *show* me how you don't need a Russian for that."

Ask anyone, the Big Dig hadn't made anything easier. These days, getting onto the expressway, north or south, from the end of West Broadway, never before a problem, now McCauley almost needed a map. Passing over the Fourth Street Bridge, going under the highway, turning left onto Albany Street, he followed a maze-like configuration that eventually funneled him to 93 South. Accelerating between Jersey barriers onto the expressway past the Fortress, the huge inflatable gray padlock in front rippling in the breeze, he thought about Mackey, how now he had a reason to call her.

True, she'd only been on Cotter's payroll for a week, knew nothing about the disc, but she could be in danger. He thought about Cotter and his possible connection to two murder victims. About McLintock, was he killed for the disc? Passing beneath the Savin Hill overpass, he tightened his grip on the wheel. Decided to call Mackey, grabbed his phone off the passenger seat.

Five rings later, she hadn't picked up but, as he wondered what to leave for a message, she suddenly did.

"Del," Mackey said, "what a pleasant surprise." McCauley felt good as cars in the same lane ahead of him accelerated, one after the other, around a slow-moving truck.

"Got a moment to talk?" he said, down-shifted to second and stomped on the gas, the howl of the Paxton supercharger almost drowning out her response.

Turns out she did, telling him, "I'm sitting on what you'd call a stakeout." Paused for a second. Asked if he was okay, was anything up?

The exit at Neponset coming up fast, McCauley mentioned the Teamsters, his run-in with Janowski. The stress was evident in Mackey's voice when she said he had to go to the police. Then he told her about Lilly.

He mentioned the CD, but not what was on it. About Cotter's possible connection to two recent murder victims. That both had been charged with first-degree murder, then later been adjudicated insane by the court.

Now Mackey gasped. She said, "*Both?*"

McCauley said, "Cotter was council for one, we're trying to find out if it was both." He said, "I'm not trying to scare you, but there's a good chance somebody's already been killed over this thing."

"Who was killed, over what?"

He took the Neponset exit and told her.

Passing a strip mall, McCauley went under the 93 North overpass, over the bridge and stayed right, took the Hancock Street exit.

"The killer," Mackey said, "you know who it is?"

"I think so," McCauley said, "I'm on my way to meet him now." Bearing right at the bottom of the ramp, the throaty exhaust of the Mustang's 5.0 engine accelerating into Newport Avenue's only curve.

"Del, you're crazy, let the police handle this."

"You're right."

"You'll let the police?'

"No, I'm crazy. I'll call you later." He tossed the phone on the seat.

Following Newport Aveenue for a mile, McCauley turned right at the T station onto Brooks Street and followed it until it went across Taylor, banged a U-turn. He pulled over on the corner of Taylor and Brook next to a green chain-link fence. Had a bird's- eye view of 182 Taylor, the address that Huffington gave him.

Timing is everything.

He'd just killed the engine when the front door swung open

and out stepped a twenty-something brunette: tanned and petite, tight-fitting pink T-shirt, white low-cut shorts, long legs toned like a runner's, pink flip-flops. She held the door open with the edge of her foot, accentuating the muscular curve of her butt as she said something to someone inside. Big smile, blowing a kiss, she turned for the stairs as the inside door closed.

Descending, she stopped in the middle and opened her pocketbook and pulled out what looked like a wallet. She opened and closed it, continuing down, turning left at the sidewalk heading south towards Beale.

When she had gotten to the end of the block, across from the school, McCauley reached back between the seats and grabbed the canvas bag off the floor, with the laptop protruding, and got out of the car. Pressed the door gently shut and crossed the street, following the sidewalk down.

On the opposite side of the street, a row of tidy houses sprouted up to the edge of an asphalt playground, from somewhere within it, children's laughter, the echo of a basketball bouncing.

As McCauley got close to the house, he checked the windows, no movement of the blinds to indicate somebody watching, he climbed the white steps and pulled opened the storm door, put the bag down in front of it, and knocked on the door. Inside, footsteps approached.

"Ya, what?" a gruff voice said through the wood. "Who is it?"

"Quincy water and sewer, got a leak in your basement?"

"Got a leak . . . what? Who told you we got . . ."

"Says here," McCauley said, "number one eighty-four, pressurized water coming in through the wall, probably a broken main in the street. It's pooling out here by the curb."

"First off, this one eighty-*two*," Catchy said, angrily ripping open the door, glaring. "What you talkin' about, *pooling*?" Looking past him, at the bag, at McCauley again. Inching closer, his hand edging towards the small of his back. "Don't see no water *poolin'* out there." Catchy's eyes narrowed. "Know guys that do and you don't *look* like you work for the city."

"Used to," McCauley said, pointing up, Catchy's eyes following the finger. McCauley bent slightly, crossed the threshold and twisted into a right uppercut that caught Catchy square on the chin. With a sigh, Catchy collapsed into the door frame, Mc-Cauley bounced a short left hook off his temple to finish him off.

"Actually, I worked for the *state*," McCauley said, bending and dragging Catchy from under the armpits into the house.

Catchy woke up on the floor on his side with hands tied behind him. The first thing he thought was, What the hell hit me? The side of his face felt like he'd slept on a golf ball. Second was the heat.

October and in the middle of Indian summer it had to be eighty outside, with the breeze from the ceiling fan barely making it down. Moving just his eyes, taking in McCauley's workbag a few feet away, he shifted them to the open laptop on the orange chair by the window.

Tried to remain calm.

Until the floor creaked behind him and a five-inch folding knife chunged into the wood near his chin. Footsteps, and a pair of black suede Air Jordans stopped in front of his face, a hand reached down twisted and pulled out the blade.

Catchy looked up at McCauley. The big, thick-necked dude said, "You weren't planning to use that on me?"

Catchy kicked out with his legs, also secured by tie-wrap, and tried to sit up but only succeeded in flopping around. McCauley bent over, grabbed the front of his shirt, flipping him onto his back, jerked him up close to his face.

"I'm going to ask you this once. The disc you took from McLintock, where is it?"

Hey, how'd this guy . . .?

Twisting his shoulders, Catchy snarled, "I don't know what the fuck you're . . ."

McCauley slammed him into the floor, pinning his chest with his knee, put his full weight behind it. He reached into the tool bag beside him.

Turning his head, Catchy watched McCauley fish through the bag, look down at him, wink. "Hey, what the fuck you got a beef with me, why?" McCauley coming out with a pair of needle-nose pliers.

Holy Jesus. Don't show him no fear. Catchy said, "Hey, motherfucker, I asked you a question. You better . . ."

McCauley grabbed a fistful of hair and savagely twisted the head, slipped the pliers lengthwise onto an ear. "No," he said, "me, *I* ask the questions."

Catchy thinking, Gotta keep this guy talking, said, "What did . . . aar — aarrghh!" McCauley squeezing, the pliers crushing through flesh, he covered Catchy's mouth, pulled him close, whispered into his good ear, "Shssh, don't want the neighbors to hear — the disc."

"Owmmwoohh, Christ, you, you're tearin' it off."

Releasing the grip on the blue-and-,red ear, McCauley shifted the bite inward squeezed harder this time.

Like he was hit with a Taser, Catchy convulsed. "Aaaarrrgh, all right, all right, you son-of-a-bitch, son-of-a . . ." His eyes flooding with tears, he indicated with his head. "The bookshelf over there, next to the dictionary." Closed his eyes, grimaced.

McCauley came back opening a square plastic case. He took out the disc, loaded it into the laptop, stood there tapping the keys with one hand, opened and closed the pliers with the other, looked at Catchy. "This isn't the right one, you've got problems, my friend." Turned back to the screen, leaned closer, examined a folder marked ESH, the lines in his brow growing deeper.

It was a list of eight names.

Some of the names fancy-sounding, like Charlton Brookings and Edmund Fenton Gunn III. Others weren't, like the last one, Michael Ciampa. The murder victim, Lilly said, in Weymouth.

The entire file was some kind of log.

A dollar amount followed each name. After Brookings was five hundred thousand, the amounts increasing after every name. Following the seventh, Caleb Whitehead, was seven hundred thousand. After Ciampa, the last name on the list, one-and-a-half million. Whatever the business was, business was good.

Following the dollar amounts was a single-spaced paragraph detailing what appeared to be arraignment and adjudication dates for each man in Suffolk, Norfolk, and Essex Counties — but there wasn't a clue what the crime was. McCauley knew about Ciampa and had read about Whitehead — figured each must have been charged with first-degree murder.

Brookings had been adjudicated thirteen years earlier; Ciampa, less than two years before. And something McCauley found interesting: each man had received the same finding, NGI — not guilty by reason of insanity — each followed by the letters ESH. McCauley subtly recoiled as he recognized those letters. Edgewater State Hospital, the state maximum-security hospital/prison for the criminally insane.

Tossing the pliers into the bag, McCauley said, "Have you seen this?" Looking at Catchy, the blood running in thin fingers down his ear, cheek, and chin. Turned back to the screen.

"No," Catchy snapped, "I haven't seen nothin'. Just take the damn disc and get out." Squirmed against the restraints, said softer, "You ain't planning to kill me, are ya?"

McCauley ignored him and continued to read what appeared to be some kind of installment plan: dates and times, places where payoffs were made — all to the same person, Dr. Noah Durning.

In Ciampa's case, the first four hundred thousand was paid in Revere across the street from Kelly's Roast Beef, six days after his arraignment. Even described the weather that day. McCauley knew the spot well. On the beach, lots of foot traffic, cars pulling in, pulling out, no one would notice.

The second, three hundred and fifty thousand delivered in Medford, the day after the finding, like all of the rest — not guilty by reason of insanity — in the parking lot of the Glen Meadow Mall. Together they added up to half the amount next to Ciampa's name. Where did the other half go? It didn't take long to figure. McCauley took out the disc.

Catchy tried to sit up, clipped the corner of a low bamboo table, and he fell back onto his side. He looked at McCauley, made a face like a flashbulb went off, gasped, "*Knew* that I knew you, your name's . . . McCauley. Seen you back in the system." His courage dribbling back with the name recognition.

McCauley closed the computer. Trying to play we're-all-convicts here?

"You were just coming into Norfolk, me and Dizzy Riles were going out, got lugged for fighting — not with each other, a couple of spooks. We passed each other in the doorway to the Ad Building that day, remember? Naww, but *he* did. You'd *pinched* him before, and he pointed you out."

Sticking the laptop into the bag, McCauley rummaged around

the bottom and came out with an industrial razor blade still in the brown paper wrapper. He dropped it near Catchy's belt and crossed to the window. "Don't cut your wrists," McCauley said, twisting the blinds open, checking the street. Closing them, he picked up his bag.

"What about my knife?" Catchy said.

"It's coming with me," McCauley said, patting his pocket. He started to reach for the doorknob and paused, made a fist, turned it over. "You know, maybe you *should* think about cutting your wrists." He opened the door and started to go through it.

"Son-of-a-bitch," Catchy said, fighting to sit up. "I'm still bleedin'. You was a cop, ain't supposed to do this."

McCauley stopped on the threshold and threw a thumb towards the bookcase. "The dictionary, over there? After freeing yourself, look up *was*," he said, and walked out.

FORTY-FIVE

J ARVIS REEMS TURNED THE IGNITION KEY to accessory and flicked on the radio. AM talk radio. ". . . mean to tell me that taking guns away from private law-abiding citizens makes the streets any safer?" he heard an angry voice saying.

The cheap stereo burped up a soft chuckle. The moderator, named Howie, said, "Ed, from Somerville, what don't you *get*? Taking all the guns off the streets means *all* the guns — so even the *creeps* won't be able to get 'em."

Ed came back on saying the time comes for them to confiscate his legally owned weapon, better bring backup. The soft chuckle again. Howie saying Ed just don't get it, what do *you* think, folks? Call me, and rattled off a number.

For the past forty minutes Jarvis had been listening to the same number as he sat in Amrhein's parking lot in the black Chevy van. Watching the red Mustang, waiting for the six-foot, young-side-of-middle-age man to exit the District Six police station, cross the street, and get in. The same argument over and over: guns don't kill people, people kill people. Jarvis was thinking he couldn't agree more.

A hour before that, while he was in the drafty boathouse in Quincy, the empty containers of microwaved meals around him, Jerry Springer on the tube, he got the text message from the doctor: the address in South Boston, the description of the car, and a name — McCauley. Then the message: Clean Up the Mess. Already aware, from the doctor, of who McCauley was, it would be the first time he actually *saw* him.

He closed his eyes and turned off the radio, pressed his head back into the cushion. Tired lately, and not used to the feeling, he'd been like this since he was weaned off the drug — that allowed him to sleep.

And *dream* when he was awake.

First he'd take care of the one in the house, then he'd head over to where the other one lived. He'd reconnoitered McCauley's house already. Knew every room.

Measure twice, cut once.

Half a block up Taylor, on the other side of Brooks, Jarvis sat on a milk crate in the back of a beat-up Dodge van. From between the front seats he watched McCauley exit the house, get into the Mustang, and leave. Decided not to follow him now, he needed to be certain that he had the disc.

Pulling on a thin pair of gloves, slipping on a pair of black-rimmed safety glasses, grabbing a toolbox, he opened the rear door and got out. Closing the door, tugging the zipper at his neck down a foot, he reached into the gray denim jumpsuit he wore, shifted the M1911-style Springfield Defender .45 in its holster.

Thanks to an old contact in Manhattan, part of a cache recently arrived from New York, the small but powerful weapon allowed for the use of an extra-large silencer that extended almost down to his waist. He pulled up the zipper, casually swinging the tool box as he walked down the sidewalk, nonchalantly checking the blank sheet of paper he took from his pocket, at the numbers of the houses he passed.

Just a repair man trying to find the right address.

It was a bitch, but by using the wall Catchy was able to get to his feet. He hopped to the window, put his head to the blinds, and tried to look out. What if McCauley, that fucking maniac, came waltzing back in? He hopped to the door and, wrenching his shoulder, twisted the deadbolt behind him. Thought to himself, What the hell happened to Leda?

He wanted to call the cops. Hello, of-fi-cer? I'd like to report a house *invasion*. Big guy, ugly, slammed me around and tied me up, squeezed my head with fucking pliers. Noticed the razor on the rug and dropped to his knees. His fingers fumbling behind him for it. What did he take from me, officer? Nothing. Can't tell ya about the disc I *killed* a guy for. 'Course you guys know nothing about that. You're saying you already do? On his side on the floor now, the blade nipping his wrist as he sliced at the wrap. And you guys written it off as *aliens* that done it? Gee, ain't *they* shifty.

I know you, McCauley, the next time you see me, my hands won't be tied.

The storm door creaked open, a heavy knock on the door. Jesus, he's back. Cutting his ankles free, Catchy stood up.

"McCauley," he said, "you got what you came for, what you want?" Looking around for something to use as a weapon.

"Quincy police."

What the . . . ? Catchy saying, Excuse me? Didn't call no police. The cop telling him, We got a call from your neighbor, reported a scream, please open the door. The door knob twitched, the wood popping briefly from pressure.

The guy doesn't *sound* like McCauley. Catchy put the chain on the door and cracked it a few inches.

Peeking out through the gap, a really *big* guy in a jumpsuit? The gorilla leaned back and thrust out with his foot, the force of it jerking his shoulders. No time to react, the door exploded inward, caught Catchy at the hairline, launching him, splitting him there.

Now on his back, through a haze, Catchy tried to focus on a guy who filled the whole door frame. Had the vague feeling of being pulled from the floor, then suddenly around him there was nothing but air.

He hit the kitchen floor rolling.

Almost soundlessly, footsteps approached. Catchy, one arm crumpled under his stomach, the other bent over his head, heard the voice.

"Anyone else home?"

"Huh?" Lifted his head off the floor, struggling to wipe the blood from his eyes. "What the . . . ?"

"The disc, where is it?"

Beginning to believe in karma, Catchy said, "Hey, got the shit kicked outta me over that thing. It's gone, for chrissakes, a guy named McCauley just took it."

He started to blubber, rolled over, the pain in his shoulder like a wound from a saber, and tried to sit up, said, "Look what he did to me, now what *you've* done," wiped the blood from his chin, turned his bloody palms over. "I'm bleeding all over again."

"Not enough," Reems said, pulling a pistol that took forever to come out. From the hip he shot Catchy under one eye, then through the forehead. Catchy collapsed back on the floor. Using a foot to turn the chin down, the suppressor almost touching, Jarvis gave him one more in the ear.

Picking up the spent shells, he reentered the hallway, paused at the sound of a key sliding into a lock, and slid into the bedroom.

Leda entered the house clutching a bag, blinking as she looked down the dark hallway. "Catchy," she said softly, closing the door with her ass. Two more steps in, louder this time. "Catchy?" Scowling, stamping her foot. "Ya know, I'm tired of keeping the blinds closed around here." Raising her nose, sniffing. "What's that *stink*?" she said, clopping towards the kitchen.

Reems stepped into the hall. "Cordite," he said. Just like a woman, smells everything. "Comes when you fire a gun."

Leda stiffened, the bag hit the floor. "Who are you, whaddaya want?" she said, wrapping herself in her arms. She tried to look past him, the tiny voice wavering. "Catchy. You haven't hurt Catchy?" Rising up on her feet looking.

Jarvis lifted the weapon, nudged her back towards the door. He said, "Into the front room."

Now wrist-flicking the gun towards the orange chair, he said, "Sit."

Still holding herself, Leda fell more than sat into it.

Eyes brimming, she said, "You ain't gonna hurt me?" tilting her head still attempting to look down the hall. "Catchy . . . down there?"

"Catchy's fine," Reems said, slide-stepping in front of her, extending his arm. He fired once. The Black Talon slug caught her between the breasts, pounded her back in the seat. Leda looked down and gasped, fingers tugging at either side of the hole in her chest.

Confused, she looked up at him, gasped, "You . . . ssshot . . . *why*?"

With a sound like a burst of steam escaping, the .45 Defender coughed twice. The first round through the chin, scattering teeth, exiting high in the neck. The second punching a quarter-sized hole between her eyes. As if a current shot through her, one leg convulsed, like it was kicking a ball, then went limp. Now her head was back like it was pinned into place, the open eyes more sad than peaceful.

Hungry, hungry hippos, get your *hun*-gry . . .

"Now you're fine too," Jarvis said.

FORTY-SIX

DRIVE," WACKO SAID and pointed the way. The hulking man behind the wheel of the black Mercury Marauder nodded once before pulling away from the Quencher Tavern on I Street.

"Where to, boss?" the other man said, keeping his eyes on the road, stopping for the lights at Fifth Street. Wacko stared at the closed St. Peter's school on the corner, like most empty buildings in Southie, soon to be converted to condos. He made a face. "Fucking yuppies," he said, "fucking yuppies and feds, all we got over here in Southie these days."

The tuned dual-exhaust hummed as the Marauder rolled on the green. "Nowhere? Anywhere? Where we headin' to, boss?" the driver said, eyeing his passenger. "Or maybe you want I should just make a sweep?"

With a flick of the wrist, Wacko motioned ahead. "Naw, just drive, no *sweeps* today, though I ain't sayin', considering the shit-bags we deal with, I wouldn't like to make one." Wacko looked out the side window envisioning something. "Did, we'd be clipping so many we'd be meltin' down barrels." Shook his head, leaned forward, he slapped the dash. "But not today, Jughead, not today."

He flicked at the windshield again. "We got money to make. Turn right on Broadway, head down Emerson, across L, then straight up the Point." He pushed back in the seat, ran his fingers through his neatly cut hair, shook his head, and said, "We're gonna go to the Mint Room and see Mr. *Cooney*."

On the corner of P and Sixth, Flavius "Flavor" Cooney stood in the sun just beyond the doorway of Jimmy's Korner Store. Swiping his thumb on his tongue, he was counting his tickets to the daily number. Usually bought thirty a day, at a buck a pop, and *never* gave them a number, Just give me the Quik-Pics he'd tell them, leaving the rest up to the gods. Flavor thinking he was destined to win.

When he was younger, winning was something that never came easy. He'd seemed like a failure from the time he was born — beginning with his first name, Flavius, the name his Italian mother forced his Irish father, a man already beset with the *curse*, to accept.

As a kid he got in a lot of fights over that name, mostly taking a beating. Other kids calling him things like "Flatty-puss," until some genius one day called him Flavor — *Flavor* Cooney, it had a nice ring. Strangely, the new nickname helped make him a winner, at least less of a loser, and became a turning point in his life.

Popular but a lousy student, Flavor dropped out of Southie High in the ninth grade and went to work for the gangster Marty Fallon, in the stockroom of Rotary Liquors. Located across from the Old Colony projects, the Rotary was a hijacking mecca.

It was there Flavor learned the art of the fence.

Stolen goods, from swag artists all over Southie and Charlestown, poured into the place. Flavor — who now had become an avid student — learned how to determine the value of all kinds of jewelry, to pick out a fine diamond, tell the difference between ermine and mink, between a good watch and a knock-off. Time went by and, with Fallon's blessing, telling him, sure kid you can open your own business, long as you *always* pay me my end, he went out on his own.

Two months shy of a year into the new business, a straw store-front selling used vacuums on Congress Street down on the waterfront, Flavor got busted. Did eighteen months in Deer Island.

While he was doing his bid, Fallon got whacked and Flavor came out to a whole new regime. On the street again, he swore he'd steer clear of selling hot goods — instead, he got into the coke.

Most cokeheads remembered the first time they tried it, how quickly it hit them, how fast they were hooked. Flavor, seeing how it turned others to toast, never tried it, but retained a shrinkwrap clear image of the first sale he made.

After picking up a quarter ounce off Leppy Mullins, he stepped on it, packaged it, and sold it down Street Lights, Hap's Lounge that same Saturday night. Sold fourteen packages in less than two hours.

Now Flavor was hooked.

Two years later, employed by the new boss Wacko Curran, Flavor had moved up quickly from quarter ounces to pounds, his territory now covering the entire South Shore.

Outside the market, on the corner of P and Sixth, Flavor leaned on a mailbox pressing a scratch ticket into the curve of its top. Working a nickel on it, blowing, Flavor glanced up and saw the black Mercury Marauder approaching a few blocks away.

Had the feeling in his balls like they'd chomped down on tin foil.

He rarely saw Wacko Curran these days, as a rule always dealt with Janowski, but Janowski *was* a day late for his pickup. Maybe Wacko had come in his place?

"Hey, Edso," he yelled, waving the ticket at the gangly twenty-year-old in a dark-blue hooded sweatshirt, gray running pants, sneakers, standing directly across the street. Edso pulled the hood from his head and lowered the phone from his ear. Lifting his chin, he said, "Whassup, Flav, got a hit?"

"Naw," Flavor said, scowling, tossing the ticket. "Go downstairs to the bar, into the cooler, the package behind the Guinness keg, get it."

Edso looked up the street, took a step, stopped. "Hey, the boss, ain't that him comin'?"

Pointing a finger at him, Flavor dragged a line to the rear of the Farragut House. "No shit, Notredamus, now go *get* the package."

Edso bolted the length of the building, disappeared at the end down a steep flight of steps.

The Marauder pulled up, stopped in front of Flavor, and the driver's-side window hummed down. Flavor slipped on a caught-by-surprise look. "*Hey*, Juggie, what's up?" he said, bending down further. "*Jack.*"

The electric door locks snapped up.

"Hey, Flav," Wacko said, sitting straight up in the seat. He turned just his head and said, "Get into the car."

Be cool, man, Flavor thinking, trying to read their blank looks. He straightened up and took a step back. "Hey, Jack, Jug, everything's cool, sent the kid Edso downstairs to pick up your . . ."

"Don't know what you're *talkin'* about," Wacko said, glaring ahead at the windshield, "get in."

On Day Boulevard, passing Marine Park and the Farragut statue, Flavor said, "I got a bad *what*?" lunging forward grabbing the head rest.

"Mailbox," Wacko said, looking back over his shoulder, "that corner you hang at, got a bad mailbox, the feds got it bugged. And at least four others in Southie, I'm told." Now he turned in the seat and stared at Flavor. "Been mentionin' my name around it?"

Swallowing hard, watching Jughead's eyes in the mirror, Flavor said, "No, Jack, I ain't, honest . . . *ever* mentioned your name."

Still on Day Boulevard, following the bulge of the Sugar Bowl, Wacko stared intently ahead. "Go all the way out to the island," he said as he looked at the ocean out the side window, the overcast sky turning the water dark gray. Folding the fingers of one hand like he was checking his nails, he said casually, "You seen Mike Janowski?"

Flavor told him no, not in days, but that he'd heard about the Teamsters, what happened. Everyone's talking, he said, shook his head. "Can't see anyone getting the drop on Janowski, must have had him outnumbered," he said, staring at the headrest, awaiting a response. But Wacko said nothing.

"Also ain't like Mike to be missing his pickups," Flavor said. "Yesterday had the package all ready, fifteen grand and no Mike. Last week the same thing, then Flippy stopped by and picked up the dough. Weird, Mike was always the one that picked up, but, of course, I had no problem giving it to Flippy," Flavor said nervously scratching his chest. "Figured it was okay, you got it, correct?"

Wacko looked at Jughead. "When we get to the island," he said, "circle the lot and head back." He threw his arm over the seat, his eyes drilling into Flavor's.

"Flippy Condon been around?"

Flavor shook his head. "Haven't seen him for days." Scratched his wrist and looked at his watch.

Wacko's eyes widened. He said, "You in a *hurry?*"

Flavor stopped scratching and covered the watch. Gave him a big stupid grin.

"Naw . . . no, Jack," he said. "Just back at the Mint Room the kid's holdin' your dough, figured you're here, why not grab it."

Wacko said, "We'll grab it later, Jughead will call you." Motioned him closer. "And you *never* said my name to the mailbox?"

Flavor recoiled in the seat, held up his left hand, palm out, "Jesus, Jack, no," switched to the right, "Never, Jack, God, I'd cut my wrists before."

Wacko nodded. "Good. Remember you do, *I'll* cut your throat after."

Turned back, facing the front.

"Sure, Jack, sure," Flavor said, nodding more than he had to. "Anything you say and, oh, I can do anything just . . ."

Without turning, Wacko held up his hand. "You see Flippy Condon, you tell him to call me. Same goes for Janowski, he stops by for the dough."

*   *   *

Stopped at the lights in Quincy, the corner of Sea Street and the Southern Artery, Wacko said, "The Stop and Shop over there, pull into the lot." The light changed to green and he checked the side mirror as Jughead made a wide left turn. Wacko said, "You notice anyone behind us on the way down?"

Jughead checked the side mirror, the rearview, shook his head slowly. "Nothin' suspicious, Jack, 'course the cops ain't that obvious when they tail guys these days, sometimes they use them transponders."

"That's why we sweep every day," Wacko said, "with that gizmo Butchie sent up from Tampa. Sure as hell saved us some headaches, remember the bug we found just before Christmas?"

Nodding, Jughead took a right into the Stop and Shop lot. "Yeah, Butchie's magic wand, boss, but at twenty-five hundred a pop, the magic ain't cheap."

"'Specially black magic," Wacko said, staring ahead as Jughead backed into a slot next to a brick ATM, killed the engine.

Wacko glanced at his watch and said, "We got some time to kill, grab us a paper."

A half hour later, following a nod from Wacko, Jughead started the car. Wacko focused on the small slip of paper he held in his lap. Looking up, folding it, he said, "Head down to Weymouth."

Heading south on the Artery, past a car dealership and strip malls, Jughead picked up the newspaper folded between them as they passed a gas station with a lighthouse behind it. He tapped Wacko's arm with it.

"Just sayin' you should read this here article, Jack. There's a big anti-snitching campaign going on in the city." Chuckled as he slowed for the Washington Street lights. "Boston cops, the D.A.'s office, man, they're *hot* over it."

Wacko looked at the headline, folded the paper, and tossed it on the backseat over his shoulder. "I'm tired of reading about rats."

At the lights, Jughead asked him which way we go. Straight, Wacko said, at Quincy Avenue turn left and follow it down to the Landing.

Wacko was quiet as they went by a school, then an apartment

complex. He stared out the side window. "A few nights ago, on the tube, seen a thing about rats." Looked at Jughead. "How they got 'em in China, almost as many as people." Wrinkled his nose. "Jesus, Jug, they *eat* the fuckers."

Jughead gave Wacko a look of disgust, said, "Them chinks are *weird* people, boss, heard they ate cats," shrugged, "so probably anything rhythms with 'em too?" He was grinning when they drove past the old Fore River Shipyard. "Ya know, maybe them chinks got something there."

Wacko looked at him, What are you, nuts?

"Seriously, Jack, Marty Fallon was a big goddamn rat, would have fed twenty easy. Maybe we should eat the next rat we whack, wouldn't that send a hellava message." Smirked. "Go ahead, tell me I don't got a point."

"Got a point," Wacko said, nodding.

Jughead's eyes widened. "Really?" Looked over but it was obvious Wacko's thoughts already were far beyond the edge of the Mercury's hood.

Looking down, tapping his watch crystal, Wacko said, "Know what, Jug? All this talk about rats made me hungry, you?"

Past a Mexican restaurant, descending the hill into Weymouth Landing, Jughead shrugged twice and said, "Ya . . . I *guess.*"

Through the lights at the bottom, they passed the burnt ruins of Sacred Heart Church. Jughead glanced at it, shuddered. "Ma says bad luck passing a church that's burnt out."

Wacko gave a look of disgust. He said, "These days seems like its worse luck for some who go in." He nodded ahead. "Go straight up the hill, then turn left at the fire station, Broad Street, half a block down on the left's Jimmy's diner." He crumpled the paper.

"Pretty hungry there, boss?"

Wacko gave Jughead's shoulder a pat. "Could say my appetite's building," he said.

Jughead parked near the front door of Jimmy's, next to a handicapped spot. Read from the hand-painted sign near the door. "Says open seven days a week," he said.

Wacko glanced at him as he cracked his door open. "Ya, so are we, so what?" And got out.

Jughead killed the engine, pulled out the keys, opened his door, and said, "I'm hungry too."

Wacko said, "No, you stay put and keep an eye on the door. Anyone you recognize goes through it you come in behind them *fast*, you got it?"

Inside he barely heard the hostess say, Sir, any particular place that you'd like to sit? Lifting his chin and scanning the room, Wacko caught a hand signaling to him from a booth in the corner.

"Think I'm all set," he said, heading towards it.

"Thanks for coming, directions okay?" Flippy Condon said, partially standing, the first one to offer his hand. Taking the hand, Wacko looked back toward the door. Released it, slid in opposite.

Nodding as he looked around the place, Wacko said, "They really fixed this joint up. Wasn't it once . . ."

"A bakery," Flippy said. "Been empty for years 'til these guys stepped in. Food's great. Me and the other guy meet here some times."

Wacko rested his forearms on the table, hunched over them, glanced towards the door. "And you ain't worried that *he* might show up?"

Flippy shook his head just a little. "Ain't worried a bit, the reason I asked you to come here," he said.

A middle-aged woman with a boyish haircut, didn't look bad on her, came over holding a pad. Her blue dress showed she still had a figure. "This gentleman's all set," she said. Nice smile. "But what about you, love, know what you want?"

Flippy lifted the menu. He said, "For him coffee, black, something to eat, Jack?"

"Two tunas, whole wheat, lettuce and tomato and a large Coke to go." Wacko said, looking up at her briefly.

Scribbling, the woman's eyes drifted up from the pad. "And nothing right now to nibble . . .?

"That's *it* — thanks," Wacko said, staring at Flippy. Watched her receding figure a moment before returning his attention to Flippy. He said, "I'm not here for the tuna fish, whaddaya got?"

"It's Mike, Jack," Flippy said, taking a sip of his coffee, putting the cup down. "You ain't gonna like . . ."

"Spit it out."

Looking embarrassed, Flippy lifted the cup briefly, recentered it on the saucer. Used the same hand to gingerly finger the thick patch of gauze he had taped to his forehead.

"That part of it?" Wacko said, staring, moving a finger.

A little flush of red in his cheeks, his voice rising, Flippy said, "Okay, its my fault I got caught with a bottle — a couple, okay? But it was Janowski's I was there in the first place."

Wacko glanced towards the front of the room, his hand patting the air center table. "Whoa, you broadcasting or *talkin'*? Tone it the fuck down."

His whole body sunk an inch and Flippy said softer, "Ya, Jack, sure, sorry," crimson spreading in his cheeks.

Wacko said, "You're telling me that Michael fucked up, so what? You perfect, me?" Glanced up at the waitress as she slipped his coffee in front of him. He handed back the two small containers of cream.

She took them and looked at him strange. "Tuna'll be up in just a few minutes," she said, turning.

Flippy picked up his cup, looked at it like he was thinking, I'm wired enough. Put the cup down. His eyes rose and met Wacko's. "Mike's fucking up, Jack."

"Fucking up, how?"

I know he's fucking up, where is he right now?

"He ain't doing his pickups no more."

Wacko straightened, thinking, What are you talking about? He said, "But the money's being dropped at the bar twice a week."

Flippy jabbed his chest with a finger. "Me, *I* do the pickups, by myself, and drop 'em off at the Pen, have been for weeks." He wiped his mouth with a napkin, angrily balling it in his fist.

"Mike don't do shit." Bounced the napkin off the table, sank back into the cushion. "Being kind here, Jack, Mike's outta his mind's more like it. First, he's hot to find what McCauley's looking for, then he loses all interest. Now, all he talks about is killing that cop."

Wacko remembered the heat two years before. Janowski shot a cop during a hold-up they pulled. It had to be done, but after. Like someone had fired up a fucking blast furnace. It was Marty

Fallon's problem then, the rackets were his. Wacko remembered thinking at the time how all the heat maybe helped him, threw the guy off his game plan, made him vulnerable. But now it was different, all this was his.

Maybe his old pal, Michael Janowski, was looking to move up, even . . .

Like someone had stuck a lit fuse up his ass, Wacko fought to control the tsunami of anger that flashed through his body, threatening to explode from his face. He brought the cup to his lips, the dark, hot liquid burning his tongue, took another mouthful, his eyes watering as he put the cup down.

Flippy, taking it all in, sucked his chin toward his chest. He said, "You . . . *okay*, Jack?"

Wacko, thinking back on how Mike had come to him, after the fight at the Teamsters, demanding that McCauley be clipped. Saying he had it all figured out, a four-man team, two cars, maybe three, an ambush on G Street, when McCauley came home after work. How he had responded, saying, No, Mike, we can't, you can't kill a cop. Janowski screaming, Ain't a cop no more, what don't you get? The two of them almost coming to blows.

Wacko said to Flippy, "This cop, you're talkin' McCauley?"

"Ya, him," Flippy said, hitting the table edge like a bongo with the tips of his fingers, "but that ain't the worst." Both of them watched the waitress approach. She put an open white bag on the table, the check alongside it.

Flippy stopped drumming, watched her depart. He leaned closer to Wacko. "Mike's been talkin' to guys, sayin' shit about you. That you're soft, disrespect them, don't give 'em an end of what they deserve." Nodded like, there, he'd gotten it out. He picked up his cup. Downed the last of it, his blue eyes darting like something was giving them shocks.

Tell him the rest, Flippy.

"Thing is those guys are *listenin'*, Jack, and he's talkin' about — *his* words — takin' you out." Dragged the back of his hand across his mouth..

"Really?" Wacko said, his face a blank slate, just a hint of a smile.

You're telling me this, why?

Wacko tugged on the edge of the bag. "Two sandwiches," he said, looking in, "good." The smile gone now, he watched Flippy's eyes.

"My brother, Kevin, liked tuna," Wacko said. Pressed the edge of the bag with a finger, looked in again, up at Flippy. Pursed his lips, little look of surprise. "'Magine, put a straw in there too." Settled back in the seat. "See, sometimes they forget the little things."

With the back of his fingers he pushed his cup and saucer towards Flippy, hitting the Sweet'N Low bowl. Folding his hands in its place, he subtly shifted his head and said, "'Course ain't as bad as forgetting the big things, like who picked them up when they came out of the can, made them rich, gave them power."

"Boss, what can I say, I —"

Wacko waved a finger, shut up. "Who's with him?" he said, struggling to keep his voice even, refolding his hands.

"Me — he thinks," Flippy said, licking his lips. "The Hughes twins for sure, and probably the little crew they got down on P Street, you know near Kemble Place, where they like to hang out?"

"Anyone else? You gotta be sure." The face now a stone mask.

Flippy pushed down with both hands, shifted uncomfortably. "Might be others, Jack, don't *know* for sure, Christ, I can't *ask* him . . . don't want him thinkin' I'm thinkin' too much."

Never knew that I paid you to think.

"Know what *I'm* thinkin', Flip," Wacko said, "the reason you're tellin' me this . . . why?"

Flippy turned his head and looked towards the front, his eyes picking up on the Marauder and Jughead.

Feeling trapped, Flippy boy?

Looking at Wacko. "Man complains about you, Jack, how you treat him like shit. But Mike treats me worse." Almost whining. "Can't figure the guy out, I'm there when he needs it, for *anything*," stared at him, the eyes widening, "know what I'm sayin'?"

He fingered the bandage on the back his head, grimaced. "At the Teamsters, after I got whacked with the bottles, Mike left me outside. Just jumped in the car and roared off. Me, I took a cab to the hospital. Can you believe a fucking *cab*? And Janowski wants me to jump ship?" He shook his head. "I can't trust him no more." Checking the Marauder again.

"And *if* you could trust him?" Wacko said, his blue eyes searching, trying to filter deceit.

Flippy looked at him, shook his head slowly. He said, "No, Jack, you're the boss. Mighta' worked for the guy, but I'm with you, fact," Flippy said.

FORTY-SEVEN

BY THE TIME HE'D GOTTEN TO THE BRIDGE at Neponset, McCauley had already called Mackey and Lilly. Left both of them a message but didn't say much. Figuring this was something that had to be seen.

Cotter was involved in some kind of unholy relationship with at least one doctor, Noah Durning, at Edgewater. Over the years he'd made payoffs that guaranteed his high-brow clients, who had been charged with homicide, were delivered an easy way out — not guilty by reason of insanity. Judging by the dollar amounts, the service didn't come cheap, but there weren't alternatives. Without the doctor's help, Cotter's clients would have faced a straight-up conviction for first-degree murder.

McCauley thinking that it wouldn't have been hard. Cotter providing defense psychiatrists who'd testify his wealthy clients were crazy, while Durning's office, representing the state, provided Edgewater doctors who'd concur. Found not guilty by reason of insanity, Cotter's clients would be committed to Edgewater State Hospital for an indeterminate period of time.

Durning, in his position as head of forensics, had the final word regarding when they were *cured* and fit to return to society. From what McCauley had seen on the disc, it rarely took more than a year.

One hellava bang for the buck.

On the Dorchester side of the bridge, with the ramp to 93

North backed up, McCauley took Morrissey Boulevard north towards South Boston, pulled into a small strip mall on the right. He had Catchy's knife in his pocket and, from his past as an investigator, knew how some criminals hated to part with their weapons, even ones used in a murder. According to Lilly, Catchy was a known cutter. There was a chance he had formed a bond with his weapon.

Catchy's knife seemed to be clean, but there was a chance that traces of blood would be found on it matching the DNA of a guy named McLintock. In a kind of two-for-one, after making a copy, he'd turn the disc over to Lilly, along with the knife. He pulled the knife from his pocket, stuck it under the seat, and pulled back into traffic.

He had just passed the Phillip's Candy House when his cell rang. It was Mackey.

"Hey, Del, what's cooking?" she said, then asked him if he had spoken to Catchy. He told her that things had gone smoothly but he'd explain it all later. Then he said, "Where are you now, working?"

"Brewer's Corner," Mackey said, "in Quincy, you know it? I'm in the process of following this lame." Explaining how she, involved in a workmen's compensation case, had been following a parks and recreation worker for the city of Quincy. He was out on disability with, supposedly, a bad back.

"He's a busy little bee, doing side work as a roofer," she said, "in the city whose insurance carrier he's suing. Can't *believe* it, the gall. As we're speaking, he's across the street working a job and I'm standing here taking pictures of him."

McCauley said, "Be careful, don't let him see you."

"The camera's hidden, a little bitsy thing in a purse that has a hole in its side." Mackey was silent for a moment, then said, "Oh no, oh no, Del, he's *coming* this way." McCauley pulled the phone away as she burst into laughter. "Oh, *no*, Mary, that's hysterical, you're such a *bad* girl, what's John going to say?"

"I take it he's close?" McCauley said.

"Yes, he *certainly* is, Mike's such a good man, but, personally, I think you should rethink the relationship. You know . . ." Her voice suddenly hushed. "He just entered this little store behind me. Holy moly, I'm thinking he made me, Del, and he's got this horrible-looking hammer-hatchet thing hanging off his belt. God, why am I *doing* this?" She giggled, and McCauley smiled. "Because it's *fun*?" she said, and giggled again. "I'm so nervous, I almost peed myself."

"Relax," McCauley said, "don't be paranoid, you've got your weapon?"

"Great, don't be paranoid, but are you packin'? Yes, I've got it and . . . so, *Mary*, darling, are we going to meet at the airport? Ken's *so* excited, Fort Lauderdale in October, my honey's little bag's been packed for three weeks."

"Criminy, looks like this jerk bought a *six-pack*, and he's going back up the ladder? The bus has come and gone, *again*, and I'm looking suspicious. I'm packing it in."

McCauley said, "Good, can I meet you?"

"Del, tonight I don't know, I'm supposed to meet my father." *No good way to say this.*

McCauley said, "I'm not trying to scare you, but you may be at risk."

"Risk?" She sounded more curious than scared. "You can't tell me more over the phone?"

"I know about phones and don't trust them," McCauley said. "You'll understand more when I show you."

"Okay, Del, okay, but where?"

"You're in Quincy, not far from the center? I'm in Dorchester, right over the bridge. Know the Thomas Crane Library?" Mackey told him she did.

"I'll meet you on the second floor of the new addition, the computer workstations in front near the windows, twenty minutes, okay?"

"About my father," Mackey said, "should I still tell him I'll meet him?"

Nodding, McCauley said, "Lady, this is one night I think you *should* meet him."

Behind a desk, shoulder to shoulder, the laptop in front of them, a row of bright ceiling lamps reflecting off the dark glass beside them, McCauley said, "Close your mouth, people are staring."

Ducking a little, Mackey's eyes got even bigger. "But that's *house* invasion, Del, are you out of your mind?" she said in an Irish whisper. "You could get life, the courts won't care the guy was a felon."

McCauley opened the laptop and centered it between them. He pushed the on button and faced her and said, "Did you really expect me to knock on the door? After*noon*, Mr. Davis, you've got something I want, give it up or . . . I'm *leavin'*?" He snorted. "Its classic ends-justify-the-means," McCauley said, working the touchpad. "After you view this, you'll see what I mean."

Mackey focused on the screen as McCauley scrolled down.

"If you're wondering," McCauley said, "what you're looking at are *payoffs*." Explained to her the way he thought the game worked.

Mackey just sat there staring when he had finished. She said, "My poor father trusted . . . *hired* this guy." She shook her head slowly, turned back to the screen.

"That's not all," McCauley said, pointing. "In the past three weeks, two of the men on this list have been murdered — not counting Dinny McLintock. I'm thinking *because* of this list, he was murdered." He looked at her, realized he was seeing something new.

The first tendrils of fear taking root in her face.

"You said . . . I may be at risk too."

McCauley shrugged. Tried to appear casual, calm. "I said might be," he said, believing it was way more than might. "Could be anyone associated, you, me, hell, even Lilly."

"I've seen enough," she said and started to get up, paused for a moment, and dropped back in her seat. She grabbed her pocketbook and threw back the flap. "He'll want to know, I'm calling my father." Coming out with the phone.

McCauley touched her forearm gently. He said, "You can't, except for us, no one can know anything until I talk to Lilly." He looked at his watch, frustrated. "I called him almost an hour ago, where the hell is he?"

"And after you do, then what?"

"Cotter's his friend, it's up to him how he wants to handle this thing. My guess, he'll try to convince Cotter he's finished, give him the chance to flip on Durning . . . before the good doctor can do it to him. Shouldn't be hard. I only met Cotter once. Didn't strike me as a killer, but anything's possible."

"You said three men have been killed, Del, why?" Mackey said.

Her curiosity is keeping her fear under control. The girl's cool under pressure.

"Enfield Higgins's a sharpie," McCauley said. "He knew he had something as soon as he looked at the disc. For Higgins and McLintock, it was just blackmail. They hadn't a clue they'd be facing a tiger. Higgins was the lucky one, he got himself jailed. McLintock got killed holding the bait."

McCauley shrugged. "The other two, *patients*? I don't know why they're dead. Might be the same thing — blackmail — it's a good enough reason to kill for some," he said, shutting down the computer and removing the disc.

"And what do you want me to do?"

"What I don't want you to do is to go back to your place in the South End tonight. Could you stay at your dad's house?"

"I keep a travel bag in the trunk," Mackey said, "change of clothes, toothbrush. Never know where you'll end up when you're working a case, have to stay overnight in the area."

"Good."

"What should I tell him? Daddy's a worrier, and he doesn't take things sitting down."

"CIA guys rarely do," McCauley said, "but for now there's no need to involve him. Make something up, tell him that you're meeting a client in, say, Dover tomorrow and would he mind if you slept in your old bed, he'll love it."

"What about you?"

"I'm hungry. I'll grab a bite to eat around here, then, if I haven't heard back from him, I'll reach out to Lilly again. Then I'll head home, burn a copy of the disc on my desktop."

Mackey said, "But even you can't feel safe." Her eyes meeting his, worry sparking like flares in her eyes. She scanned the room, made sure no one was close, lowered her voice, and said, "I went to the Braintree Gun Club this morning. My favorite weapon, the 9mm, is in my trunk, along with a few others: a .32 Beretta and a .22 Magnum. Take one."

McCauley wanted to but couldn't — the guns were registered

to Mackey. If anything happened, as a convicted offender he'd do five years and Mackey's career would be over.

He took her hand like he intended to shake it, but instead held it firmly and looked into her eyes. He said, "Nice of you, thanks, but me and guns don't mix anymore."

The streetlights were on and the night air cool, maybe fifty degrees, when McCauley and Mackey came out of the library, heading south through the parking lot along Washington Street. Parked on the same side near the entrance, Mackey's red Audi RS4 was in front of the Quincy Driving School, where the last class of the day seemed to be wrapping.

Inside of its brightly lit interior, a small group of boys and girls, high school age mostly, laughed and bumped shoulders as a guy with a beard, probably a teacher, talked to them from behind a small desk.

Mackey got in and left the door open. She said, "Del, meant to ask you, the front-left tire seem low to you?" McCauley examined the tire against the curb, but in the poor light, it was hard to tell. "Mind checking it, please?" Mackey said, pressing her palms together. "There's a gauge in the trunk, one of those chrome things you stick on the tire, I never learned to use it, sorry." Gave him an aren't-I-silly grin before hitting the trunk- lock release.

McCauley lifted the rear deck. On the left, under the arc of the interior light, a folded pink beach chair, in a heap on it, a colorful beach towel that partially obscured the shoebox behind it filled with a collection of small tools.

As McCauley fished through it he noticed, in the open gym bag beside it, the glint from the black plastic handle of the holstered .32 Beretta, the rubber grip of the .22 Magnum beneath it. Mackey called from inside the car. "See anything you like back there, take it, got some great tools."

Sticking his head around the rear deck, McCauley grinned into the side mirror. "Your persistence is admirable, thanks, but no thanks — again." Wiggled the tire gauge at her. "It's the only tool I'll be needing tonight."

As Mackey pulled away from the curb, she watched McCauley,

in the rear mirror, follow the sidewalk in the same direction. He waved at her and she waved back but knew, in the darkness, that he couldn't have seen it.

As she passed the post office on the left, she thought about all that had happened since the first time they met: the fight in the Pen, Janowski's death threats, the murders and their possible connection to Cotter, and now she'd actually seen the disc. Mackey tried to put things into perspective.

Raised to be independent, she could take care of herself, but people were dying, and Cotter, a man she had trusted, her *father* had trusted, was looking more like he couldn't be.

She was glad that McCauley was in her corner, she had never met anyone like him before. Most of the men in her life, at least the ones she dated her own age, were in the process of "finding" themselves — *after* graduating college then moving back in with their parents.

There was never a plethora of strong male role models in her life. There was her loving though absentee father, and a succession of private school teachers, then later college professors, sure, most of them men, but none like McCauley. McCauley was different.

It was true he was older, though certainly not her father's age, and there was his background, what he'd done or not done; still, she trusted him, his judgment.

He had a sureness about him that didn't seem cultivated, more like something innate. And it was infectious. She had no problem following his lead, and if McCauley said there was cause for concern — and he certainly made the point stronger — there was little doubt that there was.

She followed Hancock Street through the square, turning right then left, heading west on McGrath Highway. Curiously, the same car had remained behind her since she passed city hall. Mackey sped up, exceeding the speed limit, then dropped down below it, watching the other car keep pace while remaining the same distance apart.

Maintaining the speed limit, she switched to the right lane and reached into her handbag and pulled out the Beretta she laid on the armrest. Accelerating towards the green light at the West

Quincy T station, a queasiness spread in the pit of her belly as she'd watched the light turn from yellow to red.

At the lights, the car was directly behind her now, but it was too close to make out the plate, the headlights, the bright blue ones, obscuring the model. Mackey pressed on the brakes and brought up the revs, kept her hand on her gun as she watched the side mirrors.

She burned through the green.

Heading uphill now at sixty, seventy, closing on eighty, she switched to the left lane heading towards 95 South. The other car, in the rearview, far behind her now, took the right at the split towards 93 North.

Mackey wiped her forehead with the back of her hand and cracked two windows for air. She picked up the phone to call her father. She wouldn't be stopping until Wellesley.

FORTY-EIGHT

JANOWSKI COULDN'T BELIEVE how easy it was, the three-family house at seventy-three G Street, a damn cracker box to get into. The end of the day, him dressed like a car salesman, carrying a clipboard — blend in brother, blend in — he first hit the buzzer and got no response. Scribbled some stick figures, tic-tac-toe — you *lose* — on the pad, he went through the green gate at the side of the house, up the alleyway, climbed the fire escape of seventy-five G, went onto the flat roof, then right up the gabled roof, running off the flat, its peak a little more than two feet from McCauley's rear deck.

Hop, skip, *jump*.

The rear door was locked, but the window, to the left of it, was open a few inches. Climbing through it, he ended up in a room that seemed like a small office. He couldn't tell for sure, the house was dark, like every shade had been pulled. Hey, McCauley was a bartender, right? Probably slept late, liked it dark in the morning.

Worked for McCauley, would work better for him.

From a pocket, Janowski pulled out a pencil-sized flashlight and started to move towards the door, kicked something over that sounded like a bowl, scattering little hard things all over the floor. Crunching cat food, dog food, some fucking animal.

Down a short hallway, a bedroom on the left, kitchenette on the right, he came to the foyer and the front door. Hmmm. So many choices, where's the best place to whack this ex-cop asshole? The living room.

Be the greeter when Daddy comes home.

He swept the thin beam around the room. On his left, a black leather recliner faced a little TV in the corner. Against the wall on the right, a cheap particle-board bookshelf filled with dead paperbacks. Man liked to read. Directed the beam around the back of the TV. Not much to watch without cable.

Next to the bookshelf, a scarred wooden box, long legs, little door, something old men kept cigars in. On top of it, magazines, looked like scandal rags, *National Enquirer*, *Globe*, *Star*. Janowski grinned. McCauley liked dirt. Good, he'd be taking a nap in it soon or . . . his eyes coming to rest on a frazzled, blue fabric chair in the corner — something Ma gave him when he got out of the can? Maybe he should have just let him live — like this — probably worse than him ending it quick. Janowski knew the drill well. Defense attorneys had taken everything McCauley had, left the guy broke.

He sank into a soft leather recliner, the only thing in the place not old or worn out, wrapped his hand around the trigger guard of the .22 Ruger auto, with silencer, a little beauty he had machined down in Georgia. For backup? *Always* have backup — a two-incher, a five-shot .38 on his ankle.

He gazed at the ceiling, in the darkness barely able to make out the overhead fan. He imagined his future like it was up there suspended on a screen, one of them flat ones, plasma. Couple of days after McCauley, assuming it took the cops a few days to find him, Wacko would get it. Parting on bad terms the last time they spoke, he needed some time to set the guy up.

Janowski stroked the bandage on his now-level ear. Then, that little cocksucker Flippy was next — maybe before, depending.

The Hughes boys saying they'd take him out for him. But, in the past couple of days, he hadn't seen Flippy — not since the Teamsters — when he didn't watch his back like he should have. And after, outside, him whining about a ride to the hospital. Shut up and grow up, he should have said then. Muttered to himself softly, shut up and *grow up*.

Now Flippy's lost the chance to.

But all that's tomorrow, the next day, whatever. It was McCauley's turn now, and Janowski had his number — fifty-six, sir? Come on down.

All comfy now, all he had to do was sit here and wait for the sound of footsteps on stairs. When McCauley came in, he'd put on the light, and he'd step out from the wall. Howdy-do. No warning, no bullshit Hollywood speech, just pulling the trigger, the CCI 36-grain mini-mags turning McCauley's brain into slush.

After, he'd do it smart and take a different way out. Through the back door, to the roof and the fire escape down. Through the backyard to Thomas Park, follow that down to Old Harbor, to the car he'd parked across the street from the Marion Manor. Geezers ain't looking out the windows at night.

He'd done his homework. McCauley wasn't working, should be home any minute. It was almost seven when he looked at his watch. The chair wasn't bad, pretty comfy.

Janowski jerked up in the chair, his finger now on the trigger. Damn, fell asleep. Good way to shoot yourself, asshole.

Darkness had its disadvantages too.

Disoriented, he reached for the side handle, lowered his feet to the floor. Turning his wrist in front of his face he squeezed the watch with two fingers, its face glowing a green seven thirty.

Then he remembered what woke him.

Way off in the distance, or — like from inside a closet — a little kid's voice singing . . . about hippos. *Hippos?* He felt a breeze behind him and straightened. But every window was closed, except for the . . .

When Janowski began to push himself up, the pressure began on the top of his head, stinging, like he was under the ass of some huge goddamn hornet. From behind him with both hands, like he was pulling the rope of a heavy church bell, Jarvis drove the blade of the fourteen-inch Bowie through the top of his head.

Carving a channel down the length of his throat, it severed his tongue, and Janowski choked once before dying.

With a grunt, Jarvis yanked out the knife. Would have preferred to have shot him, but the cordite. The woman hadn't recognized it, but McCauley would, and it would give him time to react.

Jarvis picked up the Ruger, sniffed the end, grinned. Bent over and, like a sack of dry leaves, hoisted Janowski out of the chair, dropped him on the floor alongside it. The legs flopped comically as he flipped the corpse over, wiped the blade on the back of its shirt. Three hours under the kitchen table. It was his turn now for the chair.

FORTY-NINE

WIPING HIS MOUTH WITH A NAPKIN, McCauley exited Liberty Bell Roast Beef on West Broadway. He wiped his fingers with it, balled it, and flipped it into a bucket. Looked up the street towards District Six and thought about Lilly. How would he take the news about Cotter? He owed the guy, sure, but how far was he planning to take it?

McCauley got in the Mustang and fired it up. Wasn't his problem, he wasn't a cop anymore, right?

Who was he kidding?

It was his problem. In the street now, heading towards District Six, the captain's space out front empty, went by it, passed Triple O's on the right. The former gangster joint closed now, its windows as dark as some of the patrons who once drank there. McCauley shook his head thinking just another yuppie joint soon. Snorted. At least the damn gangsters were interesting.

Cracking open the window, turning left at the lights at Dorchester Avenue, his cell rang. It was Lilly.

"Bill's House of Pizza," McCauley said with a Greek accent.

First there was silence, then, "What? McCauley, that *you?*"

"Ya, me, just wanted you to feel like you got the wrong number."

"Why's that?"

"Because that's how I felt dialing yours, leaving messages that don't get returned, like I was dialing the wrong fucking number."

Lilly, all apologies, explained how he was at a command staff meeting at headquarters, the new building in Roxbury, telling him how much he hated the place, the air-conditioning dried out his sinuses, felt like someone had sandblasted his throat.

"Ya know," Lilly said, "if you *had* called my office instead of my cell phone, you would have gotten a recorded message instructing you to call Fred Laracy the acting area commander's extension, he would have *told* you where I was.

"So, what's up?" Lilly said. "You owe me an address, where's Catchy Davis, you talk to the bum?"

McCauley told him he had, but there was more, a lot more. He'd gotten the disc.

"Am I on it?" Lilly said.

"No," McCauley said, passing over a railroad bridge, "and it's a good thing you're not."

"That's a relief."

"Believe me, Lil, there's no relief here except maybe, in the future, for the families of more than a half dozen murder victims."

Lilly's voice dropped an octave, "What are we talking?"

"I'm not *talking* about anything, you have to see for yourself."

"Bad news regarding my friend?"

"No more on the phone."

"Understand, can you come down the station? I'm on Melnea Cass now, should be back there in ten, fifteen minutes."

McCauley said, "It's not something I'd view on the stationhouse computer. Anyone could be tapped into that thing."

"It's that bad, huh?"

"If I told you could be worse, it would have to come with a disclaimer," McCauley said. "Can you swing by the house, I'll buy the coffee?"

Lilly told him he could but, expecting him to sign off on some paperwork there, he had to stop at the station house first. It shouldn't take long.

"See you then," McCauley said, closing the phone, turning left onto Old Colony.

He pulled into Dunkin' Donuts, ordered at the drive-through, pulled around to the window. John, the owner, was standing there, putting covers on the large regulars to go.

"What's the matter, boss," McCauley said, "little short on help?"

John pushed his glasses up the bridge of his nose, looked down it, and grinned. He said, "How we *doin'*, Del? Two of my regulars called in sick," shrugged, "two more of 'em did, be working this joint with my six-year-old twins." He passed him the coffees. "Could be worse, my friend, could be worse."

McCauley tried to hand him money, but John shook his head, blocked the window with the palms of his hands, "Cops don't pay here . . . ever," he said.

Extending the money, McCauley said, "Thanks, John, but can't. I'm not a cop anymore."

John, tapped the side of his head with a finger. He said, "In here, McCauley, *always* a cop. Those bastards might have gave you a screwin', but, in my place . . ." Dipped his head toward the coffees. "So, who's the other one for?"

"Captain Lilly."

Big grin. "*Another* good cop." The face suddenly grew serious, he waved a finger. "Tell him he should watch his ass too. The IA? The bums that did you? Do *his* ass in a heartbeat too." John threw a thumb across his chest. "Now get outta here, enjoy the coffee, got payin' customers behind ya." Winked. "Make *plenty* offa them."

Heading east on Dorchester Street, catching the green arrow at the West Broadway merge, McCauley headed up Little Broadway's first hill, turning right at the lights onto G Street. The streetlamps, white points among the towering elms, struggled to dispel darkness along the length of the street that slowly ascended to Dorchester Heights.

Lucky, McCauley found a space half a block from his house. Acutely aware of the knives in his pocket as he twisted in his seat backing into it. He thought about Doctor Mario as he pulled the key from the ignition. According to Mario, a true knifer *always* carried multiple knives. He got out of the car. But was he really a true knifer?

He thought maybe at one time, but he was also a good cop then too. A true knifer? No, believing that knives might be more of a magnet for trouble, he was more of a dabbler these days. Thinking, as he pointed the remote lock behind him, he'd be glad when this whole thing was over.

Near Fifth Street he cut diagonally across G, checking the shadows, thinking he should have asked Mackey to call him when she got to her father's. Would she think he was bugging her? Shook his head no, figuring under the circumstances.

He came in through the front door, shoving it closed with his butt, picked up the mail: some Macy's brochures, a flier for The Neighborhood Watch, bills, mostly for him, one for Mrs. Slattery, the second-floor tenant. One final tug on the doorknob and he ascended the stairs, slipped the bill under Mrs. Slattery's door.

He keyed open the front door, the back of his hand searching for the switch on the left, the light chasing the darkness to the end of the hall. He stepped inside and looked at his watch, closed the door with his heel. Still reading a brochure when he twisted the deadbolt, he decided to wait a half hour before calling Mackey.

Hanging his jacket on a hook in the hallway he moved up it, stopping at the kitchen to toss the mail on the table. Took another step and froze, the hair on the back of his neck rising. At the end of the hall, scattered like buckshot across the threshold of the doorway, Nuala's cat food. In less time than it took to exhale, McCauley had his knives out, the blades open before passing his hips.

A slight breeze behind him, something big, moving soundlessly, *fast*.

Crouching, McCauley pivoted around to the left. Just ahead, coming at him, a dark silhouette. Moving too quickly to make out the face he could see the knife — fucking *sword* — in its right hand, thrusting down like a matador at an angle to his face.

Your body's a weapon, your knives an extension.

Shoving off of the right foot, McCauley stepped in blocking with a left age-uke, his arm catching the giant's inside of the elbow, halting the Bowie an inch from his neck. Reversing the blade in his right hand, McCauley slid closer and back-cut him up the middle, paring open the other man's chest, chin, cutting off a piece of his nose.

Just a grunt, like a bear that had stepped on a briar.

Almost in the same motion McCauley loosened his block, sliding right, the left blade in a down stroke now cutting across the carotid, notching the clavicle. Turning the giant's elbow, McCauley slid past him, took a step left, reversing the blade that had just cut the carotid and savagely swung it, like a pendulum stroke backwards, burying it deep near the kidneys.

Now the bear roared.

Somebody tell him he's dying.

McCauley bolted for the door, dropped one of his knives as he fought with the deadbolt. Felt the same rush of air and instinctively ducked, the Bowie hacking deep into the door frame above him. He wildly slashed back with his own knife and missed. Picked up like a rag doll and slammed into the wall, he climbed it on his back as he rose towards the ceiling.

He heard the bear panting as he went suddenly airborne, crashing into and crushing the bookshelf, landing on his back in front of the TV.

Briefly stunned, he came to, a paperback, *Get Shorty*, tumbled from his chest as he sat up and spat blood. He tried to focus on a door that wasn't blocked by a bear — looked more like a monster. The face drenched in blood had shadows for eyes, its dark clothes wet looking, shiny.

Holding a hand to its neck, the blood, like water in summer through a length of flat hose, pulsed in thin streams through its fingers. The huge blade in the other, it grinned at McCauley, took a halting step towards him, leaned into the next one, rushed in to end it.

Rolling to his feet, McCauley grabbed the humidor's legs and gave it a home-run swing. Bobbing beneath it, the humidor splintering against the wall, the giant sprung out of his crouch and back-cut with the knife, slashing the front of McCauley's shirt. McCauley staggered off-balance backwards, stumbled over the recliner and hit the floor hard. The wind knocked from his lungs, turning his head he noticed Janowski — and the gun exposed by the pant leg curled up.

He willed his hand towards it.

Jarvis reversed the blade in his hand, moved in to finish him, suddenly stopped, dropped the hand from his neck and examined the palm. The eyes slowly rising, he glared at McCauley, the mad grin, white teeth dividing the gore, raised the Bowie again, swept the recliner out of the way.

Backed into the corner, his knees to his chest, McCauley double gripped the weapon and extended his arms. His lungs fought for air as he aimed center mass.

The sound deafening as small flames sprouted from the short-barreled gun.

Bang, bang . . . bang, bang — bang, click!

Knocked back a step, Jarvis first looked confused, then down at his chest. He looked at McCauley, the eyes, barely human, now registering pain. Raising the blade he croaked, "*Hippos*," and shuffled towards him, went down on a knee, lunged, the blade arcing before burying itself deep in the floor. Still gripping the handle, Jarvis tugged himself closer. Now inches away, the grin bubbling blood, he said, "Feed . . . *them*."

And McCauley lashed out with both feet.

FIFTY

UNIFORMED COPS FLEW PAST THEM, taking the steps two at a time, as they stood at the bottom of the outside steps leading up to Seventy-three G Street.

"Just another two minutes," Lilly said, shaking his head, "I'm passing the courthouse and figured I'd call you I'd be there in a minute, and *you* pick up like nothing had happened." The head shook again. "Just another two minutes, and I might have helped you."

"And done what?" McCauley said, wincing as he sat down on a step, gingerly fingering the back of his head. "Would have killed him, and not me." Touched his ribs as he gazed down the street that was now filled with police vehicles, radios squawking, blue lights scattering shadows like cat-scared birds. Cops telling the neighbors to get back in their homes.

Lilly said, "Any idea how Janowski got in? Did you see him before the big guy attacked?"

An oversized van that said CITY CORONER on its side snaked its way slowly up G Street, past cops pulling hands towards their faces like they were trying to get air.

"He was dead when I got there," McCauley said. "Did they come in together?" He shrugged, "Who the hell knows."

"What about the goon, you recognize him?"

McCauley rubbed the back of his head. "No," he said, "never seen him before."

Close to his ear, Lilly whispered, "And the disc?"

McCauley lifted his shirt, displaying the top of a thin plastic case at the belt-line. "It's safe, thank God, I put it in my jacket." Leaned towards the railing, Lilly stepping back allowing the EMTs carrying two gurneys, entirely shrouded by sheets, down the steps past them.

Another siren in the distance, getting closer, added to the cacophony around them. "Your ambulance," Lilly said, looking west towards Little Broadway.

McCauley stopped rubbing and looked at him, irritated. "*Told* you I was okay."

Laying a hand on his shoulder, Lilly said. "Double homicide, remember, *ex-con*? *You're* injured too . . . it will help your defense."

"I was attacked in my own house, remember?" McCauley said bitterly, shoulders sinking, looking down at his feet. "Was righteous, don't need it."

"I know it was, brother, just trying to help," Lilly said gently. "The captain's right on this one, and you know it."

McCauley looked at him, grinned. He patted the hand on his shoulder. "You're right, brother, let's get my damaged butt to the hospital," he said.

Pretending to rub his stomach, McCauley pulled out the disc, slipped it to Lilly. "Just make me a copy after you view it."

Lilly nodded, "Count on it," he said, signaled to a cop in the street who, turning from him, looked down it, nodded back, fanned the air towards him as the ambulance, red lights flashing, slowly weaved its way up.

Rocking the glass in small circles, mindful of the Jameson washing over the ice, Cotter stood at the window eyeing the moon. Like a cheap plastic plate above Boston Harbor. Cheese. Wasn't long ago they thought it was *cheese*. Cotter brought the glass to his lips, held the whiskey in his mouth feeling it burn.

Cheese? Be *rancid* if it were — a lot like his life. He swallowed the whiskey, brought the glass up again.

When the telephone rang, he turned his head slightly, like he was trying to work out a kink. Teetered slightly as he turned. "Kandy," he said softly. He carefully shifted his feet so that now all of him was facing the desk. "The phone, I'm not in," brought the glass to his lips, paused, "not *really*," he said, sipping.

On the fourth ring now.

"Kandy," he shouted, unsteadily approaching the desk. Almost there was when he stumbled into it. Grabbing the long-necked brown bottle in front of the phone, he shouted, "Kandy, please take a message, and get-me-some-ice." Then he said, "Forget it," and fell into his seat, dropped his head back, and laughed. "Oh, Kandy, silly cow, *I'll* get it," he said, and picked up the phone, refilling the glass as he listened.

"Cotter . . . you there?"

Recognizing the voice, Cotter pressed the phone to his chest, saying, "It's okay, Kandy, I'll take the call, it's my old pal from the precinct house, *Lilly*." Held the phone out. "Is you, Lilly, isn't it?" Put it back to his ear.

"I've seen the disc, Esmond," Lilly said. "We have to talk — at the station house, *tonight*."

Pressing the phone to his neck, Cotter said, "Oh, Jeesus, he's *seen* it, the copper knows effferything." Dropped it on the floor, hit the speakerphone button.

"Cotter, you still there . . . *Cotter*?"

"Much as I was," Cotter murmured, circling the whiskey in the glass. "Conway, think Kandy should cancel my appointments?" He giggled, took a belt, swallowed, clenched his teeth.

"Listen to me, Cotter, Kandy left the office hours ago."

Cotter wrinkled his nose and giggled. He said suspiciously, "How'd you know?" Glared at the phone. "You f-f-fucking my secretary?" And giggled again.

Lilly said, "Esmond, I'm putting on my jacket and coming to get you. Put the glass down and don't drink any more."

Cotter held the glass up, stared. He said, "Knows that *too?*" shrugged, and pulled himself out of the chair. Weaved his way to the windows, big ones, hurricane-proof, hard to break with a hammer. He pressed a palm to the window and gazed down at the street. Looky there, on the avenue, teeny cars, little bugs, going, going . . . leaning forward his cheek to the glass . . . *gone.*

Stepping back, Cotter filled his eyes with the moon. Wavered a little.

Nothing was easy these days, everything was so . . . *hard.*

The voice from the box on the desk — so distracting — he listened to Lilly telling him, too loudly, "The disc, Esmond, we've got things to discuss: the money transactions, your connection to Durning — especially that — and other, more serious things." Sounding so desperate. "I'll help if I can, but you've got to help me."

Cotter laid a hand alongside his mouth and shouted, "So, you're saying we're in for a *bumpy* night?" and broke into dry laughter. "Bette Davis, Conway, isn't that what she said? Fashen your *seat belts.*" He toasted the moon, downed the rest of the whiskey

Lilly continued. "I'm outside the station, getting into my car. I'll be there in less than ten minutes, just me, I'm not sending a squad car or anyone else, but you've *got* to stop drinking."

Cotter dropped the glass on the floor, Lilly hearing it shatter.

"You're right, Conway, I've had *quite* enough," Cotter said over his shoulder as he jerked the battle-ax down off the wall. Dragged it towards the window.

Just like the little cars, going, going . . . *gone.*

As he passed, Cotter said to the desk, "Damnit, Lilly, the fucking *moon's* rancid, is anything left?"

Eighty miles an hours down D Street, the new convention center a blur on the left, approaching the Summer Street lights, Lilly hit the wig-wags, the siren.

"Cotter? Talk to me," he said, blowing through them, the Crown Vic bottoming out, almost losing control, continuing down D.

"Cotter, you there? *Cotter . . .?*" he said.

FIFTY-ONE

IN A DOUBLE ROOM of Boston's Brigham and Women's Hospital, McCauley sat on a wooden chair with blue vinyl seat. As he pulled on a cross-trainer, he winked at the older guy across from his bed. "*Sure* they ain't broke?" the other man said, lifting his head from the pillow. He lowered his paper, fingered up his glasses, stared at McCauley.

"The ribs? They're not broke, just badly *bruised*," McCauley said with a grimace as he laced up the other.

The other man nodded gravely. "Been there myself, *busted* 'em, fell off a ladder onto a paint can. Wife wasn't, You *okay*, honey? Just bitched I got blue paint all over the lawn."

Both men turned their heads and stared when Mackey appeared in the doorway, tight black jeans, white blouse, short black leather jacket, hips cocked at an angle, hands resting on them, she said, "Then *I'll* have to say it," she grinned at McCauley, "you *okay*, honey?"

His mouth hanging open, sitting up in the bed, the older man looked at McCauley. "Hey, partner," he said, "could you get her to say that to me?"

Heading towards the elevators and Mackey asked, "Are you sure it's over, could any more of them be out there waiting for you?" Meeting her eyes, McCauley told her that he hoped that it was, but he couldn't be certain until after he contacted Lilly — who was supposed to call Cotter last night.

"Oh, Lilly *called* him, all right," Mackey said, her voice rising. "I got up this morning and put on the news — and it was horrible, Del — cameras panning your house, flashing to the scene when they took out the bodies." Her eyes filling, turning her head towards the window. McCauley touched her wrist, stopping her, saying, hey, twice. She looked back at him, dabbed her eyes with a tissue, a little smile. She said, "I'm okay, really. Just this morning, the memory, the way I felt then. It all just caught up to me . . . silly."

McCauley patted the small of her back. "It's okay, pal," he said. "It's not silly at all. Actually, it was scary." Urged her ahead with his chin. "So, tell me, you spoke to Lilly this morning?"

As she followed the corridor, Mackey talked with her hands.

She said, "When I called District Six this morning I couldn't believe that Lilly was still there, he'd been up all night with this thing."

McCauley thinking, Look at her scared but still keeping it together.

He said, "What did he tell you about Cotter."

They stopped in front of the elevator doors, Mackey hit the already-lit down button. She said, "I got the feeling as we talked there was a lot *more* to the story. He did tell me they had Cotter in custody." She stared at him steadily, a strange glint in her eyes. "They brought him in drunk," she said.

McCauley's eyes widened. "Drunk?"

Up the corridor behind them, McCauley recognized the woman's voice that said, "Mr. McCauley." Turning, both of them watched a tall, brown-haired woman, no makeup, wearing a lab coat, holding a clipboard to her breast, approach. "You're not leaving us?" she said pleasantly, adjusting her glasses.

McCauley sheepishly looked at Mackey. "Good morning, Doctor Berman, matter of fact, yes, I am."

Dr. Berman looked at her clipboard, smiled at Mackey. Began talking to her before shifting her eyes back to McCauley. "You're fully aware I prefer you remain here, at least for another day," she said, "you suffered a slight concussion, and four ribs are bruised." Looked at Mackey again, frowned, I need some help here. Refocused on McCauley. "But if you must leave us, please take it easy, no heavy lifting at least for five days."

"No problem, Doc, the only thing I'll be lifting are sixteen-ounce Buds," McCauley said.

The doctor wagged a finger at him. "And no drinking," she said sternly. "The concussion, remember?"

McCauley waved a finger back. "Not drinking, Doctor, I'm a bartender by trade."

Making a notation on the clipboard, her eyes rose and met McCauley's. One eyebrow floated up. "A *bartender*, Mr. Mc-Cauley? I watched the *news* this morning, you could have fooled me."

The elevator doors dinged opened.

Stepping inside, McCauley tapped the control panel, looked at Mackey. He said, "What you're telling me," lowered his voice, "is that Lilly took a statement from him drunk." He chewed his lip and shook his head. Finally he said, "Lilly should know better. No judge is going to consider a statement taken from a guy the cops *knew* was drunk."

"Lilly didn't," Mackey said, the doors opening at the lobby, McCauley stepping out, Mackey hurrying to catch him. "Or, more accurately, I should say, Cotter *wasn't* — no longer, at least — they let him sleep it off, until, two, three o'clock this morning. He told me that Cotter woke himself up."

"And just decided to talk."

Touching his arm, slowing him down, Mackey said, "Look, Cotter's a lawyer, he *knows* what he's doing. Once Lilly informed him they had direct evidence — the disc — linking him to extortion and murder, he made his own decision, you ask me, the right one, to flip on the other guy first. He *demanded* the cops take his statement, then talked for three hours."

Just before the revolving door, Mackey cut in front of him and looked into his eyes, "You don't look good," she said, turned, and pushed through them. Faced him outside. "You sure you're okay?"

McCauley winced, pressed a hand to his ribs, "Yeah, I'm fine," he said, looking towards Francis Street. "How far are you parked?"

"Half a block down," Mackey said.

*   *   *

Mackey had told him you shouldn't in your condition, as he held the Audi door for her. He'd walked around the front of the car and was opening his own when the black Mercury Marauder pulled up alongside.

"Hey, McCauley," Wacko said, over the top of the descending dark glass, Jughead crowding the wheel, staring.

McCauley straightened and winced, the hand dropping automatically to the ribcage stopped — don't give him anything — let the hand swing to the side.

Turning his gaze to the windshield, Wacko said tiredly, "Get in the car, McCauley, we gotta talk."

"Del, *frig him*, get in the car, please," Mackey shouted, grabbing her phone, glaring at Wacko, "I'm calling the police, *Mister.*" she said, and turned back to McCauley. "Del, ignore him, get into the . . ."

McCauley extended his palm towards her and stared over the roof. "Gotta *talk*? About what?"

"Get in and find out," Wacko said, and stuck his arm out the window, pointing his fingers at the street, rotating his wrist. He said, "Little spin around the block." Patted the door skin, looked at Mackey. "Girly, *re-lax*, its broad daylight, plenty of witnesses. Ain't nothin' happenin' to no one today."

Through the Mercury's rear window as the car pulled away, McCauley watched Mackey jump from the Audi and run briefly behind them as she wrote on a pad, her figure getting smaller and smaller.

Through the dark rising glass, Wacko caught the play in the side mirror. His arm over the seat, he started to turn, but not all the way, like the effort was too much. He spoke to the empty seat next to McCauley. "Broad thinks it's a movie. Ain't, is it, Mc-Cauley. Should be so lucky." He turned back to the front and jerked his thumb to the side. "Brookline Ave'," he said to Jug-head, who glanced at him, nodded, settled back in the seat.

Wacko said nothing for almost a block, then finally, as Jug-head turned right onto Brookline Avenue, spoke to the wind-shield. "So, McCauley, the job, how's it goin'?" he said.

McCauley attempted to hunch himself closer, grimaced with pain. He straightened and said, "If you talking about T.K.'s, it's going all right." Winced as he gingerly fingered his ribs. "But it's my day off. You want a free drink, stop by tomorrow."

Wacko's head twitched and he started to turn, stopped. McCauley watching his ears turning red.

"Not talking about T.K.'s, the other thing," Wacko said, "the *thing* you were lookin' for, ever find it?" He popped Jughead's bicep with the back of his hand. "Next up's Longwood, go right." Threw his arm over the seat, twisted until he looked at McCauley. "You don't mind me askin', you know, since I helped."

"Don't mind a bit," McCauley said. "It will all be in the papers."

He told Wacko everything he knew.

When he had finished, they were still on Longwood in heavy traffic. Passing the Massachusetts College of Pharmacy, Wacko whistled. "Be a son-of-a-bitch," he said. "We're talkin' millions, McCauley." Looked at Jughead. "Turn right on Huntington, then again at the lights." Turned back to the front. "Fucking *millions*," he said.

At the corner of Francis, Jughead slowed for pedestrians, turned right on the green. Wacko shook his fist at the windshield and said, "Ennie Higgins — that fucking *junkie* — had it all figured out. Knew the lawyer would be willing to pay, then he would have gone after the doctor." Wacko chuckled, turned his head, and gazed out the window. "Coulda made 'em pay easy a *couple* times."

McCauley spotted Mackey half a block down leaning against the Audi's driver-side door. She turned towards them when she spotted them, stepped into the street like she was preparing to leap on the hood. Wacko chuckled and pointed a finger. As they began to slow down, he said, "Tough little broad, cute."

Throwing the arm back over the seat again, turning his chin to his shoulder, Wacko said, "There's one more little thing," the eyes dark now and focused as he stared at McCauley. McCauley thinking it was the last thing more than a few men had seen as the Marauder pulled alongside the Audi.

"Janowski," Wacko said, "*you* kill him?" The eyes searching, giving him nothing.

"I missed the chance," McCauley said. "He was dead when I got there."

The electric door locks snapped up.

"Too bad," Wacko said, turning back to the front. "Mighta had a reason to like ya."

FIFTY-TWO

LILLY GOT UP AND CLOSED HIS OFFICE DOOR, returned to his desk, and sat down. He said, "So, she let you crash at her pad . . . *overnight*?" Took a sip of his coffee. "All right, so you're in there all comfy and cozy, then what?" Pulled just his fingers towards him.

McCauley said, "What? Don't get enough gutter on the job, Lilly?" Scowled at him. "Get your mind out of it, it's not that kind of relationship."

Lilly's eyebrows climbed towards his hairline. "But it is a *relationship*." Wink. "Cute little cupcake, can't say I blame ya, but if you had kids, Del, she'd be what, about your *daughter's* age now?" He laughed, waved a finger at him. "Fucking *dog*."

"Ya, arff, arff," McCauley said and gave him the finger. "Hell, what was I supposed to do? Your Crime Scene Services was tossing my place, I couldn't go back. I had to make do, and was lucky she offered."

Lilly jerking the eyebrows again. "Even in your shape, looks like you *do* pretty well, arff, arff," he said.

McCauley looked to the side at the wall of badges and plaques, looked at Lilly. "Can we knock this shit off? For the past two hours we've gone over the events leading up to the shooting." He tapped beneath his chin with the backs of his fingers. "I've had it to here, Lilly, now it's your turn. Tell me what happened with Cotter last night."

Lilly's face softened. He shook his head sadly. "Ya, Cotter," he said, but perked up when he told him Cotter only needed eight stitches.

"Stitches?" McCauley said. "What the hell happened?"

Lilly telling him how Cotter was drunk when he called him,

loaded, he said. Sounded despondent, was talking really weird, enough so he figured the guy might make a meal of a gun, maybe jump out a window.

McCauley said, "Stitches? You had to restrain him?"

"Restrained himself," Lilly said, "after a two-step with a battle-ax."

"Battle-ax?"

"The one on the wall, he swung it at the window but the glass didn't give, deflected it," Lilly said. "The end of the handle caught him under the chin. He shrugged. "Got caught with a medieval uppercut, was out cold on the floor when I found him. Took him to Boston Medical."

Lilly tugged himself forward, lifted his coffee cup. "He's doing the right thing now, giving us everything."

He raised the cup a little before bringing it to his lips. "When they arraigned him yesterday morning they used his own statement against him. For starters, charged him with conspiracy to murder and extortion. After the arraignment, they shipped him to South Bay. No bail's been set yet and I don't think he'll get any. After I leave here I'm heading over to see him, along with a couple of the homicide boys — they're just *dying* to meet him — wish I could take you."

The phone on his desk rang.

Snatching it up, he said, "Captain Lilly," and looked at McCauley. "Going down there, when?" Lilly nodded and rolled his eyes. "Christ, they *should* have enough, Cotter's his partner." He grinned and winked at McCauley. "Sounds good, go get the bum." Nodded again. "Okay, call me when you've got him in custody? Thanks for the head's up." His eyes twinkled as he hung up the phone.

Said to McCauley, "You're going to love this, your old team? Got a warrant for Durning. There's an MSP convoy streaming out to Edgewater as we speak." He clenched his fist and said, "Yes!"

"This will blow the roof off the Department of Corrections?" McCauley said.

"Too fucking bad," Lilly said.

"What's the first question you think they'll ask Durning?"

Lilly stamped the floor and gave a ta-*daa* with his hands. "For starters," he said, "how about, Who was Godzilla?"

McCauley shuddered, touched his ribs. "That guy knew his stuff, Janowski wasn't what you'd call *easy*."

Lilly pointed when he said to McCauley, "And he almost got *you*."

"Had a hell of a game, if he had a gun I'd be dead."

Wondering why he didn't?

"Just be glad you did," Lilly said. Telling him about other guns they'd found, a big .45, a .22, each with silencers, professional stuff.

Why weren't they used?

McCauley said, "Did Cotter ever mention the guy, talk to him, see him?"

Lilly shook his head, saying, "He claims he never did, but that Durning once told him about him. Was supposedly former Navy SEAL, CIA, some kind of fucking assassin, but the weird thing, he allegedly came out of Edgewater." Lilly rested his hands on his belt buckle, leaned back the chair, creaking.

"That doesn't make sense," he said, "Edgewater's maximum security." He tilted his cup towards him, looked in it, and frowned, set it back down. "Don't matter, if Godzilla was committed, we'll find out. The staties are grabbing all of the files."

"But if he was committed," McCauley said, "and somehow got out, how come nobody noticed and sounded the alarm?"

"Might be bullshit he was CIA," Lilly said, "but if he was and had outlived his usefulness . . . what if they put him in there? I've heard about things like that happening before."

"And because Durning was the high mucky-muck of the joint, he could do whatever he wanted with him."

"At best, Godzilla would have been no more than a number. He couldn't escape if he never existed."

The phone rang again. Lilly made a face when he picked it up. He listened, said into it, "Downstairs, now?" Tugged at his collar and nodded. "Okay, tell them I'll be down in a couple of minutes, we're almost finished up here." He laid the phone on the desk and looked at McCauley. "Homicide boys," scratched his cheek lightly like there were hot ashes on it. "Just *itchin'* to get at him," he said, putting the phone in its cradle. Pointed at the ceiling.

"Al-most forgot," he said, "before you go back to work — personally, I think you're crazy, take another goddamned day off — Catchy Davis's address, I want it." Tossed a small sticky pad at McCauley. "Because Catchy's the *second* stop on the blue line today."

McCauley said, "I'm only at the bar until four, if you're off when I am, stop in for a beer."

Lilly slapped his palms on the desk, stood, and said, "A beer with you? What? And that's going to be, what, your *one* for the month?"

McCauley finished writing and passed him the address. "Ya, and the hot tip of the month? I've got Catchy's knife in my car. Give it to homicide to bring to the lab, my bet it'll test positive for McLintock's blood."

"And you came across it how?" Lilly said, putting his hands on his hips.

McCauley shrugged. "He *gave* it to me." Lifted himself painfully from the chair at an angle. "Amazing, huh? That a hard rock like him has a heart."

FIFTY-THREE

McCAULEY PULLED INTO A SPOT in front of Thornton's Flowers and killed the Mustang's engine. Checked his watch, it was a little after ten. He looked across the street at T.K. O'Malley's. With no keys to get in, he hoped Stuffa was still in the place cleaning.

He got out. Halfway across heard a horn and a blue Mazda pulled up. Bobby Kiley, his face layered with genuine concern, lowered the window. "McCauley," Kiley said, "how're ya feelin'? Haven't seen ya since the beef at the Teamsters."

McCauley held out his arms and turned his hands over; checking himself out, he said, "Can't complain, Bobby, I'm still standing while a couple of others who used to be aren't."

Kiley shook his head and tightened his two-fisted grip on the wheel. "Heard the bad news," he said, "what happened up G street."

McCauley glanced east towards the merge, looked at Kiley. "Can't discuss it, Bobby, but I want to thank you again for the help."

Kiley stared blankly at him. What are you talking about? Dragged his nails across his cheek, squinted when he said, "Didn't help *you*, McCauley. I mean, how could me, an ex-con, help you, an ex-cop, against a gangster like I used to be?" Shook his head. "Naw, you got it wrong, McCauley, I was drunk, took a fall, that's it." Put the hand back on the wheel, revved the engine a little. "Things that happen in bars. Wouldn't want *Mister* Curran thinking I set up his man."

"Yeah, his *man*," McCauley said and looked up the street watching an old woman pushing a cart crossing. Looked back at Kiley. "Wouldn't worry about that I was you, Bobby."

Kiley stared hard at the instrument cluster. "Ya, maybe," he said.

A horn sounded behind them, and McCauley waved, said to Kiley, "You gotta go, and I have to work." He put out his hand.

"Me too," Kiley said, taking it.

Releasing it, McCauley said, "*You*, work? Where?"

"The Teamsters," Kiley said, putting the Mazda in gear. "My *job's* makin' your cousin's life miserable."

Stuffa shook a tall garbage bag as he walked out of the kitchen. Spotting McCauley at the window, he held up a finger and grinned.

Opening the door, he said, "Wasn't sure you were comin' today, you okay, Cuz?" His eyes searched for something. "Hey, don't see no keys, you lose 'em?"

McCauley stepped past him. He said, "Ask the Boston cops, they shredded my place, couldn't find my keys, nothing." Fingered his ribs and winced. "'Least this place hasn't changed."

Stuffa gave him a look like his eyebrows were smoking, jingled his own keys as he turned for the bar. "You only missed what, three days the past couple of weeks? What's gonna change?"

At the bar, McCauley pulled a stool towards him. He said,

"It's only two weeks I've been involved in this thing?" Shook his head as he sat. "Fucking Lilly," he said.

"This *thing*," Stuffa said, "over? You get what you wanted?" Put a soda water and lime in front of McCauley.

McCauley winced as he pulled off his jacket. "I did, that and more," he said, resting his forearms on the bar. "So tell me, who filled in for me, my slot?"

Grinning, Stuffa stabbed himself with his thumb. "Who'd you think, Cuz? Me," he said proudly. "Well, not completely, Walter was here too, saying he wants to bring me along . . ." pressed his hands towards the floor, "*easy*," he said, "bottled beers, pulling drafts what I did mostly." He clapped and pointed up with both hands, seesawed the fingers at the ceiling. "It was easy and it was a start," he said.

"Let's hope today's *easy*, McCauley," said as the bar phone rang. Stuffa snatched it off the wall and said, "Yeah," and listened. He turned and faced McCauley, nodded, handed the phone to him. "Your buddy, Captain Lilly," he said softly.

McCauley fanned the air in front of his face, whispered, "I'm-not-here-yet."

Stuffa put it back to his ear and started to say something, cringed, said, "Said he can *hear* you," extended the phone, whined, "Take it, Cuz, *please*."

McCauley took it, "Yes, *Captain* Lilly."

"You sitting?" Lilly said.

A nervous shift in his stomach.

"Give it to me, Lil," McCauley said, glancing at Stuffa.

Like he was trying to get it all out in one breath, Lilly said, "I just got a call from Eddie Burke, one of your academy classmates? Eddie's part of the crew that went down to Edgewater."

"Eddie's a good man."

"Yeah? Too bad, because he's having a *bad* day."

"Eddie all right?"

"Physically, ya."

"Then what are we talkin'?"

"A half-hour ago an inmate-slash-patient buffing the floor outside of Durning's office heard a sound like a gunshot. As he's running for help, the fire alarm goes off. The COs bust into the office, run into a wall of smoke, and find Durning dead behind his desk. Not from smoke inhalation — the guy inhaled a *bullet*.

There are two fires burning: a big pile of papers in front of the file cabinet, and a smaller one inside of the bucket. Before they could nail them with the fire extinguishers, whatever was burning went up pretty good."

McCauley started to stand up and felt dizzy. "Have you told Cotter?"

"Haven't yet."

"Good luck," McCauley said, and tossed Stuffa the phone.

Eyeing him, Stuffa said, "Sorry, bad news?"

"Just more in a long string of it."

Stuffa grinned and hung up the phone. "Well, I got some good. Forgot to mention, yesterday? You got a phone call, a guy named Donovan, Jimmy, I think, ring a bell? Said that you knew him."

"I know him," McCauley said, settling back on the stool. "What'd he want?" Pulled the glass towards him, squeezed the lime into it.

"Said, tell you thanks, and to give you a message." Stuffa looked up like it was scrawled on the ceiling. "There's a preliminary hearing next week on the thing you guys discussed, and . . ." jabbed his finger towards the cue card, "said his lawyer has talked with the assistant D.A. and . . . it looks like they're getting a deal. He sounded real happy, Del." Stuffa went up on his toes. "Hey man, thought you'd be happy."

"Glad somebody is," McCauley said, and stared into the glass.

"McGarrity," McCauley said, putting a thick white ceramic plate, thin-sliced corned beef on rye on it in front of him, "every day, exactly ten minutes to twelve, you plop your soggy ass down on my bar stool. Ever think of hanging at the Quencher instead?"

Eyeing the sandwich, McGarrity pulled off his ball cap, used a single digit to scratch the top of his head. He said, "You ever been next to Morgan Daly on a hot summer day?" Made a face like he'd been sprayed by a skunk, waved the hat at his face. "And the man's always in there takin' his *bets*."

"He's a bookie, they do that," McCauley said, wiping his

hands with a bar towel, dropping it next to McGarrity. "Morgan's a big guy, he sweats, can't help it. Besides, its fall now, not summer."

"It *lingers*," McGarrity said, keeping his eyes on McCauley, opening his mouth wide enough to back in a van. He took his first bite, looked down at the plate as he chewed. "What's the matter, McCauley, no chips or pickle?" Rolled his eyes. "Suppose I should be thankful I got mustard," he said.

"The ingratitude," McCauley said, tugging a small bag of chips off a rack, firing them into McGarrity's chest. "And here I was just about to ask you the rest of the story, the one you started about Kookie Keveany, and you're getting fresh."

The cell on his hip rang.

McCauley pretended to glare at him as he flipped it open. He said, "Lilly, what's up?"

"Your ears must be burning."

"No, got Caller ID," McCauley said, stabbing a fork into a pickle jar, swinging it towards McGarrity.

"You sitting?"

"I'm *working*, Lil, and kind of busy," McCauley said, tossing the fork in the sink.

Lilly said, "I don't quite know who to thank yet, but the Commonwealth was just saved the cost of a trial."

McCauley pushed through the swinging doors into the kitchen. After the door swung behind him he said, "Spit it out," and stared at a calendar, Rooney's Realty, on the door of the walk-in freezer

"Two things, both of them connected. First, I need a time frame from you, when you got to Catchy's house, and, of course, when you left."

"There's a problem?"

"More than that, we're inside the house now. Catchy's deceased, a female's with him, also deceased, both of them shot."

Waited for that to sink in.

McCauley walked to the rear of the kitchen and opened the door, his eyes followed the alleyway towards Silver Street. A cool breeze caressed his face, carrying with it the faint stench of garbage as he told Lilly the times.

When he finished he said, "Remember, I called you as soon as I left there. Then I called Mackey. Check your messages, Lil, everything should match."

Kicked the door closed, walked back towards the front.

"Del, you're not a suspect, I didn't mean to imply."

"Yeah, that makes me feel better. You said there were two things, Lil."

"That's right, about a block from your house, on Pacific, we found something."

"Okay." McCauley getting aggravated now, come on, Lilly, spit it out. He nudged the swinging door open with his knee, checked out the two men his end of the bar both staring back. One made the peace sign and mouthed the word, Bud. McCauley shifted his gaze to McGarrity. The older man a short distance up, quietly singing to himself, rocking his empty glass near his face.

"We'd checked every license plate around your house in a three-block radius," Lilly said, "figured Janowski could have been dropped off or walked there, but Godzilla must have had wheels.

"Yesterday, couple of uniform guys ran the plates of a van parked down on Pacific. Nothing. Don't ask me what happened, maybe the computer was down or they put it in wrong, but they went back today and tried it again. Who do you think?"

"Just tell me, I'm working, remember?" McCauley said, pulling McGarrity's draft, yanking two long-necked Buds from the cooler.

"The good doctor, Noah Durning, it's registered to him. And a peek through the windshield revealed a gym bag in back. The D.A.'s been contacted. We're waiting for a search warrant."

McCauley rang up the Buds, turned, got a wave from the pair, threw the change in the tip jar.

"And the van is *registered* where?" he said, holding the phone to his ear with his shoulder as he mixed a Cape Codder. He put the drink down on a napkin in front an overweight woman in a meter maid's outfit, sheepish look on her face, a couple of seats down from McGarrity. Waved a finger at her, said, "Told you before Angie, whether I'm out here or not, no smoking."

"What?"

"Sorry, Lil, you said registered . . ."

"To an address in Quincy, looks like Hough's Neck."

McCauley scanned the bar, is everyone all set?

"We've got a call into the Registry of Deeds up in Dedham, we're trying to determine who owns the house, might be the same guy. Staties and the Quincy police will be hitting that place with a search warrant too. I get off in time, I'll be *needing* that beer."

"I'd say more than one," McCauley said. "And here I was hoping for an easy day."

"Don't shoot the messenger," Lilly said, "I'll try not to call you again."

"Yeah, you're a pal," McCauley said.

FIFTY-FOUR

HEADING EAST ON STORROW DRIVE in a gray, un-marked Crown Victoria, Sergeant John Graziano, of the Internal Affairs Division of the Massachusetts State Police, hit the turn signal, checked the rearview, and cut to the right lane. He looked at his partner, said, "The way people don't use their turn signals these days drives me fucking crazy," hit the turn signal again, passing a white Volvo and Mass General Hospital, before he pulled back into the center lane.

Passing an apartment complex where a sign out front read, If You Lived Here You'd Be Home Now, Trooper Phineas O'Rourke nodded his head. "Fifteen years ago, in the day, fresh out of the academy," he said, "Chapter 90, motor vehicle law, was all the brass pushed. You *had* to write eight violations for eight hours' work, or be in deep shit. Believe me, we *got* these assholes who don't use their turn signals." Looked at Graziano, at the rotary now keeping right, following the signs to 93 South. "These days, the only time you see blue lights on the road's when somebody's working a damn *detail*."

Graziano sang loudly off-key, "And the times they are a-changing," scowled, and checked the side mirror, followed the road down into the tunnel.

The overhead incandescent lights illuminating the knees of his khaki pants, O'Rourke said, "Stay in the right lane, get off in South Station. Go Summer Street to L, turn right onto Broadway. They tell me McCauley's joint's down on the left, after the merge at West Broadway."

Coming up on a sign above them reading, South Station Right, Graziano said, "Never thought we'd see *him* again," hitting the turn signal and almost out of the lane when he was passed too close by a red Ford pickup.

Asshole wouldn't have done it if I was driving a marked cruiser.

"But you're right about the details," Graziano said, "the new braves, a lot of them, that's all they do, that's why they're on the job, details. Get out there and do some police work, make arrests? Shiiiiit. It's a real fucking shame," he said.

O'Rourke fanned him with a thick manila folder. "Here's a guy, Sarge, John O'Halleran, who won't be working details no more." Made the sign of the cross. "Jesus, *thank you*," he said, "they assigned it to me, 'magine, scanning the Internet for fourteen-year-old boys, one of us, a fucking *state trooper?*" Hammered his knee with a fist. "Gonna be fun getting this son-of-a-bitch."

Traveling up Summer Street, passing the Federal Reserve Bank on the left, Graziano looked at him, said, "Almost feels like the time we went after McCauley."

O'Rourke slipped the folder into his briefcase, emphasized snapping it shut. He looked at Graziano. "How do you think McCauley will take it?"

Staring through the windshield, barely shaking his head. "How would *you?*" Graziano said, accelerating over the bridge at the Fort Point Channel.

*   *   *

Walter Collins sat at the end of the bar going through the day's receipts, punching the keys on a small calculator. It was almost three thirty as he watched McCauley pack beers in the cooler. Earlier that day, a little after two, when Stuffa stopped by for his check, McCauley had asked him if he could please watch the bar and went up to Walter's second-floor office. He gave his boss a truncated version of everything that had happened the past couple of weeks, including the specifics of the phone calls that day. When he finished, Walter felt the need to get out of that room, headed downstairs for some air.

Outside in the street, Graziano, the first to get out of the unmarked gray cruiser, gave the lapels of his sports coat a yank. He fiddled with the knot in his tie. "How'd I look?" he said to no one in particular.

O'Rourke got out the other side and opened the rear door, grabbed his sport coat off a hanger. "Hey, Graz, we need the paperwork," he said, "doctor's notes, anything?"

In the middle of the street, without turning, Graziano waggled his hand near his head like he was shooing away flies. "Just bring yourself, Phinny, just yourself," he said.

With two fingers Walter lifted a page from the clipboard. His eyes roaming up and down the next page, he said, "The schedule next week, Del, you're back with us regular?"

McGarrity chuckled while he piled crumpled bills on the bar. "So, ya *through* runnin' around Southie like a fucking *bant*-shee, McCauley?" Tried to focus on the bar bill he held in front of his face but like there was a tug-o-war going on for his head.

McCauley came over and leaned close to his face. "Think its *ban*-shee McGarrity."

"The *female* persuasion," McGarrity said, glaring back, his runny eyes dropping back down to the tab.

When the men in suits entered, McCauley pushed from the bar and stiffened. He fought the urge to leap over as he stood there glaring, hands on his hips.

Graziano said, "Afternoon, Lieutenant," and nodded at Walter, who gazed blankly back.

McCauley pointed at the men, said, "Walter, let me introduce Sergeant Graziano and Trooper O'Rourke, Mass State Police Internal Affairs, these are the two *bums* who came after me like I was Marty Fallon." He pushed up his sleeves. "Got a problem, boys, lost? Look around you're in *Southie*. Probably looking for

Deer Island, where they process the shit. It's more up your alley."

O'Rourke growled, "Hey, McCauley," and took a step towards him, the other man blocking his chest with an arm.

In one fluid motion, McCauley vaulted the bar and faced them both at an angle.

Walter slid off the stool, flipped his glasses onto the bar, and came alongside McCauley.

Graziano took a step back and showed his palms. He said, "Hey, boys, hey, not here for a brawl," looked at O'Rourke, then back at the bar. "On the contrary, McCauley, we gotta *talk*." Turning his head, taking in the rest of the room. "In *private*," he said.

"In the kitchen, Del," Walter said, throwing a thumb over his shoulder. "I'll get the bar." Kept an eye on the cops as he came around the end.

Inside the kitchen, McCauley turned at the sink and faced the two cops blocking the door. He said, "Say what you have to, then get the hell out."

"Hear us out, McCauley," O'Rourke said, "you might change your mind."

Graziano casually took in the kitchen, said a little wise, "Considering recent events, McCauley, you probably could use some good news."

McCauley said, "*Good* news from you two? And you want for it, what? My firstborn?" Started to move towards them like he was planning on walking right through. "Sorry, I don't have any kids."

Neither man moved. "Out of the way," McCauley barked, stopping just before them, "my fucking shift's over."

Graziano showed his palms shoulder height, gently pushed the air. "Hold up, McCauley, listen. The DEA agent in your case, Doyle? He's been out of his coma for over a week."

McCauley looked at O'Rourke. Bastards, this some kind of trick?

"It's the truth, McCauley."

"Over a week?" McCauley said softer than he had intended, almost took a step back, caught himself. "Why wasn't I told this before?"

The cops looked at each other, back at McCauley. "We were

afraid that he might relapse," Graziano said finally, and shrugged. "That happened, what would we say?"

McCauley looked at the floor. "How about he relapsed," he said, sliding a stool out from beneath a stainless steel table and lowering himself onto it.

"You'd probably want to know if he's talking," O'Rourke said. "The answer is, yes — and he remembers that night, every day, more and more's coming back to him."

"Most importantly, he corroborates your story," Graziano said, "that you were too far back in the alley, couldn't have been there when the beating took place. It was all like you said, Mc-Cauley." He pulled out his wallet, took out a card.

Like he was nodding, falling asleep, McCauley's head dropped. His body was going numb, it was an effort to stay on the stool. "This is me," Graziano said, reaching out, touching his forearm, slipping the card up between his finger and thumb.

He said, "Ever hear of the Justice Initiative? It's a new program, launched out of the A.G.'s office in 2004. It promises a review of erroneous convictions. With your permission, McCauley, we're recommending they look at your case." His eyes went to O'Rourke's. "We'll be in touch, any questions, just call me — like to help if in any way we can."

The doors swung behind them.

A few moments later, McCauley came out. "You okay?" Walter said. "Christ, you don't look good."

"Like he seen a damn bant-shee," McGarrity said, the face floating, the liquid eyes staring.

McCauley sat down beside him and barely gave him a look. "No need to muscle me," McGarrity said sourly, shifting his ass. He waved a fistful of crumpled bills. "I'm *payin'* my damn tab."

McCauley turned his head slowly, looked at him, and said, "McGarrity, shut the fuck up."

Walter jerked his head towards the door. "Those other two left without saying a word." He came over closer and studied Mc-Cauley's face. "You *okay,* Del?" he said, put his hand on the other man's shoulder.

"Don't tell me you started before me, McCauley," said a voice from the front. As he came towards them, tan sport coat draped over an arm, Lilly tugged at the knot in his tie.

Turning in the seat, McCauley said, "Wouldn't think of it, Lil," and held out his hand. "I got 'em on ice right behind me."

Shaking it, Lilly jerked back his head. "Those two just left here, cops?"

McCauley nodded. "IA, my old job," he said, stretching over the bar, grabbing two Buds from the bin. He wiped the ice from them over the floor.

Lilly sucked in his chin, his eyes narrowing. "Internal Affairs?" he said. "What'd *they* want?"

Like he couldn't believe it himself, McCauley said, "They brought me good news." Handed one to Lilly, twisted his own cap off.

"Sure as shit could use some today, going to tell me?" Lilly said, clinking the bottles, studying his face.

McCauley took a slug of his beer. He said, "Think *you* better sit down."

FIFTY-FIVE

STANDING IN FRONT OF A WEATHERED, gray railing bordering the promenade at Marina Bay in Quincy, Delray McCauley, in jeans, black turtleneck, blue Barracuda, boat shoes, released the hand he'd just cautiously shook. Mackey, in a black leather Jones of New York waistcoat, Lucky jeans, violet blouse, held the position a moment before letting her arm drop to the side.

McCauley said, "What did you want me to say?" Mackey's other hand rose to her forehead, whisked away stray hairs there that played in the breeze. She stared briefly into his eyes before turning, folded her arms as she followed the boardwalk along past a law office on the right.

When McCauley caught up, she said, "How about, I would have called you sooner but there's been a lot going on, things have been crazy." She stopped in front of a hypnotist joint and turned towards him, reached out to touch the sleeve of his jacket, hesitated, pulled the hand back, indignant. "You know, it's not like I wasn't a part of this thing. The police have been to my office twice already."

McCauley looked away towards the ocean, the marina's slips, most of them empty now, but a few boats remained. One, a thirty-five-foot cigarette boat *Lil Dancer,* belonged to a friend of his, Freddy Ciovacco, from Southie. It was the beginning of November, wondered why Freddy had left it in this long?

Wondered too why he hadn't called Mackey. What was he afraid of?

Two weeks before, he was just another ex-con. Had accepted the fact that no matter what else he did with his life, it was the way that he'd always be labeled. Content with existing, he'd stopped having dreams, learned to keep it simple: a job at a bar, an apartment somewhere, a half-decent car. Lonely, but the thought of a relationship scared him knowing he had nothing to offer — especially to someone like Mackey. But that was two weeks ago.

Everything had changed.

Less than a day after meeting with the state police, a lawyer, an old friend, George McMahon, had contacted him. Told him what he already knew — he had grounds now to flip the case.

On a contingency basis, George went to work. Interviewed Graziano and O'Rourke, doctors at the Spaulding Rehab Center where the DEA agent, Doyle, had been transferred.

George even spoke briefly to Doyle, who, getting stronger every week, his memory returning, was eager to help McCauley in any way possible. Paperwork was filed with the court to vacate McCauley's finding and petition for a new trial. So intense was the lawyer's belief that the DA would refuse to retry him, more paperwork was filed with the state police requesting a hearing on reinstatement.

But, concerning the job, would he even want to go back? McCauley didn't think so. He'd learned a hard lesson, something he'd heard about but never believed — the state police had a habit of eating their young.

And there was the issue of backpay. Over three years at a lieutenant's rate, not including overtime and details missed. And the other of reparation. The county would have to pay for its mistake. The going rate for wrongful incarceration: $250.00 a day — multiplied by three years. Between them, McCauley was looking at close to three quarters of a million.

And there were other distractions.

Walter, the owner of T.K.'s, interested in building a chain, had been looking at a new location on Front Street in Scituate. Wanted a partner. Would McCauley be interested in buying half ownership of the T.K.'s in Southie?

There were reasons he hadn't called Mackey.

Mackey was the first woman to capture his attention since Carolyn died. In the months following Carolyn's death, people would ask him, Why aren't you dating? He'd tell them he was in mourning, to leave him alone. But as time went by, he had to ask himself, who exactly was he mourning for? Was it the loss of himself? Had he been so tied up in the life of another, unable to imagine a life without her, that he had fallen out of touch with who he was? Was he afraid that with Mackey it might happen again?

Following the boardwalk, turning left past a restaurant named Siros, he guided her to a bench facing the ocean a short distance down. He started to sit, noticed she wouldn't, straightened his knees, and faced her. "If you're wondering," he said, "how the police got your name, they probably got it from Cotter, it must have come up when he made his statement. We're talking about murder here, Mackey. It's standard procedure that they'd want to talk."

Mackey stared out across the harbor towards the Boston skyline in the distance. Stepping in front of the bench, she plopped down more than sat. "I understand that," she said, refolding her arms. "It's just that I thought we were friends, if not *friends*," using her fingers to make quote marks, "working associates. It didn't seem right me finding out about you, this DEA guy coming out of the coma able to testify you had nothing to do with putting him there, from the front page of the *Globe*." When he sat down beside her, Mackey hugged herself tighter. "It's been on every station, all of them saying the same thing." She turned her head and looked at him. "You're an innocent man, Del. You got screwed."

She crossed her legs, folded her hands in her lap, and looked away from him. Hurt, and a little angry too, she didn't know what else to say. Hadn't their relationship — relationship? — their *working* relationship been a good one? She admired Mc-Cauley and believed he thought the same of her, at least seemed to, her professionalism, work ethic, but it never carried beyond that.

He was never a flirt, at least not directly, not that she would have minded, he always stopped at the edge, kept it professional. Still, there was something there — on her part too. The guy was interesting — and, she believed, interested — even though she hadn't heard from him in almost two weeks.

She'd left him messages, at the bar, on his cell, and had gotten no response, so when he called her this morning, she almost ignored it. Now here she was sitting at Marina Bay in a jacket too light for the weather. What was she thinking? Maybe it was because she wasn't.

McCauley said, "Remember at the Fat Belly Deli when I gave you my *frame-a-logue*, explained how I was an innocent man?" Mackey glanced at him, nodded.

"Seems the idea's caught on . . . finally," he said with a shrug, eyeing a seagull, hearing its cry as it descended in tightening circles above them. He shielded his eyes and watched it. "Things are looking up," he said. Dropped his hand, looked at her. "Hey pal . . . I'm sorry I didn't call you sooner."

Mackey nodded once. "Apology accepted," she said, staring straight ahead. "It's not like you *owe* me, I . . ." McCauley put his hand on her wrist.

"You're wrong, I do owe you," he said. Tapped the side of his head with a finger. "Just lately there's been a lot banging around up here."

"I can't imagine," she said, turning her head to look at him. Her eyes dropped like she wasn't quite sure what to say next. Then she looked at him again. "They tell me I'm a good listener," she said.

"Think I could use one," McCauley said, standing. He offered his hand. "I'm hungry, you?" She took it and stood, the cries of the gulls echoing above them.

"I could something light," Mackey said, looking up. She shielded her eyes, trying to spot them. "Funny," she said, "most birds are gone before winter, but gulls hang around."

"Maybe they know something."

Mackey turned her head, looked at him, pointed the eyebrow. "How do you mean?"

Touching her elbow, McCauley gently turned her, the hand remaining there as he guided her back up the boardwalk. He said, "I don't know, there's something to be said for hanging around."